The Dolfin Chalice

Michael Smith

Published by Michael Smith, 2024.

This is a work of fiction. Similarities to real people, places, or events are entirely coincidental.

THE DOLFIN CHALICE

First edition. September 23, 2024.

Copyright © 2024 Michael Smith.

ISBN: 979-8227430670

Written by Michael Smith.

Prologue: The Dolfin Chalice

Cumberland, 1666

The great hall of Lowther Castle echoed with the sound of raucous laughter and the clinking of goblets. Lord William Lowther, his face flushed with wine, raised his cup in a toast to his guest of honour.

"To Dolfin, descendant of Vikings and new friend to the Lowther name!"

Dolfin, a towering figure with hair the colour of straw and eyes as blue as the northern seas, inclined his head in acknowledgment. His weathered hand, more accustomed to the hilt of a sword than the stem of a goblet, tightened around his drink.

"Your hospitality honours me, Lord Lowther," Dolfin replied, his accent still carrying traces of his Norse ancestry despite generations in Cumberland. "May our families' fortunes be forever entwined?"

As the night wore on and the wine flowed freely, Dolfin found himself drawn into conversation with Lord Lowther's younger brother, Edmund. The two men stood apart from the revelry, their heads bent close in hushed discussion.

"You say you have knowledge of ancient rites?" Edmund asked, his eyes gleaming with interest. "Passed down from your Viking forebears?"

Dolfin nodded slowly, glancing around to ensure they weren't overheard. "Aye, secret rituals of power and prophecy. But such knowledge comes at a price, my friend."

Edmund's hand moved to a pouch at his belt. "Gold is no object. But tell me, can these rites guarantee the success of our family? Can they secure our place in history?"

A slow smile spread across Dolfin's face. "Gold is good, but I speak of a different price. Are you willing to pay it, Edmund Lowther? Are you willing to bind your family's fate to powers beyond mortal understanding?"

For a moment, Edmund hesitated. Then, with a quick nod, he sealed the pact that would shape generations to come. "Tell me what must be done."

In the shadows of the great hall, unnoticed by the revellers, a serving girl named Agnes listened with wide eyes. She clutched a heavy bone china chalice, an heirloom of the Lowther family, her knuckles white with tension. As she heard talk of rituals and ancient powers, the chalice, studied with semi-precious gems seemed to grow warm in her hands, as if awakening to long-forgotten purpose.

Little did Agnes know that the conversation she overheard would set in motion a chain of events that would echo through centuries? The pact made that night between Dolfin and Edmund Lowther would intertwine the fates of multiple families, weaving a tapestry of power, secrecy, and dark rituals that would culminate in the mysteries of Egremont three hundred years later.

As the night deepened and the moon rose high over Cumberland, the foundations of a legacy were laid - a legacy that would touch the lives of Paul Brankenwall and Mary Postlethwaite in ways they could never have imagined.

The Viking's blood, the nobleman's ambition, and the servant's witness - three threads in a complex weave of destiny that would unravel in the rolling hills and mist-shrouded valleys of Cumbria, where ancient secrets lay buried, waiting to be unearthed.

Chapter 1

The morning mist clung to the Black Mountains like a gauzy veil as Ravenglass stirred to life. A fine, persistent drizzle – typical of Cumbria's capricious weather – painted the coastal village in muted hues. Nestled in the shadow of the imposing peaks, this sleepy hamlet was home to more than just fishermen and shopkeepers. It was the beating heart of the Postlethwaite Pottery business, a family legacy that had shaped the community for generations.

As the reluctant sun climbed higher, its weak rays glinted off the smokestack of the sprawling brick building that dominated the village skyline. Once the local school, it now housed the dreams and livelihoods of the Postlethwaite family and their employees, its windows fogged with the breath of creativity within.

In the distance, the shrill whistle of the "Laal Ratty" pierced the misty air. The Ravenglass and Eskdale Railway, with its narrow gauge track and tenacious little steam engines, was as much a part of the village's charm as the pottery itself. Its rhythmic chug-chug-chug provided a comforting contrastt to the day's labours, a reminder of the outside world beyond their creative cocoon.

Inside the pottery, the air thrummed with energy, a stark contrast to the dreary day beyond its walls. The rhythmic thud of pottery wheels mingled with the Beatles' "Hey Jude" playing on the crackling radio, barely audible over the patter of rain on the roof and the distant huffing of the steam engine. The heady scent of clay hung in the air, punctuated by the acrid tang of kiln smoke – a perfume that spoke of creation and transformation.

In one corner, Maggie, a skilled craftswoman with calloused hands and sharp eyes, hunched over a delicate porcelain figurine. Her fingers danced across the surface, coaxing out details with a precision born of decades of practice. The gentle tap of her tools was a counterpoint to the rain's steady rhythm.

"Oi, Maggie!" called out Jim from across the room. He stood before a massive potter's wheel, his muscular arms caked with clay up to the elbows, rivulets of water from his rain-soaked hair creating abstract patterns on his apron. "Reckon this vase is big enough for the Haddon Hall order?"

Maggie squinted at the towering form taking shape under Jim's hands. "Any bigger and they'll be using it as a bloody bathtub, Jim!"

Their laughter, warm and genuine, cut through the grey mood set by the weather outside. It was cut short by a resounding crash from the kiln room, followed by a string of colorful curses that would make a sailor blush.

"Sounds like Old Tom's dropped another load," Jim chuckled. "That's the third time this week."

Maggie shook her head, a fond smile playing on her lips. "Ah, leave him be. His hands ain't what they used to be, poor soul. This damp weather does him no favours."

As if summoned by the commotion, Steve Postlethwaite emerged from his office, a cardigan thrown hastily over his shoulders to ward off the chill. The eldest of the Postlethwaite siblings, Steve was the steady hand on the tiller, his quiet authority a counterpoint to the creative chaos around him.

"Everything alright out here?" he asked, his eyes scanning the factory floor with the practiced ease of a captain surveying his ship.

"Right as rain, Mr. Steve," Maggie assured him, then chuckled at her own unintended pun. "Just Old Tom having a bit of a fumble."

Steve nodded, his brow furrowing slightly. He'd been poring over the financial ledgers all morning, and the numbers were far from comforting. The lingering effects of Prime Minister Edward Heath's

Three-Day Week still cast a long shadow over the business, as grey and oppressive as the clouds outside.

As if reading his thoughts, the lights flickered ominously. A collective groan rose from the workers, echoing the rumble of distant thunder.

"Not again," Steve muttered, pinching the bridge of his nose.

From the design studio, a voice called out, tinged with equal parts exasperation and amusement. "Another bloody power cut, Steve? At this rate, we'll be back to firing our pots over campfires!"

Andrew Postlethwaite, the youngest of the siblings, emerged from his creative lair. His wild hair and paint-splattered smock were a stark contrast to Steve's pressed shirt and polished shoes. He carried with him the scent of turpentine and possibility.

"Don't give them any ideas, Andrew," Steve retorted, but there was a hint of a smile playing at the corners of his mouth. "Your last 'innovative firing technique' nearly burned down the east wing."

Andrew grinned unrepentantly. "But think of the unique patterns it created! We could market it as our new 'Flame-Kissed Collection'. Perfect for brightening up these dreary Cumbrian days."

Their banter was interrupted by Bert, the grizzled old foreman, his face a roadmap of wrinkles earned through years of hard work and hearty laughter. He limped slightly, his old injury acting up in the damp weather.

"Boss," he said, addressing Steve, "there's a call for you. It's your sister."

The brothers exchanged puzzled glances. "Mary?" Steve asked, surprise evident in his voice. "What on earth does she want?"

As Steve headed back to the office, Andrew turned to Maggie, his eyes twinkling with curiosity. "Well, this is unexpected. Our prodigal sister calling from the hallowed halls of Strasbourg. Think she's finally seen sense and is coming back to get her hands dirty with real work?"

Maggie snorted. "That'll be the day. That girl's got her head in the clouds and her feet planted firmly on foreign soil. Though I suppose even Strasbourg must seem appealing in weather like this."

The distant whistle of the Laal Ratty sounded again, as if in agreement. Andrew grinned, "Maybe we should send her a ticket for the railway. A ride through the hills in this weather might remind her what she's missing."

In the quiet of his office, Steve picked up the receiver, the old rotary phone a testament to the pottery's blend of tradition and innovation. "Hello, Mary. What's up? How's life in Strasbourg?"

There was a pause at the other end of the line, long enough for Steve's confusion to turn to concern. When Mary's voice finally came through, it was filled with a mixture of determination and trepidation that set alarm bells ringing in Steve's head.

"I'm here in Egremont," she said, the words tumbling out in a rush. "Staying with Mum for a few days. I need to talk to you both about something important."

Steve's grip on the receiver tightened, his knuckles whitening. "What on earth for? You know how busy we are here, Mary. The business—"

"I'll explain everything when I get there," Mary cut him off, her tone brooking no argument. "Probably early next week. The weather forecast looks a bit clearer by then."

Before Steve could protest further, the line went dead. He stared at the receiver for a long moment before replacing it, his mind racing. Whatever Mary was up to, it was clear she was serious. And in Steve's experience, a serious Mary meant trouble with a capital T.

As he stepped back onto the factory floor, Steve's eyes were drawn to the large portrait hanging on the far wall. It showed Uncle Brian, their father's brother, who had taken over as CEO after their father's untimely death. Though retired now, his presence still loomed large over the pottery, much like the mountains that watched over Ravenglass.

Steve's gaze shifted to the old school bell that hung beside the portrait, a relic from the building's previous life. It seemed to him a fitting symbol – a call to order in a world of creative chaos, a reminder of the legacy they were all tasked with preserving.

The Postlethwaite Pottery was more than just a business. It was a family saga written in clay and fire, each piece that left the factory carrying with it a piece of their history. As Steve watched his brother gesticulate wildly to a group of amused workers, no doubt outlining his latest outlandish idea, he couldn't help but wonder what new episode Mary's return might herald.

Whatever it was, one thing was certain – change was coming to Ravenglass, as inevitable as the tide that lapped at its shores. The Postlethwaite family would need all their skill, creativity, and stubborn determination to weather the storm ahead, both literal and metaphorical.

Outside, the rain continued its relentless percussion, a fitting backdrop to the uncertainty that hung in the air. But within the walls of the old school, now a crucible of art and commerce, the warmth of family and tradition held the chill at bay – for now. And beyond, the Laal Ratty chugged on, a steel thread stitching together past and present, much like the Postlethwaite legacy itself.

Chapter 2

The summer of 1974 brought an unexpected respite from Cumbria's typically capricious weather. As the newly christened county basked in an unusual spell of sunshine, the rain that had drenched Egremont for days finally ceased. The forecast promised an unprecedented stretch of clear skies, though with a caveat – temperatures were expected to fall in the hills, adding a crisp edge to the air. As the first light touched Egremont, painting the slate roofs in hues of pink and gold, Mary Postlethwaite stood on her mother's doorstep, her heart a tumult of anticipation and trepidation. The fresh, cool breeze carried the scent of damp earth and possibility, mirroring the mix of hope and uncertainty that swirled within her.

"You sure about this, love?" Her mother, Margaret, a woman of quiet strength, stood in the doorway, her eyes a mixture of pride and worry.

Mary forced a smile. "Absolutely, Mum. It's just a bike ride."

Margaret sighed, shaking her head. "A bike ride, she says. To Cold Fell, no less. You know what your Aunt Beatrice said when I told her?"

"Let me guess," Mary replied, rolling her eyes. "Something about it not being proper for a young woman?"

"She said you'd gone mad, living in France all those years," Margaret chuckled, then grew serious. "But truly, Mary, are you certain? It's a long way, and-"

"And what?" Mary interrupted, a hint of defiance in her voice. "I'm not a child anymore, Mum. I've lived abroad, worked for the European Commission. I think I can handle a bike ride."

Margaret reached out, straightening the collar of Mary's jacket. "I know, love. It's just... with Howard gone..." Her voice trailed off, the unspoken grief hanging between them.

Mary's expression softened. "I know, Mum. That's part of why I need to do this. For Howard."

Just then, a voice called out from next door. "Oi, Mary! You're not really going through with this madcap idea, are you?"

Mary turned to see Mr. Thompson, their elderly neighbor, leaning over the fence. His wife, Edna, peered out from behind him, curiosity evident on her face.

"Good morning, Mr. Thompson," Mary called back, forcing cheerfulness into her voice. "Indeed I am. Beautiful day for it, don't you think?"

"Beautiful day for a picnic, maybe," Edna chimed in. "Not for gallivanting across the countryside alone. It's not safe, dear."

Mary bit back a retort. Instead, she smiled sweetly. "I appreciate your concern, Mrs. Thompson. I'll be sure to wave as I pass by on my triumphant return."

Turning back to her mother, Mary saw a glimmer of amusement in the older woman's eyes. "Well, don't be too reckless," Margaret said, her voice softening. "And promise me you'll stop at the Shepherds' Arms for a pint on your way back. Your father always said it was the best reward after conquering Cold Fell."

Mary laughed, a genuine sound that seemed to lighten the morning air. "I promise, Mum. One pint at the Shepherds' Arms, in Dad's honor."

With a final wave, she turned and pushed off, her bicycle rolling smoothly down the quiet street. As she pedalled away, she could hear Mr. Thompson's voice fading behind her.

"Mark my words, Margaret, that girl's going to give you grey hairs before your time!"

Mary grinned, the wind whipping through her hair as she picked up speed. The biting Cumbrian dawn nipped at her heels, but the exhilaration of the open road warmed her spirit. As Egremont receded behind her, the road stretched out before her like a ribbon of infinite possibility.

Her mind wandered to the events that had brought her back after so many years away. Howard's death, claimed by cancer at the tragically young age of 29, had left a void that seemed to echo with each turn of her bicycle's wheels. Then there was Uncle Brian's summons, his words still ringing in her ears: "What we need is a trained economist with a cool head."

Mary snorted at the memory. "Trained economist, indeed," she muttered to herself. "If only they knew."

As she pedalled on, memories of her reckless youth bubbled to the surface. She could almost hear the roar of David's motorbike, feel the wind rushing past as they hit a hundred miles an hour on this very road. They were sixteen then, invincible and utterly fearless.

"Oh, David," she whispered to the wind, "if you could see me now."

The road began to incline, the first hint of the challenge that lay ahead. Mary leaned into her handlebars, her determination growing with each push of the pedals. Cold Fell loomed in the distance, a silent sentinel waiting to test her resolve.

"Well, old friend," she said to the mountain, her voice carrying a hint of challenge, "let's see what you've got in store for me this time."

With the sun climbing higher in the sky and the weight of expectations - both others' and her own - on her shoulders, Mary Postlethwaite pressed on. The journey ahead was more than just a physical challenge; it was a declaration of independence, a quest for solitude, and a way to honor the memory of her brother.

Little did she know, as she approached the base of Cold Fell, that this journey would lead her to an encounter that would change the course of her life forever.

As Mary approached Ennerdale village, the quaint cluster of slate-roofed houses nestled peacefully under the midday sun. The imposing silhouette of the Black Mountains rose majestically beyond, their peaks seemingly brushing the clouds. Feeling the need for a brief respite, she decided to seek refuge in a traditional pub tucked away from the main road.

The moment she stepped inside, the pub enveloped her in a warm embrace. Its interior was low-ceilinged and dimly lit, with a worn wooden bar and a collection of hunting trophies adorning the walls. The air was thick with the scent of ale and wood smoke.

A group of locals were gathered around the fire, their voices raised in animated conversation. A woman with a shock of red hair was holding court, her laughter filling the room.

Mary approached the bar, catching the eye of the grizzled bartender.

"What can I get you, love?" he asked, his voice gravelly but kind.

"A half pint of bitter and a plate of ham and cheese sandwiches, please," Mary replied, settling onto a bar stool.

As the bartender busied himself with her order, Mary's attention was drawn to the lively group by the fire.

"I'm telling you, Maggie," a portly man in a tweed cap was saying, "if this weather holds, it'll be the best harvest we've had in years."

The red-haired woman, presumably Maggie, scoffed. "Don't count your chickens, George. Remember '72? We thought the same thing and then the rains came."

"Aye, but that was then," George countered. "Times are changing. Did you hear about that new tractor old Wilson's got? They say it can do the work of ten men!"

"Here you are, love," the bartender said, setting down Mary's order. "You're not from around here, are you?"

Mary shook her head. "No, I'm from Egremont originally. Just passing through on a bike ride."

The bartender's eyebrows shot up. "Egremont? That's quite a journey. Where are you headed?"

"I'm doing a round trip to Calderbridge across Cold Fell," Mary explained, taking a sip of her bitter.

The conversation by the fire suddenly hushed, and Mary found herself the centre of attention.

"Did you say Cold Fell?" Maggie asked, her eyes wide. "On a bicycle?"

Mary nodded, feeling a mix of pride and self-consciousness. "It's been a dream of mine since I was a teenager."

George let out a low whistle. "That's quite the adventure for a young lady. You sure you're up for it?"

Mary felt a familiar spark of defiance. "I've lived in Strasbourg for years, working for the European Commission. I think I can handle a bike ride."

There was a moment of impressed silence before Maggie burst out laughing. "Well, aren't you full of surprises! Come on over here and tell us more about this grand adventure of yours."

As Mary joined the group, sandwich in hand, she found herself opening up about her reasons for the trip, her return to Egremont, and the complex tangle of emotions she was navigating.

"I attended the all-girls' school in Egremont until I was eleven," she explained, "before leaving for Whitehaven Grammar. It feels like a lifetime ago."

"And now you're back," Maggie said softly. "That can't be easy, love."

Mary sighed. "It's... complicated. My brother Howard passed away recently, and the family pottery business needs attention."

George nodded sympathetically. "Ah, the Postlethwaite Pottery. Fine work they do there. Your brother was a good man."

"He was," Mary agreed, feeling a lump in her throat. "But now, well, everything's up in the air. My older brother Steve wants to keep things as they are, while my younger brother Andrew has all these grand ideas for expansion."

"And where do you fit in all this?" Maggie asked, her eyes kind but searching.

Mary took another sip of her bitter, considering the question. "That's what I'm trying to figure out. This ride, it's not just about fulfilling an old dream. It's about finding my place in a world that's shifted beneath my feet."

The group nodded, understanding etched on their faces. For the next hour, they swapped stories of family obligations, personal aspirations, and the challenges of balancing the two. Mary found herself drawn into discussions about local politics, the changing face of rural life, and yes, the vagaries of Cumbrian weather.

As the afternoon wore on, Mary glanced at her watch and realized she needed to get back on the road.

"I'd better be off," she said, standing up. "I've still got Cold Fell to conquer."

"Well, good luck to you, lass," George said, raising his pint in salute. "You've got more gumption than half the young ones around here."

Maggie stood and gave Mary a quick hug. "You take care out there. And remember, sometimes the answer you're looking for is right where you started."

As Mary stepped back out into the sunshine, she felt a renewed sense of purpose. The connections she'd made, however brief, had grounded her, reminding her of the warmth and resilience of the community she'd left behind.

Mounting her bicycle, Mary took a deep breath of the crisp Cumbrian air. The road ahead was challenging, but for the first time since she'd returned home, she felt ready to face whatever lay around the next bend.

As she pedalled on, the landscape transformed around her. The road wound its way through a densely wooded plantation, creating a cool green tunnel that enveloped her. Sunlight filtered through the leaves, casting a hypnotic dappled pattern on the path ahead.

"It's like cycling through a living, breathing painting," Mary murmured to herself, her voice barely audible over the crunch of gravel beneath her tires.

When she finally emerged from the tree line, Mary gasped audibly. There, sprawling before her in all its majesty, was Ennerdale Lake. Its surface was a perfect mirror, reflecting the vibrant blue sky and fluffy white clouds with startling clarity. She pulled over, her legs trembling slightly as she dismounted.

"Oh, Howard," she whispered, her throat tight with emotion. "I wish you could see this."

As she stood there, drinking in the view, a surge of emotion washed over her. This landscape, wild and beautiful, was more than just scenery. It was her heritage, the backdrop to generations of Postlethwaite history. For the first time since her return, Mary felt a deep connection not just to her family, but to the land itself.

"Maybe this is what you were trying to tell me all along, little brother," she said softly, imagining Howard standing beside her. "That our roots run deeper than just the pottery."

As the day's light began to wane, casting long shadows across the still waters, Mary decided to make camp for the night. She found a secluded spot sheltered by a cluster of silver birch trees, their leaves rustling gently in the evening breeze like nature's own lullaby.

With practiced hands, she erected her small tent, a compact shelter that had accompanied her on many European adventures. But here, on the shores of Ennerdale Lake, the experience was profoundly different.

Chapter 3

The convent garden basked in the warm Breton sunshine, its meticulously trimmed hedges casting intricate shadows across the weathered stone paths. Amélie Bouchard sat on a wrought-iron bench, her habit rustling softly in the breeze as she gazed at the oleander bushes nearby. Their delicate pink flowers seemed out of place against the austere backdrop of the convent walls.

"Amélie!" Sister Claire's voice broke through her reverie. "There you are. We've been looking for you."

Amélie turned to see Sisters Claire and Elise approaching, their faces alight with curiosity. She smiled, grateful for their company. They had been her closest confidantes since childhood, the sisters she never had.

"How was your trip south?" Elise asked, settling beside her on the bench. "We missed you at vespers."

Amélie's eyes brightened. "It was... enlightening," she said, choosing her words carefully. "Annie's funeral was beautiful, but sad. She was always so kind to me."

Claire nodded sympathetically. "May she rest in peace. Did you meet any of her family?"

"I did," Amélie replied, a hint of excitement creeping into her voice. "Her son, Paul. We talked for hours after the service. He's... different from anyone I've ever met."

Elise leaned in, intrigued. "Different how?"

Amélie paused, considering. "He understands what it's like to feel... out of place. He spoke of his concerns about his father, about feeling disconnected from his family history. We have so much in common."

"And?" Claire prompted, sensing there was more.

Amélie took a deep breath. "He's going to England to find his family, to uncover the truth about his past. And I... I think I should do the same."

Her friends exchanged worried glances. "Amélie," Elise began gently, "you know your family is here, with us."

"But what if it isn't?" Amélie countered, her voice rising with passion. "I've had dreams, visions. In one, Paul was my brother. I know it sounds crazy, but—"

Claire chuckled, shaking her head. "Oh, Amélie. Always dreaming, always seeing visions. Next, you'll tell us the oleanders spoke to you."

Amélie frowned, stung by the dismissal. "You don't understand. I made some calls after I returned. I spoke to a Mr. Benn in England. He says... he says my real name is Angela Benn, and that he's my cousin."

Her friends fell silent, shock evident on their faces.

"It's so exciting," Amélie continued, her words tumbling out in a rush. "I'm leaving for England. I have to know the truth about who I am, about my family."

"Amélie, think about what you're saying," Elise pleaded. "This is your home. We're your family. You can't just leave based on a phone call and some dreams."

Claire's brow furrowed with concern. "And what about your mother? Have you spoken to Sister Ada about this?"

Amélie's expression softened at the mention of her mother. "I... I haven't told her yet. You know she moved to the monastery to dedicate herself to prayer. I don't want to disturb her peace."

"But surely she should know," Elise insisted. "She's your mother, after all."

Amélie nodded, a mix of emotions playing across her face. "I know. I'll write to her once I'm in England. Once I have some answers."

"Speaking of England," Claire said, her tone cautious, "is your English good enough for this trip? It's been years since your mother taught us."

A small smile tugged at Amélie's lips. "It may be a bit rusty, but it is my mother tongue, after all. I'll manage."

The memory of those English lessons flooded back – Sister Ada's patient voice guiding them through unfamiliar words and phrases, the laughter as they stumbled over pronunciation. It had been one of the few times Amélie had felt truly connected to her mother, sharing a part of her past with her daughter and the other young nuns.

"I remember those lessons," Elise said softly. "Your mother had such a beautiful accent. So different from the English we heard from tourists."

Amélie nodded, her eyes distant. "Yes, she did. Sometimes, when I dream in English, I hear her voice."

But Amélie's mind was made up. She stood, her eyes blazing with determination. "I have to do this. I've never felt like I truly belonged here. This is my chance to find out where I do belong."

In the days that followed, the convent buzzed with whispers of Amélie's decision. Sister Agnes, the Mother Superior, called her to her office, her kind eyes filled with concern.

"My child," she said, her voice gentle but firm, "I urge you to reconsider. The world outside these walls can be harsh and unforgiving. Are you certain this is what you want?"

Amélie nodded, her resolve unwavering. "I am, Mother. I'm grateful for everything you've done for me, but I need to find my own path."

On the morning of her departure, Amélie stood at the convent gates, a small rucksack containing her meager possessions slung over her shoulder. She had exchanged her habit for a pair of faded jeans and a simple blouse, the clothes feeling strange against her skin after so many years.

Sisters Claire and Elise embraced her tearfully, whispering words of caution and love. Even Sister Agnes was there, her face a mask of worry and resignation.

"Remember, Amélie," the Mother Superior said, pressing a small silver cross into her hand, "no matter what you find out there, you will always have a home here."

Amélie nodded, her throat tight with emotion. She took one last look at the convent, at the garden where she had spent so many hours shaping the hedges into fantastic forms. The oleander flowers seemed to wave goodbye in the morning breeze.

With a deep breath, she turned and stepped through the gates, leaving behind the only world she had ever known. The road ahead was uncertain, filled with both promise and peril. But as she set off towards her new life, towards the mysteries of her past and the family she had never known, Amélie felt a surge of exhilaration.

For the first time in her life, she was truly free. And with every step, the English words her mother had taught her so long ago echoed in her mind, a bridge between her past and her uncertain future.

Chapter 4

The pre-dawn chill nipped at Mary's nose as she emerged from her tent, the fabric rustling softly in the gentle breeze. The world around her was cloaked in a diaphanous mist, transforming the familiar landscape into something otherworldly. Ennerdale Lake stretched before her, its surface a mirror of quicksilver, broken only by the occasional ripple of a jumping fish.

Mary stood transfixed, drinking in the ethereal beauty. The distant call of a curlew pierced the silence, its mournful cry echoing across the water. She closed her eyes, inhaling deeply. The air was crisp and clean, tinged with the earthy scent of damp leaves and the faint aroma of wood smoke from her dying campfire.

"This," she whispered to herself, "this is what I've been missing."

With renewed energy, Mary set about breaking camp. Her movements were deliberate, almost meditative. As she worked, her mind wandered to the family pottery, to the decisions that lay ahead. But here, in this moment, those worries seemed as insubstantial as the mist that was slowly lifting from the lake.

A quick breakfast of crusty bread and sharp Cumbrian cheese fortified Mary for the day ahead. She savored each bite, the flavors more intense somehow in the crisp morning air. As she sipped her tea – strong and sweet, just as her father had always made it – Mary felt an overwhelming urge to share this moment with her mother.

Gathering her things, she set off down the road, keeping an eye out for a public phone box. After about half a mile, she spotted the familiar red kiosk standing sentinel by the roadside. Its vibrant Colour stood out against the muted tones of the Cumbrian landscape.

As she approached, Mary couldn't help but smile at the quintessentially British sight. The phone box was surprisingly well-maintained for its remote location, with only a few faded posters adorning its glass panels. She stepped inside, the smell of damp wood and metal filling her nostrils.

Fishing in her pocket, Mary pulled out the coins she'd set aside for this purpose. With slightly trembling fingers, she inserted the money and dialed her mother's number. The mechanical whir and click of the rotary dial seemed oddly comforting in its familiarity.

As she waited for the connection, Mary's eyes wandered over the graffiti etched into the wooden frame of the box. Declarations of love, crude jokes, and mysterious initials told silent stories of past callers.

Finally, the ringing tone gave way to her mother's voice. "Hello, Postlethwaite residence."

"Hi Mum," Mary replied, surprised by the peace she heard in her own voice. "It's me, Mary. I'm okay, don't worry. I've survived my first night in the wild."

There was a pause, then, "Wild? You're camping? I thought you were staying in a hotel."

Mary couldn't help but chuckle. "I wanted to get away from it all, Mum. It's been lovely. No traffic, no crowds, just me and nature."

She could almost hear her mother's frown through the crackly line. "Well, I suppose it's good for you to get out and about. But do be careful, Mary. And don't forget to eat properly."

"I will, Mum. I promise." Mary's voice softened. "And Mum? Thank you. For everything."

"Oh, love," her mother's voice wavered slightly. "Just come home safe, alright?"

As the pips sounded, signalling the end of her call time, Mary quickly said her goodbyes and hung up. She stood in the phone box for a moment longer, the echo of her mother's voice lingering in her mind.

Stepping back out into the morning air, Mary took a deep breath. The call home had grounded her, connecting her journey to the life and people she'd left behind. As she walked back to her campsite, her steps felt lighter.

Turning her attention to packing, Mary found that each item seemed to carry a memory: the sleeping bag Howard had given her for her first solo trip to France, the battered old compass that had been her father's. As she secured her rucksack to the bicycle, she was struck by how much lighter it felt. Perhaps, she mused, it wasn't the pack that had changed, but her.

The open road beckoned, promising new adventures and, perhaps, answers to the questions that had driven her on this journey. With a smile, Mary mounted her bicycle and set off, the red phone box receding in her rear-view mirror – a small splash of civilization in the vast, wild beauty of the Cumbrian landscape.

The sun was cresting the horizon as Mary set off, its golden rays setting the lake ablaze with Colour. A family of ducks paddled by, their ducklings trailing behind like a string of feathered pearls. Mary couldn't help but smile at their antics.

As she pedalled, the landscape began to change. The gentle slopes of the Lake District gave way to the more austere beauty of the fells. The road twisted and turned, each bend revealing a new vista more breathtaking than the last.

It was as she rounded one such bend that Mary saw it: the Druids Stone Circle. The prehistoric monument stood silently on the moorland, a testament to the enduring mystery of the human spirit. Mary felt drawn to it, compelled by some force she couldn't quite name.

Dismounting her bicycle, she approached the circle with reverence. The stones loomed above her, their weathered surfaces telling tales of millennia gone by. Mary reached out, her fingers tracing the lichen-covered surface of the nearest monolith. The stone was cool to the touch, and she fancied she could feel the weight of history thrumming beneath her fingertips.

"If only you could talk," she murmured to the ancient sentinel. "What stories you could tell."

As she walked slowly around the circle, Mary's mind wandered. She thought of the countless generations that had stood where she now stood, of the rituals and ceremonies these stones had witnessed. In that moment, her own troubles seemed to shrink, put into perspective by the vastness of time.

The tranquility of the moment was broken by the distant bleating of sheep. With a start, Mary realized she had been lost in contemplation for far longer than she'd intended. The sun was now high in the sky, casting long shadows across the moorland.

As she remounted her bike, Mary cast one last look at the stone circle. Something had shifted within her, though she couldn't quite put her finger on what. The sense of wonder lingered as she pedalled on, the road ahead stretching out like a promise of adventures yet to come.

Chapter 5

The road ahead stretched like a ribbon of asphalt, leading Mary towards the rugged expanse of Cold Fell and onwards to Calderbridge. The memory of the stone circle lingered in her mind, transforming her journey into something more profound – a pilgrimage of sorts. To what end, she wasn't quite sure, but as the wind whipped through her hair and the Cumbrian landscape unfolded before her, Mary felt a surge of readiness to face whatever lay ahead.

As the gradient steepened and the wind picked up, Mary gritted her teeth, her legs burning with exertion. "Come on, old girl," she muttered to herself, "you've faced tougher challenges than this."

With each twist and turn, the landscape grew more dramatic. The fells, once distant silhouettes, now loomed as towering giants on the horizon. Mary pushed on, her determination fuelled by the raw beauty of her surroundings.

Finally, she arrived at a five-bar gate, the stark boundary between civilization and wilderness. Dismounting her bicycle, Mary paused, her breath held in anticipation. The paved road gave way to a rough, dirt track that disappeared into a vast expanse of moorland.

"Well, this is it," she said aloud, her voice carried away by the wind. "No turning back now."

Leaning her bicycle against a dry stone wall, Mary took a moment to catch her breath. As she stepped onto the ridge, a gasp escaped her lips. Before her lay a panorama of breathtaking beauty: a vast, undulating sea of green broken only by patches of golden gorse. The sky above was a canvas of blues and whites, and a soft breeze carried the sweet scent of heather.

With each step upward, the world seemed to expand, revealing new vistas of awe-inspiring grandeur. Mary felt a profound sense of peace and freedom wash over her, as if she had stepped into a different world entirely.

The air was filled with the constant bleating of sheep, their woolly bodies scattering in surprise as she rounded each bend. Mary couldn't resist a chuckle. "Sorry, ladies," she called out to a particularly startled group. "Just passing through!"

As she continued her journey, her mind drifted to the fabled Matty Benn's Bridge, also known as Monk's Bridge. The memory of a past boyfriend's tales about this historical landmark brought a bittersweet smile to her lips.

"I wonder if it's as magical as David made it sound," she mused, quickening her pace. The physical exertion of the climb was invigorating, a welcome contrast to the mental journey she was undertaking.

As she walked on, the dissimilarity between her structured life in Strasbourg and this untamed landscape became increasingly apparent. The open moorland, with its wild beauty and sense of freedom, was a stark contrast to the confines of her existence abroad.

"God, I've missed this," Mary whispered, her eyes drinking in the rolling hills and distant mountains. The allure of this place was intoxicating, a balm for her weary soul.

As she drew closer to Matty Benn's Bridge, a flicker of movement caught her eye. An old shepherd was herding his flock nearby, his weathered face a map of the harsh Cumbrian elements.

"Afternoon, miss," he called out, tipping his cap. "Fine day for a walk."

Mary smiled, grateful for the human interaction. "It certainly is. I'm headed to Matty Benn's Bridge. Am I on the right path?"

The old man's eyes crinkled with amusement. "Aye, that you are. Not far now. Heard the story of old Matty, have you?"

Mary shook her head, intrigued. "Only bits and pieces. Something about her building the bridge herself?"

The shepherd leaned on his crook, a twinkle in his eye. "Oh, aye. They say Matty was a woman of extraordinary strength. Built that bridge with her own two hands, she did. Her twelve children helped her, or so the story goes. Their laughter echoed through the valley as they worked."

Mary listened, captivated by the tale. "Twelve children? And they all helped build the bridge?"

The old man chuckled. "So they say. Course, some folks'll tell you it was the monks from Calder Abbey who built it. Hence the name Monk's Bridge. But I prefer Matty's story myself. Shows what a determined woman can do, doesn't it?"

As they parted ways, Mary felt a renewed sense of purpose. The story of Matty Benn, whether true or legend, resonated deeply with her own journey.

Finally, the old packhorse bridge came into view. A graceful arch of weathered stone traversed Friar Gill, spanning a deep chasm where rushing water tumbled over rocks far below. Mary stood transfixed, marveling at the bridge's simple yet enduring beauty.

"WELL, MATTY," SHE SAID softly, placing a hand on the cool stone, "I hope I can find even half the strength you had."

As she crossed the bridge, each step felt significant. She wasn't just crossing a physical divide; she was bridging the gap between her past and her future, between the life she had known and the one that lay ahead.

Chapter 6

Mary stood at the edge of Matty Benn's Bridge, her hand still resting on the cool, weathered stone. The old shepherd's tale of Matty Benn and her twelve children echoed in her mind, blending with the rushing sound of Friar Gill below. As she turned to look back at the bridge one last time, its ancient stonework seemed to call to her, a siren song of history and legend that threatened to swallow her whole.

A sudden burst of laughter cut through the tranquillity, startling Mary from her reverie. She turned to see a pair of hikers making their way across the moor, their backpacks laden with camping gear. As they drew closer, Mary could make out more details. The man was tall and lanky with a shock of unruly red hair. Beside him trudged a teenage girl, her expression vacant and disinterested.

"Enjoying the fresh air?" the man called out, his voice carrying on the breeze.

Mary nodded, a smile spreading across her face. "It's beautiful here," she replied.

The man's eyes lit up with recognition as he glanced at the bridge. "You've been to see Matty Benn's Bridge, haven't you?" he said, his voice tinged with a hint of local pride. "My name's Gordon Benn, by the way. Great-great-great grandson of the original Matty. And this is my daughter, Freda."

Mary's eyes widened in surprise. "No way!" she exclaimed, her mind racing back to the shepherd's story. "Matty Benn as in the bridge builder?"

Gordon grinned, clearly pleased by her reaction. "The very same. My old man used to tell me stories about her. Tough as old boots, they say she was. Built like a brick shithouse."

Throughout the exchange, Freda remained silent, her eyes glazed over with boredom. She idly kicked at loose stones, seemingly oblivious to the conversation or the historic surroundings.

Mary couldn't help but chuckle at Gordon's description. "I just heard a story about her from a shepherd. He said she built the bridge with her twelve children. Is that true?"

Gordon's eyes twinkled with amusement. "Ah, old Tom's been spinning his yarns again, has he? Well, the truth is probably somewhere in between. Matty was indeed a force of nature, but I doubt she single-handedly built the bridge. More likely, she organized the local community to pitch in. Still, it makes for a better story to say she did it all herself, doesn't it?"

As they chatted, Mary found herself studying Gordon and Freda more closely. At thirty-two, she was acutely aware of the contrasts in her own appearance - her slim figure and long auburn hair at odds with her practical attire of worn jeans and sturdy hiking boots. Gordon, with his easy manner and weathered outdoor gear, seemed perfectly at home in this rugged landscape. Freda, on the other hand, looked like she'd rather be anywhere else.

"So, what brings you out here?" Gordon asked, his curiosity evident.

Mary hesitated for a moment before answering. "I'm on a bit of a... personal journey, I suppose. Trying to reconnect with my roots and figure out my next steps."

Gordon nodded understandingly. "Sometimes you need to step away from everything to see it clearly. That's why I drag this one out here," he said, gesturing to Freda, who rolled her eyes in response. "There's something about this place that puts things in perspective."

As they talked, Mary's attention was caught by a glint of white in the distance. Nestled beneath the shade of a sprawling oak tree stood a car - an immaculate white Audi, its gleaming surface reflecting the afternoon sun like a polished mirror.

"That's an unusual sight out here," Mary remarked, nodding towards the car.

Gordon followed her gaze and nodded. "Ah, yes. Spotted that a couple of days ago when we were up here. Bit out of place, isn't it? Left-hand drive too. Didn't see the driver though. Mysterious, that."

Freda, showing the first signs of interest, piped up. "Can we go now, Dad? You promised we'd be back for tea."

Gordon chuckled, ruffling his daughter's hair affectionately. "Right you are, love. Well, Mary, it's been a pleasure. We're heading back to Calderbridge. If you're going that way, you're welcome to join us."

Mary glanced at her bicycle leaning against the dry stone wall. The offer was tempting, but there was something about completing the journey under her own steam that felt important.

"That's very kind of you," she said finally, "but I think I'll stick with my bike. This journey... I need to finish it the way I started."

Gordon nodded, respect evident in his eyes. "I understand. Well, Mary, it's been a pleasure meeting you. Perhaps our paths will cross again in Calderbridge?"

As Gordon and Freda continued on their way, Mary turned back to her bicycle. The encounter had left her with a strange mix of emotions - a connection to the past through the Benn family legend, and a curiosity about the mysterious car and its unseen owner.

Mary Postlethwaite leaned her bicycle against a weathered dry stone wall, her eyes drawn to the vast expanse of Cold Fell stretching before her. The wild Cumbrian landscape, with its rolling hills and patchwork of green fields, seemed to mirror the tumultuous state of her mind. The mysterious white Audi gleamed in the distance, a stark contrast to the rugged surroundings.

She inhaled deeply, savoring the crisp air. "Just what I needed," she murmured, closing her eyes briefly.

"It certainly is breath-taking, isn't it?"

The rich, masculine voice startled her. Mary turned to find a man perched on a nearby rock, his appearance as unexpected as his presence. Tall, with sun-kissed blonde hair and piercing blue eyes, he exuded an air of sophistication that seemed at odds with the rugged surroundings. He was dressed in hiking gear that looked barely worn, as if it had just come off a designer rack.

"I'm sorry, I didn't mean to startle you," he said, his lips curving into an apologetic smile. A hint of a French accent coloured his words. "I'm Paul. Paul Brankenwall."

"Mary Postlethwaite," she replied, finding herself drawn to his easy charm despite her initial wariness. "I didn't expect to find anyone else up here."

Paul chuckled, the sound warm and inviting. "Neither did I. It's usually just me and the sheep. Although they're not nearly as good conversationalists."

As they talked, Mary found herself opening up about her dilemma, surprised by her own candour with this stranger. There was something in Paul's attentive gaze that made her feel... understood.

"I'm at a crossroads," she admitted, running a hand through her wind-tousled hair. "My brother Howard passed away recently, leaving our family pottery business without a CEO. I have a stable job with the EU in Strasbourg, but..."

"But you're torn," Paul finished for her, his eyes reflecting a depth of understanding that caught Mary off guard.

Mary nodded, a lump forming in her throat. "Exactly. The pottery's been in our family for generations. It feels wrong to let it go, but I'm not sure I'm cut out to run it. And then there's the life I've built in Strasbourg..."

Paul listened attentively, occasionally asking thoughtful questions that made Mary consider aspects of her situation she hadn't before. As the conversation flowed, he reached into a small cooler by his feet and produced a bottle of white wine.

"Care for a glass? It's from my vineyard in Roussillon," he offered, a hint of pride in his voice.

Mary hesitated only briefly before accepting. As Paul poured the wine into two crystal glasses he seemingly produced out of nowhere, she couldn't help but marvel at the surreal nature of the situation.

"Your own vineyard? That sounds fascinating," she said, accepting the glass.

As they sipped the crisp, fragrant wine, Paul shared his own story, his voice taking on a nostalgic tone.

"I understand the pull of family legacy," he said, his gaze distant. "I was educated at a private school in Oxfordshire, but my roots are in France. The vineyard near Perpignan has been in my family for generations."

"What brings you to Cumbria, then?" Mary asked, intrigued by the parallels in their situations.

Paul's expression turned wry, a shadow passing over his features. "Family business, much like yourself. It seems we're both trying to balance duty with personal desires. Sometimes I wonder if it's possible to have both."

As the afternoon wore on, Mary found herself increasingly drawn to Paul's wit and charm. The wine loosened her tongue, and she shared more about her fears and hopes for the future, surprised by her own openness.

"It's not just about the business," she confessed, her voice barely above a whisper. "It's about finding my place in the world. Do I belong in Strasbourg or Ravenglass? Am I betraying my family's legacy if I choose my career in Europe?"

Paul nodded thoughtfully, refilling their glasses. "Sometimes the hardest choices are between two good options. But remember, Mary, you're not just choosing a place or a job. You're choosing a life, a future. And sometimes, the right path isn't always the obvious one."

As the sun began to dip towards the horizon, casting long shadows across the fell and painting the sky in hues of orange and pink, Paul glanced at his watch, an expression of regret crossing his face.

"I should be going," he said, a note of reluctance in his voice. "But I've enjoyed our conversation immensely. Would you like to continue it over dinner tomorrow? Say, at the Pennington Arms in Ravenglass?"

Mary felt a flutter of excitement, mixed with a tinge of caution. This man was virtually a stranger, yet she felt a connection she couldn't quite explain. "I'd like that," she replied, surprised by her own eagerness.

Paul smiled, the warmth of it reaching his eyes. "Excellent. Shall we say seven o'clock?"

As he gathered his things and walked towards the sleek white Audi parked a short distance away, Mary called out, "Thank you, Paul. For listening, and for the wine. It's been... unexpected, but wonderful."

Paul turned back, his smile enigmatic. "The pleasure was all mine, Mary. Sometimes the most beautiful things in life are the unexpected ones. I look forward to tomorrow."

As Paul's car disappeared down the winding road, the rumble of its engine fading into the distance, Mary turned back to the panoramic view. The decision before her still loomed large, but somehow, it felt less daunting. With a small smile, she stood up and stretched her aching legs, her muscles protesting from the long bike ride.

The sun was sinking lower, painting the sky in vibrant hues of orange and pink. But as if on cue, the infamous Cumbrian weather began to assert itself. A chill wind picked up, carrying with it the promise of rain. Mary shivered, pulling her jacket closer around her. She knew it was time to set up camp for the night, and quickly.

As she began to unpack her tent, the first droplets of rain began to fall. By the time she had the tent erected, the drizzle had turned into a steady downpour. The pitter-patter of raindrops on canvas created a soothing rhythm, almost drowning out the whistle of the wind across the fell.

"Welcome to Cumbria," Mary muttered to herself, a wry smile on her face as she ducked into the tent, grateful for its shelter.

As night fell, the rain showed no signs of letting up. The moor, which had been awash in twilight Colours just hours ago, was now a dark, sodden expanse. Yet, as Mary peered out of her tent, she gasped. A full moon, a colossal, luminous orb, had ascended, its light piercing through gaps in the rain clouds. It cast an almost daylight brilliance across the desolate landscape, creating a ethereal interplay of light and shadow, mist and rain.

Inside her tent, Mary huddled in her sleeping bag, the chill of the night seeping into her bones despite her layers. The physical discomfort of sleeping rough was a stark contrast to her comfortable life in Strasbourg, yet she couldn't deny the exhilaration of this wild experience.

As she lay there, listening to the relentless rain and the occasional gust of wind that shook her tent, her mind raced. The unexpected encounter with Paul, the promise of tomorrow's dinner, and the looming decision about her future intertwined in a complex knot of emotions. The weight of her choices, momentarily forgotten in the excitement of the day, now pressed down on her with renewed force.

Morning arrived with a bitter tang and a bone-deep chill. The world outside was shrouded in a thick, damp mist, and a sense of unease settled over Mary as she emerged from her tent, stiff and shivering. Her heart sank as her eyes scanned the area. Her bicycle was gone.

"No, no, no," she muttered, panic rising in her throat. "Where can it have gone? Why would anyone steal my old bike?"

The reality of her situation hit her like a bucket of cold water. Without transportation, she was stranded in the middle of nowhere, miles from civilization, with the promise of more rain hanging heavy in the air.

Resigned to her fate, Mary packed up her sodden tent and set off on foot, following the winding country lanes. The walk was a test of endurance. The damp mist clung to her clothes and hair, and intermittent showers left her thoroughly drenched. The beauty of Cold Fell that had so enchanted her yesterday now seemed foreboding and alien.

An hour and a half later, her legs aching and her spirit dampened, Mary reached the small village of Calderbridge. The cluster of stone buildings was a welcome sight after the desolate expanse of the moor. Exhausted and disoriented, she made her way to the village's sole bus stop, gratefully sinking onto the bench under its small shelter.

As she waited for the bus to Ravenglass, Mary's mind wandered to the dinner invitation from Paul. Would she even make it? And more importantly, had this misadventure changed her perspective on the decision she faced?

The bus arrived with a hiss of brakes and a spray of water from the puddle-strewn road. As Mary climbed aboard, she cast one last look at the mist-shrouded fells behind her. Despite everything, a small smile played on her lips. This journey had certainly not gone as planned, but perhaps that was the point. Life, like the Cumbrian weather, was unpredictable. And sometimes, it was in facing those unexpected challenges that one found their true path.

Chapter 7

Detective Inspector Harry Williamson stood at the edge of the beck, his eyes fixed on the pale form lying on the muddy bank. The grey morning seemed to mirror the grim mood that had settled over the scene. A cold wind whipped across the fell, carrying with it the mournful cries of distant sheep.

A man approached, his weathered face etched with concern. He was tall and lean, with hands roughened by years of toil. This was Thomas Carter, a tenant farmer on the Earl of Egremont's land. His father had run the farm before him, until his untimely death five years ago.

"Inspector, I'm the one who called it in," Carter said, his voice thick with a local accent. "My dog found her just over an hour ago."

Williamson turned to face him, his gaze sharp. "Tell me everything you saw and heard, no detail too small."

Carter nodded, his eyes fixed on the tragic figure. "Right, well, it was about 6:15 when my dog started barking like mad near the bridge. I called 999 straight away and didn't touch a thing." He paused, frowning. "Oh, and last night, around 1 am, I heard a car on the fell. Unusual, that."

Williamson's interest piqued. "A car? Can you describe it?"

Carter shook his head. "Not much to tell, I'm afraid. Just saw it heading towards Egremont from my window."

Williamson pressed further, his tone urgent. "What about Saturday? Notice anything out of the ordinary?"

Carter scratched his chin, trying to recall. "Come to think of it, there was a fancy white car parked near the main gate. Foreign, I reckon. Had different number plates."

Yeah, and I had a bit of a chat with a young lass, looking at the bridge."

Williamson made a note in his pocketbook.

"Did she have red hair?"

"No, I don't think so." Replied Carter.

"Mr. Carter, I'd like to ask you to come into the station later today to make a formal statement. This information is crucial to our investigation."

Carter nodded solemnly. "Of course, Inspector. Anything to help."

Sergeant Thompson approached, his face ashen. "Sir, I don't recognize her. Young lass, I'd say 18, maybe 20. That red hair would make her easy to identify."

Harry Williamson nodded slowly, his jaw clenched. "Any signs of violence, Thompson?"

"Nothing obvious, sir. It's... strange. Almost like she just lay down and..."

"And what, Thompson? Decided to have a kip in the nude by a freezing river?" Williamson's voice was sharp, his frustration palpable.

"No, sir. Of course not. I just meant-"

Williamson sighed, running a hand through his thinning hair. "I know what you meant. Sorry, lad. It's too early on a Sunday morning. This case... it's getting to me."

As they watched the forensic team at work, Thompson ventured, "What's your gut telling you, sir?"

Williamson was quiet for a moment. "That we're dealing with something far more complex than we initially thought. No obvious signs of violence... it doesn't fit any profile I've seen before."

"Could it be an accident?" Thompson suggested.

"An accident that left her naked and washed up downstream from Matty Benn's Bridge? Unlikely." Williamson's brow furrowed. "No, there's more to this. We're missing something crucial."

Thompson's eyes widened as he spotted something. "Sir, we've found a rucksack under the bridge. Looks like it might contain her clothes."

Williamson's eyebrows rose. "Her clothes? Interesting. Anything else?"

"Yes, sir. There's a bike leaning against a tree nearby. Oh, and two more items of interest - a lighter with the initials 'PB' engraved on it, and a crucifix necklace with 'AB' on the back."

Williamson's eyes narrowed. "AB - PB? Now that's intriguing. What do you make of all this, Thompson?"

The sergeant hesitated. "Well, sir... it's odd, isn't it? Her clothes neatly packed away, the bike... it's almost as if-"

"As if she came here voluntarily," Williamson finished. "But then why end up by the river? And who does that lighter belong to? Remember, Thompson, she was found ten yards from the bank, like she was sheltering from the wind behind a bush."

"Could be a boyfriend we don't know about," Thompson suggested.

Williamson shook his head. "Possibly. But let's not jump to conclusions. A young girl doesn't just strip off and die for no reason. There's more to this story, Thompson."

"What's our next move, sir?"

Williamson straightened his coat against the chill. "We need to identify that 'PB'. Check local records, school rosters, anything you can think of. And I want to know everything about this girl's movements in the last 48 hours. Who she spoke to, where she went, what she ate for breakfast - everything."

"Yes, sir. And the post-mortem?"

"I'll be there first thing tomorrow," Williamson said grimly. "Something tells me it's going to be crucial to this case. For now, let's get back to the station and get the team working on this. We've got precious few leads, and I want them all followed up. This girl deserves justice, Thompson, and by God, we're going to get it for her."

As they walked away from the scene, both men felt the weight of the mystery settling on their shoulders. They knew this was just the beginning of a complex and challenging investigation.

Back at the station, Williamson and Thompson were briefing their team when a young constable burst into the room, slightly out of breath.

"Sir, we've got something," he panted. "A lead from the Blue Bell pub."

Williamson's eyebrows shot up. "Well, don't keep us in suspense, lad. Out with it."

The constable nodded, catching his breath. "A barmaid remembers a girl with striking red hair in the pub on Saturday night. She was with a man - blonde, long hair, good-looking type."

Thompson leaned forward. "That's promising. Anything else?"

"Yes, sir. This is where it gets interesting," the constable continued. "They were speaking French."

Williamson's eyes narrowed. "French, you say? Now that's unexpected in these parts. Go on."

"They ordered a bottle of wine, but neither seemed impressed. The barmaid said, and I quote, 'They were proper wine snobs, those two.'"

Thompson chuckled. "Sounds like they knew their vintages."

The constable nodded. "They asked for the wine list and ordered something expensive. Shared a meal, stayed until last orders at 11."

Williamson stroked his chin thoughtfully. "And the man? Any more details?"

"Yes, sir. He drove a white Audi."

Williamson and Thompson exchanged meaningful glances. "A white Audi," Williamson mused. "Just like our sheep farmer mentioned. Thompson, I want that CCTV footage from the pub, and I want it yesterday."

As the team dispersed to follow up on the new lead, Williamson pulled Thompson aside.

"Something's not adding up here, Thompson. A French-speaking couple, expensive tastes, and now she's found dead by a beck? It doesn't fit."

Thompson nodded. "You think there's more to this than a date gone wrong?"

Before Williamson could answer, his phone rang. His face grew grave as he listened.

"Right, thank you," he said, ending the call. He turned to Thompson, his expression grim. "That was the lab. Preliminary tox screen shows traces of a rare poison in her system. Derived from a plant not native to the UK."

Thompson's eyes widened. "Murder, then?"

Williamson nodded slowly. "Aye, and a sophisticated one at that. But why here? Why her?"

Just then, another officer approached with a file. "Sir, we've identified the girl. Her name is Amélie Bouchard. She's a French exchange student, supposed to be staying with a local family."

Williamson took the file, his brow furrowing. "Amélie Bouchard? But the crucifix had the initials 'AB'..."

Thompson's face lit up with realization. "Angela Benn. Sir, what if..."

Williamson nodded, catching on. "What if our victim isn't who we thought she was? Thompson, get me everything you can on Angela Benn. And find out where Amélie Bouchard is supposed to be right now."

As Thompson hurried off, Williamson stared at the photo of the red-haired girl in the file. "Who are you really?" he muttered. "And what have you got yourself into?"

The case had just taken a turn into international waters, and Williamson had a sinking feeling that this was only the tip of the iceberg.

Chapter 8

Mary arrived in Ravenglass, her emotions a tumultuous mix of anticipation and apprehension. The prospect of dining with Paul sent a thrill through her, but it was tempered by the nagging awareness of her limited wardrobe options. She'd packed for a camping trip, not a dinner date with a sophisticated stranger.

In her room at the Pennington Arms, Mary surveyed her meager choices. She could swap her muddy walking boots for trainers and had a clean shirt, but her jeans were far from ideal for what promised to be an upscale evening. "He'll just have to understand," she muttered, hoping Paul wouldn't judge her too harshly.

As she changed, her eyes drifted to the window, where she could just make out the silhouette of Postlethwaite Pottery at the far end of town. The family legacy loomed large, a constant reminder of the decision that awaited her. Mary pushed the thought aside, determined to postpone her visit to the pottery until tomorrow. Tonight, she wanted to savor this unexpected encounter and explore the quaint charm of Ravenglass.

Descending the stairs to the hotel bar, Mary was struck by an unsettling change in atmosphere. The usual cheerful buzz of conversation had been replaced by hushed, urgent whispers. Concerned faces huddled over tables, their usual jovial demeanor replaced by something more somber.

As she hesitantly approached the bar, a local man turned to her, his face etched with worry. "Terrible business, this," he said, his voice low and gravelly. "Young woman found murdered on the fells."

The news hit Mary like a physical blow. Her mind raced, recalling her own recent solitary wanderings on those same fells. She listened intently as theories circulated – a tragic accident, a crime of passion, or something more sinister. Each speculation seemed to heighten the sense of unease that had settled over the room.

Amidst this unsettling atmosphere, Mary spotted Paul entering the bar. His presence, normally so reassuring, now seemed incongruous with the gravity of the situation. As he approached, smiling warmly, Mary felt caught between two worlds – the excitement of a new connection and the shocking reality of a community in turmoil.

She stood to greet him, suddenly self-conscious of her casual attire. "I'm sorry," she began, gesturing to her jeans and trainers. "I'm afraid I didn't pack for fine dining."

Paul's smile didn't falter. "You look lovely," he assured her, before his expression turned more serious. "But I sense something's amiss here. Shall we find a quiet corner and you can fill me in?"

As they moved to a secluded table, Mary felt a mix of relief at Paul's understanding and a growing sense of unease about the events unfolding around them. This dinner, she realized, would be about far more than getting to know each other better.

The soft glow of candlelight seemed to flicker uncertainly, as if sensing the shift in mood.

Mary fidgeted with the hem of her clean but casual shirt, acutely aware of its inadequacy for the setting. "I'm sorry about..." she gestured vaguely at her outfit, a rueful smile playing on her lips. "Someone nicked my bike. Can you believe it? Right there on the fells. I had to hoof it to Calderbridge and catch the bus."

Paul's eyebrows shot up, his fork pausing midway to his mouth. "Your bike was stolen? Out there in the middle of nowhere?" He shook his head, bewildered. "That's more than just opportunistic theft. It's... deliberate."

A chill ran down Mary's spine at his words. The vast, wild beauty of the fells that had so enchanted her now seemed tinged with menace. She took a sip of wine, hoping it would steady her nerves.

Paul leaned forward, his blue eyes intent on her face. "Mary," he said softly, reaching across to cover her hand with his. "There's more troubling you than a stolen bike. What is it?"

Mary hesitated, then the words tumbled out in a rush. "There's been a murder. A young woman, found on Cold Fell." She watched as Paul's expression shifted from concern to shock.

"Cold Fell?" he repeated, his voice low. "Where we met yesterday?"

The implications hung in the air between them, unspoken but impossible to ignore. The romantic tension that had simmered between them since their first meeting now mingled with a darker, more dangerous undercurrent.

Paul sat back, running a hand through his hair. "This is... quite a coincidence," he said, his tone carefully neutral.

Mary nodded, her appetite vanishing. "I can't help but wonder..." she began, then trailed off, unsure how to voice her suspicions without sounding paranoid.

The news of the murder hung over Mary and Paul like a heavy shroud, transforming what should have been a romantic dinner into something far more sombre.

Their desserts arrived, an incongruously cheerful interruption. The waiter's forced smile suggested he, too, was affected by the grim news circulating through the small town.

As they contemplated their untouched sweets, the restaurant door swung open with a decisive thud. The chatter in the room died instantly as a tall, broad-shouldered man strode in, his keen eyes sweeping the room. Even without the tell-tale badge glinting on his lapel, his air of authority would have marked him as Detective Inspector Williamson.

His gaze locked onto Mary and Paul's table, and he began to make his way towards them with purposeful steps.

Paul straightened in his chair, his face a mask of polite inquiry. "It seems our evening is about to take another unexpected turn," he murmured to Mary.

Mary felt her heart rate quicken. As the Inspector approached, she couldn't shake the feeling that their lives were about to become far more complicated than either of them had anticipated when they'd agreed to this dinner.

The restaurant fell silent as Detective Inspector Williamson entered. His imposing figure, coupled with the seriousness of his demeanour, commanded attention. He was a man clearly accustomed to authority, and his presence filled the room with an air of tension.

He stopped at their table, his presence looming over them. "Ms. Postlethwaite? Mr. Brankenwall?" he said, his voice gravelly and authoritative. "Good evening, I'm afraid I'm going to have to ask you both some questions."

the inspector began, his voice cutting through the silenceI'd be happy to expand on this scene.

"I'm Detective Inspector Williamson from the local police force," the man announced, his stern gaze sweeping across the dining room. "I apologize for interrupting your dinner, but I'm here on a matter of utmost importance."

A collective intake of breath swept through the room as people shifted uncomfortably in their seats. The inspector's eyes settled on Mary and Paul.

"I'm investigating a murder that occurred last night on Cold Fell," he continued, his voice low and deliberate. "The victim is a young woman, not yet identified. We're in the process of gathering all possible information."

A hush fell over the restaurant as the gravity of the situation sank in. Mary felt a cold dread creeping over her. The idyllic evening she had been anticipating had taken a sinister turn.

The inspector turned his attention back to Mary and Paul. "I believe this belongs to one of you," he said, producing the silver lighter.

A gasp escaped Mary's lips. The lighter was undoubtedly Paul's.

Williamson continued, "We found it near the victim's body. We believe it may be connected to the case."

Paul's face paled. "That's mine," he managed to say, his voice barely a whisper.

"I see," the inspector said, his eyes narrowing. "Can you explain how it ended up at the crime scene?"

Paul swallowed hard. "I... I must have dropped it while we were walking on the Fell."

The inspector nodded, jotting down notes. "Can you provide more details about your exact location and the timeframe of your stay?"

MARY INTERJECTED, HER voice trembling slightly. "Yes, we were there... camping on the moor."

"Camping?" Williamson's eyebrow raised. "Where exactly were you camping?"

"We arrived in the late afternoon," Mary began, but Paul cut her off.

"I think we should consult with a lawyer before making any further statements," he said firmly.

The inspector regarded them both with a steady gaze. "That is your right," he replied. "However, I must remind you that any delay in providing information could hinder our investigation. Did you see or hear anything unusual during your stay on Cold Fell?"

MARY AND PAUL EXCHANGED glances, the tension palpable between them.

"We didn't notice anything out of the ordinary," Mary said cautiously.

Williamson's pen scratched across his notepad. "And what time did you leave the area this morning?"

"Early," Paul replied tersely. "I had an appointment in town."

The inspector's eyes narrowed. "What kind of appointment?"

Paul hesitated. "A personal matter. I'd rather not discuss it without legal counsel present."

Williamson nodded slowly. "I understand. However, I must ask you both to come to the police station tomorrow morning to make a formal statement. Any information you can provide, no matter how insignificant it may seem, could be crucial to our investigation."

He reached into his pocket and produced two business cards. "Here's my direct contact information. If you remember anything else or have any questions before our meeting tomorrow, please don't hesitate to call."

As he handed them the cards, his gaze lingered on the silver lighter still on the table. "I'll be taking this as evidence," he said, carefully placing it in an evidence bag.

With that, he turned to leave but paused at the door. "Oh, and I strongly advise against leaving town until we've concluded our initial questioning. Good evening."

As Inspector Williamson's footsteps faded, the hushed whispers of the other diners gradually returned, filling the air with nervous energy. Mary and Paul sat in stunned silence, the weight of the situation settling over them like a heavy shroud.

Mary glanced at the business card in her hand, then at Paul, her mind reeling with questions and fears about what the coming days might bring.

Mary and Paul sat in stunned silence, the remnants of their meal forgotten.

Mary's hands trembled slightly as she reached for her wine glass. "Paul," she whispered, her voice strained, "what just happened?"

Paul's face was a mask of calm, but his eyes betrayed a hint of worry. He leaned in, speaking softly. "It's alright, Mary. We've done nothing wrong. But in situations like these, it's best to be cautious."

Mary nodded, trying to process the whirlwind of events. "The lighter..." she began, her brow furrowed in confusion.

Paul's jaw tightened almost imperceptibly. "An old memento," he said dismissively. "I must have dropped it yesterday. But that's hardly important now."

He signaled for the bill, his movements deliberate and controlled. "We should leave. This isn't the place for this conversation."

As they stepped out into the cool evening air, the quaint charm of Ravenglass seemed to have evaporated, replaced by an atmosphere of suspicion and unease. The street lamps cast long shadows, and Mary couldn't shake the feeling of being watched.

Paul guided her towards a small, secluded garden behind the hotel. The scent of night-blooming jasmine hung in the air, a stark contrast to the tension between them.

"Mary," Paul said, his voice low and urgent. "I need you to trust me. There's more going on here than a simple murder investigation."

Mary's heart raced. "What do you mean? Paul, do you know something about this?"

He ran a hand through his hair, a gesture of frustration. "It's complicated. I can't explain everything right now, but I promise I will. For now, we need to be careful about what we say to the police."

Mary took a step back, her mind reeling. "You're scaring me, Paul. First the murder, then the lighter, and now this? What aren't you telling me?"

Paul reached for her hand, but she pulled away. His expression softened, a mixture of concern and something else – determination, perhaps. "I know how this must look, but please, give me a chance to explain. Not here, not now, but soon."

A cold breeze rustled through the garden, sending a shiver down Mary's spine. She wrapped her arms around herself, suddenly feeling very alone despite Paul's presence.

"I think," she said slowly, choosing her words carefully, "that I need some time to think. This is all too much."

Paul nodded, resignation clear in his eyes. "I understand. But Mary, promise me you won't speak to the police alone. Wait for me in the morning. We'll go together, with a lawyer."

As Mary turned to leave, Paul called out softly, "And Mary? Be careful. Trust no one."

She hurried back to her room, her mind a whirlwind of questions and fears. As she locked the door behind her, Mary couldn't help but wonder what she had stumbled into. The peaceful bike ride that had led her to Cold Fell now seemed like a distant memory, replaced by a web of mystery and danger she couldn't begin to unravel.

Lying in bed, sleep eluding her, Mary stared at the ceiling. The events of the past two days played on repeat in her mind. What had started as a simple decision about her future had morphed into something far more complex and potentially dangerous. As the first light of dawn crept through her window, Mary made a resolution. She would get to the bottom of this, no matter where it led her.

Chapter 9

Mary jolted awake, her heart racing. The events of the past day crashed over her like a tidal wave, leaving her gasping for breath. As she fumbled to get dressed, her mind reeled with the impending police interview. Suddenly, she froze, a crucial detail slamming into her consciousness - her stolen bike. She'd completely forgotten to mention it to Inspector Williamson.

"Oh God," she whispered, her hand trembling as she buttoned her blouse. The theft, once a mere inconvenience, now loomed large in the shadow of murder.

She hurried to the pottery, her steps quick and uneven on the familiar path. The quaint charm of Ravenglass now felt oppressive, as if the very buildings were watching her.

Steve was at his desk when Mary burst in, her face pale and drawn. "Steve," she gasped, "I need to talk to you. Now."

Concern etched across his features as he ushered her into a private office. "What's wrong, Mary, we didn't expect you until next week? You look like you've seen a ghost."

The words tumbled out of her in a torrent. She told him everything - the solitary night on Cold Fell, her stolen bike, the gruelling walk to Calderbridge. Then came Paul, the enigmatic stranger who'd captivated her, followed by the chilling interruption of their dinner by Detective Inspector Williamson.

"And now," Mary concluded, her voice barely above a whisper, "I have to go to the police station. Steve, I'm terrified. What if they think I'm involved somehow?"

Steve listened intently, his brow furrowed. When Mary finished, he leaned forward, his voice low and steady. "Mary, this is serious. You can't go alone. I'm coming with you."

"But Paul," Mary started, then hesitated. "He said he'd meet me there, with a lawyer."

Steve's eyes narrowed. "Paul? The man you just met? Mary, think about this. You barely know him. And now he's suddenly involved in a murder investigation? Something doesn't add up."

Mary felt a flicker of doubt. "But he was so kind, so understanding..."

"Maybe so," Steve conceded, "but right now, you need family. Someone you can trust completely. Let me come with you. We'll face this together."

The sincerity in Steve's eyes broke through Mary's hesitation. She nodded, feeling a wave of relief wash over her.

As they drove to the station, Mary stared out the window, the familiar landscape blurring past. "What about the pottery?" she asked suddenly, guilt creeping into her voice.

Steve squeezed her hand reassuringly. "The pottery's been around for generations, Mary. It can survive without us for a morning. This is more important."

They pulled up to the station, its stark facade looming before them. Mary's heart raced as she spotted Paul pacing near the entrance, his usually composed demeanour now tense and agitated.

Steve noticed her gaze. "Remember, Mary," he said softly, "you don't owe him anything. We're here for you, to protect you. Let's go in together and tell the truth. That's all that matters now."

Mary took a deep breath, drawing strength from her brother's presence. As they stepped out of the car, she felt a curious mix of fear and determination. Whatever lay ahead, she knew she wasn't facing it alone.

Paul's eyes widened in surprise as he saw Mary approach with Steve. She could see the questions forming on his lips, but Steve stepped forward, placing himself protectively between them.

"Mr. Brankenwall, I presume," Steve said, his tone polite but cool. "I'm Steve Postlethwaite, Mary's brother. I'll be accompanying her today."

As they entered the station, Mary caught Paul's hurt and confused expression. But Steve's steady presence beside her reinforced her decision. Family first, she thought. Everything else could wait.

Chapter 10

With her plans disrupted, Mary decided to focus on the pottery business, hoping that immersing herself in work would distract her from the growing unease. As she stepped into the Postlethwaite Pottery, a wave of nostalgia washed over her. The familiar scents of clay and kiln smoke brought back memories of childhood Saturdays spent helping her father. Back then, the pottery had seemed like a magical place, filled with wonder and creativity.

She was met with a cold reception from her uncle, Brian. The once jovial man who had taught her the basics of pottery seemed distant and preoccupied. His eyes, usually filled with a calculated shrewdness, held a hint of something darker today. It was clear that the family business was in trouble, and Brian was under immense pressure. The weight of the family legacy seemed to be crushing him, and Mary could sense the storm brewing beneath the surface.

"Where have you been, Andrew said he saw you this morning with Steve," he said, his voice flat, breaking the tense silence.

Mary ignored the implicit criticism. "I had a bit of trouble this morning," she replied, her voice carefully neutral. "My bike was stolen."

Brian nodded, his expression unreadable. "The bank called," he said, his voice heavy with disappointment. "Another missed payment. We're running out of options, Mary."

The news was a heavy blow. The pottery, once a thriving business, was now on the brink of collapse. How could a business with such a rich history be in such dire straits? A surge of anger and frustration swept through her. This was her family's legacy, and it was crumbling before her eyes.

Determined to make a difference, Mary threw herself into the work. She spent hours at the potter's wheel, rediscovering a passion she hadn't known she possessed. The physicality of the task was therapeutic, providing a much-needed distraction from the turmoil in her mind. As her skills developed, so did her confidence. She began to see the pottery not just as a business, but as an art form, a way to express her creativity and connect with her family's heritage.

The more she worked, the more she realized the depth of the problems facing the pottery. Costs were rising, competition was fierce, and consumer tastes were changing. It was clear that a radical overhaul was needed.

As she worked, Mary couldn't help but think about the enigmatic Paul. His words about following one's heart echoed in her mind. Perhaps it was time to stop playing it safe and take a risk. After all, what did she have to lose?

As days passed, Mary managed to arrange another meeting with Paul. They agreed to meet for an evening walk along the coastal path, both eager for a respite from the tension that had built up since their encounter with Detective Inspector Williamson.

The salty air whipped around them as they made their way along the rugged coastline. The rhythmic crash of waves against the shore provided a soothing backdrop, momentarily drowning out their worries. As they walked, Paul's usual reserve began to soften, and he started to open up about his family and recent experiences.

"I made a statement to the police," Paul said, his voice barely audible above the wind and waves. Mary felt her heart skip a beat, but she remained silent, allowing him to continue. "They questioned why I hadn't stayed the night camping with you."

Mary nodded, remembering how abruptly Paul had left that evening on Cold Fell. She had wondered about it herself but hadn't found the right moment to ask.

Paul took a deep breath before continuing. "I told them I had an appointment at the Registry office the next morning. I've been searching for records of my family history." He paused, glancing at Mary to gauge her reaction. "It's partly why I came to this area in the first place."

Mary's curiosity was piqued. "Your family history? What are you hoping to find?"

Paul's gaze turned to the horizon, his expression a mix of hope and uncertainty. "I'm not entirely sure. There are gaps in my family tree, mysteries that have been passed down through generations. I'm hoping to fill in some of those blanks, to understand where I come from."

As they continued their walk, Paul shared more about his family's past, the fragments of stories he'd heard growing up, and the questions that had driven him to this search. Mary listened intently, feeling a growing connection to Paul as he revealed this vulnerable side of himself.

Their conversation meandered, touching on Paul's research, Mary's work at the pottery, and their shared experience of being caught up in the murder investigation. Neither mentioned the lighter with the initials 'PB' that the detective had shown them, but its presence hung unspoken between them.

As the sun began to set, casting long shadows across the coastal path, Mary found herself torn. On one hand, she felt a deepening bond with Paul, a shared understanding forged through their recent ordeals. On the other, questions lingered in her mind about his sudden departure that night on Cold Fell and the true nature of his connection to the ongoing investigation.

They turned back towards town, the sky ablaze with the Colours of sunset. Mary realized that while this evening had provided a temporary escape, it had also added new layers of complexity to her already complicated situation. As they said their goodbyes, Mary couldn't shake the feeling that there was still much more to Paul's story than he had revealed.

Mary's mind buzzed with thoughts of clay and kilns, of family secrets and unexplained murders. She knew that tomorrow would bring another day of work at the pottery, another opportunity to lose herself in her craft. But she also knew that the mystery surrounding Paul and the events on Cold Fell would continue to simmer beneath the surface, waiting to be unraveled

Paul spoke of his childhood in France, a world away from the structured rigidity of the Postlethwaite family. He painted a picture of a household without a father but filled with love and laughter. His mother, a devoted housewife; his father an absent nobleman. It was a life immersed in creativity and passion, a stark contrast to the practical, grounded existence Mary had known.

In contrast to Paul's idyllic childhood, Mary had grown up in a more traditional environment. Although her family had enjoyed a comfortable lifestyle, there had been an underlying sense of duty and responsibility. Her father's untimely death had cast a long shadow over her upbringing, leaving her with a deep-rooted sense of obligation to the family business.

As they talked, a sense of camaraderie grew between them. They were both outsiders in a way, each carrying their own burdens and searching for a sense of belonging. In the fading light of the evening, as the waves crashed against the shore, they found solace in each other's company.

Mary listened intently, finding herself drawn to the warmth and openness of his family life. In contrast, her own family seemed shrouded in secrets and unspoken resentments. As they walked, a sense of peace washed over her, a brief respite from the turmoil of her own life.

Their relationship deepened with each meeting. Paul was a constant source of support and encouragement, and Mary found herself relying on him more and more. As they walked along the cliff path, hand in hand, she felt a sense of belonging she hadn't experienced in a long time.

Meanwhile, the investigation into the murder on Cold Fell seemed to have hit a dead end. The police were no closer to identifying the killer, and the case had faded from the headlines. But for Mary, the memory of the crime remained a constant presence, a reminder of the fragility of life.

Mary's initial enthusiasm for diving into the world of pottery was gradually tempered by the stark realities of running a family business. Her uncle Brian, a man of rigid principles and even more rigid routines, proved to be a formidable adversary. His scepticism towards her, thinly veiled as concern, was palpable.

There was a growing sense among the older generation of the family that Mary, an outsider with a career in the European Union, was an interloper, meddling in affairs she knew nothing about. Her ideas, born out of a fresh perspective, were often met with resistance. Her suggestions for modernizing the business, exploring new markets, and incorporating sustainable practices were dismissed as impractical or too costly.

Yet, Mary persisted. She was determined to breathe new life into the struggling pottery. She began by analyzing the company's finances, poring over spreadsheets and balance sheets. The picture that emerged was bleak. The pottery was losing money, and the debt was piling up.

Despite the challenges, Mary found a strange satisfaction in the work. There was a rhythm to the business, a cyclical nature that mirrored the seasons. She spent countless hours in the pottery, learning the intricacies of the craft. Her hands, once soft and delicate, became rough and calloused, a testament to her dedication.

As the weeks unfolded, the Postlethwaite family dynamics revealed themselves in all their complexity. Mary found herself at the centre of a web of conflicting interests, each sibling harboring their own agenda for the pottery's future.

Amidst this familial tumult, Mary's connection with Paul deepened, offering a welcome respite. One crisp evening, as they strolled along the windswept beach, their conversation veered into more personal territory.

Mary hesitated, then spoke softly, her words nearly carried away by the rhythmic crash of waves. "There's something I should tell you, Paul. I was married once before."

Paul's eyebrows raised slightly, but his voice remained gentle. "Oh? I sense there's quite a story there."

Mary nodded, a rueful smile playing on her lips. "It was a whirlwind romance. We were young, idealistic, full of grand plans. But..." she trailed off, searching for the right words.

"But life had other ideas?" Paul prompted softly.

"You could say that," Mary chuckled without humor. "Two months in, Freddy realized he was gay. The divorce was quick, at least."

Paul whistled low. "That's quite the plot twist. How did you handle it?"

Mary paused, considering. Her gaze grew distant as she remembered those tumultuous days. "At first? Terribly. I was devastated, embarrassed, angry... you name it. I felt like a fool, like everyone must have known except me."

She took a sip of her drink before continuing. "The hardest part was that Freddy had been such a close friend of my brother Howard. They'd known each other since university. So when Freddy came out, it wasn't just my marriage ending - it felt like I was losing a part of my family too."

Paul leaned in, his expression sympathetic. "That must have been incredibly difficult."

Mary nodded. "It was. But Howard and his wife Jenny were amazing. They supported both of us through it all. Jenny became my rock during those days."

She sighed, a mix of emotions playing across her face. "The real test came at Howard's funeral. Freddy showed up with his boyfriend, Sam. He wanted to introduce him to the family."

"Oh wow," Paul murmured. "How did that go?"

Mary's lips quirked in a wry smile. "It was... surreal. There I was, grieving my brother, and suddenly I'm face to face with my ex-husband and his new partner. I felt this bizarre mix of anger, sadness, and... oddly enough, relief."

"Relief?" Paul asked, curious.

"Yeah," Mary replied, her voice softer now. "Seeing Freddy happy, just being himself... it made me realize our divorce wasn't my fault. We were both just trying to figure out who we really were, you know?"

She straightened in her chair, a newfound strength in her posture. "That day, standing there with my family, Freddy, and Sam, I felt this weight lift. I realized I had survived one of the most challenging periods of my life. It taught me self-reliance, the value of independence."

Paul nodded thoughtfully. "Life's best lessons often come wrapped in its hardest challenges."

Mary smiled, a genuine warmth in her eyes now. "Exactly. It wasn't easy, but I came out stronger on the other side. And now, Freddy and I have managed to salvage a friendship. It's different, of course, but there's a mutual respect there."

She laughed softly, shaking her head. "Life certainly has a way of surprising you, doesn't it? I never imagined I'd be sitting here, years later, able to talk about all this without feeling that old pain."

Paul reached across the table, gently squeezing her hand. "You're an incredibly strong woman, Mary. Thank you for sharing that with me."

Mary felt a warmth spread through her at his touch and his words. For the first time in a long while, she felt truly seen and understood. As they sat there, the conversation flowing easily between them, Mary realized that her past, with all its twists and turns, had led her to this moment - and she was grateful for every step of the journey.

They walked in companionable silence for a moment, the rhythm of the waves a soothing backdrop. Then Paul spoke again, his tone casual but his eyes intent. "I've taken a flat in Whitehaven."

Mary's eyebrows shot up. "Oh? I thought you were heading back to France soon."

Paul shrugged, a mischievous glint in his eye. "Plans change. I've still got some loose ends to tie up here. Speaking of which..." he turned to face her, his expression warm. "I'd love for you to see the place. How about dinner tomorrow? I'll cook."

Mary felt a flutter of excitement. "Dinner cooked by the mysterious Paul Brankenwall? How could I refuse?"

Paul grinned. "Excellent. I'll pick you up at your mother's around 7? And maybe over supper, I can fill you in on why I'm lingering in this lovely corner of the world."

Mary matched his grin. "It's a date. And I'm counting on some answers, Mr. Brankenwall. You can't dangle mysteries in front of me and expect me not to bite."

As they turned back towards town, Mary felt a sense of anticipation building. Tomorrow promised not just a lovely evening, but perhaps some long-awaited answers about the enigmatic man beside her.

Chapter 11

The candlelight flickered, casting an ethereal glow on Mary's face as she leaned in, captivated by Paul's tale. He took a deep breath, steeling himself for the revelation.

"Mary, my story isn't a fairy tale," Paul began, his voice low and intense. "It's more of a Gothic novel, full of dark secrets and family shame."

Mary's eyes widened. "Go on," she urged softly.

Paul nodded, his gaze distant. "My father, William Wyndham, the sixth earl, was barely out of his teens when he met my mother, Annie. A chambermaid, if you can believe it."

"A forbidden romance?" Mary breathed.

Paul's laugh was hollow. "They called it love. A whirlwind affair that ended with her pregnant and exiled to France. Quite the convenient arrangement to preserve the precious family name."

"That's terrible," Mary said, her voice filled with sympathy.

"Oh, it gets worse," Paul continued, his tone bitter. "The great and noble Wyndhams couldn't possibly acknowledge a maid, let alone as a potential bride for the heir. So, they shipped her off, a dirty little secret to be buried."

He paused, taking a long sip of wine. "But my father... he couldn't let it go entirely. Visited in secret, even married her in a monastery in France. Romantic, isn't it?"

Mary frowned. "But if they were married..."

Paul's smile was razor-sharp. "Ah, but here's where it turns truly dark. The same man who swore eternal love to my mother later exercised the monstrous 'droit du seigneur' on countless women. Can you imagine the hypocrisy?"

"My God," Mary whispered, shock evident in her voice.

"Indeed," Paul nodded. "While I grew up in France, oblivious to my heritage, my father built a new life in England. Complete with a 'legitimate' wife and children."

Mary reached out, touching his hand gently. "And now you're back. Why?"

Paul's eyes met hers, burning with determination. "My father is dying of cancer, Mary. With him goes my chance to claim what's rightfully mine. But it's not simple. There's a half-brother, Nigel, who thinks he's the sole heir. And who knows how many other illegitimate children are out there, each with their own claims?"

"It sounds dangerous," Mary said, concern evident in her voice.

Paul nodded grimly. "It is. A battle for identity, for justice, for a legacy stolen before I was born. The road ahead is long and treacherous, but I'm prepared to walk it, whatever the cost."

He leaned forward, his gaze intense. "Now you know my secret, Mary. The question is, where do you stand in all of this?"

Paul drained his glass, his eyes blazing with resolve. "This isn't just about money or titles, Mary. It's a fight for my very identity, for justice long denied. I'm reclaiming a legacy that was snatched away before I drew my first breath."

Mary reached across the table, her fingers intertwining with his. "You won't face this alone, Paul. I'm with you, come what may."

He squeezed her hand, a ghost of a smile touching his lips. "Your support means more than you know. But the path ahead is treacherous. I need to confront my father face-to-face, force him to acknowledge the truth. And the family archives... they could hold the key to everything. I'll need a crack legal team to navigate this minefield."

MARY'S BROW FURROWED in thought. "Actually, I might be able to help with that. My work in Strasbourg... I've crossed paths with some top-notch inheritance lawyers. This is their bread and butter."

Paul's eyebrows shot up. "Really? That could be invaluable."

Mary nodded, her voice taking on a note of determination. "Trust me, I know first-hand how crucial the right legal support can be.

"Mary, you're a godsend," Paul breathed, his eyes shining with gratitude. "I'll start by consulting a local solicitor in Egremont, but having an international perspective could be a game-changer."

As they drove through the twilit countryside, a comfortable silence settled between them. Paul felt the weight on his shoulders lighten, buoyed by Mary's unwavering support.

Pulling up outside Mary's mother's house, Paul turned to her. "Two days," he said, his voice filled with purpose. "Let's meet then. I should have a clearer picture of our next move."

He helped Mary out of the car, then hesitated, caught between leaving and staying. "Mary, I... thank you. For everything."

Mary smiled, reaching up to touch his cheek. "We're in this together, Paul. Whatever comes next, we'll face it side by side."

As Paul drove away, his mind raced with possibilities. The road ahead was uncertain, fraught with challenges, but with Mary by his side, he felt a glimmer of hope. The battle for his birth right was just beginning, but for the first time, he truly believed he could win.

Chapter 12

Mary sat at the table in the staff rest room, her tea long forgotten, as she stared out at the rain-washed landscape. The air was crisp and clean, but the weight of the pottery's future hung heavy in the room.

She sighed, running a hand through her hair. "Oh, Howard," she murmured, "what would you do?"

The sudden loss of her brother, the driving force behind Postlethwaite Potteries, had left a gaping hole in the family business. Her father's passing years earlier had already been a blow, mitigated only by Uncle Brian's willingness to step out of retirement.

"Bless him," Mary said aloud, thinking of her uncle's kind but overwhelmed demeanor. "He's doing his best, but it's not enough."

The door creaked open, and Steve, her eldest brother, wandered in. "Talking to yourself again, sis?" he teased, but his smile didn't reach his eyes.

Mary turned to face him. "Just thinking aloud. About the pottery."

Steve's face hardened. "Andrew's been at it again, hasn't he? Talking about selling?"

"Can you blame him?" Mary asked, her voice weary. "He sees the numbers, Steve. We can't ignore them forever."

"Numbers!" Steve spat. "Is that all it is to you? Cold, hard figures? What about our heritage, our family's legacy?"

Mary stood, her frustration bubbling over. "Of course it's not just numbers! But passion alone won't keep the doors open. We need a plan, Steve. A real, workable plan."

Steve deflated, sinking into a chair. "I know, I know. But I can't bear the thought of losing it all. Dad and Howard... they poured their lives into this place."

Mary's expression softened. She placed a hand on her brother's shoulder. "I miss them too. And I'm not ready to give up. But we need to think creatively."

"What do you mean?" Steve asked, a glimmer of hope in his eyes.

Mary paced the staff rest room, her mind racing. "What if we diversified? Offered pottery workshops, classes for adults and kids. Corporate events, even."

Steve's brow furrowed. "You really think people would be interested?"

"Why not?" Mary's eyes lit up with enthusiasm. "People love getting their hands dirty, creating something. And we could showcase our family's history, tell the Postlethwaite story."

Steve nodded slowly, a smile spreading across his face. "You know, that's not half bad. It could bring in a new crowd, maybe even revitalize interest in our traditional pieces."

Mary grinned, feeling a spark of hope for the first time in weeks. "Exactly! We're not giving up on our heritage, we're building on it."

As they continued to brainstorm, the weight on Mary's shoulders began to lift. The road ahead would be challenging, but with creativity and determination, there was hope for Postlethwaite Potteries yet.

THAT EVENING AT HOME she nursed a cup of tea in the kitchen. Her mother entered, eyes curious. "You've got that look, Mary. What's brewing in that head of yours?"

Mary hesitated, then took a deep breath. "Mum, I think I might have a solution for the pottery."

Her mother sat down, eyebrows raised. "Oh? Do tell."

"Well," Mary began, her words rushing out, "what if we turned the pottery into more than just a shop? We could offer workshops, tell our family's story, make it a real destination."

Her mother nodded slowly. "That's... actually quite interesting. But it would be a big change."

"I know," Mary admitted. "But think about it. We're in the heart of the Lake District. Tourists are always looking for authentic experiences."

Just then, Steve walked in, catching the tail end of the conversation. "What's this about tourists?"

Mary's eyes lit up. "Steve! Perfect timing. I was just telling Mum about my ideas for the pottery."

She launched into her explanation again, this time adding, "And what if we partnered with the Laal Ratty railway? We could offer combo tickets - a pottery workshop and a scenic train ride."

Steve whistled low. "That's ambitious, sis. But I like it. It could really put us on the map."

Their mother looked between her children, a mixture of hope and concern on her face. "It sounds wonderful, but it's a big undertaking. We'd need a solid plan."

"I know," Mary nodded. "I'm already working on it. We'll need to do market research, look into funding options..."

"Don't forget about Uncle Brian," Steve interjected. "He'll need to be on board."

Mary's face fell slightly. "Right. Uncle Brian. That might be a tough sell."

Their mother reached out, patting Mary's hand. "Leave Brian to me. You focus on fleshing out this plan of yours."

"Thanks, Mum," Mary smiled. Then, turning to Steve, "What do you think about a pottery trail? Linking up with other local ceramicists?"

Steve's eyes widened. "Now that's an idea! We could make the Lake District the ceramics capital of the UK!"

As they continued to brainstorm, the kitchen filled with an energy it hadn't seen in months. Ideas bounced back and forth, each one building on the last.

"You know," their mother said softly, "your father would be proud. This is exactly the kind of innovative thinking he always encouraged."

Mary felt a lump form in her throat. "I wish he was here to see it."

"He is, in a way," Steve said, squeezing her shoulder. "In every pot we throw, every glaze we fire."

Mary nodded, blinking back tears. "Right then," she said, her voice strong. "Let's make this happen. For Dad, for Howard, for all of us."

As the evening wore on, Mary's jotter was filled with notes and to-do lists. The challenges ahead were daunting, but for the first time in months, the future of Postlethwaite Potteries looked bright.

Chapter 13

"Let's go Mum..." Mary gripped the steering wheel tightly as she drove to Ravenglass, her mind racing faster than the car. The stunning Lake District scenery blurred past, barely registering as she rehearsed her arguments.

As she pulled up to the family business, she took a deep breath. "Here goes nothing," she muttered.

The conference room was thick with tension when Mary entered. Uncle Brian, looking every bit his age, sat at the head of the table. Andrew's face was set in stone, while Steve offered a weak smile.

Mary cleared her throat. "Right, thank you all for coming. I know we're at a crossroads with the pottery, but I think I have a solution."

Andrew snorted. "Let me guess, more artsy workshops?"

Mary bristled but kept her cool. "Actually, yes, but it's more than that. We could create a whole experience - workshops, tours, even partner with the Laal Ratty railway."

Their mother leaned forward, interest sparking in her eyes. "Go on, dear."

As Mary outlined her plans, she could see the room dividing. Steve nodded enthusiastically, while Andrew's scowl deepened.

When she finished, Andrew cleared his throat. "That's all very nice, Mary, but this isn't a charity. I've got a buyer in Spain offering good money. We need to think practically."

The room erupted.

"Practically?" Steve shouted. "What about our heritage?"

"Heritage doesn't pay the bills!" Andrew retorted.

Their mother tried to intervene. "Please, let's not fight-"

"We're not fighting," Andrew cut in. "We're facing reality."

Mary slammed her hand on the table. "Reality? The reality is that this pottery is more than just a business. It's our family's legacy!"

Uncle Brian, who had been quiet, suddenly spoke up. "Your father... he always said the pottery was about more than money."

Andrew rolled his eyes. "Dad's not here anymore, Uncle Brian. Times have changed."

The argument raged on, voices rising and falling like stormy waves. Hours passed, and the initial hope Mary had felt began to crumble.

Finally, exhausted, Mary stood up. "This isn't working," she said, her voice cutting through the chaos. "We're all too emotional right now."

She looked around at the tired, angry faces. "Let's take a week. Cool off, think about what we really want. Then we'll meet again and try to find a solution that works for everyone."

The room fell silent, then slowly, heads began to nod.

As they filed out, Mary caught her mother's eye. The older woman squeezed her hand. "You did well, love. Your father would be proud."

Mary managed a small smile. The battle wasn't over, but at least now they had a chance to regroup. As she walked to the car, she couldn't help but wonder what Paul would think of all this. His steady presence would have been a comfort in the storm of family drama. With a sigh, she started the engine. One week to save the pottery. The clock was ticking.

Chapter 14

Paul settled into the plush leather chair in Mr. Hartley's office, the weight of generations pressing on his shoulders. The solicitor's keen eyes studied him from across the polished oak desk.

"So, Mr. Brankenwall," Hartley began, his voice measured, "you believe you're related to the Wyndham estate. That's quite a claim. How did you come by this information?"

Paul leaned forward, his voice low. "It was my mother, Annie. On her deathbed, she revealed a secret she'd guarded for decades. My father... he was William Angus Charles Wyndham, the sixth earl."

Hartley's eyebrows shot up. "The Wyndhams? Well, that's... unexpected. I assume you have some evidence to support this?"

Paul reached into his briefcase, producing a worn document. "This is a copy of my parents' secret marriage certificate. It's in French, dated November 1941."

Hartley examined the paper, frowning. "My French is a bit rusty. Could you translate the key points?"

As Paul explained the document's contents, Hartley's frown deepened. "Mr. Brankenwall, while this is intriguing, it's far from conclusive. Have you considered DNA testing?"

Paul nodded. "I'm prepared to do whatever it takes. There's more, though. The expensive school in Oxford, the vineyard in Perpignan... I always wondered how my mother afforded it all. Now I know - my father must have been supporting us in secret."

Hartley leaned back, stroking his chin. "This is a complex situation, Mr. Brankenwall. The Wyndham estate is vast, and any claim will face fierce opposition. Are you prepared for that?"

Paul's jaw set. "This isn't just about money or titles, Mr. Hartley. It's about my identity, about justice for my mother. About confronting a past that's been buried for too long."

Hartley nodded slowly. "I understand. But we need to approach this carefully. We'll need to verify this document, search for official records, consider the implications of other potential heirs..."

He paused, studying Paul intently. "Mr. Brankenwall, given the complexity of your case and the high-profile nature of the Wyndham family, I believe we need to bring in a specialist."

Paul's heart raced. "A specialist? Who did you have in mind?" He couldn't help but think of Mary, wishing she was here to steady him in this storm of revelations and possibilities.

Paul exhaled, his shoulders visibly relaxing. "That's... that's a weight off my shoulders. Do you have someone specific in mind?"

Mr. Hartley leaned back in his chair, a glimmer of satisfaction in his eyes. "As a matter of fact, I do. There's a solicitor in London, Doreen Thornton. She's made quite a name for herself handling complex inheritance cases, particularly those involving the nobility. Discretion is her middle name, and she's got a knack for navigating these... shall we say, delicate waters."

"Sounds like just what we need," Paul said, leaning forward eagerly. "How quickly can we get her on board?"

"I'll put out feelers today," Mr. Hartley replied, already reaching for his phone. He paused, his expression growing serious. "Now, about this desire of yours to meet your father..."

Paul's jaw tightened. "It's not just a desire, Mr. Hartley. It's a necessity. I need answers, and I need them from him. How do we make this happen?"

Mr. Hartley's brow furrowed. "Tread carefully, Mr. Brankenwall. Marching up to Wilton Manor unannounced... well, it could be seen as an act of aggression. The family might circle the wagons, so to speak."

"Damn it," Paul muttered, raking his fingers through his hair. "But he's got lung cancer. Every day we wait is a day too long."

"I hear you, I do," Mr. Hartley said, his tone softening. "But let's not rush in half-cocked. My advice? We wait for Ms. Thornton's input. She might have some tricks up her sleeve that could get you through those gates without raising hell."

Paul's eyes narrowed. "And if she doesn't?"

Mr. Hartley drummed his fingers on the desk. "Then we get creative. A letter, perhaps, through official channels. Makes it harder for them to brush you off. Or..." he paused, a sly smile crossing his face, "we could always crash a garden party. Your father's bound to show his face at some public shindig sooner or later."

Paul leaned forward, his mind whirring. "What about events at Wilton Manor? Any chance they open their doors to the public?"

Mr. Hartley's eyes lit up. "Now there's an idea. Many of these old estates do host charity dos or tours. Keeps the coffers full, you know. I'll dig around, see what I can unearth."

"Perfect," Paul nodded, a plan crystallizing. "And while you're at it, please reach out to Ms. Thornton. I'll start penning a letter to my father, just in case. He needs to know I exist, even if I can't see him face-to-face."

As Paul rose to leave, Mr. Hartley's voice turned grave. "One last thing, Mr. Brankenwall. Brace yourself for pushback. Your sudden appearance... well, it's bound to ruffle some very expensive feathers."

Paul's jaw clenched, a fire kindling in his eyes. "I appreciate the heads up, Mr. Hartley. But I've been a ghost in my own life for far too long. It's high time for the truth, come hell or high water."

Stepping out onto the bustling street, Paul felt a curious mix of exhilaration and dread. The path ahead was murky, but he was inching closer to unraveling the Wyndham family's web of secrets. His thoughts drifted to Mary, a lifeline in this storm of uncertainty.

Back at his flat, the silence felt oppressive. Paul's hands shook as he poured a generous measure of whiskey. He stared at his phone and dialled Mary's number.

"Mary? It's me. I... I need you. Can you come over?"

When she arrived, concern etched on her face, Paul felt a wave of relief. He recounted his meeting with Mr. Hartley, his voice rising and falling with barely contained emotion.

"Christ, Mary," he choked out, "my entire life... it's all been smoke and mirrors."

Mary's hand found his, her touch grounding him. "Hey, look at me. You're not alone in this, Paul. Not anymore."

Gratitude washed over him. He leaned in, kissing her softly. "I don't know what's coming," he murmured against her lips, "but with you by my side, I feel... invincible."

As night fell, they sat in companionable silence. Paul's mind raced with possibilities, both thrilling and terrifying. Mary's voice cut through his reverie.

"Your father," she said softly. "Are you going to confront him?"

Paul exhaled slowly. "God, I don't know. Part of me wants to kick down his door and demand answers. But then... what if I don't like what I hear?"

Mary squeezed his hand. "Whatever you decide, whatever happens... I'm in this with you. All the way."

As the street lights flickered outside, Paul felt a strange sense of calm settle over him. The road ahead was fraught with uncertainty, but for the first time in years, he felt like he was exactly where he needed to be. With Mary anchoring him, he was ready to face whatever storms lay ahead in his quest for truth.

Chapter 15

A glimmer of hope pierced through Paul's mounting frustration when he discovered Wilton Manor was hosting a charity gala. It was a long shot, but it offered a chance to breach the walls that had kept him at bay. With a mixture of trepidation and determination, he secured an invitation.

The night of the gala arrived, and Paul found himself thrust into a world of ostentatious wealth. Wilton Manor loomed before him, a behemoth of stone and history. As he ascended the grand staircase, his heart hammered in his chest.

Inside, the opulence was staggering. Crystal chandeliers cast a soft glow over the assembled aristocracy, their laughter tinkling like the champagne in their flutes. Paul moved through the crowd, feeling like a spectre in a world that should have been his birthright.

His gaze was drawn to a portrait in the grand hall - a young woman with an uncanny resemblance to his mother. The similarity was so striking that Paul felt the air leave his lungs.

"Beautiful, isn't she?" a voice beside him said.

Paul turned to find an elderly woman, her eyes twinkling with a hint of mischief. "The resemblance to my... to someone I know is remarkable," he managed.

The woman nodded, a shadow passing over her face. "That's Annie. She was my dearest friend. Like a sister to me."

Paul's pulse quickened. "What happened to her?"

The woman's gaze grew distant. "They say consumption took her at twenty-two. But there are whispers of a different story."

Before Paul could probe further, a hush fell over the crowd. He turned to see a distinguished gentleman descending the staircase -

his father, the Earl of Egremont. The resemblance was undeniable, yet there was a hardness to the older man's features that Paul didn't recognize in himself.

As the night wore on, Paul found himself drawn back to the elderly woman. She sat alone in a quiet corner, her eyes fixed on the portrait of Annie.

"I don't believe we've been properly introduced," Paul said, taking a seat beside her. "I'm Paul."

"Constance," she replied, her voice tinged with warmth. "You're not from around here, are you, Paul?"

He shook his head. "No, I'm... exploring my roots, you could say."

Constance's eyes narrowed slightly. "Curious timing. There have been... murmurs in certain circles."

Paul leaned in, his voice low. "What kind of murmurs?"

She glanced around before answering. "About a long-lost heir. About secrets buried deep." Her gaze locked onto Paul's. "About a young woman who didn't die of consumption, but fled with a child in her womb."

Paul's world tilted on its axis. "Are you saying... Annie didn't die?"

Constance's eyes glimmered with unshed tears. "I'm saying, young man, that the past has a way of resurfacing. And that you bear a striking resemblance to someone I once knew."

As the gala wound down, Paul's mind reeled. He had come seeking answers, only to uncover more questions. But as he cast one last glance at his father - the man who had never acknowledged his existence - he felt a renewed sense of purpose.

The truth was out there, hidden in the shadows of Wilton Manor. And Paul was determined to bring it into the light, no matter the cost.

The morning after the gala, Paul sat at his modest kitchen table in Whitehaven, his mind a whirlwind of thoughts. The coffee in his mug had long gone cold, forgotten in the wake of last night's revelations.

"Christ," he muttered, running a hand through his dishevelled hair. The portrait of Annie, his mother's doppelganger, seemed to hover before his eyes. "What the hell have I stumbled into?"

The shrill ring of the telephone cut through the silence of Paul's flat. He glanced at the clock - just past midnight. With a sense of anticipation, he reached for the receiver.

"Hello?" he answered, his voice hushed in the quiet of the night.

"Paul? It's Mary." Her voice crackled slightly over the line, concern evident in her tone. "How did it go? Are you okay?"

Paul sank into the armchair beside the phone table, cradling the receiver against his ear. He stared out the window at the moonlit street below, unsure how to respond. How could he explain the maelstrom of emotions, the sense of being adrift in a sea of secrets?

"Paul? Are you there?" Mary's voice prodded gently.

He cleared his throat. "Yes, I'm here. It's... it's bigger than we thought, Mary. I need to go back."

There was a pause on the other end of the line. When Mary spoke again, her voice was soft but firm. "Be careful, Paul. Don't lose yourself in this."

A faint smile tugged at Paul's lips. Mary always knew what to say, even when she didn't know the full story. "I'll try," he promised.

"Do you want to talk about it?" Mary offered.

Paul sighed, running a hand through his hair. "Not over the phone. It's too complicated. But thank you for calling, Mary. It means a lot."

"Of course," she replied. "That's what friends are for, right? Just... take care of yourself, okay?"

"I will," Paul assured her. "Goodnight, Mary."

"Goodnight, Paul."

As he placed the receiver back in its cradle, the soft click seemed to echo in the empty flat. Paul stood up, a new sense of determination settling over him. "Time to dig deeper," he said to the quiet room.

He moved to his desk, pulling out a notepad and pen. As he began to jot down his thoughts and plans, the phone call with Mary lingered in his mind, a reminder of the connection and support he had, even in the midst of this complex and potentially dangerous situation.

The night stretched ahead, full of questions and possibilities. But for now, Paul focused on the task at hand, the gentle ticking of the clock and the scratch of pen on paper the only sounds in the otherwise silent flat.

The second day of the Wilton Manor charity gala felt different. Paul moved through the crowd with purpose, his eyes scanning for familiar faces. He felt like a detective in a murder mystery, each interaction potentially hiding a clue.

Then he saw him - Nigel, his half-brother. The man who had grown up with everything Paul had been denied. Taking a deep breath, Paul approached.

"Nigel," he said, his voice steady despite the adrenaline coursing through his veins.

Nigel turned, his expression morphing from polite interest to barely concealed disdain. "Well, if it isn't the charity case. Enjoying the party?"

Paul ignored the jab. "We need to talk. Privately."

Something in Paul's tone must have registered because Nigel's smirk faltered. He led them to a secluded alcove.

"What's this about?" Nigel demanded.

Paul met his gaze unflinchingly. "It's about our father. William Angus Charles Wyndham, the sixth Earl of Egremont."

The Colour drained from Nigel's face. "What did you say?"

"You heard me," Paul continued, his voice low but intense. "And that portrait everyone's been admiring? That's my mother, Annie."

Nigel's world seemed to tilt on its axis. He gripped the wall for support. "You're lying," he hissed, but there was a tremor in his voice.

"Am I?" Paul challenged. He pulled out a folded document from his jacket. "Our father married Annie Brankenwall in November 1941. I was born in January 1942."

Nigel snatched the paper, his eyes wild as he scanned it. "This... this can't be real."

"It is," Paul said, a hint of sympathy creeping into his voice. "And it changes everything."

Nigel looked up, his face a mask of conflicting emotions. "Do you have any idea what this means? What it will do to our family?"

Paul's expression hardened. "Our family? For years, I've been shut out, denied my birth right. I'm not here to destroy anything, Nigel. I'm here for the truth."

A tense silence stretched between them. Finally, Nigel spoke, his voice barely above a whisper. "What do you want?"

"I want to meet our father," Paul said. "Properly. And I want answers."

Nigel nodded slowly, the fight seeming to drain out of him. "This won't end well, you know. For any of us."

As they stood there, two brothers united by blood but divided by circumstance, the sounds of the gala faded away. The real battle, they both knew, was just beginning. The rest of the evening was a blur. The glittering world of the charity gala had transformed into a battlefield, with Paul and Nigel at the centre of the conflict. As they navigated the complexities of their newfound relationship, they were both acutely aware that their lives would never be the same again.

After their initial confrontation, Paul and Nigel retreat to a quiet corner of the library. The tension between them is palpable, but there's also a grudging recognition of their shared predicament.

Nigel paces, running a hand through his hair. "This is madness. Absolute madness."

Paul watches him, his voice steady. "It's the truth, Nigel. Whether we like it or not."

Nigel whirls around. "Do you have any idea what this will do to our Father's reputation?"

"Our Father?" Paul repeats, bitterness in his voice. "I've been out of his family my entire life."

Nigel stops, really looking at Paul for the first time. He sees the resemblance to their father, and something in him shifts. "God, you really are his son, aren't you?"

Paul nods silently.

Nigel sighs deeply. "Alright. Here's what we're going to do. I'll arrange a meeting with Father. But this stays between us for now. No press, no lawyers. Agreed?"

Paul considers for a moment. "Agreed. But I won't be silenced forever, Nigel. I deserve answers."

Nigel extends his hand. "Then let's get you those answers. Together."

As they shake hands, both men feel the weight of history shifting around them.

Chapter 16

The Earl's study is a sanctuary of old-world charm - leather-bound books, a crackling fireplace, and the heavy scent of pipe tobacco. Paul stands before the imposing mahogany desk, his heart hammering in his chest. The Earl, William Angus Charles Wyndham, sits behind it, his face a mask of carefully controlled emotion.

"So," the Earl begins, his voice gravelly with age and perhaps a hint of fear, "you're the boy."

Paul swallows hard. "I'm your son," he says, his voice stronger than he feels. "Why did you abandon us?"

The Earl's hand trembles slightly as he reaches for a silver cigarette case on his desk. He withdraws a cigarette and lights it, the flame of the ornate lighter briefly illuminating the deep lines on his face.

From the corner of the room, Nigel speaks up, his tone a mixture of concern and exasperation. "Father, you shouldn't be smoking. The doctors said your lung cancer—"

The Earl cuts him off with a dismissive wave of his hand. "I'm dying anyway, Nigel. What does another cigarette matter?" He takes a long drag, the smoke curling around him like a shroud.

Paul watches this exchange, the reality of his father's mortality adding another layer of complexity to his tumultuous emotions. The Earl turns his attention back to Paul, his eyes narrowing as he exhales a plume of smoke.

"Abandon you?" the Earl scoffs, but there's a hint of defensiveness in his tone. "I provided for you, didn't I? Made sure you and your mother wanted for nothing."

"Money isn't everything," Paul retorts, his fists clenching at his sides. "We needed a father, not a distant benefactor."

"Then why?" Paul demands, years of pent-up emotion spilling out. "Why did you let us go?"

The Earl stands slowly, moving to the window. "Our world... my responsibilities... They were different times, Paul. Marrying beneath one's station was more than just scandalous. It could ruin everything we'd built over generations."

Paul feels a surge of anger. "So you chose your title over your own child?"

The Earl turns, his eyes glistening. "I chose wrong. And I've lived with that choice every day since."

As the confrontation continues, the layers of family secrets begin to peel away.

"Your mother didn't die of consumption," the Earl says quietly.

Paul freezes. "I know .. you shipped her off to France."

The Earl moves to a hidden safe behind a painting. He retrieves a bundle of letters, his hands shaking slightly. "Annie was forced to flee. To protect you."

"Protect me? From what?"

"From those who saw you as a threat. To the family name, to the inheritance." The Earl's voice is heavy with regret. "There were powerful people, Paul. People who would have gone to any lengths to... remove the problem."

Paul feels the room spinning. "So you sent us away? To save us?"

The Earl nods, handing Paul the letters. "These are from your mother. She wrote to me in secret, for years. Telling me about you, how you were growing. I... I couldn't risk replying, but I kept every one."

Paul takes the letters with trembling hands. His mother's handwriting stares up at him, a ghost from the past.

"She never stopped loving you," the Earl says softly. "And neither did I. Even if I was too much of a coward to show it."

The tension in the room is palpable, the smoke from the Earl's cigarette adding to the hazy atmosphere of unspoken truths and long-buried secrets.

As Paul begins to read, tears blurring his vision, he realizes that the truth he's sought for so long is far more complex and heart-breaking than he ever imagined. The story of his family, of love and loss, of duty and sacrifice, unfolds before him in his mother's own words.

Chapter 17

Doreen Thornton's London office was a study in contrasts: sleek, modern design tempered by the warm glow of antique brass accents. The woman herself was equally intriguing. Tall and elegant, with sharp, intelligent eyes, she exuded an air of quiet authority.

As Paul Brankenwall sat across from her, he felt a surge of nervous anticipation. Doreen's piercing gaze seemed to dissect him.

"Mr. Brankenwall," she began, her voice rich and measured. "Your case is... shall we say, deliciously complex."

Paul shifted in his seat. "Is that a good thing?"

A ghost of a smile played on Doreen's lips. "For me? Certainly. For you? That remains to be seen." She leaned forward, her eyes boring into his. "Tell me, what's driving this quest of yours? Is it the allure of the Wyndham fortune, or are you chasing ghosts of a different kind?"

The question caught Paul off guard. "I... I suppose it's both," he admitted. "The truth about my father, yes. But the estate... it's tangible proof of my identity."

Doreen nodded slowly. "Identity. A powerful motivator. But tell me, Mr. Brankenwall, are you prepared for what that identity might entail?"

Paul frowned. "What do you mean?"

"Family trees have many branches, Mr. Brankenwall. Some bear fruit, others... thorns. How many potential heirs do you think we might uncover?"

Paul's stomach dropped. "I... I hadn't considered..."

"Precisely," Doreen interjected. "Legitimate children, illegitimate ones, adopted siblings, perhaps even grandchildren. It's a veritable Pandora's box we're about to open. The inheritance rights, especially for illegitimate children of noble families like an earl, are notoriously complex."

Paul swallowed hard. "And the Wyndhams? They won't take this lying down, will they?"

Doreen's laugh was sharp and brief. "Oh, my dear Mr. Brankenwall. 'Not taking it lying down' would be a gross understatement. Prepare for war. You must understand, until quite recently, illegitimate children had very limited rights to inherit titles or estates. The law has been changing, but nobility tends to cling to tradition."

Paul frowned. "But surely, if I'm the earl's son—"

"It's not that simple," Doreen cut in. "Titles and entailed estates typically pass through legitimate male heirs. Without explicit inclusion in a will or some form of legal acknowledgment from your father, your claim could be tenuous at best. The Legitimacy Act of 1926 and subsequent laws have improved matters, but they don't necessarily apply to titles of nobility."

Despite the gravity of her words, Paul felt a surge of determination. "I'm ready. I've lived in shadows long enough. If it comes down to it, we'll fight this through every court in the land."

Doreen nodded approvingly. "That's the spirit. But be prepared for a long and bitter struggle. The Wyndhams will use every legal loophole and societal prejudice to their advantage. We're not just fighting for an inheritance here, we're challenging centuries of aristocratic tradition."

Doreen's eyes glinted with approval. "Good. We'll need that fight in you. Now, let's talk strategy..."

As Paul left Doreen's office an hour later, his mind was reeling with the enormity of the task ahead. He was so lost in thought that he almost missed the two men waiting by the elevator.

"Paul Brankenwall?" one of them asked, flashing his warrant card.

Paul's heart lurched. "Yes?"

"You may remember me.... I'm Detective Sergeant Thompson and I'm arresting you on suspicion of the murder of Angela Benn."

The world seemed to tilt on its axis. "Murder? What... I don't understand..."

As the detective began to recite his rights, Paul's mind raced. "Angela Benn who the hell is Angela Benn?

The last thing Paul saw as he was led away was Doreen Thornton, standing in her office doorway, her expression unreadable. The quest for his identity had just taken a dark and unexpected turn.

Chapter 18

The cell door clanged shut behind Paul, the sound echoing in the small space. He sank onto the hard bench, his mind reeling.

"I want to make a phone call," he called out to the retreating officer. "It's my right, isn't it?"

The officer paused, then nodded. "One call. Make it count."

In a plush London hotel bar, Detective Inspector Harry Williamson nursed a whiskey, his brow furrowed in thought. The ice clinked against the glass as he raised it to his lips, the smoky liquid burning a path down his throat.

The bar was quiet at this late hour, with only a few patrons scattered about. Soft jazz played in the background, providing a stark contrast to the gravity of Williamson's thoughts.

A young man in a hotel uniform approached his table. "Excuse me, sir. There's an urgent call for you at the front desk."

Williamson nodded, draining the last of his whiskey before following the attendant to the lobby. Behind the ornate front desk, a smartly dressed woman handed him the receiver of a heavy, black rotary phone.

"Williamson," he answered gruffly.

"Sir, it's Thompson," came the voice on the other end, slightly distorted by static. "We've secured the suspect. Transfer is scheduled for 0800 hours tomorrow. Do you have any further instructions?"

Williamson's grip tightened on the receiver. "Good work, Thompson. Keep him isolated. I want to see his face when we lay out the evidence."

"Understood, sir. Anything else?"

Williamson paused, considering. "Yes. Send a telegram to my hotel room first thing in the morning. Confirm the transfer details and any last-minute changes. Use the usual code."

"Will do, sir. Goodnight."

Williamson replaced the receiver, nodding his thanks to the desk clerk. As he made his way back to the bar, his mind raced with the implications of tomorrow's transfer.

The next morning, Williamson was awoken by a sharp knock at his hotel room door. A bellboy stood outside, holding a small yellow envelope.

"Telegram for you, sir," the young man said, handing over the envelope.

Williamson tipped the boy and closed the door. Tearing open the envelope, he unfolded the telegram and read:

SUSPECT SECURE STOP

TRANSFER 0800 AS PLANNED STOP

NO COMPLICATIONS STOP

AWAITING YOUR ARRIVAL STOP

A grim smile played across Williamson's face. He folded the telegram and tucked it into his jacket pocket. It was time to end this game of cat and mouse. With determined steps, he gathered his things and headed out, ready to face whatever the day might bring.

Back at the station, Paul's hands shook as he dialled Mary's number.

"Paul? What's wrong? Where are you?" Mary's voice was thick with concern.

Paul took a deep breath. "Mary, listen. I've been arrested. They're saying I murdered Angela Benn ...you know...The girl they found dead on Cold Fell."

"What? That's ridiculous! You didn't-"

"Of course I didn't," Paul cut in. "But they think I did. I'm being transferred to Cumbria in the morning. Can you... can you come? And maybe arrange a lawyer?"

Mary's voice steadied. "Of course. I'll be there. And I'll call Doreen Thornton. If anyone can help, it's her."

As Paul was led back to his cell, he overheard two officers talking.

"Long drive tomorrow, eh? Six hours with a murder suspect."

"Yeah, should be fun. Williamson's got a bee in his bonnet about this one."

The next morning, as Paul was being escorted to the transport vehicle, he saw Williamson approaching.

"Mr. Brankenwall," Williamson said, his voice cold. "Ready for a little road trip?"

Paul met his gaze. "I didn't kill her, Detective. You're making a mistake."

Williamson's smile was humourless. "We'll see about that, won't we? You've got six hours to think about what you're going to tell me when we get to Cumbria."

As they set off, Paul in handcuffs in the back of the police car, he couldn't shake the feeling that he was being swept along by forces beyond his control. The search for his true identity had led him here, to this moment, accused of a crime he didn't commit.

He closed his eyes, picturing Mary's face, clinging to the hope that she and Doreen would find a way to clear his name. But as the miles rolled by, a nagging doubt crept in. What if the truth about his past was even darker than he imagined.

Chapter 19

Mary's hands shook as she dialled Doreen Thornton's number. The phone rang three times before Doreen's crisp voice answered.

"Thornton speaking."

"Ms. Thornton, it's Mary Postlethwaite, Paul's girlfriend.... Paul's been arrested for murder. I don't know what to do."

There was a pause on the other end of the line. "I saw the arrest from my office. I was afraid this might happen."

Mary's voice cracked. "Can you help him?"

"I'm not a criminal lawyer, Mary. But I know someone who is. James Hetherington in Carlisle. He's the best in the business."

Mary scribbled down the name. "Thank you. Will you... will you tell him what you know about Paul's case?"

"Of course. I'll brief him immediately. But Mary, there's something else you should know."

Mary's heart sank. "What is it?"

Doreen's voice was measured. "I've been digging into the Wyndham family tree. There are multiple illegitimate children, each with their own claim. But Paul's link... it's not as clear-cut as we hoped."

"What does that mean for Paul?"

"It means we have a fight on our hands. But I'm not giving up. Neither should you."

As Mary hung up, she felt a mix of hope and dread. She immediately dialled Hetherington's number, praying he could help Paul.

The office recorded voice message told her the office was closed.

Meanwhile, Doreen returned to her research, poring over documents and family records, bringing new revelations and complications.

Then, late in the evening, Doreen's phone rang. It was the lab.

"Ms. Thornton? We have the DNA results you requested."

Doreen's heart raced. "Go on."

"There's a match. The sample from Mr. Brankenwall is a direct match to the unidentified body found on Cold Fell."

Doreen's blood ran cold. "Are you certain?"

"Yes, ma'am. The probability of relation is over 99%."

Doreen thanked the technician and hung up, her mind reeling. She had to tell Paul, but how? And what did this mean for his case?

Steeling herself, Doreen dialled the number for the Cumbria police station where Paul was being held.

"This is Doreen Thornton. I need to speak with Paul Brankenwall immediately. It's regarding new evidence in his case."

After a brief wait, Paul's voice came on the line, sounding tired and strained.

"Ms. Thornton? What's happening?"

Doreen took a deep breath. "Paul, I have news. The DNA results are back."

"And?" Paul's voice was tense with anticipation.

"There's a match, Paul. Your DNA... it's a direct match to the unidentified corpse found on Cold Fell."

The silence on the other end of the line was deafening.

"Paul? Are you there?"

His voice, when it finally came, was barely a whisper. "What does this mean, Doreen?"

Doreen's voice was grim. "It means, Paul, that the victim was almost certainly a close relative. A sibling, perhaps. And it means that your connection to the Wyndham family is now irrefutable."

———◉———

AFTER DELIVERING THE news, Doreen knew she had to act quickly. She immediately reached out to James Hetherington, the renowned criminal defence lawyer she had recommended earlier.

"James, I'm forwarding you all the details on the Brankenwall case. It's taken a turn, and I need you to take over."

Hetherington's response was swift. "Consider it done, Doreen. I'll get to work on this right away."

As Doreen waited for Hetherington to review the case file, she couldn't help but feel a sense of dread. The DNA evidence was damning, and it threatened to unravel everything Paul had been fighting for. But she refused to give up. If anyone could get to the bottom of this, it was James Hetherington.

Meanwhile, in his cell, Paul stared at the blank wall, his mind racing. The DNA match meant he was related to the victim, but how? And did that make him a murderer in the eyes of the law? He knew he had to be completely honest with Hetherington, no matter how painful the truth might be.

The road ahead was paved with uncertainty, but Paul was determined to find a way to prove his innocence and uncover the Wyndham family's deepest secrets.

Doreen's fingers trembled slightly as once again she dialled the number for the Cumbria police station. Her voice was steady when she spoke, "This is Doreen Thornton. I need to speak with Paul Brankenwall immediately. It's regarding new evidence in his case."

After a tense wait, Paul's voice crackled through the line, heavy with exhaustion and worry. "Ms. Thornton? What's happening?"

Doreen inhaled deeply, steeling herself. "Paul, I'm afraid the situation has taken a turn. The pathologist found traces of poison in her body. They're treating it as murder now."

"Christ," Paul breathed. "What else?"

"I've brought James Hetherington on board. He's been briefed on everything we know so far." Doreen paused, her tone grave. "But

Paul, the forensic results... they're not in your favour. They found her hair and fingerprints in your car."

Paul's voice cracked. "That's impossible. I never... I mean, I didn't..."

"I know what you're going to say," Doreen interrupted gently. "But the police know about your meeting at the Blue Bell. The waitress saw you together."

"God, I should have mentioned that I'd had dinner with Amélie ," Paul groaned, frustration evident. "I didn't think-"

"Why didn't you?" Doreen pressed, her voice sharp. "What really happened that night, Paul?"

There was a long pause before Paul spoke, his words carefully measured. "We talked. About my family, about her connection to the Wyndhams. But I swear on my life, Doreen, I didn't hurt her."

Doreen's tone was neutral, professional. "The police found your lighter near the body. And Gordon Benn claims Amélie was going to meet you after leaving him."

"Gordon Benn, who's that ....?" Paul's surprise was palpable. "...What's he got to do with this?"

"He mentioned a ritual at Matty Benn's Bridge. Apparently, Amélie was interested in it. She introduced herself as Angela Benn, claiming to be his cousin."

Paul's confusion was evident. "Ritual? What ritual? She told me she was meeting an old family friend on Cold Fell. I offered to drive her – those country roads are treacherous at night."

"So you're saying you didn't poison her at the pub and then drive her out there?" Doreen asked pointedly.

"Of course not!" Paul's voice rose in panic. "Doreen, you have to believe me. I didn't kill her. There has to be another explanation."

Doreen sighed heavily. "I want to believe you, Paul. But the evidence is damning. If you want my help, I need the whole truth. What aren't you telling me?"

Paul took a shaky breath. "Alright. I'll tell you everything."

As Paul recounted the events of that night, Doreen listened intently, her mind racing to connect the dots.

"So you kept quiet about meeting her to protect your claim on the Wyndham estate," Doreen concluded, her tone a mixture of understanding and disappointment.

"I know it was stupid," Paul admitted, shame Colouring his words. "I was so close to uncovering the truth about my family. I didn't want to jeopardize that."

"Well, Paul," Doreen said, her voice firm but not unkind, "your silence has only made things worse. Now we need to prove you didn't kill Angela Benn – or Amélie Bouchard, whatever her real name was."

"How?" Paul sounded defeated. "All the evidence points to me."

"Then we find evidence that points elsewhere," Doreen stated, determination in her voice. "Because if we don't, you're looking at a long time behind bars."

"What should I do now?" Paul asked, desperation creeping into his tone.

"James will be there first thing tomorrow morning," Doreen assured him. "Until then, remember this: say nothing. If the police question you, answer with 'No comment.' Can you do that for me, Paul?"

"Yes," Paul agreed, sounding slightly more composed. "Thank you, Doreen. I don't know what I'd do without you."

"Just hang in there," Doreen said softly. "We'll get to the bottom of this. I promise."

As the gravity of the situation sank in, Paul felt a sense of dread wash over him. He had come so far, only to find himself trapped in a web of deceit and suspicion. But with Doreen in his corner, he knew he couldn't give up. The truth was out there, and he was determined to uncover it, no matter the cost.

Chapter 20

Mary's brother Steve burst through the door, his face etched with concern. "Mary, I just heard on the TV. Are you alright?"

"They've taken him in for the murder of Angela Benn – the girl found on Cold Fell." Mary's words hung in the air, heavy and surreal.

Mary stumbled to the couch, her legs giving way beneath her. "This can't be happening. Paul wouldn't hurt a fly, let alone..."

MARY LOOKED UP AT HIM, her eyes brimming with tears. "It's not true, Steve. It can't be."

Steve sat beside her, his voice gentle but firm. "I know it's hard to hear, but the evidence... it doesn't look good. His lighter at the scene, witnesses at the pub..."

"No," Mary interrupted, her voice gaining strength. "I don't care what they think they've found. I know Paul. He's innocent, and I'm going to see him right now."

Uncle Brian, who had been silently observing, spoke up. "Mary, love, I understand you want to help, but we need you here. The pottery—"

"To hell with the pottery!" Mary snapped, surprising even herself. "Paul needs me."

Steve placed a hand on her arm. "Mary, think about this. We're in the middle of a crisis ourselves. The business—"

"Can wait," Mary finished, her jaw set with determination. "I'm sorry, but I have to do this. Paul would do the same for me."

Brian tried one last time. "Mary, please. Let the lawyers handle this. You rushing off won't change anything."

Mary stood, grabbing her coat. "Maybe not, but I won't let him face this alone. I'll be back as soon as I can."

Before either man could protest further, Mary was out the door, her car keys jingling in her hand. The drive to the police station was a blur, her mind racing with thoughts of Paul, alone and scared.

Bursting through the station doors, Mary approached the desk, her voice quavering but resolute. "I need to see Paul Brankenwall. Now."

The officer behind the desk looked up, startled by her intensity. "I'm sorry, ma'am, but Mr. Brankenwall is in custody and not allowed visitors at this time."

Mary leaned forward, her eyes flashing. "I don't care about your procedures. That man is innocent, and he needs support. I demand to see him."

"Ma'am, please calm down," the officer said, rising from his seat. "I understand you're upset, but—"

"No, you don't understand," Mary cut in, her voice rising. "Paul Brankenwall is a good man, and he's being wrongly accused. I won't leave until I see him."

As other officers began to take notice of the commotion, a voice called out from behind her. "Mary Postlethwaite I presume?"

She turned, expecting to see Doreen, but instead found herself face-to-face with a tall, distinguished-looking man in his early fifties. His piercing blue eyes regarded her with a mix of curiosity and concern.

"I'm James Hetherington, Paul's lawyer," he introduced himself, extending a hand. "Doreen Thornton referred me to the case. I've read about you, but we haven't had the pleasure of meeting until now."

Mary shook his hand, her eyes lighting up with hope. "Mr. Hetherington, thank God you're here. Can I see Paul? Please, I need to talk to him."

James considered for a moment, his expression softening. "Well, I was just about to meet with him myself. Perhaps... yes, I think we could arrange for you to join us. But first, I need to check with Paul to make sure he's comfortable with that. Would you mind waiting here for a few minutes?"

Mary nodded eagerly, her heart racing. As James disappeared down a corridor, she paced nervously, ignoring the curious glances from the officers around her.

After what felt like an eternity, James returned, a slight smile on his face. "Good news, Mary. Paul's agreed to see you. Follow me, please."

They were led to a small, stark interview room. The walls were a dull beige, adorned only with a large mirror that Mary suspected was two-way. A simple metal table sat in the centre, flanked by four uncomfortable-looking chairs.

As they entered, Mary's eyes immediately locked onto Paul. He looked pale and exhausted, dark circles under his eyes betraying his lack of sleep. The moment he saw her, his face crumpled with emotion.

Mary rushed forward, enveloping Paul in a fierce hug. She could feel his body shaking as he broke down, quiet sobs muffled against her shoulder. "It's okay," she whispered, stroking his hair. "I'm here now. We're going to get through this together."

James cleared his throat softly, reminding them of his presence. "I hate to interrupt, but we don't have much time. Paul, are you ready to talk?"

Paul nodded, wiping his eyes as he and Mary took their seats across from James. He took a deep breath, his voice hoarse as he began to speak.

"I guess I should start at the beginning," Paul said, his eyes meeting Mary's for a moment before focusing on James. "It all started when I first learned about my connection to the Wyndham family..."

As Paul launched into his backstory, Mary listened intently, her hand never leaving his. She silently vowed to stand by him, no matter what challenges lay ahead. In that cold, impersonal room, a flame of hope and determination burned brightly between them.

Paul leaned forward, his voice low and intense. "It all started when I was twenty-nine. I'd been running the vineyard in Saint Genis, near Perpignan for 11 years. My mother, Annie, was diagnosed with incurable pancreatic cancer. In those final weeks, she revealed secrets she'd kept hidden my entire life."

We had moved to a vinery estate house near a small village near Perpignan

He paused, running a hand through his hair. "She told me about my father William Angus Charles Wyndham, the sixth earl of Egremont. They'd had a secret marriage, a love story I'd never known about. It was... overwhelming, to say the least."

Mary squeezed his hand encouragingly, and Paul continued. "Mum also mentioned her friend, Ada Benn. Similar story - sent away to a convent in Brittany when she fell pregnant. They'd kept in touch over the years."

Paul's gaze met the lawyer's. "Before she died, Mum gave me the name of a priest in Brittany who'd officiated their wedding. She said he could provide proof of my legitimacy. It felt like... like a mission, you know? A way to honor her memory."

He took a deep breath. "At Mum's funeral, I met this girl, Amélie Bouchard Red hair, fiery personality. She claimed Ada Benn her mother, was now a staunch Catholic nun living in a monastery in Brittany. She also told me she thought we might be related. We hit it off, exchanged numbers. I told her about my plans to investigate the Wyndham estate."

"So that's what brought you to Egremont?" James prompted.

Paul nodded. "I booked into the Blue Bell hotel, spent days researching in the library and church records. That Saturday, I took a drive into the countryside. That's... that's when I met Mary." He smiled softly at her before continuing.

"Later that evening, back at the Blue Bell, I had dinner with Amélie Bouchard. We talked about our similar backgrounds - her mother was Ada Benn, also pregnant by an Earl and sent away. Amélie mentioned meeting someone she believed was her cousin, I guess that was Gordon Benn."

Paul's brow furrowed. "She said she was meeting him at Cold Fell that night, before 1 AM. I tried to talk her out of it - it seemed dangerous, wandering the fells alone at night. But she was adamant."

He sighed heavily. "In the end, I gave in. I drove her up to the five-barred gate, watched her walk away. I was back at the hotel by half past midnight. That's... that's all there is to it. I swear."

James nodded slowly, processing the information. "And you're certain you didn't see or hear from Amélie after that?"

"Positive," Paul insisted. "I had no idea anything had happened to her until the police showed up at my door."

Mary leaned in, her voice gentle but firm. "We believe you, Paul. We'll figure this out, I promise."

As they continued to discuss the details, the gravity of the situation hung heavy in the small interview room. But amidst the uncertainty, there was a glimmer of hope - the truth was out there, waiting to be uncovered.

James Hetherington leaned forward, his expression serious. "Paul, I need to ask you some difficult questions. The post-mortem revealed that Amélie was poisoned. Is there any possibility her food or drink could have been tampered with during your dinner?"

Paul's eyes widened, clearly shocked by this information. "Poisoned? I... I had no idea. We ate and drank the same things, I think."

James nodded, encouraging him to continue. "Take me through the meal. What did you order? Did anything unusual happen?"

PAUL FURROWED HIS BROW, his mind reaching back to that fateful evening. "We ordered wine first, as we always do. The waiter recommended a Bordeaux, but when it arrived..." He trailed off, his face scrunching up at the memory.

"What was wrong with it?" James prompted, leaning forward slightly.

Paul's eyes refocused on the present. "Well, the waitress poured it, and right away something seemed off. It looked a bit cloudy in the glass. Amélie, she's seemed to be more of a wine connoisseur than me, I was impressed me being the professional wine grower." He smiled and continued, "she stuck her nose in the glass and frowned immediately."

"Did she say anything?" Mary asked softly, her pen poised over her notepad.

Paul nodded. "Yeah, she muttered something about it smelling 'corked' or 'off'. I took a small sip to see for myself and..." He shuddered slightly. "God, it was awful. Tasted like wet cardboard mixed with vinegar."

James leaned back, his expression thoughtful. "So what happened next?"

"We called the waitress over and explained the issue. She was very apologetic, took the bottle away immediately. I decided to play it safe and ordered a Spanish Rioja from their limited wine list. I'd had it before, you see."

Mary interjected, her voice gentle but probing. "Paul, this is important. The first bottle, the bad one – do you remember how much of it you and Amélie actually consumed?"

Paul shook his head emphatically. "Barely anything at all. Just that small sip each. We didn't even finish what was in our glasses before sending it back."

James nodded slowly, his fingers drumming on the table. "And the Rioja? How was that served?"

"Oh, very properly," Paul replied. "The waiter brought it out himself this time. Showed us the bottle, opened it right there at the table. We both had a glass with our appetizers."

Mary and James exchanged a significant look.

"Paul," James said carefully, "I hate to ask this, but we need to consider every possibility. Is there any chance the first bottle could have been tampered with?"

Paul's eyes widened. "Tampered with? You mean... intentionally?" The gravity of the situation seemed to hit him anew. "I... I suppose it's possible. But why? Who would do such a thing?"

Mary placed a comforting hand on Paul's arm. "We don't know yet. But every detail helps us build a clearer picture. Can you remember anything else about that first bottle? The label, perhaps, or how the waitress handled it?"

Paul closed his eyes, concentrating. "The label... it was dark, I think. Maybe a deep green? And the waitress, she seemed a bit nervous now that I think about it. Fumbled with the corkscrew a bit."

James nodded, jotting down notes. "Excellent, Paul. These details might seem small, but they could be crucial. We'll need to follow up with the restaurant, get a list of their staff that night, check their wine inventory..."

Paul slumped in his chair, the weight of the situation evident in his posture. "I can't believe this. We were just having a nice dinner, and now..." He trailed off, shaking his head.

Mary squeezed his arm gently. "We're going to figure this out, Paul. One step at a time."

James made a note, then looked up at Paul. "This is important, Paul. Did you notice anyone paying particular attention to your table? Or did Amélie mention feeling unwell at any point during the meal?"

Paul thought for a moment. "No, nothing like that. The restaurant was quiet, and Amélie seemed fine throughout dinner. She was animated, talking about her family history and her plans to meet her cousin later."

James leaned back, processing the information. "Alright. We'll need to investigate this angle thoroughly. The type of poison used could be crucial to your defence."

He turned to Mary. "You mentioned something about plants in the South of France?"

Mary nodded. " I've heard oleander is common in Mediterranean areas and highly toxic."

"Well, you raise an interesting point Mary, but Brittany is not on the Mediterranean, but Perpignan is, so your suggestion could equally apply to Paul.

"I suppose it can be found in parts of Brittany, it would be worth checking." Said Mary,

James raised an eyebrow, impressed. "That's a good point, Mary. Oleander poisoning could indeed be mistaken for other causes of death initially. We'll need to get more details on the exact toxin found in her system."

He turned back to Paul. "This information about the wine could be vital, Paul. It suggests that if poison was administered at the restaurant, it likely wasn't in the wine you shared. We'll need to look into every aspect of that meal, including the food you ate."

Paul nodded, looking slightly overwhelmed. "I'll try to remember every detail I can."

James gave a reassuring smile. "That's all we can ask for now. We're building a picture, piece by piece. Remember, the burden of proof is on the prosecution. Our job is to create reasonable doubt, and I think we're making progress."

As the interview continued, the atmosphere in the room shifted slightly. While the situation remained grave, there was now a sense of purpose and direction to their efforts.

James paused, then shifted gears. "Now, Paul, I'd like to ask about Gordon Benn. What can you tell me about him?"

Paul shook his head. "Not much, I'm afraid. I've never actually met him. Everything I know came from Amélie."

James leaned forward, intrigued. "And what did Amélie tell you about him?"

"She said he claimed to be her cousin," Paul replied. "She seemed excited about the connection, but I got the impression she didn't know him well. The meeting at Cold Fell was supposed to be about some family history, I think."

Mary suddenly sat up straighter. "Wait, did you say Gordon Benn?"

James turned to her, eyebrow raised. "Yes. Do you know something about him?"

Mary nodded slowly. "I think I might have met him. It was a few weeks ago, when I was hiking near Matty Benn's Bridge."

Paul looked at her in surprise. "You never mentioned this."

"I didn't think it was important at the time," Mary explained. "But now... Well, this man I met, he introduced himself as the great-great-great-grandson of Matty Benn. He was with a women, a young girl, probably in her mid to late teens. He was very interested in local history, especially anything related to the Benn family."

James leaned forward, his interest piqued. "Can you describe this man, Mary?"

Mary closed her eyes, trying to recall details. "He was tall, lanky maybe in his late fifties or early sixties. Unkempt curly red hair,. He had an intense way about him, very passionate when he talked about history. Said his Dad had told him lots of weird stories about Matty Benn....Seems she was quite the celebrity in her day."

James scribbled notes furiously. "And did he mention anything about rituals or meetings at Cold Fell?"

Mary shook her head. "No, nothing like that. He mostly talked about Matty Benn and some old family legends. Rumour has it she had 12 children But..." she hesitated.

"But what?" James prompted.

"There was something... off about him," Mary said slowly. "I can't put my finger on it, but he made me uneasy. And the girl, she just stood there looking blank, didn't say a word. It was weird... I cut our conversation short and continued back to my bike."

James nodded thoughtfully. "This could be significant. It provides a potential connection between Gordon Benn and the area where Amélie's body was found."

He turned back to Paul. "Did Amélie mention any specifics about why she was meeting Gordon at Cold Fell? Any details about what they planned to do?"

Paul shook his head. "No, she was pretty vague about it. Just said it was about family history and some old ritual. I thought it was odd, meeting so late at night in such a remote place, but she seemed determined."

James made a few more notes, then looked up at them both. "This information about Gordon Benn could be crucial. It gives us another avenue to explore, another potential suspect. We need to find out more about him and his connection to both Amélie and the Cold Fell area."

He closed his notebook and gave them a determined look. "I think we've made some real progress today. Paul, I'm going to work on getting these new leads investigated. Mary, if you remember anything else about your encounter with this man claiming to be Gordon Benn, no matter how small, please let me know immediately."

As the meeting wound down, Mary's determination was palpable. She turned to Paul, her eyes fierce with loyalty. "I know you're innocent, Paul. I knew it the moment you drove away that Saturday evening, leaving me on Cold Fell. I felt... I felt I'd found something real, something true."

Paul's eyes softened, a mix of gratitude and pain crossing his features. "Mary, I—"

She cut him off gently. "No, let me finish. I'm going to clear your name, whatever it takes."

James raised an eyebrow. "Mary, I appreciate your dedication, but we need to be careful—"

Mary's eyes glinted with determination as she spoke. "I understand the risks, but I've already taken some initiative. I found Gordon Benn's address in the phone book and I've arranged to meet him tomorrow."

Paul's face paled, his grip tightening on Mary's hand. "Mary, no. It's too dangerous. We don't know what this man is capable of."

James leaned forward, his brow furrowed with concern. "I have to agree with Paul. Meeting Gordon Benn alone could be incredibly risky. We should approach this through proper channels."

Mary shook her head, her jaw set. "We don't have time for proper channels. Every day Paul spends in here is another day his life is being torn apart. I'll be careful, I promise."

Paul's eyes searched hers, a mix of admiration and fear evident in his gaze. "I couldn't bear it if anything happened to you because of me. Please, Mary, reconsider."

"I have to do this, Paul," Mary said softly, squeezing his hand. "I won't stop until we uncover the truth and clear your name."

James sighed, recognizing the futility of arguing further. "If you're determined to go through with this, at least let me give you some advice on how to handle the conversation. And promise me you'll meet him in a public place."

As James began to outline some safety precautions, a guard appeared at the door. "Time's up," he announced gruffly.

The reality of their situation came crashing back. Paul was to be returned to his cell, their brief reunion cut short. Mary stood, pulling Paul into a tight embrace. She kissed him, pouring all her love and determination into the gesture.

"I'll let you know what happens after my meeting with Mr. Benn tomorrow," she whispered, her voice thick with emotion. "Stay strong, Paul. We'll get through this."

Paul nodded, unable to speak as the guard led him away. Mary watched him go, her heart breaking at the sight of him in handcuffs.

Turning to James, she extended her hand. "Thank you for everything, Mr. Hetherington. I promise to keep in touch and let you know what I learn."

James shook her hand, his expression grave. "Be careful, Mary. And call me immediately if you feel threatened or discover anything significant. Remember, we're walking a fine line here."

As Mary left the police station, the weight of her mission settled heavily on her shoulders. Tomorrow's meeting with Gordon Benn could change everything – for better or for worse. With each step, her resolve strengthened. For Paul's sake, for the truth, she would see this through to the end, whatever the cost.

Chapter 21

The Blue Bell pub hummed with the lazy chatter of the lunchtime crowd as Mary pushed open the heavy oak door. She spotted Gordon Benn immediately, his weathered face and calloused hands marking him as a man accustomed to hard work.

"Mr. Benn?" Mary approached, extending her hand. "I'm Mary. Thank you for meeting me."

Gordon nodded, his handshake firm. "Call me Gordon. Shall we sit?"

As they settled into a corner booth, the waitress approached, greeting Gordon with familiarity. "The usual, Gordon?"

He grinned. "You know me too well, Lizzy. Chicken nuggets and chips, and a pint of bitter."

Mary ordered the scampi and chips, hesitating over the drink. "I'll have a glass of red wine, please."

Gordon's eyebrows shot up. "I wouldn't if I were you. The red here is rubbish."

"Oh?" Mary's interest was piqued. "How do you know?"

Gordon leaned in, lowering his voice. "Well, I was up at Wilton Manor last week, fixing a leak. The Earl, Nigel, he tells me to drop off a box of red to the Blue Bell. Said it wasn't 'vintage' enough for his posh cellar." He chuckled. "Guess that's what you get when you drink where the toffs offload their cast-offs."

Mary nodded, switching her order to white wine. As their food arrived, she steered the conversation carefully. "Gordon, I wanted to ask you about Ada Benn. Angela's mother?"

Gordon's face clouded. "Aye, I knew her. My dad's sister, she was. Worked as a maid up at the Manor." He paused, taking a long pull of his bitter. "Got herself in trouble, if you catch my meaning. They shipped her off to France, must be... oh, about 18 years ago now."

Mary's heart raced. This aligned perfectly with Amélie's age. "That must have been hard for your family."

Gordon shrugged, finishing his pint and signaling for another, adding a whiskey chaser this time. As he sipped the amber liquid, his tongue seemed to loosen. "Hard? It's the way of things around here. The Earls, they've always had a... taste for young girls. Pretty little things, fresh-faced."

Mary struggled to keep her expression neutral. "What do you mean?"

Gordon's voice dropped to a conspiratorial whisper. "Sometimes, I'd get asked to find new staff. You know, when girls ran off or got in trouble. They always wanted virgins, see. Said they were 'purer.'" He made a disgusted sound. "Load of bollocks, if you ask me."

Feeling slightly nauseous, Mary pressed on. "Gordon, what can you tell me about the rituals at Matty Benn's Bridge?"

His eyes lit up. "Ah, now that's a tale! Old family tradition, that. They say if a virgin bathes in the moonlight at the bridge, she'll see Matty's ghost. Brings fertility and good health, supposedly." He winked. "Load of nonsense, but the young'uns still do it sometimes."

Mary took a deep breath, steeling herself for the crucial question. "Gordon, did you meet Amélie – or Angela, as you knew her – on Cold Fell the night she died?"

Gordon's face went blank for a moment. "No," he said slowly. "No, I didn't see her that night."

"What time were you there?" Mary pressed.

"About 1 AM, I reckon," Gordon replied, his eyes not quite meeting hers.

"Did you see anyone else? Any cars on the fell?"

Gordon shook his head. "Nah, place was dead quiet. Just me and the sheep."

Mary leaned in, her voice low and probing. "Gordon, if you had met Angela as you said you planned, what would you have done together?"

Gordon shifted uncomfortably in his seat, his eyes darting around the pub before settling back on Mary. He took a long swig of his drink before answering.

"Well, you see," he began, his voice a bit unsteady, "I was going to show her the old ways. The rituals, like I mentioned. She was keen on learning about her heritage, you know?"

He paused, as if considering his words carefully. "We were going to do a small ceremony at Matty Benn's Bridge. Nothing too fancy, mind you. Just a bit of the old magic, connecting with our ancestors. She seemed right excited about it when we talked earlier."

Gordon's eyes took on a distant look. "I had it all planned out. Candles, some herbs, the whole bit. Was even going to bring a special bottle of wine – an old vintage from the Manor's cellar. Nigel... I mean, the young Earl, he wouldn't miss it."

He shook his head, as if coming back to the present. "But she never showed up. I waited for hours, freezing my arse off by that bridge. Eventually gave up and went home. Didn't know what had happened to her until I heard the news later."

Mary studied Gordon's face carefully as he spoke, noting the mix of emotions that played across his features – nostalgia, excitement, and something else she couldn't quite place. Was it regret? Or perhaps fear?

"That's quite a detailed plan for someone you'd only just met in person a few hours earlier," Mary observed, keeping her tone neutral.

Gordon shrugged, a bit too casually. "Family's family, innit? Even if we'd never met proper, we shared blood. That means something in these parts."

As Gordon signalled for another drink, Mary couldn't shake the feeling that there was more to this story than he was letting on. The mention of the wine from the Manor's cellar, the elaborate plans for a ritual with a virtual stranger – it all seemed a bit too convenient, too rehearsed.

She made a mental note to look into the connection between Gordon, Nigel, and this mysterious bottle of wine. Something told her it might be a crucial piece of the puzzle she was trying to solve.

As they continued their meal, Mary's mind raced. Gordon's story didn't quite add up, and his revelations about the Earl were disturbing, to say the least. She knew there was more to uncover, more threads to pull. But for now, she'd have to tread carefully, balancing her need for information with the growing sense that she might be stepping into something far more dangerous than she'd initially imagined.

Mary took a sip of her wine, carefully considering her next question. "Gordon, how long have you worked at the manor?"

Gordon leaned back, a nostalgic glint in his eye. "Oh, let's see... I started when I was just a lad of 16. Missed the war, thanks to the old Earl. Said I was too valuable to send off to fight."

"That's a long time," Mary remarked. "Who was your boss back then?"

Gordon snorted. "In those days, you answered to the Earl himself, or the Countess if you were unlucky." His face darkened. "That woman was a right harridan, hated by everyone, including the Earl himself."

"How so?" Mary prodded gently.

Gordon leaned in, his voice dropping to a conspiratorial whisper. "Picture this: a fat, ugly bitch with a temper like a rabid dog. Treated the staff like dirt beneath her feet. Even the Earl couldn't stand her, but he was stuck with her, wasn't he?"

Mary nodded, trying to keep her expression neutral. "And now? Who's in charge these days?"

"Now?" Gordon rolled his eyes. "It's Nigel, the Earl's son. Spoilt brat if ever there was one. Thinks he owns the world, that one."

Mary steered the conversation back to more sensitive territory. "Earlier, you mentioned girls running away. What happened to them?"

Gordon's expression grew guarded. He took a long swig of his whiskey before answering. "Look, things happen in big houses. Girls get ideas above their station, or they get in trouble. Some run off to the city, thinking they'll make it big. Others..." He trailed off, his eyes darting around the pub.

"Others what, Gordon?" Mary pressed, her heart racing.

Gordon sighed heavily. "Some just... disappeared. One day they're there, the next, gone without a trace. The official story was always that they'd found better positions elsewhere, but..." He shrugged, leaving the implication hanging in the air.

Mary felt a chill run down her spine. "And no one ever questioned this?"

Gordon laughed bitterly. "Question the Earl? In those days? You must be joking. Besides, most of these girls were nobodies. No family to speak of, no one to kick up a fuss if they vanished."

As Gordon signaled for another drink, Mary's mind whirled with the implications of what she'd heard. The picture emerging was far darker and more complex than she'd imagined. She knew she was treading on dangerous ground, but she couldn't stop now. Not when Paul's freedom - and perhaps the truth behind years of hidden crimes - hung in the balance.

"Gordon," she said carefully, "I need to know more about what happened on Cold Fell that night. Are you sure you didn't see Angela... or anyone else?"

Gordon's eyes narrowed, a flicker of something - fear? guilt? - passing across his face. "I told you, I didn't see nothing. Why are you so interested anyway? What's all this got to do with you?"

Mary realized she'd pushed too far. She forced a smile, trying to deflect. "Just curious about local history, that's all. You've been so helpful, Gordon. Thank you for sharing your stories with me."

As their lunch drew to a close, Mary knew she'd only scratched the surface of the secrets lurking beneath the respectable facade of Wilton Manor. She'd have to tread carefully from here on out – but she was more determined than ever to uncover the truth, no matter the cost.

Chapter 22

Detective Inspector Williamson paced the cramped briefing room, his weathered face creased with concentration. Sergeant Thompson stood by the whiteboard, marker in hand, ready to jot down ideas.

"Right, let's go over this again," Williamson began, addressing the assembled murder squad. "What do we know for certain?"

Thompson cleared his throat. "Victim: Amélie Bouchard, also known as Angela Benn. Cause of death: poisoning. Toxicology report suggests oleander."

A young detective piped up. "Sir, we've checked and confirmed there are no traces of the poison in the red house wine from the Blue Bell pub."

"How many bottles did you check?"

"Eleven full bottles still in the box non appeared to be tampered with, One bottle missing the one they had, ended up in the bottle bank, it'll be in the recycling plant now, no way to check it.

Williamson nodded. "Okay,...Good work. Now, let's talk suspects. Paul Brankenwall is our prime focus. What's his connection?"

"He owns a vineyard in southern France," Thompson replied. "Easy access to oleander plants. Plus, he was seen with the victim at the Blue Bell on the night of her death."

Another detective chimed in. "We've got CCTV footage of Brankenwall at the bar while the victim was in the restroom. Perfect opportunity to spike her drink."

Williamson's eyes narrowed. "Motive?"

Thompson consulted his notes. "Here's where it gets interesting, sir. We've uncovered evidence suggesting that Amélie Bouchard was actually the Earl of Wyndham's illegitimate daughter."

A murmur rippled through the room. Williamson held up a hand for silence. "And Brankenwall's connection to the Wyndham estate?"

"He claims to be the Earl's son," Thompson explained. "If Bouchard was legitimate, she could challenge his claim to the title."

Williamson nodded slowly. "So, we're looking at a premeditated murder. Brankenwall meets Bouchard at his mother's funeral, learns of her connection to the Wyndhams, and plans her elimination."

"It fits, sir," Thompson agreed. "He lures her to Cumbria under the guise of exploring their shared history, poisons her, then dumps her body on Cold Fell."

As the team continued to discuss the case, a junior officer burst into the room, slightly out of breath. "Sir! We've just received an anonymous tip. Someone claims they saw Gordon Benn, a local handyman, on Cold Fell the night of the murder, and, we've traced the call to a public box in Wilton village."

Williamson's eyebrows rose. "Wilton? That's very interesting."

The constable nodded, breathless. "We're running the call through forensics now, but the caller sounded young, possibly female, and very frightened."

"Gordon Benn? What do we know about him?" asked Williamson

Thompson quickly flipped through his notes. "Benn has connections to Wilton Manor, sir. Works there occasionally. And… wait, there's a family connection. His aunt was Ada Benn, who……who was the victim's mother," Williamson finished, his mind racing. "Well, well. Looks like Mr. Benn might have some explaining to do. Thompson, bring him in for questioning. And someone get me more information on his relationship with the Wyndham family."

As the room buzzed with renewed activity, Williamson couldn't shake the feeling that they'd just stumbled onto something much bigger than a simple murder case. The web of connections between Brankenwall, Bouchard, Benn, and the Wyndhams was growing more complex by the minute.

"One more thing," Williamson called out as the team dispersed. "I want to know everything about a woman named Mary who's been visiting Brankenwall. She might be our key to unravelling this whole mess."

As the door closed behind the last detective, Williamson turned to Thompson. "What do you think, Sergeant? Is Brankenwall our man, or are we missing something?"

Thompson hesitated. "The evidence points to him, sir, but..."

"But?"

"It almost feels too neat, doesn't it? Like someone wanted us to reach exactly this conclusion."

Williamson nodded grimly. "My thoughts exactly, Thompson. My thoughts exactly."

Williamson leaned back in his chair, his brow furrowed in concentration. "You might be onto something there, Thompson. Let's explore this angle. What if Brankenwall wasn't the killer, but the intended victim?"

Thompson nodded eagerly, warming to the idea. "It makes sense, sir. The wine could have been spiked before it even reached their table. And Nigel Wyndham certainly has a motive for wanting Paul out of the picture."

"Exactly," Williamson agreed. "If Paul proves his rightful inheritance, Nigel loses everything. But if Paul goes down for murder..."

"He'd lose his claim to the estate anyway," Thompson finished. "It's a win-win for Nigel, regardless of who actually dies."

Williamson stood up, pacing the room. "But where does Gordon Benn fit into all this? What's his angle?"

Thompson hesitated, then spoke slowly, piecing together the puzzle. "Well, sir, if Angela - or Amélie - was Gordon's cousin, her death might actually benefit him in some way."

"How so?" Williamson prodded.

"Think about it," Thompson continued, his excitement growing. "If Amélie was the Earl's illegitimate daughter, she might have had a claim to the estate too. With her out of the picture..."

Williamson's eyes widened. "Gordon moves up in the line of succession. Clever, Thompson. But there's more to it, I'm sure."

He paused, then snapped his fingers. "What do we know about Gordon's relationship with Nigel?"

Thompson consulted his notes. "Gordon's worked at the manor for years. He's known Nigel since he was a boy."

"And he's been doing the 'dirty work' for the family for just as long, I'd wager," Williamson mused. "What if Nigel promised Gordon a piece of the pie in exchange for his help?"

Thompson nodded slowly. "It fits, sir. Gordon could have been the one to spike the wine, thinking he was targeting Paul. But when Amélie died instead..."

"He panicked," Williamson finished. "That's why he was seen on Cold Fell that night. He was trying to cover his tracks, maybe move the body."

The two detectives stared at each other, the implications of their theory sinking in.

"This is bigger than we thought, Thompson," Williamson said gravely. "We're not just looking at a murder anymore. We're looking at a conspiracy involving one of the oldest families in the county."

Thompson swallowed hard. "What's our next move, sir?"

Williamson's eyes glinted with determination. "We bring in Gordon Benn for questioning. But we do it quietly. If we're right about this, there are powerful people who'll want to keep this under wraps."

As Thompson moved to leave, Williamson called after him. "And Thompson? Keep an eye on that Mary woman. If she's digging into this, she might be putting herself in danger. We might need to bring her in too - for her own protection."

As the door closed behind Thompson, Williamson turned to stare out the window, his mind racing. They were on the verge of uncovering something big - something that could shake the very foundations of Cumbrian society. But at what cost? And who else might get caught in the crossfire before this was all over?

Chapter 23

The thick glass of the prison visiting room muffled the sounds of the outside world, creating a sterile, impersonal atmosphere. Mary sat across from Paul, her heart heavy. The man who had filled her world with warmth and promise was now a prisoner, accused of a crime she knew he couldn't have committed.

"I'm going to France, Paul," she said, her voice steady despite the turmoil within. "I have to find out more about Angela, or Amélie. I need to talk to Ada."

Paul's eyes widened in surprise. "That's a good idea, Mary. I think it's our best shot." He paused, his gaze filled with concern. "Are you sure you'll be safe? The police might be watching you."

"I'll be careful," Mary assured him, her determination unwavering. "I need to know what happened to her. If Ada is still alive, she might know something."

"If the police have finished with the car, you can take the Audi," Paul offered. "It's got a good engine and it'll get you there quicker."

Mary nodded, grateful for his support. "I'll let you know as soon as I have something."

THE AUDI'S ENGINE FELL silent as Mary pulled up to the imposing gates of the convent. The Brittany coastline, with its rugged beauty, had given way to a serene countryside that seemed frozen in time. Mary took a deep breath, her hand hesitating on the door handle. The weight of her mission pressed heavily upon her shoulders.

As she approached the gate, a nun with kind eyes and a welcoming smile greeted her. "Bonjour, mademoiselle. Comment puis-je vous aider?"

Mary mustered her best French. "Bonjour, Sister. Je suis ici pour voir la Mère Supérieure. C'est... c'est au sujet d'Amélie Bouchard."

The nun's smile faltered for just a moment before she nodded. "Suivez-moi, s'il vous plaît."

As they walked through the serene gardens, Mary couldn't help but wonder about the secrets these ancient walls held. The nun led her to a modest office where an older woman sat behind a simple desk.

"Mother Superior, this is..." the nun paused, realizing she hadn't asked Mary's name.

"Mary," she supplied quickly. "Mary Postlethwaite.

Mother Superior, introduced as Sister Agnes, gestured for Mary to sit. Her eyes, though kind, held a wisdom that seemed to look right through Mary.

"What brings you to our humble convent, Miss Postlethwaite?" Sister Agnes asked, her English accented but clear.

Mary leaned forward, her voice low and urgent. "I'm here about Amélie Bouchard. I need to understand who she was, where she came from. A man's life depends on it."

Sister Agnes's face clouded, a mix of sadness and something else – was it guilt? – passing across her features. "Ah, Amélie," she sighed. "That poor, troubled child."

"Can you tell me about her?" Mary pressed gently.

Sister Agnes nodded slowly. "Amélie was born within these very walls. Her mother, Ada, came to us in a delicate condition, you understand. From the moment she could walk, Amélie was... different."

"Different how?" Mary asked, leaning in.

"She had a restless spirit," Sister Agnes explained. "Always searching for something, though I don't think even she knew what. And then there were the... visitations."

Mary's eyebrows shot up. "Visitations?"

Sister Agnes nodded gravely. "Amélie claimed to communicate with spirits. At first, we thought it was a child's fantasy, but as she grew older..." She trailed off, lost in memory.

"What happened when she got older?" Mary prodded.

"Her rebellious nature grew stronger," Sister Agnes continued. "But strangely, she never left us. It was as if she was drawn to the familiar, even as she railed against it. Until recently, that is."

Mary's heart raced. "Recently?"

Sister Agnes nodded. "Just a few weeks ago, she announced she was leaving. Said she was going to visit relatives in England. We tried to dissuade her, but..." She spread her hands in a gesture of helplessness.

Mary's mind whirled with the implications. "Sister Agnes, did Amélie ever mention names? Paul Brankenwall? Or perhaps Gordon Benn?"

A flicker of recognition passed across the nun's face at the second name. "Gordon Benn... yes, I believe she mentioned him. Said he was a cousin, though we had no record of such a relation."

As Mary opened her mouth to ask another question, a commotion in the hallway interrupted them. The door burst open, revealing a flustered young nun.

"Pardon, Mother Superior, but there's a man at the gate. He's asking about Amélie too, and he seems... agitated."

Mary's blood ran cold. Who else could be here, asking about Amélie? As she turned back to Sister Agnes, she saw fear in the older woman's eyes.

"Miss Postlethwaite," Sister Agnes said urgently, "I think there's much more to Amélie's story than we realized. And I fear you may have stirred up something dangerous by coming here."

MARY FELT A PANG OF sympathy for the young Amélie. Turning her attention back to Sister Agnes, she asked, "And what about Ada Benn, Amélie's mother? Is she still here at the convent?"

Sister Agnes hesitated, her eyes clouding with a mix of emotions. "Sister Ada, as we came to know her, is no longer with us here. After... certain events, she chose to dedicate her life to prayer. She now resides in a monastery not far from here."

A flicker of hope ignited in Mary's heart. Perhaps Ada could provide the missing pieces to this tragic puzzle. She thanked Sister Agnes and left the convent, her mind racing with possibilities.

The drive to the monastery was short but seemed to stretch on forever as Mary's thoughts swirled with questions. The building itself was a picture of tranquility, its stone walls standing in stark contrast to the turmoil that had consumed Mary's world.

A gentle-faced nun led Mary to a small, austere room where Sister Ada waited. The woman was frail, her face lined with years of contemplation, but her eyes held a depth of wisdom that immediately struck Mary.

"Sister Ada," Mary began softly, "I'm here about your daughter, Amélie."

Ada's eyes widened, a mix of surprise and concern crossing her features. "Amélie? What about her?"

Mary took a deep breath, steeling herself. "I'm afraid I have some difficult news. Amélie... she's passed away."

A look of shock and profound sorrow passed over Ada's face. "My child," she whispered, her voice trembling. "I cannot believe this. How? When?"

Mary reached out and took her hand, offering what comfort she could. "It happened recently, in England. I'm trying to understand what led her there. Did you know anything about her life outside the convent?"

Ada closed her eyes, as if reliving a painful memory. When she spoke again, her voice was barely above a whisper. "I told her the truth about her father, about the life he denied her. I left her in the care of the nuns, hoping she would find peace and happiness. But I never imagined this..."

AS ADA'S VOICE TRAILED off, Mary gently prodded, "Can you tell me more about that time? About Amélie's connections in England?"

Ada's eyes refocused, a flicker of recognition passing through them. "Annie Brankenwall," she said suddenly. "Of course, I remember Annie. A kind soul, taken far too soon. It was at her funeral that Amélie met her son, Paul, wasn't it?"

Mary's heart skipped a beat at the mention of Paul's name. "Yes, that's right. Did Amélie speak of him?"

Sister Ada continued, oblivious to Mary's internal turmoil. "Amélie did mention him. She spoke of his wife's illness, how it had taken a toll on him. She said he seemed like a good man, burdened by sorrow."

The words hit Mary like a physical blow. Paul's wife? She felt the room spinning around her as the implications sank in. All this time, she'd been falling for a married man. The Paul she thought she knew suddenly felt like a stranger.

As Mary struggled to maintain her composure, Sister Ada continued to reminisce, unaware of the emotional bombshell she had just dropped. Mary listened with half an ear, her mind reeling, as she tried to reconcile this new information with everything she thought she knew about Paul Brankenwall.

The news of Paul's marriage hung heavy in the air. It was as if a veil had been lifted, revealing a side of him she never knew existed. And with each passing moment, the man she thought she knew and loved was fading away, replaced by a stranger.

Mary forced herself to continue. "Did Amélie have any close friends here in the convent? Someone who might know more about her life, her thoughts?"

Ada's expression softened. "There were two, I believe. Sister Claire and Sister Elise. They were like true sisters to Amélie. They might be able to shed some light on her troubled heart."

Mary leaned forward, her heart racing. "And Amélie? Did she know about her heritage?"

Ada nodded slowly. "I told her everything when she turned eighteen. Perhaps it was a mistake, but I believed she deserved to know the truth. She was so angry, so determined to claim what she saw as her birthright."

"Is that why she left for England?" Mary pressed.

"Partly," Ada admitted. "But there was more to it. She spoke of visions, of a calling she couldn't ignore. She mentioned rituals, ancient family traditions. I thought it was just her imagination running wild, but now..."

Mary's mind raced, connecting the dots. "Sister Ada, did Amélie ever mention Gordon Benn?"

Ada's brow furrowed. "Gordon? Yes, she spoke of him. Said he was a distant cousin who'd reached out to her. He filled her head with stories of family legacies and hidden truths. I warned her to be cautious, but she was so eager to belong somewhere."

As Mary absorbed this information, she couldn't help but return to the revelation about Paul. "Sister Ada, you mentioned Paul's wife. Can you tell me more about her?"

Ada looked surprised. "Oh, my dear, I'm afraid I don't know much. Amélie said she was ill, that's all. Is something wrong?"

Mary forced a smile, trying to mask her turmoil. "No, no. It's just... I'm trying to understand everything that was happening in Amélie's life."

Ada reached out, taking Mary's hand. "My dear, you seem troubled. Is there something you're not telling me?"

Mary hesitated, then decided to be honest. "I... I've grown close to Paul. But I had no idea he was married. It's come as quite a shock."

Ada's eyes widened with understanding. "Oh, my child. The heart is a complex thing, isn't it? But remember, appearances can be deceiving. In matters of the heart, it's best to seek the truth directly."

As they continued to talk, Mary's mind whirled with new information and unanswered questions. The mystery surrounding Amélie's death had only grown more complex, and now her own feelings for Paul were thrown into doubt.

Ada's face paled. "My dear," she whispered urgently, "I think it's time for you to leave. There are forces at work here that are beyond your understanding. Be careful, and trust no one completely."

As Mary rose to leave, she felt the weight of secrets and lies pressing down on her. She had come seeking answers, but had only found more questions. And now she realized that her quest for the truth had become far more dangerous than she could have imagined.

A renewed sense of purpose filled Mary. She thanked Sister Ada for her time and left the monastery, her mind racing. The pieces of the puzzle were slowly coming together.

Back at the convent, Mary requested to see Sisters Claire and Elise. The two nuns, now in their early twenties, welcomed her with gentle smiles. As she shared Amélie's story, their eyes filled with sorrow. They spoke of a young woman searching for her place in the world, a soul torn between the sacred and the secular.

"Why not take a walk around the garden?" suggested Elise. "We can talk more easily there, walls have ears, you know."

"Amélie was a complex child," Sister Claire said softly. "Brilliant but troubled. She often spoke of running away, of finding a life beyond these walls."

Sister Elise added, "She was drawn to the world outside, the allure of freedom. But she always returned, seeking solace in the familiar."

"What was her job here in the convent?" Mary asked, curious about Amélie's daily routine.

"We all shared the housework, but Amélie had a particular love for the garden," Sister Claire replied. "She found a strange kind of peace tending to the plants. She was especially skilled at topiary, shaping the hedges into intricate forms. It was a fascinating way to add a unique touch to the landscape."

They paused, gesturing towards the meticulously trimmed hedges that lined the garden path. Intricate shapes of animals and birds emerged from the green foliage.

"She would spend hours out here, her hands gentle as she pruned and shaped," Sister Elise added. "There was a certain magic to the way she transformed the ordinary into something extraordinary."

As they walked, Mary couldn't help but notice the vibrant green of the hedges, punctuated by the stark white of the convent walls. The contrast was striking, almost jarring. And then she saw it, a small cluster of oleander bushes, their delicate pink flowers a stark contrast to the severe architecture of the convent. A shiver ran down her spine. Oleander was known for its toxic properties. A dangerous plant to have in a place where children lived.

Mary's heart pounded as she sought out Father Bétron. His room was a simple cell, filled with the quietude of a life dedicated to prayer. The old priest, his face etched with the lines of age, looked at her with gentle eyes.

"Father Bétron," she began, her voice trembling slightly, "I'm looking for information about a marriage. A secret marriage between the Earl of Egremont and a woman named Annie Brankenwall."

The old priest's eyes widened in surprise. "You're not the first person to ask about that in the last week," he said, his voice low. "It's a delicate matter, young lady."

Hope ignited within Mary. "I understand. But I need to see the marriage certificate. It's important."

Father Bétron sighed. "The certificate exists, it's a record of a sacred union. But it's not something I can simply hand over. It's a matter of trust, and I'm not sure I trust you."

Mary felt a surge of frustration. "I understand your concerns, Father. But I promise, I'll only use it to prove Paul's legitimacy. He's been accused of murder, and I believe this certificate could be the key to clearing his name."

The old priest studied Mary's face for a long moment. Finally, he nodded, a flicker of reluctance crossing his features. "Very well," he said, his voice low. "I will make an exception in this case."

A surge of relief washed over Mary. "Thank you, Father," she said, her voice filled with gratitude.

"But understand," the priest continued, "the original document will remain in my safekeeping. Only a judge or someone in a position of high authority can access it. I will make a copy for you, but it must be handled with the utmost care."

Mary nodded solemnly. "I understand. Thank you."

As she left the convent, a sense of purpose and determination filled her. The marriage certificate was the key she needed to unlock the truth, to prove Paul's innocence, and to uncover the secrets of the Wyndham family.

Mary thanked the sisters for their time, her mind racing with the information she had gathered. The image of Amélie, a young woman caught between two worlds, became clearer. With each piece of the puzzle falling into place, Mary felt a growing sense of determination. She would find the truth, no matter the cost.

Chapter 24

Doreen Thornton was deep in the rabbit hole of the Wyndham family tree. Surrounded by papers and her computer, she was piecing together a complex puzzle.

"Quite a tangled web," she muttered, running a hand through her hair. "Let's see, the first Earl of Egremont was Algernon Seymour, but it was his nephew, Charles Wyndham, who really got the ball rolling."

She paused, scrolling through digital documents. "Then there's George Wyndham, the third Earl. A real player, by all accounts. Lots of children, but only one legitimate heir. Can you imagine the drama?"

Her focus sharpened. "Next up, Henry Wyndham. His reign was short-lived, but his son, George, became the first Baron Leconfield. An interesting side note there."

She tapped a few keys. "Now, the sixth Earl is where it gets complicated. William Angus Charles Wyndham, that's him. His father, Sir Winston Wyndham, was a friend of Major Terrance Lonsdale. There's a rumour they cooked up a plan for William to inherit the Earldom, even arranging a marriage to secure the title."

Doreen leaned back, her eyes narrowing. "So, the current Earl would have been around eighteen in 1940. That would make him... let's see, that's about fifty-four now."

A thoughtful expression crossed her face. "Ada Benn worked at the manor around that time. Could there be a connection? If the current Earl is the father as she claims, it would explain a lot."

Doreen leaned back in her chair, her mind racing. "This also means that Nigel, who's currently running things at the Manor, must be his son. And if Paul's claim is legitimate, he would be... what? A half-brother to Nigel? But what about the others, the illegitimates? How many are there and do they have any claim to the estate?"

A complex web of possibilities unfurled before her. "If Paul's claim that his father was legally married to his mother Annie is true, then he would be the eldest son and rightfully claim the title. On the other hand, if Nigel can disprove the legality of the marriage, then the power dynamic shifts dramatically."

She paused, considering the implications. "And then there's the question of the Earl's status. Bigamy is a serious offense. His scandalous behaviour might warrant some action to remove his title."

A chill ran down her spine. This wasn't just about a family feud or a property dispute. It was about power, greed, and possibly even murder.

Doreen reached for her phone, her mind racing. She needed to update James Hetherington. "This is bigger than we thought," she murmured to herself. "Much bigger."

As she dialed the number, she couldn't shake the feeling that they were on the brink of something monumental. Something that could change everything.

Chapter 25

The cell door clanged open, and James Hetherington strode in, his normally impeccable suit slightly rumpled. Paul looked up from the uncomfortable cot, hope and anxiety warring on his face.

"James," Paul said, standing quickly. "Any news?"

Hetherington shook his head, setting his briefcase down. "I'm afraid not much has changed since yesterday, Paul. But I'm here to discuss our next steps."

Paul ran a hand through his disheveled hair. "Have you heard from Mary? She mentioned a meeting with Gordon Benn. Said it might be useful."

A flicker of concern crossed Hetherington's face. "No, I haven't. When did you last speak with her?"

"Before all this," Paul gestured around the cell, his frustration evident in every movement. "She said she was taking the Audi to France after meeting Benn. I don't understand why she hasn't been in touch. It's not like her."

Hetherington, Paul's lawyer, frowned, his brow furrowing in concern. "That is odd. We should inform Detective Inspector Williamson about this. It could be relevant to your case."

He turned to the uniformed officer standing guard. "Officer, we need to speak with DI Williamson immediately. It's urgent."

As they waited, Paul's anxiety grew with each passing minute. The fluorescent lights buzzed overhead, casting harsh shadows on the institutional green walls of the small interview room they'd been moved to.

Finally, Harry Williamson entered, his face a mask of professional detachment. "Mr. Hetherington, Mr. Brankenwall, what's this about?"

Hetherington quickly explained the situation. Williamson's expression grew serious as he listened.

"I see," Williamson said, stroking his chin thoughtfully. "This could indeed be significant. I'll need to place some calls."

He turned to the officer. "Bring me a phone, will you?"

When the phone arrived, Williamson dialled the operator. "This is Detective Inspector Williamson. I need to place a call to France, please." He rattled off a string of digits.

Paul and Hetherington watched anxiously as Williamson waited for the connection. The detective's fingers drummed an impatient rhythm on the table.

Finally, Williamson spoke into the receiver. "Hello, is this the Hotel Méditerranée? This is Detective Inspector Williamson from the British police. I'm trying to reach a guest, Mary Postlethwaite. She should have checked in yesterday."

After a moment, Williamson's frown deepened. "I see. And she hasn't left any messages? ... Yes, if she does check in or contact you, please ask her to call this number immediately." He recited the police station's number, then hung up.

He turned to Paul and Hetherington, shaking his head. "She hasn't checked in. The hotel hasn't heard from her at all."

Paul's face paled. "That's not possible. She would have called if there was a change of plans. Something's wrong, Inspector."

Williamson nodded gravely. "I agree. This changes things." He turned to the officer. "Get me the paperwork for a missing persons report. And contact the French police. We need to put out an alert for Mary Postlethwaite and that Audi."

As the officer hurried off, Williamson fixed Paul with a stern gaze. "Mr. Brankenwall, I hope you understand that this development may impact our investigation. I'll need you to tell me everything you know about Miss Postlethwaite's plans."

Hetherington interjected, "My client is willing to cooperate fully, Inspector. But I must insist on being present for any further questioning."

Williamson nodded curtly. "Of course."

As they left the room, Paul's mind raced with worry. The absence of communications suddenly felt painfully acute, leaving them fumbling in the dark for answers about Mary's whereabouts.

Paul's face fell. "James, what if something's happened to her? With everything going on..."

Hetherington held up a hand. "Let's not jump to conclusions. There could be a perfectly reasonable explanation. I'll have my office look into it."

Paul nodded, but the worry didn't leave his eyes. "What about the case? Where do we stand?"

Hetherington sighed, leaning against the cell wall. "The good news is, the police are lacking in facts. They suspect you poisoned Angela, but they have no concrete proof. It's all circumstantial at this point."

"But I didn't do it!" Paul exclaimed, frustration evident in his voice.

"I know, Paul. And that's what we need to focus on." Hetherington's voice was calm but determined. "They think they have a motive, but they can't prove anything. Not really."

Paul slumped back onto the cot. "So what now?"

Hetherington straightened his tie, a glint of determination in his eye. "Now, I plan to confront the police. Demand they release you. They can't hold you indefinitely without charges, and their case is flimsy at best."

"You think that'll work?" Paul asked, a hint of hope creeping into his voice.

"It has to," Hetherington replied. "We need you out of here so we can properly investigate what really happened to Angela. And," he added, his voice lowering, "find out what's going on with Mary."

Paul nodded, standing again. "James, there's something else. Something that's been nagging at me."

Hetherington raised an eyebrow. "Go on."

"The night Amélie ... died. There was a moment, just before we left the restaurant. I saw someone outside, watching us. I didn't think much of it at the time, but now..."

Hetherington leaned in, intrigued. "Can you describe this person?"

Paul closed his eyes, concentrating. "It was dark, but... a man, I think. Tall, wearing a dark coat. He seemed to be talking on a phone."

Hetherington jotted this down in his notebook. "Good, Paul. This could be important. Anything else you remember? Any distinguishing features?"

Paul shook his head. "No, it was too dark. But there was something... familiar about him. I can't put my finger on it."

Hetherington nodded, closing his notebook. "Alright. I'll add this to our investigation. For now, try to rest. I'm going to speak with the detective in charge. With any luck, we'll have you out of here by this evening."

As Hetherington gathered his things to leave, Paul called out. "James? Thank you. For everything."

Hetherington offered a small smile. "We're not out of the woods yet, Paul. But we will get to the bottom of this. All of it."

As the cell door closed behind Hetherington, Paul sat back on the cot, his mind racing with questions about Angela's death, Mary's disappearance, and the mysterious figure outside the restaurant. Despite Hetherington's reassurances, he couldn't shake the feeling that this was all part of something much bigger – and much more dangerous – than he had initially thought.

Chapter 26

After leaving the police station, James Hetherington sat in his car, deep in thought. His gaze fell on the bulky car phone installed in the centre console - a rare and expensive piece of technology he'd had fitted just last month. On a hunch, he picked up the receiver and dialed the number for the Hotel Mediterranée in France.

"Good afternoon, Hotel Mediterranée," came the accented voice of the receptionist.

"Hello, this is James Hetherington. I'm trying to reach Mary Postlethwaite. Has she checked in yet?"

There was a shuffling of papers. "Ah, yes, Miss Postlethwaite checked in about an hour ago. Would you like me to put you through to her room?"

Hetherington's heart leapt. "Yes, please. Thank you."

After a series of clicks and buzzes, Mary's voice came through the line, tinny but unmistakable.

"Mary, thank God. We've been worried sick," Hetherington said, relief evident in his voice.

There was a pause before Mary spoke, her voice tight with emotion. "James, I... I don't know what to do."

Hetherington frowned, gripping the receiver tighter. "What's wrong? Are you alright?"

"I'm fine, physically," Mary replied. "But James, I've learned some things here in France. I met with Ada Benn and..." She trailed off.

"And what, Mary?" Hetherington pressed gently, aware of the exorbitant cost of the international call but too concerned to care.

Mary's voice cracked slightly. "She told me Paul is married. Has been for years. How could he not tell me? And then I found out about his meeting with Angela Benn. How many other things has he kept from me?"

Hetherington's mind raced. This was unexpected and complicated matters significantly. "Mary, I had no idea. Have you spoken to Paul about this?"

"No," Mary said firmly. "I can't face him right now. I love him, James, but how can I trust him after this? My family is telling me to forget about him, to move on."

Hetherington sighed, running a hand through his hair. The complexity of the situation was growing by the minute. "Mary, listen to me. Don't make any hasty decisions. I know you're hurt and confused, but there might be more to this story. Can you stay put for now? I'll try to get to the bottom of this."

"I don't know, James. I feel so lost," Mary's voice wavered.

"I understand. Look, I'll call you back at the hotel tomorrow. Try to get some rest, and don't do anything rash. Can you promise me that?"

There was a long pause before Mary responded. "Alright, I promise. But James, please... find out the truth. I need to know."

As Hetherington hung up the phone, he sat back in his seat, his mind whirling. The situation had just become far more complicated than he'd anticipated. He started the car, determination setting in. It was time to have a very serious conversation with Paul Brankenwall.

Hetherington sighed, "What the hell is going on here"

After ending the call with Mary, He drove to his office, his mind working overtime. He needed to verify Mary's claims and figure out how this fit into the larger picture.

At the office, Hetherington's assistant handed him a file. "Sir, we've got something on that mysterious figure Paul mentioned."

Hetherington opened the file to find several grainy CCTV images. They showed a tall man in a dark coat outside the restaurant on the night of Angela's death. The man's face was partially obscured, but there was something familiar about his stance and build.

Hetherington's eyes widened as he realized why the figure seemed familiar. He quickly dialled Detective Inspector Thompson.

"Thompson," Hetherington said urgently, "I need to speak with Paul immediately. And I think we need to look into Gordon Benn's whereabouts on the night Angela died."

"Benn?" Thompson sounded surprised. "What's he got to do with this?"

Hetherington stared at the CCTV image. "I'm not sure yet, but I think he might be our mysterious watcher. And if I'm right, this case just got a lot more complicated."

As he hung up, Hetherington's mind raced. Paul's hidden marriage, Mary's distress, Angela's death, and now Gordon Benn's possible involvement – the pieces were starting to form a picture, but it was far from clear. One thing was certain: there were more secrets to uncover, and time was running out.

———◦———

HETHERINGTON SAT IN his office, staring at the phone. He had just finished a revealing conversation with the administrator of a private hospital in Paris France. The pieces were starting to fall into place, but the picture they formed was heart-breaking.

He dialled Paul's number at the detention centre, his mind reeling from what he'd learned. When Paul answered, Hetherington didn't mince words.

"Paul, we need to talk about Yvette."

There was a sharp intake of breath on the other end of the line. "How... how do you know about Yvette?"

Hetherington's voice was gentle but firm. "I know everything, Paul. About your marriage, the accident, the coma. Why didn't you tell us?"

There was a long pause before Paul spoke, his voice heavy with emotion. "I couldn't... I can't..." He took a shaky breath. "It's my fault she's there, James. That night, ten years ago... our first anniversary..."

As Paul recounted the events of that fateful night, Hetherington listened intently. The celebratory dinner that devolved into an argument about Paul's obsession with the vineyard. Yvette storming out, deciding to walk the three miles home. Her declaration that she was going to leave him. And then, the devastating news just five minutes from their house - Yvette had been hit by a drunk driver.

"She's been in a coma ever since," Paul finished, his voice barely above a whisper. "The doctors say there's no chance of recovery. But I can't... I can't let her go."

Hetherington nodded, even though Paul couldn't see him. "The insurance company of the drunk driver - they're pushing you to switch off life support, aren't they?"

"How did you know?"

"It's costing them a fortune, Paul. Hundreds of thousands each year. They want to cut their losses."

Paul's voice hardened. "I won't do it. I can't. It's my fault she's there. If I hadn't been so obsessed with the vineyard, if we hadn't argued..."

Hetherington interrupted gently. "Paul, you can't keep blaming yourself. It was a tragic accident, but it wasn't your fault. The drunk driver is the one responsible."

There was silence on the other end of the line.

"Paul," Hetherington continued, "there's something else we need to discuss. Mary knows about your marriage."

Paul's sharp intake of breath was audible. "Oh God. How... how did she find out?"

"Ada Benn told her in France. Mary's devastated, Paul. She feels betrayed."

"I never meant to hurt her," Paul said, his voice cracking. "I love her, James. I love her so much. But how could I tell her about Yvette? How could I explain?"

Hetherington sighed. "You're going to have to, Paul. If we're going to clear your name in Angela's death, we need Mary's help. And for that, we need the truth. All of it."

There was a long pause before Paul spoke again. "You're right. I've been living with this guilt for so long... I thought I could keep my past separate from my present. But I can't. Not anymore."

"I'll arrange for Mary to visit you," Hetherington said. "You need to tell her everything. About Yvette, about the accident, about your feelings. It's the only way forward."

As Hetherington ended the call, he couldn't help but feel a mix of sympathy and frustration. Paul's situation was undoubtedly tragic, but his secrecy had complicated matters enormously. Now, with Angela's death looming over everything, the tangled web of Paul's past and present threatened to unravel completely.

Hetherington picked up his phone again. It was time to dig deeper into Gordon Benn's involvement and the mysterious figure outside the restaurant. He had a feeling that somewhere in this complex tapestry of love, guilt, and secrets lay the key to solving Angela's murder - and clearing Paul's name.

AS HETHERINGTON WORKED tirelessly to unravel the mystery surrounding Angela's death, Mary found herself in the eye of an emotional storm. She sat in her family's living room, surrounded by concerned but frustrated faces.

"Mary, you need to cut ties with Paul," Steve, her brother, insisted. "He's lied to you, he's mixed up in a murder investigation. How much more trouble do you need?"

Uncle Brian nodded in agreement. "Love's made you blind, girl. It's time to see reason."

Mary opened her mouth to protest, but was cut off by Andrew, her other brother. "And it's not just about Paul. We need you focused on the family business. Howard's widow has decided to side with me on selling the pottery."

Mary felt as if she'd been punched in the gut. "What? But she promised Howard she'd keep it in the family!"

Andrew shrugged, his casual demeanor a stark contrast to the tension in the room. "People change their minds. Especially when there's a good offer on the table."

As the argument escalated, the shrill ring of the telephone cut through the air. Mary hurried to answer it, grateful for the interruption.

"Hello?" she said, trying to keep her voice level.

"Mary, it's Hetherington," came the lawyer's voice, sounding urgent even through the slightly crackly line. "I need to speak with you immediately. There have been some important developments. Can you meet me?"

Mary's heart raced. "Yes, of course. Where?"

"The café on Church Street, in an hour. It's crucial, Mary."

"I'll be there," she promised, then hung up.

Turning back to her family, Mary took a deep breath. "I have to go. This discussion isn't over, but I need some air, and I have an urgent meeting."

Steve opened his mouth to protest, but Mary held up a hand. "We'll continue this later. I promise."

An hour later, Mary pushed open the door of the small café on Church Street. The bell above the door jingled softly, announcing her arrival. The place was nearly empty, save for an elderly couple in the corner and Hetherington, sitting at a table near the back, a steaming cup of tea in front of him.

As Mary approached, Hetherington stood, pulling out a chair for her. "Thank you for coming so quickly," he said, his voice low.

Mary sat down, noticing the concern etched on Hetherington's face. Her eyes were red-rimmed from the earlier argument, but her voice was steady as she spoke. "What's so urgent, James?"

Hetherington leaned in, his voice barely above a whisper. "I've received some information that could change everything. It's about Paul, and it's... well, it's complicated."

The waitress approached, and Hetherington paused, ordering another cup of tea for Mary. As soon as the waitress left, Mary leaned forward, her heart pounding. "Tell me everything, James. What's happened?"

Hetherington pulled his chair closer to the table. "Mary, I know you're hurt and angry with Paul, but there's more to the story than you know. Paul's wife, Yvette... she's been in a coma for ten years."

Mary's eyes widened as Hetherington explained the tragic circumstances of Yvette's accident and Paul's on-going guilt.

"He needs to tell you himself," Hetherington finished, "but I wanted you to have some context. There's more at stake here than just Angela's death."

Mary sat back, her mind reeling. "I... I don't know what to think. Why didn't he tell me?"

"Guilt, shame, fear of losing you," Hetherington suggested. "But Mary, we need your help to clear his name. And there's something else..."

He produced the CCTV images of the mysterious figure outside the restaurant. "We think this might be Gordon Benn. Does this look familiar to you?"

Mary studied the image, her brow furrowing. "It could be... the build is similar. But why would Gordon be there?"

"That's what we need to find out," Hetherington said. "And it might tie into your meeting with Ada Benn. What exactly did she tell you?"

As Mary recounted her conversation with Ada, a new picture began to form. There were whispers of financial troubles at the Benn estate, rumors of Gordon's gambling debts, and hints of a long-standing rivalry between the Benns and Paul's family.

"Mary," Hetherington said seriously, "I think there's more to Angela's death than we initially thought. And I believe you might be the key to unraveling it all."

Mary took a deep breath, her mind racing. On one side, her family's pressure to abandon Paul and focus on saving the pottery business. On the other, the complex web of secrets, lies, and possible murder that Paul was entangled in.

"What do you need me to do?" she asked finally.

Hetherington smiled grimly. "First, we need you to talk to Paul. Hear his side of the story. Then, I think it's time we pay a visit to Wilton Manor. Something tells me Nigel might know more than he's letting on."

As they left the café, Mary felt a mix of dread and determination. She was walking into a storm, but she was beginning to see that it might be the only way to clear the air - and possibly save more than just Paul's reputation.

"One more thing," Hetherington added as they parted. "Be careful. If Gordon is involved in this, he might not take kindly to our investigations. Watch your back."

Mary nodded, her resolve strengthening. She had decisions to make - about Paul, about her family's business, about her own future. But first, she had a mystery to solve and a man to save - if he was indeed worth saving.

As she drove home, Mary couldn't shake the feeling that the next few days would change everything. For better or worse remained to be seen.

Chapter 27

Detective Sergeant Thompson sat across from Gordon Benn in the stark interview room. Benn's lawyer, a stern-faced woman in her fifties, sat quietly to his right.

"Mr. Benn," Thompson began, "we appreciate you coming in to answer some questions. Let's start with your recent encounter with Mary Postlethwaite on Cold Fell. Can you tell us about that?"

Gordon shifted in his seat. "It was just a chance meeting. I was out for a walk with my daughter. She'd been to see Matty Benns Bridge"

"Your daughter?" Thompson raised an eyebrow. "Can you elaborate?"

"Freda Benn," Gordon replied. "She's 16. We often walk together in that area."

Thompson made a note. "I see. And where exactly do you live, Mr. Benn?"

"Wilton Cottage," Gordon answered promptly. "It's on the edge of Wilton village, on the road to Cold Fell. About a 20-minute walk from Matty Benn's Bridge."

Thompson nodded. "Now, regarding Angela Benn. Did you meet with her in France recently?"

Gordon shook his head. "No, I didn't meet her in person. She called me on the phone, though. Her English was heavily accented. I found her quite difficult to understand, to be honest."

"Interesting," Thompson mused. "What about the day before she died? We have information suggesting you met with Angela at Wilton Cottage."

Gordon's lawyer leaned in, whispering something in his ear. Gordon nodded before responding. "Yes, that's correct. She wanted to discuss some family matters."

"And later that evening, Angela was seen meeting Paul Brankenwall at the Blue Bell pub. Were you aware of this?"

Gordon's face tightened almost imperceptibly. "I heard about it afterwards. Small village, word gets around."

As the interview continued, Thompson pressed Gordon on his whereabouts the night of Angela's death, his relationship with Paul Brankenwall, and any financial difficulties he might be experiencing. Gordon's answers were measured, revealing little, but Thompson couldn't shake the feeling that there was more beneath the surface.

After Gordon and his lawyer left, Thompson turned to his colleague. "What do you think?"

"He's hiding something," the other detective replied. "But what?"

Chapter 28

Mary stood in front of the hallway mirror, adjusting her collar one last time. Her conversation with Hetherington had left her conflicted, but she knew she needed to hear Paul's side of the story. The visit to the detention centre weighed heavily on her mind.

Just as she reached for her coat, the shrill ring of the telephone pierced the quiet of the house. Mary hesitated for a moment, then moved to answer it.

"Hello?" she said, cradling the receiver between her ear and shoulder as she continued to put on her coat.

"Mary, it's Andrew," came her brother's voice, urgency clear in his tone. "We need to talk. Howard's widow has officially sided with me. We're moving forward with the sale of the pottery."

Mary felt her heart sink. Her hand gripped the phone tighter. "Andrew, you can't! This business has been in our family for generations!"

"It's not just my decision, Mary," Andrew replied, a note of frustration in his voice. "The majority of the shareholders agree. It's time to let go."

Mary leaned against the wall, closing her eyes. "But what about our heritage? What about all the people who depend on the pottery for their livelihoods?"

"Times change, Mary," Andrew said, his voice softening slightly. "The pottery isn't profitable anymore. We can't keep running it on sentiment alone."

"There has to be another way," Mary insisted. "Have you looked into modernizing the production? Or finding new markets?"

Andrew sighed. "We've been over this. The investment required would be enormous, and there's no guarantee of success."

Mary felt torn. Her planned visit to Paul suddenly seemed less urgent in the face of this family crisis. "Andrew, can we meet to discuss this further? Maybe if we put our heads together, we can find a solution."

"I'm sorry, Mary, but the decision's been made," Andrew replied firmly. "I just thought you should hear it from me first."

As the conversation ended, Mary replaced the receiver in its cradle, her mind whirling. She glanced at the clock on the wall, realizing she was now running late for her visit to Paul.

With a heavy heart, she grabbed her keys and headed out the door. As she walked to her car, parked on the street, she couldn't help but feel that her world was shifting beneath her feet. The family business, Paul's situation, her own uncertain future – everything seemed to be coming to a head at once.

Starting the car, Mary took a deep breath. She had decisions to make, and time was running short. As she pulled away from the curb, her mind raced with possibilities and fears. The drive to the detention centre would give her time to think, but she knew that sooner or later, she would have to face the harsh realities that awaited her.

AT THE DETENTION CENTRE, Paul was waiting, his face a mask of anxiety and hope. As Mary sat down across from him, she knew that whatever he said next would change everything.

"Mary," Paul began, his voice barely above a whisper. "I'm so sorry. I should have told you everything from the beginning. About Yvette, about the accident... about everything."

Mary leaned forward, her heart pounding. "I'm listening, Paul. Start from the beginning."

As Paul began to speak, unravelling the tangled threads of his past, Mary listened intently. Little did they know that their conversation was about to uncover a truth that would shock them both - a truth that would tie together the Benns, the pottery business, and a decade-old tragedy in ways they could never have imagined.

Chapter 29

James Hetherington strode purposefully through the police station, his briefcase clutched tightly in one hand. He nodded curtly to the desk sergeant before being escorted to Detective Inspector Williamson's office.

Williamson looked up from his desk, his face a mask of professional neutrality. "Mr. Hetherington, what brings you here today?"

Hetherington placed his briefcase on the desk and clicked it open. "I have new evidence that I believe will change the course of your investigation, Inspector. And I'm here to demand the release of my client, Paul Brankenwall."

Williamson leaned back in his chair, eyebrow raised. "That's a bold statement, counselor. Let's hear what you've got."

For the next thirty minutes, Hetherington laid out his findings. He presented expert analyses of the oleander traces, reports from botanical specialists, and a detailed breakdown of the weather conditions on the night of Angela's death.

"As you can see, Inspector," Hetherington concluded, "the traces of oleander in Angela's system were far too minute to have caused her death. Our experts believe she likely ingested these traces while trimming oleander hedges on the estate, or possibly by inhaling smoke from burning hedge clippings."

Williamson frowned, leafing through the reports. "If not poisoning, then what's your theory?"

"Hypothermia," Hetherington stated firmly. "The evidence suggests Angela went for a late-night swim at Matty Benn's Bridge - a local tradition, as I'm sure you're aware. The water was exceptionally cold that night. She likely became disoriented, couldn't find her clothes, and succumbed to the cold before she could seek help."

Williamson sat back, his face thoughtful. "It's an interesting theory, Hetherington. But it doesn't explain everything. Why was she there? Who was she meeting?"

"Those are valid questions, Inspector," Hetherington conceded. "But they're not grounds to keep Paul Brankenwall in custody. Your case against him is circumstantial at best. You have no solid evidence linking him to Angela's death, which we now have reason to believe was a tragic accident rather than murder."

Williamson stood, pacing behind his desk. "You're asking me to release a prime suspect, Hetherington."

"I'm asking you to follow the law, Inspector," Hetherington countered. "You can't hold Paul indefinitely without charges. And based on this new evidence, I don't believe you have grounds for charges."

After a tense moment, Williamson nodded slowly. "I'll need to review all of this with the Crown Prosecutor. But... you may have a point about holding Mr. Brankenwall."

Hetherington allowed himself a small smile. "Thank you, Inspector. I trust you'll make the right decision."

As he left the station, Hetherington's phone buzzed. It was a text from Mary Postlethwaite: "Any news? My family's pushing to sell the pottery business again. Need to talk."

Hetherington sighed, his mind racing. He had to get Paul released, continue investigating what really happened to Angela, and now deal with Mary's family crisis. As he headed to his car, he couldn't shake the feeling that all of these threads were somehow connected, leading back to the shadows of Wilton Manor and the surrounding community.

The battle was far from over, but Hetherington felt a glimmer of hope. They were one step closer to the truth, and soon, Paul would be free to help unravel the rest of this complex mystery.

Two days after Hetherington's meeting with Inspector Williamson, Paul Brankenwall stood outside the police station, blinking in the bright sunlight. He inhaled deeply, savoring his first breath of freedom in weeks.

James Hetherington stood beside him, a satisfied smile on his face. "How does it feel, Paul?"

"Surreal," Paul replied, his voice hoarse. "I can't quite believe it's over."

"Not over," Hetherington corrected gently. "Just entering a new phase. The charges have been dropped, but there are still many unanswered questions."

As they walked towards Hetherington's car, a familiar figure approached - Mary Postlethwaite, her face a mixture of relief and concern.

"Paul!" she called, quickening her pace. She hesitated for a moment before embracing him tightly. "I'm so glad you're out."

Paul returned the embrace, closing his eyes briefly. "Mary, I don't know how to thank you for everything you've done."

As they separated, Mary's expression grew serious. "Paul, James, we need to talk. There's been some... developments."

Hetherington nodded, opening the car door. "Let's go to my office. We'll be able to speak freely there."

Twenty minutes later, they were seated in Hetherington's office, cups of strong coffee in hand.

"So," Hetherington began, "what's on your mind, Mary?"

Mary took a deep breath. "It's about the pottery business. My family is really pushing to sell. There's a Spanish ceramics company making a very attractive offer."

Paul frowned. "But the pottery's been in your family for generations. Surely you can't just sell it off?"

"It's complicated," Mary sighed. "I don't want to sell, but the pressure is mounting."

Hetherington nodded thoughtfully. "I see. And how does this relate to our current situation?"

Mary hesitated. "I'm not sure it does, exactly. But with everything that's happened, I can't shake the feeling that there's more going on than meets the eye. The timing of this offer feels... convenient."

Paul leaned forward. "You think there might be a connection?"

"I don't know," Mary admitted. "It could just be coincidence. But after everything with Angela and Wilton Manor, I'm starting to question everything."

Hetherington sat back, his fingers steepled. "It's worth looking into. We can't afford to overlook any potential connections, no matter how tenuous they might seem."

Just then, Hetherington's phone rang. He answered, listening intently for a few moments before hanging up.

"That was Inspector Williamson," he said, his expression serious. "They've received an anonymous call from a young woman. She claims Gordon Benn was at Matty Benn's Bridge the night Angela died."

Paul and Mary exchanged startled looks.

"Gordon Benn?" Paul asked. "The handyman from Wilton Manor?"

Hetherington nodded. "The very same. This could be a significant development. It places a potential witness - or suspect - at the scene."

Mary's brow furrowed as she recalled her lunch meeting with Gordon Benn. "Actually, there's something I need to tell you both about Gordon," she said, her voice low. "I met with him for lunch a few days ago, trying to gather information."

Paul and Hetherington leaned in, their attention focused on Mary.

"Gordon admitted he was at Matty Benn's Bridge that night," Mary continued, her voice tinged with unease. "He claimed he didn't see Angela, but... something about his manner felt off."

Hetherington's eyes narrowed. "What exactly did he say?"

Mary took a deep breath, recounting the conversation. "He said he was there around 1 AM. Claimed the place was 'dead quiet, just me and the sheep.' But when I pressed him about what he would have done if he had met Angela as planned, things got... strange."

"Strange how?" Paul asked, his face tense.

"He started talking about showing her 'the old ways,'" Mary explained. "Mentioned something about rituals at the bridge, connecting with ancestors. He even said he'd brought candles, herbs, and a special bottle of wine from the Manor's cellar."

Hetherington frowned. "That's quite elaborate for a meeting with someone he'd supposedly just met."

Mary nodded. "Exactly. And there's more. Earlier in our conversation, he made some disturbing comments about the Earl having a 'taste for young girls.' He talked about being asked to find new staff when girls 'ran off or got in trouble.' The way he spoke about it... it was chilling."

Paul's face had gone pale. "My God. You don't think..."

"I don't know what to think," Mary admitted. "But combining what Gordon told me with this anonymous call the police received... it paints a disturbing picture."

Hetherington stood, pacing the room. "This is significant, Mary. Gordon's admission places him at the scene, contradicting what he told the police. And these hints about rituals and the Earl's behavior... we need to look into this further."

"But we need to be careful," Paul interjected. "These are serious allegations, especially against the Earl."

Hetherington nodded gravely. "Indeed. We'll need to corroborate everything. Mary, can you write down everything you remember from your conversation with Gordon? Every detail could be crucial."

Mary agreed, already reaching for a notepad.

"This changes things," Hetherington mused. "We now have a potential witness - or suspect - admitting to being at the scene. And these implications about Wilton Manor and the Earl... we may be dealing with something far bigger than we initially thought."

The room fell into a tense silence as the implications of Mary's revelation sank in. The mystery surrounding Angela's death had just deepened considerably, and they all knew that unraveling it could lead them into dangerous territory.

Chapter 30

The early morning mist hung low over Wilton Manor as Detective Inspector Williamson's car crunched up the gravel driveway. He'd been roused from his bed by an urgent call – a body had been found in one of the estate cottages.

As he approached, he saw the flashing lights of police vehicles and an ambulance. Uniformed officers were already securing the perimeter. A young woman with red-rimmed eyes sat on the cottage steps, wrapped in a blanket.

"Inspector," a constable greeted him. "Victim is Gordon Benn, the estate handyman. Found by his daughter, Freda, there." He nodded towards the young woman.

Williamson's eyes narrowed. "Freda Benn? The name's familiar..."

"Yes, sir," the constable confirmed. "She's admitted to being our anonymous caller from the other day. Says she has more information now."

Williamson nodded grimly. "Right. Let's have a look inside first."

The cottage interior was a scene of violence. Gordon Benn's body lay crumpled on the floor, a pool of congealed blood surrounding his head. The forensics team was already at work, photographing and collecting evidence.

"Blunt force trauma to the head," the lead forensic officer reported. "Multiple blows. Weapon appears to be missing, but from the wounds, I'd guess something like a heavy candlestick or fireplace poker."

Williamson absorbed the information, his mind already racing. "Time of death?"

"Preliminary estimate, between 10 PM and midnight last night."

After a few more minutes examining the scene, Williamson stepped back outside. It was time to talk to Freda.

The young woman looked up as he approached, her face a mask of grief and fear.

"Miss Benn," Williamson began gently, "I'm Detective Inspector Williamson. I'm sorry about your dad. I know it's hard, but I need to ask you some things. Is that okay?"

Freda nodded, sniffling and wiping her nose with her sleeve. "Yeah... I gotta tell you stuff. 'Bout the phone call, and what Dad said... and Nigel."

Williamson's eyebrows rose at the mention of the Earl's son. "Alright, let's start at the beginning. You called us a few days ago, didn't you? Didn't say who you were?"

"Uh-huh," Freda mumbled. "Dad came home real late that night. He'd been up on Cold Fell. He was all... jumpy-like. Said he saw a girl swimming with no clothes on at Matty Benn's Bridge. Then next day, we heard she was dead. Dad got real scared, said he didn't do nothing, but..."

"But you were worried enough to call us," Williamson finished. Freda nodded, looking miserable.

"What can you tell me about your dad and Nigel, the Earl's boy?"

Freda's face scrunched up. "Weren't just Nigel. The old Earl too, 'fore he got sick. Dad... he'd find girls for 'em. Young ones. He said it was just for work at the big house, but I knew... I knew it weren't right."

Williamson felt a chill run down his spine. "What else, Freda?"

"They had parties, down in the cellar where the wine is. Dad helped set 'em up. Sometimes girls'd go missing after. Dad said they just left, got better jobs and that. But..." Freda's voice cracked, and she started crying again.

As Williamson gently coaxed more information from her, a horrifying picture began to take shape. Since her mum died having

THE DOLFIN CHALICE

her, Freda had seen things no kid should see. Years of bad stuff happening, everyone keeping quiet, and at the middle of it all, them Wyndhams and their big fancy house.

Just then, a commotion at the estate gates drew their attention. A sleek black car was pushing its way past the police cordon. As it pulled up, Nigel Wyndham, the current Earl of Egremont, stepped out, his face a mask of aristocratic disdain.

"What is the meaning of this?" he demanded. "This is private property. I insist you leave at once."

Williamson straightened, meeting the Earl's gaze coolly. "I'm afraid that won't be possible, my Lord. We're investigating a murder."

As Nigel's face paled, Williamson knew that this case was about to blow wide open. The grim discovery in the cottage was just the beginning. The real challenge would be unravelling the web of secrets that had ensnared Wilton Manor for generations.

As Nigel Wyndham's face paled, Williamson pressed his advantage. "Lord Wyndham, I understand your father, the Earl, is unwell. Perhaps we should continue this conversation inside?"

Nigel hesitated, his aristocratic composure faltering for a moment before he nodded stiffly. "Very well. We can use my father's study."

As they walked towards the main house, Williamson couldn't help but recall his conversation with Paul Brankenwall about his encounters with both the ailing Earl and Nigel. Paul's descriptions of the two men – the Earl's frailty and Nigel's barely concealed ambition – took on a new significance in light of recent events.

Inside the opulent study, Nigel poured himself a generous measure of whiskey, not offering any to Williamson. "Now, Inspector, what's this about a murder?"

Williamson kept his voice level. "Gordon Benn was found dead in his cottage this morning. Brutally clubbed to death."

Nigel's hand tightened on his glass. "Good God. How dreadful. But surely you don't think—"

"At this point, Lord Wyndham, we're not ruling anything out," Williamson interrupted. "Mr. Benn's daughter has provided us with some... concerning information about activities here at the manor."

Nigel's face hardened. "I'm sure I don't know what you mean. The Benns have always been prone to wild stories and flights of fancy."

"Perhaps," Williamson conceded. "But we take all leads seriously, especially when they involve multiple disappearances and potential abuse."

Just then, a knock at the door interrupted them. A elderly man in a dressing gown shuffled in, supported by a nurse. It was the Earl himself, looking gaunt and frail.

"Father," Nigel said, surprise and irritation warring in his voice. "You should be resting."

The Earl waved a trembling hand. "Nonsense. I heard raised voices. What's happening, Nigel?"

Williamson stepped forward. "Your Lordship, I'm Detective Inspector Williamson. I'm afraid there's been a murder on the estate. Gordon Benn was found dead this morning."

The Earl's rheumy eyes widened. "Gordon? Dead? But how... why..."

"That's what we're trying to determine, sir," Williamson replied, watching both men carefully. The Earl seemed genuinely shocked, but Nigel's expression was harder to read.

"Inspector," the Earl wheezed, lowering himself into a chair with the nurse's help, "I assure you, you'll have our full cooperation in this matter. Won't he, Nigel?"

Nigel's jaw tightened almost imperceptibly. "Of course, Father. We have nothing to hide."

As Williamson began to question both men about their relationships with Gordon Benn and their knowledge of his activities, he couldn't shake the feeling that he was only scratching the surface of a much deeper, darker mystery.

Outside, forensics teams combed the grounds, searching for the murder weapon and any other evidence. In the village, news of Gordon's death was already spreading, and with it, whispers of long-buried secrets finally coming to light.

And somewhere in Carlisle, James Hetherington's phone buzzed with an urgent message from Mary Postlethwaite: "Gordon Benn is dead. Everything's changing. We need to talk."

The investigation had only just begun, but already it was clear that the repercussions would be far-reaching, shaking the foundations of Wilton Manor and the surrounding community to their very core.

While Williamson was interrogating the Wyndhams at Wilton Manor, across town, Mary Postlethwaite found herself in the midst of a different kind of confrontation. She sat at the head of the conference table in the Postlethwaite Pottery's main office, surrounded by her siblings, Uncle Brian, and Jenny, Howard's widow.

Steve, her eldest brother, was pacing the room, his face flushed with frustration. "Mary, you're not listening to reason. This offer from Cerámica Innovadora is more than generous. It's a lifeline!"

Mary shook her head, her jaw set stubbornly. "It's more than that, Steve. It's the end of our family's legacy. Five generations of Postlethwaites have run this pottery. We can't just sell it off to the highest bidder."

"A legacy won't pay the bills," Andrew, her younger brother, chimed in. "Or have you forgotten about the loans we're struggling to repay?"

Uncle Brian leaned forward, his weathered hands clasped on the table. "Mary, love, I know how much this place means to you. It means a lot to all of us. But times are changing. We can't compete with these big international companies anymore."

Mary felt a pang of betrayal. Uncle Brian had always been her ally in keeping the pottery running. His change of heart was unexpected and painful.

Jenny, who had been quiet until now, spoke up. "Mary, I understand your attachment to the pottery. Howard felt the same way. But... I have to think about my future now." She paused, her voice wavering slightly. "My sister in Spain has offered me a place to stay. I could start over there, but I need the money from this sale."

Mary's eyes softened as she looked at Jenny. She knew Howard's death had hit her hard, both emotionally and financially. "Jenny, I had no idea things were so difficult for you."

Jenny nodded, her eyes glistening. "My brother-in-law, he's the one who found the buyer. He says it's a solid offer, better than we're likely to get anywhere else."

"What about our employees?" Mary argued, trying to refocus. "Some of them have been with us for decades. What happens to them if we sell?"

Steve waved a dismissive hand. "Cerámica Innovadora has promised to keep on most of the staff. It's all there in the offer."

"For how long?" Mary pressed. "A year? Two? Then what?"

The room fell silent for a moment. Mary's phone buzzed in her pocket, but she ignored it, focused on the matter at hand.

Andrew sighed heavily. "Mary, I know you've been distracted lately with... everything that's been going on. But we need you to focus on what's best for the family now."

Mary bristled at the implication. "I am focused on what's best for the family. This pottery is more than just a business. It's our heritage, our community."

"A community that's changing," Steve muttered. "Face it, Mary. The world's moved on. We need to move with it."

Just then, Mary's phone buzzed again, more insistently this time. With an apologetic glance at her family, she pulled it out. Her eyes widened as she read the message from James Hetherington.

"I... I need to take this," she said, standing abruptly. "We're not done discussing this. I won't agree to any sale without exploring all our options first."

As Mary stepped out of the room, she could hear her siblings' exasperated sighs behind her. She knew the fight was far from over, but right now, she had more pressing concerns.

Finding a quiet corner, she dialed Hetherington's number. "James? I'm glad you called back. Have you learned anything more about Gordon's murder?"

"Yes, Mary," Hetherington's voice was grave. "I've been in touch with Inspector Williamson. The situation at Wilton Manor is... complex. Freda Benn has been talking to the police, and her revelations are troubling, to say the least. There are implications reaching back years, possibly involving the Earl and his son."

Mary listened intently as Hetherington filled her in on the details - the questioning of Nigel Wyndham, the unexpected appearance of the ailing Earl, and the dark hints about long-standing abuses at the manor.

"This goes deeper than we imagined, Mary," Hetherington concluded. "We need to pool our information and plan our next steps carefully. Can you meet me at my office?"

Mary felt her world tilting on its axis once again. The pottery's troubles suddenly seemed both trivial and inexplicably connected to the larger mystery unfolding around them.

"I'll be there as soon as I can," she promised, ending the call.

Mary took a deep breath, steeling herself before returning to the conference room. As she pushed open the door, she was met with expectant looks from her family.

"I'm sorry," she said firmly, "but something urgent has come up. We'll have to continue this discussion later."

Ignoring their protests, Mary gathered her things and headed for the door. As she left, she couldn't shake the feeling that somehow, the fate of Postlethwaite Pottery was tied to the dark secrets of Wilton Manor. She just had to figure out how.

Chapter 31

Detective Inspector Harold Williamson sat across from Freda Benn in the sterile interview room at the police station. The young woman's eyes were red-rimmed, her hands shaking a bit as she held onto a cup of tea.

"Miss Benn," Williamson began gently, "I know this ain't easy, but we need to know everything you can tell us about your dad and what he was up to."

Freda nodded, taking a shaky breath. "I'll try. It's just... there's so much. Don't even know where to start."

"Let's begin with when you were little," Williamson suggested. "Can you tell me about your mum?"

Freda's eyes went cloudy. "She died in '53. When I was born. Dad always said she couldn't handle his 'weird ways,' but now I reckon she knew something weren't right."

Williamson made a note. "And after she was gone, it was just you and your dad?"

Freda nodded. "Yeah. He... he tried, I s'pose. But there was always summat off about him. Didn't get it when I was little."

"When did you start to think something was wrong?"

Freda's face hardened. "I was 'bout twelve. Found his stash."

"Stash?" Williamson prompted.

"Pictures," Freda whispered. "Loads of 'em. Young girls, starkers. Some at Matty Benn's Bridge, others... others in the big house."

Williamson felt a chill. "Did you know any of the girls?"

Freda shook her head. "Not then. But later, I figured some of 'em were girls who'd worked at the Manor for a bit. Girls who suddenly 'moved away' or 'got better jobs.'"

"Did your dad know you'd seen the pictures?"

"Don't think so. Never said owt to him. Was... scared, I guess. And part of me didn't want to believe it."

Williamson leaned forward. "Freda, you mentioned Matty Benn's Bridge. What can you tell me about what your dad did there?"

Freda let out a hollow laugh. "Oh, he loved that place. Said it was 'magical.' He'd go there loads, 'specially when the moon was full. Sometimes..." She stopped, looking embarrassed.

"Go on," Williamson encouraged.

"Sometimes he'd dress up. Put on a lady's wig, pretend to be Matty Benn's ghost. I reckon... I reckon he used it to get girls there."

Williamson's pen paused. "Get them there? For what?"

Freda's eyes met his, full of shame and anger. "For the Manor. For the Earl and his lad. Dad... he'd bring girls there. Young ones, usually not from 'round here. Girls no one would miss."

"And what happened to these girls?"

Freda's voice went real quiet. "Dad would sometimes moan that they 'didn't play nice.' That they made things 'hard.' And then... then they'd vanish."

Williamson felt sick. "Freda, are you saying you think these girls are dead?"

Freda nodded, crying now. "Can't prove it. But... there were hints. Things Dad would say when he'd had a few. About 'sorting it for good' and 'feeding the land.' I reckon... I reckon they're buried somewhere on the estate."

As Williamson reached for his phone, he couldn't shake the feeling they were only scratching the surface of something way darker and more twisted than anyone had thought. As the interview wound down, Williamson's mind was already racing with the new possibilities this information opened up. Tom Carter was now a person of interest in Gordon Benn's murder. But was his motive as simple as a neighbourly dispute over livestock? Or could Carter have discovered something about Gordon's more sinister activities and taken matters into his own hands?

The case was growing more complex by the minute, and Williamson knew that every new piece of information could be the key to unraveling the whole mystery. As he prepared to leave the interview room, he made a mental note to dispatch officers to Tom Carter's farm immediately. The shepherd had some serious questions to answer.

The pieces were starting to fit together – the girl on the bicycle, Gordon's late-night excursion to the fell, his frightened confession to Freda. But there were still so many questions. Was Gordon's ritual indirectly responsible for Angela's death, and who had murdered Gordon, and why?

Williamson's mind raced with the implications. They needed to search the Wilton Manor grounds for any evidence of these rituals. And they needed to re-examine every suspicious incident connected to the Manor over the past several decades, looking for patterns of exploitation rather than outright murder.

When the interview finally concluded, Williamson stepped out of the room, his mind reeling. He needed to speak with Hetherington and Mary Postlethwaite immediately. Whatever was going on at Wilton Manor, it was clear that unravelling this mystery would shake the entire community to its core.

Chapter 32

As he reached for his phone, Williamson couldn't shake the feeling that they were only scratching the surface of a much darker, more twisted story than anyone had imagined. The accidental death of Angela Benn, the deliberate murder of Gordon Benn, the hints of long-buried secrets and exploitative rituals – it all pointed to a conspiracy that reached into the highest echelons of local society.

Harry leaned back in his chair, his mind piecing together the complex web of information. He recalled the initial interviews with Mary Postlethwaite and Paul Brankenwall at the Pennington Arms Hotel on that Sunday evening. Paul had been notably reticent, offering little beyond the bare minimum. Mary, on the other hand, had seemed more forthcoming, though he now realized she had omitted the detail about her stolen bicycle.

Their follow-up statements at the police station the next day had painted a clearer picture. Mary had opened up, providing a much more comprehensive account of events. Her mention of the bicycle theft now took on new significance in light of Freda's revelation about the cyclist at Matty Benn's Bridge.

Paul's continued reluctance to disclose his dinner with Angela or their midnight trip to Cold Fell nagged at Williamson. What else might Paul be hiding? And how did it connect to the larger picture emerging around Wilton Manor?

Williamson's thoughts turned to Mary. The cyclist Freda mentioned could very well be Mary herself, unknowingly holding a crucial piece of the puzzle. If it was indeed Mary, her encounter with Gordon Benn that Saturday could be the key to understanding the full scope of the sinister activities cantered around Matty Benn's Bridge and Wilton Manor.

He needed to speak with Mary again, to clarify the timeline of her bicycle ride and her interaction with Gordon Benn. And he needed to press Paul further about his undisclosed activities with Angela. Williamson knew that unraveling these threads could potentially expose the dark underbelly of the community, reaching far beyond the tragic death of Angela Benn and the murder of Gordon Benn.

As he reached for his phone to arrange these follow-up interviews, Williamson couldn't shake the feeling that they were on the cusp of uncovering something far more insidious than anyone in the quiet village could have imagined. The question now was, how deep did this conspiracy go, and who else might be implicated as they dug further into the secrets of Wilton Manor?

Chapter 33

Mary Postlethwaite stood at the entrance of the pottery, trying to compose herself. The weight of recent events - Gordon Benn's murder, the ongoing investigation, and now this crucial meeting about the pottery's future - pressed heavily on her shoulders. She took a deep breath and pushed open the door.

Inside, she found her siblings, Uncle Brian, and Jenny already seated around the conference table. Across from them sat two impeccably dressed individuals - representatives from Cerámica Innovadora, the Spanish company interested in buying the pottery.

"Ah, Mary," Steve said, a hint of impatience in his voice. "Glad you could join us. This is Mr. Alvarez and Ms. Rodriguez from Cerámica Innovadora."

Mary shook hands with the visitors, noting their polite but eager expressions. As she took her seat, Mr. Alvarez cleared his throat.

"We're very excited about the potential acquisition of Postlethwaite Pottery," he began. "In fact, we're prepared to offer fifty percent more than the asking price."

A collective gasp went around the table. Mary's eyes narrowed. "That's... very generous," she said cautiously. "May I ask why you're willing to go so far above market value?"

Mr. Alvarez and Ms. Rodriguez exchanged a glance. "We believe in the potential of this company," Ms. Rodriguez answered smoothly. "The history, the craftsmanship - it's invaluable."

The meeting continued, with Mary's family members growing increasingly excited about the prospect of such a lucrative sale. Mary, however, couldn't shake her suspicion that there was more to this offer than met the eye.

As the meeting wrapped up, Mary suggested they all go for drinks at the local pub to celebrate the potential deal. Her true motive, however, was to get the Spanish representatives in a more relaxed setting.

Several hours and a few rounds later, Mary found herself alone at the bar with Ms. Rodriguez. The rest of the group had already departed, leaving the two women to continue their conversation.

"You know," Mary said, swirling the wine in her glass, "I can't help but feel there's something you're not telling us about your interest in the pottery."

Ms. Rodriguez hesitated, then leaned in close. "Can you keep a secret, Mary?"

Mary nodded, her heart racing.

"The truth is," Ms. Rodriguez whispered, her words slightly slurred, "we have reason to believe there's a highly valuable ceramic art piece hidden somewhere in your pottery."

Mary's eyebrows shot up. "What kind of piece?"

"A fine china chalice," Ms. Rodriguez continued, her eyes gleaming. "Stolen from monks by Vikings in the 16th century. Legend has it that it was hidden in the monastery that once stood where your pottery is now."

Mary's mind whirled. The pottery had indeed been built on the ruins of an old monastery, which had later become a school before the Postlethwaites took it over. Could this chalice really be hidden somewhere on the premises?

"This chalice," Mary pressed, trying to keep her voice casual, "it must be valuable?"

Ms. Rodriguez nodded emphatically. "Priceless. Both historically and monetarily. Finding it would be... well, let's just say it would more than justify our generous offer."

As Mary bid goodnight to Ms. Rodriguez and made her way home, her mind raced with possibilities. She knew she should tell her family about this revelation, but a part of her hesitated. If there really was a priceless artifact hidden in the pottery, finding it could change everything. It could save the business without having to sell, preserving her family's legacy.

Mary made a decision. She wouldn't tell the others, not yet. First, she would do some digging of her own. If there was a valuable piece on the premises, she was determined to find it before anyone else.

As she unlocked her front door, Mary couldn't help but smile at the irony. Here she was, in the middle of a murder investigation, and now she was about to embark on a treasure hunt. Life, it seemed, had a way of continually surprising her.

She made a mental note to visit the local historical society first thing in the morning. If anyone had information about the monastery's history and the legend of this chalice, they would. As she drifted off to sleep that night, Mary's dreams were filled with images of hidden treasures and ancient secrets, all somehow intertwined with the mysteries of Wilton Manor and Matty Benn's Bridge.

Chapter 34

D.I. Williamson and Sergeant Thompson sat across from Mary Postlethwaite in her mothers living room. The ticking of an old grandfather clock in the corner punctuated the tense silence.

Williamson leaned forward, his weathered face etched with lines of concentration. "Miss Postlethwaite, let's start at the beginning. Why did you come to Cumbria?"

Mary took a deep breath, her fingers fidgeting with the hem of her cardigan. "It's a bit complicated, actually. I came at the request of my Uncle Brian."

Thompson's pen hovered over his notepad. "Your uncle? And why did he want you here?"

"My brother, Howard," Mary's voice caught slightly, "he passed away a few months ago. He was running Postlethwaite Pottery's, our family business." She paused, collecting herself. "Uncle Brian called me, practically begging for help to save the business."

Williamson's eyebrows rose. "And where were you before this?"

"Strasbourg," Mary replied. "I had a job there as a civil servant in the EU. Steady work, but..." she trailed off, a hint of a smile playing at her lips, "frightfully boring, to be honest."

"So you left a secure position in Strasbourg to come here?" Thompson asked, skepticism clear in his tone.

Mary nodded. "I know it sounds mad, but this is home. I grew up in Egremont, where my mother still lives. And the pottery... it's been in our family for generations. I couldn't just let it fail."

Williamson leaned back, his chair creaking. "That explains why you're in Cumbria, but not why you were cycling on Cold Fell the night you met Paul Brankenwall."

A wistful look crossed Mary's face. "When I was a teenager, I once had a ride over the Fell on the back of my boyfriend's motorbike. It was exhilarating, but so fast. I always wanted to experience it more slowly, to really take in the scenery." She paused, her gaze distant. "With everything going on - Howard's death, the struggling business - I needed to clear my head. The Fell seemed like the perfect place."

"Quite a risky choice for a solo bike ride, wouldn't you say?" Thompson interjected.

Mary's eyes snapped back to the present. "I suppose it might seem that way, but I've always been drawn to solitude. And I know these fells, Detective. Or at least, I thought I did."

Williamson leaned forward again, his voice softening slightly. "Tell us about meeting Paul, Mary. What happened?"

Mary's cheeks flushed. "I was near the five-barred gate when I saw him. Or should I say when I say when I saw his car, I didn't see him at first, then he called out to me, a bit of shock at the time!! We started chatting, and..." she hesitated.

"And?" Williamson prompted.

"He was charming," Mary admitted, her voice barely above a whisper. "There was an immediate connection. It felt like..." she paused, embarrassment clear on her face, "like something out of a novel. Love at first sight, as cliché as that sounds."

Thompson's pen scratched rapidly across his notepad. "Did Mr. Brankenwall offer you any alcohol?"

Mary nodded. "He had a bottle of wine. But he only had a little, saying he needed to drive. I ended up drinking most of it."

Williamson's eyes narrowed. "Did he encourage you to drink, Miss Postlethwaite?"

"No!" Mary exclaimed, then composed herself. "No, if anything, he seemed concerned when he realized how much I'd had. He offered to drive me back, but I insisted on staying. I was... well, I was too tipsy to cycle safely."

"And the next morning?" Thompson asked.

Mary's face fell. "It was freezing. My sleeping bag was far too light. I packed up early, planning to cycle back, but..." she paused, her voice catching, "my bike was gone."

The detectives exchanged a significant look. Williamson leaned in, his voice low and intense. "What did you do then, Mary?"

"I walked to Calderbridge and took a bus to Ravenglass," Mary replied, her voice small. "I was embarrassed and confused. I didn't want to report the bike stolen because... well, because I was worried it might somehow implicate Paul. It sounds foolish now, I know."

Williamson sat back, his face unreadable. "Miss Postlethwaite, I hope you understand the gravity of this situation. Your actions that night and the following morning could be crucial to our investigation."

Mary nodded, her eyes welling with tears. "I understand. I want to help, truly. But Paul... he couldn't have done what you're accusing him of. He just couldn't have."

Mary nodded, her eyes welling with tears. "I understand. I want to help, truly. But Paul... he couldn't have done what you're accusing him of. He just couldn't have."

Detective Inspector Williamson leaned back, his chair creaking under his weight. "Miss Postlethwaite, I need you to be completely honest with us now. Have you had any contact with Mr. Brankenwall since that night on Cold Fell?"

Mary hesitated, her fingers twisting the hem of her cardigan. She took a deep breath, deciding that honesty was her best option. "Yes," she admitted. "I saw him several times after I'd made my initial statement."

Sergeant Thompson's pen scratched furiously across his notepad. Williamson's eyes narrowed. "Several times? Can you elaborate on that?"

"We... we became very close," Mary said, her voice barely above a whisper. "It wasn't planned. It just happened. We connected in a way I've never experienced before."

"And you didn't think to inform us of this development?" Williamson's tone was sharp.

Mary's cheeks flushed. "I know I should have. But by the time I realized how serious it was becoming, he was arrested. On suspicion of murder." Her voice broke on the last word. "I couldn't believe it. I still can't."

Thompson looked up from his notes. "What did you do after his arrest?"

"I did everything I could to help him," Mary said, a note of defiance creeping into her voice. "I even went to France to interview Ada Benn. I thought if I could find out more about Angela's background, it might help clear Paul's name."

Williamson leaned forward, suddenly very interested. "You went to France? What did you learn from Ada Benn?"

Mary hesitated, unsure how much to reveal. "She told me about Angela's troubled past, her connection to the Wyndham family. It was... enlightening."

"Enlightening how?" Williamson pressed.

"It made me realize there was so much more to this case than I initially thought," Mary replied carefully. "The Wyndhams, their history... it's all connected somehow."

Thompson interjected, "Did Mr. Brankenwall ask you to go to France?"

Mary shook her head emphatically. "No, it was my idea. I wanted to help."

Williamson's gaze was intense. "Miss Postlethwaite, is there anything else you've done in your... investigation?"

Mary took a deep breath. "I also had a long conversation with Gordon Benn."

Both detectives straightened in their chairs. "Gordon Benn?" Williamson repeated. "The handyman?"

Mary nodded. "Yes. He was... a very strange but interesting man. We talked about the night Angela died, about the rituals at Matty Benn's Bridge." She paused, then added quietly, "I'm sure he had something to do with Angela's death."

The room fell silent for a moment. Williamson and Thompson exchanged a significant look.

"Miss Postlethwaite," Williamson said slowly, "I hope you realize the seriousness of what you're saying. You've been conducting your own investigation, withholding information from the police, and now you're accusing a man of murder."

Mary's chin lifted slightly. "I understand how it looks, Detective. But I couldn't just sit by and do nothing. Not when I believe Paul is innocent."

Thompson leaned forward. "And what makes you so sure of Mr. Brankenwall's innocence?"

Mary's eyes met his, unwavering. "Because I know him. Because I've seen the pain in his eyes when he talks about Angela. Because..." she hesitated, then pushed on, "because I love him."

The silence that followed was heavy with unspoken implications. Williamson finally broke it, his voice grave. "Miss Postlethwaite, I'm afraid we're going to need a full, detailed statement from you about everything you've just told us. Your actions, while well-intentioned, may have seriously compromised our investigation."

As Mary nodded, a mix of emotions played across her face – fear, determination, and a flicker of something that might have been hope. She knew that her fight to prove Paul's innocence was far from over. In fact, it felt like it was just beginning.

"I'll tell you everything," she said softly. "But please, you have to promise me you'll look into Gordon Benn. There's so much more to this story than you know."

"I'll tell you everything," she said softly. "But please, you have to promise me you'll look into Gordon Benn. There's so much more to this story than you know."

Williamson nodded slowly. "We'll investigate every lead, Miss Postlethwaite. You have my word on that." He paused, reaching into a folder on his desk. "But first, there's something I need to ask you about."

He pulled out a photograph and slid it across the desk towards Mary. "Could this be your bicycle, Ms. Postlethwaite?"

Mary leaned forward, her eyes widening in recognition. "Yes, that's mine. I recognize the saddle bags. Where did you find it?"

Williamson's expression remained neutral. "It was found near Matty Benn's Bridge. But here's what's puzzling us - we found Angela Benn's fingerprints on it. Can you explain that?"

Mary's brow furrowed, a mix of confusion and concern crossing her face. "No, I can't," she said after a moment. "I suspect she must have taken it from the wall where I left it near to where I was camping. But why would she do that?"

Williamson made a note in his pad. "That's what we're trying to figure out, Ms. Postlethwaite. Now, let's start from the beginning..."

As Mary began her tale, she couldn't help but wonder what other secrets lay hidden in the mists of Cold Fell, and what price she might have to pay to uncover them. The mystery of her bicycle and its connection to Angela Benn added yet another layer to the already complex web of intrigue.

As Mary finished recounting her story to Detective Inspector Williamson, a gentle knock on the lounge door interrupted them. Mary's mother peeked in, a warm smile on her face.

"Can I interest anyone in a cup of tea?" she offered.

Williamson glanced at his watch, his eyes widening slightly. "I apologize for keeping you so late, Mrs. Postlethwaite. I'm afraid I'll have to decline the tea. I should be on my way."

He gathered his notes, thanked Mary for her time, and bid them both goodnight. As the front door closed behind him, Mary's mother settled into the chair beside her daughter.

"What was all that about, love?" she asked, concern etched on her face.

Mary sighed, running a hand through her hair. "The police are investigating that body they found near Matty Benn's Bridge. They had some questions about my bicycle – apparently, it was found there with Angela Benn's fingerprints on it."

Her mother's eyebrows rose. "Good heavens. How did that happen?"

"I'm not sure," Mary admitted. "It's all rather confusing."

Eager to change the subject, Mary remembered something she'd been meaning to ask. "Mum, have you ever heard anything about a bone china chalice supposedly held in the pottery?"

Her mother's face lit up with recognition. "Oh, yes! Many years ago, I remember your grandfather discussing it with a couple of Oxford students. They'd read about its existence somewhere."

Mary leaned forward, intrigued. "Really? What did Grandad say about it?"

"Well, that's the thing," her mother replied. "He knew nothing about it himself. But those students were quite insistent. They said it had been made in the 1100s by nuns and donated to the monks at Wilton Abbey."

Mary's mind raced with this new information. Was it just a legend, or could there be some truth to it?

"Thanks, Mum," she said softly. "That's... that's really interesting."

Her mother patted her hand gently. "You look tired, dear. Why don't you get some rest? I'm sure things will look clearer in the morning."

As Mary headed up to bed, her mind swirled with thoughts of ancient chalices, mysterious fingerprints, and the secrets that seemed to lurk in every corner of Egremont.

Chapter 35

Nigel Wyndham sat in his father's study, surrounded by the opulent trappings of generations of aristocracy. The weight of recent events - Gordon Benn's murder, the police investigation, and the whispers of long-buried secrets - hung heavy in the air. As he sifted through old family documents, hoping to find something to counter the mounting allegations against his family, his hands fell upon a weathered leather-bound journal.

The journal belonged to his grandfather, Winston Wyndham. As Nigel began to read, his eyes widened with each passing page. The truth of his family's past began to unfold before him, a story far more complex and sordid than he had ever imagined.

He learned of an agreement made between his grandfather Winston and his friend, Major Terrance Lonsdale, no blood relation but a distant cousin by marriage. The agreement centred around Winston's daughter, Margaret - Nigel's mother.

Margaret, as Nigel knew, was the daughter of the late Lord of Cumberland. What he didn't know, and what the journal revealed in stark detail, was the nature of her marriage to his father, William Angus Charles Wyndham.

Winston's words painted a vivid picture: Margaret was described as obese and unattractive, with a foul mouth and an even fouler temper. The marriage had been arranged against her will, a political and financial manoeuvre orchestrated by Winston and Terrance.

Nigel's hands trembled as he read about the grand ceremony, a lavish affair that belied the ugly truth beneath. His father, William, had been reluctant from the start, but duty and family obligation had forced his hand.

The most shocking revelation came in the description of the wedding night. William, unable to bring himself to consummate the marriage with Margaret, had instead called upon "one of his girls" - a phrase that made Nigel's blood run cold, given the recent allegations about his family's treatment of young women.

As Nigel continued to read, more pieces of the puzzle fell into place. The loveless marriage, his mother's increasing bitterness, his father's secret liaisons - it all contributed to the toxic atmosphere that had permeated Wilton Manor for decades.

He began to understand the roots of his father's behaviour, the origins of the dark secrets that now threatened to destroy everything the Wyndhams had built. But understanding didn't equal acceptance, and Nigel found himself grappling with a maelstrom of emotions - disgust, anger, and a deep-seated fear of what other skeletons might be lurking in the family closet.

As he closed the journal, Nigel's mind raced. How much of this sordid history was known to others? How did it connect to Gordon Benn's murder and the whispers about missing girls? And most pressingly, what was he going to do with this information?

The sound of approaching footsteps snapped Nigel out of his reverie. He quickly hid the journal in a drawer as his ailing father, the current Earl, shuffled into the room.

"Nigel, my boy," the Earl wheezed, "what are you doing in here?"

Nigel forced a smile, his mind still reeling from what he'd discovered. "Just looking through some old papers, Father. Nothing important."

As he helped his father to a chair, Nigel knew he had a decision to make. The truth he'd uncovered could potentially explain much about his family's dark legacy, but revealing it could also be the final nail in the coffin of the Wyndham reputation.

With the police investigation closing in and the community buzzing with rumors, Nigel realized that uncovering the past might be the key to securing his family's future - but at what cost?

Chapter 36

Mary found Professor Cowan in his cluttered office at the university, surrounded by stacks of books and ancient-looking artefacts. The elderly man's eyes lit up as she introduced herself.

"Ah, Miss Postlethwaite! Yes, yes, I remember visiting your family's pottery. Must have been... oh, nearly forty years ago now. How time flies!" He gestured for her to take a seat. "What brings you here?"

Mary leaned forward eagerly. "Professor, I'm hoping you can tell me about the Dolfin Chalice. I understand you wrote a paper on it during your studies."

"The Dolfin Chalice!" Cowan exclaimed, his eyes twinkling. "Now that's a fascinating piece of history. Let me see..." He rummaged through a drawer, pulling out a yellowed folder. "Ah, here we are. It all began in 1051, you see."

As the professor spoke, Mary listened intently, jotting down notes.

"So, these Viking raiders attacked Wilton monastery?" she prompted.

Cowan nodded vigorously. "Indeed! Stripped it bare of treasures. But two clever monks, Michael and Peter, they managed to escape with this extraordinary chalice." He paused, chuckling. "Imagine them, scurrying over Cold Fell in the dead of night!"

"And the chalice," Mary pressed, "it was made by nuns in Ravenglass?"

"Precisely!" Cowan rifled through his papers, producing a detailed sketch. "Here, look at this. It was made from an incredibly rare clay found near Muncaster. So fine, it was almost transparent."

Mary leaned in, studying the sketch. "It's beautiful. But what's this at the bottom?"

"Ah, the ruby!" Cowan's eyes sparkled. "Quite the clever trick. When water was poured in, it appeared to turn to wine. Imagine the impact in those superstitious times!"

Mary's brow furrowed. "But it didn't stay at Calder Abbey long, did it?"

Cowan shook his head sadly. "Only a year. Those persistent Vikings tracked it down in 1052. But here's where it gets interesting." He leaned in conspiratorially. "They didn't take it back across the sea. Too fragile, you see. So it remained here, in Cumbria."

"And then?" Mary prompted, captivated.

"Well, it vanishes from history for quite some time. Then, in 1666 - bit of an ominous year, eh? - it resurfaces in Carlisle. A fellow named Dolfin, claimed to be a Viking descendant, presents it to Lord William Lowther."

Mary's eyes widened. "Dolfin? That's where it gets its name?"

"Indeed! Now, after that, we lose track again until 1914. Sir Eustace Lowther mentions it in a letter, offering to sell it to the Earl of Egremont."

Mary scribbled furiously. "Professor, have you heard anything about... pagan rituals involving the chalice?"

Cowan's eyebrows shot up. "Ah, now we're getting into murky waters. There are legends, yes. Whispers of dark ceremonies. But nothing concrete, you understand."

Mary nodded, her mind racing. "And... what happened to it in the end?"

Cowan's face fell. "A sad tale, if it's to be believed. The story goes that the 6th Earl of Egremont, in a fit of rage against his wife, smashed it to pieces."

As Mary left the professor's office, her head was spinning with the chalice's long and twisted history. She couldn't shake the feeling that somehow, this ancient artifact was connected to the mysteries plaguing Egremont today. But how? And more importantly, if the chalice had indeed been destroyed, why were people still so interested in it?

Chapter 37

The sun was setting over Wilton Manor as Paul's car crunched up the gravel driveway. Nigel was waiting for him on the front steps, a tumbler of whiskey already in hand.

"Paul," Nigel nodded, his voice tense. "Thanks for coming."

Paul stepped out of the car, eyeing his half-brother warily. "You said it was urgent. What's going on, Nigel?"

Nigel gestured towards the garden. "Let's walk. I... I've discovered some things. About our family."

As they strolled through the manicured lawns, Nigel began to speak, his voice low and strained.

"Did you know about our great-uncle George? The 3rd Earl of Egremont?"

Paul shook his head. "Can't say that I do. Why?"

Nigel let out a bitter laugh. "Turns out dear old Uncle George sired no less than 40 bastards. Forty! And only one legitimate child, who died young."

Paul's eyebrows shot up. "Christ. That's..."

"Monstrous? Depraved? Welcome to the Wyndham legacy, brother." Nigel took a long swig of his whiskey. "It gets worse. Uncle George seems to have inspired our father's... proclivities."

"What do you mean?" Paul asked, though a part of him dreaded the answer.

Nigel's face darkened. "Ever heard of 'droit du seigneur', Paul?"

Paul frowned. "Vaguely. Isn't it some old feudal right? Something about lords and peasants' wives?"

"Close," Nigel nodded. "It's the supposed right of a feudal lord to take the virginity of his serfs' daughters. Our father... he seems to have taken this concept to heart."

Paul stopped walking, his face pale. "Are you saying... Nigel, is this even legal?"

Nigel barked out a humourless laugh. "Legal? Of course not. But when you're the bloody Earl of Egremont, who's going to stop you?" He paused, his voice dropping. "I think this is what Gordon Benn was involved in. Finding girls for Father."

Paul felt sick. "Jesus, Nigel. This is... I don't even know what to say."

They walked in silence for a moment before Paul spoke again. "I suppose I should tell you... Angela. She wasn't murdered. The police say she died of hyperthermia."

Nigel nodded slowly. "I'd heard rumors. It's a small comfort, I suppose. Though it doesn't change the fact that she was our sister."

Paul looked at Nigel sharply. "Our sister?"

Nigel's face twisted into a grimace. "Well, your sister. And Father's daughter. But not mine, as it turns out."

"What are you talking about?"

Nigel drained his glass. "The police did a DNA test. I'm not related to Angela. Or to Father. Or to you, Paul."

Paul stared at him, stunned. "But... how? Who...?"

"That's the question, isn't it?" Nigel said bitterly. "Mother's not exactly forthcoming about who she might have dallied with. Not that I can blame her, given what I've learned about their marriage."

Paul shook his head, trying to process everything. "This is... Nigel, this is a lot to take in."

"Tell me about it," Nigel muttered. "I've spent my whole life thinking I was the heir to this... this legacy. And now I find out I'm not even a Wyndham. Meanwhile, you..."

"Me?" Paul asked, suddenly wary.

Nigel turned to face him, his eyes hard. "You're his son. His true heir. Tell me, Paul, how does it feel to inherit all this?" He gestured broadly at the manor and the surrounding estate.

Paul held up his hands. "Nigel, I don't want any of this. I never have."

"No?" Nigel's voice was sharp. "Then why are you here, Paul? Why have you stuck around through all of this?"

Paul was quiet for a moment. "I wanted answers, Nigel. About my mother, about Angela. I never expected... this."

Nigel seemed to deflate slightly. "No, I suppose you didn't. None of us did." He sighed heavily. "What are we going to do, Paul? The police are closing in. These secrets... they're going to come out."

Paul looked at his half-brother - or was it former half-brother now? - and saw the weight of generations of secrets and sins bearing down on him.

"I don't know, Nigel," Paul said softly. "But whatever happens, we're in this together. Family or not."

Nigel nodded, a ghost of a smile crossing his face. "Family or not," he echoed. "God help us all."

As they turned back towards the house, the setting sun cast long shadows across the lawn, as if the very land itself was trying to hide the dark secrets of Wilton Manor. But both men knew that soon, very soon, those secrets would be dragged into the light of day.

As Paul and Nigel approached the manor, they saw Mary's car pulling up the driveway. Paul waved her over.

"Mary, I'd like you to meet Nigel," Paul said as she joined them. "Nigel, this is Mary Postlethwaite."

Nigel extended his hand, his aristocratic manners kicking in despite the weight of their previous conversation. "A pleasure, Miss Postlethwaite. I've heard quite a bit about you."

Mary shook his hand, her eyes curious. "Likewise, Lord Wyndham."

Nigel winced slightly. "Please, just Nigel. Given recent revelations, I'm not sure how much longer I'll be holding that title."

Paul cleared his throat. "Nigel was just about to give me a tour of the manor. Would you care to join us, Mary?"

Mary nodded eagerly. "I'd love to."

As they entered the grand foyer, Nigel began his narration. "The Wyndham family once owned Egremont Castle, you know. It's a ruin now, of course. This manor was built on the site of a 16th-century monastery."

They moved through opulent rooms, each filled with antiques and family heirlooms. Mary's eyes widened at the grandeur.

"It's incredible," she breathed. "How do you maintain all this?"

Nigel's face tightened. "With great difficulty, I'm afraid. The costs are astronomical. We've had to close off large portions of the house over the years. Only a small part of the old monastery was made habitable."

As they climbed a grand staircase, Paul noticed Mary's eyes lingering on certain architectural details. He remembered her interest in the pottery's history and wondered if she was seeing similarities.

"This wing dates back to the original monastery," Nigel explained, leading them down a long corridor. "We've found some fascinating artifacts during renovations over the years."

Mary perked up at this. "What kind of artifacts?"

Nigel shrugged. "Old religious items mostly. Some ended up in museums. Others... well, Father was never too keen on sharing family 'treasures.'"

They descended another staircase, the air growing cooler. "And now," Nigel announced with a hint of pride, "the piece de resistance - the wine cellar."

The cellar was vast, stretching further than the eye could see in the dim light. Racks upon racks of bottles lined the walls, some covered in a thick layer of dust.

"This is incredible," Paul murmured, running his hand along a nearby bottle.

As they ventured deeper into the cellar, Mary suddenly stopped short. In a small alcove, partially hidden behind some barrels, was a bed.

"Is that...?" she began, her voice trailing off.

Nigel's face darkened. "Ah, yes. That's where the Earl... entertained his 'girlfriends.'" His voice dripped with disdain.

Paul and Mary exchanged uncomfortable glances. The bed stood as a stark reminder of the dark secrets they'd been uncovering.

"It's getting late," Paul said quickly, trying to dispel the tension. "Perhaps we should head back up."

As they made their way back to the main floor, Mary lingered behind for a moment, her eyes scanning the cellar walls. Something about this place nagged at her, reminding her of the story about the Dolfin chalice being smashed by the Nigel's father.

"Mary?" Paul called from the stairs. "Everything alright?"

She shook herself out of her reverie. "Yes, coming!"

As they emerged into the fading daylight, all three were lost in thought. Paul, grappling with his newfound heritage; Nigel, wrestling with his lost identity; and Mary, her mind racing with possibilities about hidden treasures and shared histories.

The manor loomed behind them, its shadows lengthening in the evening light, secrets still tucked away in its many corners. But for how much longer?

Chapter 38

Doreen Thornton sat at her desk, surrounded by stacks of papers, old photographs, and genealogy charts. The soft glow of her desk lamp cast long shadows across the room as the night deepened outside. Across from her, Hetherington, Paul Brankenwall's lawyer from Carlisle, paced back and forth, his brow furrowed in concentration.

"Let's go over what we have so far," Doreen said, pushing her glasses up her nose. "We need to be absolutely certain before we make any accusations against the Earl."

Hetherington nodded, coming to a stop by the window. "Right. We know the current Earl of Egremont is in his early fifties now. And based on your research, there's a strong possibility he's Amélie Bouchard's biological father."

Doreen shuffled through some papers. "Yes, the timeline fits. Amélie was born in

1949, which would have made the Earl about 27 at the time. We have records of him visiting Brittany that year."

"And the connection to the convent where Amélie grew up?" Hetherington prompted.

"The Wyndham family has been making donations to that convent for decades," Doreen confirmed. "It's not definitive proof, but it's certainly suspicious."

Hetherington ran a hand through his hair. "Okay, so we have motive. The Earl wanted to keep his illegitimate daughter a secret. But why now, after all these years?"

Doreen leaned back in her chair, thinking. "That's where it gets complicated. Remember, Amélie came here under the name Angela Benn. She was looking into her past, yes, but she was also involved with our client, Paul."

"Who claims to be the rightful heir to the Wyndham estate," Hetherington added. "Paul was told by his late mother that the Earl was his father, and that they were secretly married in France."

Doreen nodded, reaching for a file. "Yes, and we have new evidence to support this claim. During Mary Postlethwaite's trip to meet Ada Benn, she also met with the priest who performed the marriage. He provided her with a copy of the marriage certificate."

Hetherington's eyes widened. "So Paul isn't just claiming to be related to the Wyndham family - he's asserting that he's the legitimate eldest son and rightful heir."

"Exactly," Doreen said, her eyes lighting up. "This changes everything. If Paul is indeed the legitimate heir, it would explain why Amélie's arrival might have been seen as such a threat. What if she knew about Paul's legitimacy?"

Hetherington nodded slowly. "It's plausible. But it also complicates our case. The Earl now has an even stronger motive - not just to keep an illegitimate child secret, but to prevent a legitimate heir from claiming his inheritance."

Doreen stood up, walking to a large cork board covered in photos and notes. "This also sheds new light on Gordon Benn's murder. If he knew about Paul's legitimacy, he would have been an even greater threat to the Earl's position."

"But we still need to prove the Earl's direct involvement in Amélie's death," Hetherington pointed out. "And let's not forget, we're not even sure it was murder. The official cause of death was hypothermia."

Doreen turned to face him, her expression serious. "What if Amélie's death wasn't the plan at all? What if the intended victim that night was Paul? Eliminating the legitimate heir would solve a lot of problems for the Earl."

As they pondered this, there was a knock at the door. Inspector Williamson and Sergeant Thompson entered, looking grave.

"Ms. Thornton, Mr. Hetherington,"

Williamson nodded. "We have some new information that might interest you."

Thompson pulled out a notepad. "We've been looking into Nigel Wyndham's background, and we've made a rather startling discovery."

Doreen leaned forward, intrigued. "What have you found?"

Williamson cleared his throat. "It involves Nigel's mother, the Countess. She's the daughter of Lord Cumberland, married to the Earl. But here's the thing - the Earl apparently dislikes her so much, he doesn't sleep with her."

"That's... interesting," Hetherington said slowly. "But how does this relate to our case?"

Thompson took over. "We've been trying to determine Nigel's parentage. The Countess refuses to reveal who his father is, but we've found a DNA match."

The room fell silent as everyone waited for Thompson to continue.

"Nigel's DNA matches with Thomas Carter," Thompson said finally. "The farmer who found Angela's body."

Doreen and Hetherington exchanged shocked looks.

"This changes everything," Doreen breathed. "The Countess, Thomas Carter, Nigel's true parentage - it's all connected to our case somehow."

Hetherington nodded, his mind racing. "We need to talk to the Countess. And Thomas Carter. They might hold the key to unravelling this whole mystery."

As the group began to plan their next moves, Doreen couldn't shake the feeling that they were on the brink of uncovering something even bigger than they had initially thought. The question of Paul's legitimacy added a new dimension to the case, one that could shake the very foundations of the Wyndham family and rewrite the future of the earldom.

"We need to proceed carefully," Williamson cautioned, his voice low. "If what we suspect is true, we're dealing with people who have a lot to lose. They won't give up their secrets easily."

Hetherington nodded grimly. "Agreed. We need to build our case meticulously. Every piece of evidence, every statement needs to be ironclad."

"And we need to watch our backs," Thompson added. "If word gets out about what we're investigating..."

He didn't need to finish the thought. Everyone in the room understood the potential dangers they faced.

Doreen looked around at her colleagues, a mix of determination and apprehension on their faces. "Then let's get to work," she said firmly. "We have a lot to do, and time may not be on our side."

As they dispersed, each lost in their own thoughts about the case, none of them could have predicted just how deep this rabbit hole would go, or the shocking truths that lay waiting to be uncovered.

Chapter 39

The investigation into the Wyndham family's secrets took an unexpected turn as more victims and witnesses began to come forward. Doreen Thornton and Hetherington found themselves working late into the night, sifting through a flood of new testimonies and evidence.

One rainy afternoon, Inspector Williamson burst into Doreen's office, his face grim. "We've got another one," he said, dropping a file on her desk. "A woman named Sarah Jennings. Says she was involved with the Earl back in the 60s."

Doreen opened the file, her eyes widening as she scanned the contents. "Good lord," she murmured. "She claims she had a child by him?"

Hetherington, who had been poring over financial records, looked up sharply. "Another potential heir?"

Williamson shook his head. "Not quite. According to Ms. Jennings, the Earl forced her to give up the baby for adoption. She never saw the child again."

"That's horrible," Doreen said, her voice tight with anger. "Do we have any leads on where the child might be now?"

"We're working on it," Williamson replied. "But that's not all. Sarah mentioned something about a 'ritual' at Matty Benn's Bridge. Sound familiar?"

Hetherington nodded grimly. "Gordon Benn mentioned the same thing before he was killed. We need to talk to this woman, and soon."

As they discussed the implications of Sarah's testimony, Sergeant Thompson entered, looking flustered. "Sorry to interrupt," he said, "but we've got a situation down at the station. A man just walked in, says he used to work as a groundskeeper at Wilton Manor in the 50s. He's asking to speak with someone about the Wyndham family."

Doreen and Hetherington exchanged glances. "I'll go," Hetherington said, standing up. "This could be the break we've been looking for."

At the police station, Hetherington found himself face to face with Albert Hodgson, a weathered old man with sharp eyes and a nervous demeanour.

"Mr. Hodgson," Hetherington began, "I understand you have some information about the Wyndham family?"

Albert nodded, his hands trembling slightly. "It's about time someone knew the truth," he said, his voice barely above a whisper. "I've kept quiet for too long, but after hearing about that poor girl's death on Cold Fell... I can't stay silent anymore."

"What can you tell us?" Hetherington prompted gently.

Albert took a deep breath. "It was in the summer of '53. I was tending to the gardens near the old wine cellar when I heard noises. Screaming, like. I went to investigate and..." he trailed off, his face pale.

"Go on," Hetherington encouraged.

"I saw the Earl and some other men. They had a young woman with them. She was crying, begging them to let her go. They took her into the cellar. I never saw her again."

Hetherington felt a chill run down his spine. "Did you report this to anyone?"

Albert shook his head miserably. "I was young, scared. The Earl caught me watching. He threatened my family if I ever breathed a word. I left Wilton Manor the next day and never went back."

As Hetherington took down Albert's statement, his mind raced. This testimony could be the key to unravelling decades of secrets and crimes.

The race was on to uncover the full extent of the Wyndham family's secrets before more lives were lost or destroyed. As night fell over Cumbria, Doreen, Hetherington, and their allies prepared for what promised to be a long and perilous journey into the heart of a decades-old conspiracy.

Chapter 40

As the investigation into the Wyndham family's secrets intensified, Mary Postlethwaite found herself facing a different kind of pressure. The Spanish company that had been circling her family's pottery business for months had finally made their move.

She sat at her desk in the pottery's small office, staring at the formal offer letter. The figure at the bottom of the page made her eyes widen. It was far more than she had expected, more than the struggling business was worth by any reasonable estimation.

She reached for the phone, her fingers hovering over the keys before she decisively dialed Doreen Thornton's number.

"Doreen? It's Mary. I need your advice on something."

Doreen's voice came through, sounding tired but alert. "What is it, Mary? Has something happened?"

Mary took a deep breath. "The Spanish company, Cerámica Innovadora, they've made a formal offer for the pottery. It's... it's a lot of money, Doreen. More than we're worth."

There was a pause on the other end of the line. "That's interesting timing," Doreen said slowly. "Have they given any reason for their sudden interest?"

"Not really," Mary replied. "Just the usual corporate speak about synergies and market expansion. But something feels off about it."

"I agree," Doreen said. "Given everything that's happening with the Wyndham case, we can't ignore the possibility that this is connected somehow."

Mary felt a chill run down her spine. "You don't think... could the Earl be behind this?"

"It's possible," Doreen admitted. "The pottery was built on an old monastery site, wasn't it? And there were those rumours about a valuable artifact hidden there."

"The chalice," Mary whispered. "But that's just a local legend. Isn't it ...and anyway I heard that the earl had smashed it during a row with the countess?"

"At this point, I'm not willing to dismiss anything as 'just a legend,'" Doreen said firmly. "Mary, I need you to do something for me. Don't respond to the offer yet. We need to dig deeper into this Spanish company."

After hanging up, Mary stared at the offer letter again. The sum that had seemed so tempting just moments ago now felt tainted, possibly even dangerous.

Meanwhile, back in his office in Carlisle, Hetherington was meeting with a contact at the local bank. As they pored over financial records, something caught his eye.

"Wait a minute," he said, pointing to a series of transactions. "These large transfers to a Spanish account... they're coming from a shell company owned by the Wyndham estate."

His contact leaned in for a closer look. "You're right. And look at the dates - they align perfectly with the timeline of the Spanish company's interest in the Postlethwaite pottery."

Hetherington felt a surge of excitement. This could be the connection they'd been looking for, a tangible link between the Wyndham family's secrets and the present-day machinations surrounding the pottery.

As he rushed back to share his findings with Doreen and the team, he couldn't shake the feeling that they were on the verge of uncovering something big. The Spanish company's offer wasn't just a business deal - it was another piece of the complex puzzle they were trying to solve.

Back at the pottery, Mary walked through the workshops, the rhythmic hum of pottery wheels and the earthy smell of clay filling the air. This place had been in her family for generations. Could she really consider selling it, especially now that it might be tied to the dark secrets they were uncovering?

As she paused by a shelf of finished pieces, a thought struck her. She sought out Uncle Brian, finding him in his usual spot by the kiln.

"Uncle Brian," she began, "have you ever heard of something called the Dolfin chalice?"

Brian's eyebrows shot up in surprise. "Now that's a name I haven't heard in a while. Funny you should ask about that now."

"Why's that?" Mary pressed.

Brian wiped his hands on his apron. "Well, a few months before your father passed, he told me about a strange occurrence. A man came to the pottery with a bone china vase, asking if we could repair it. Said it had a small chip out of the base."

Mary leaned in, intrigued. "What was so strange about that?"

"The way your father described it – said it was incredibly fine and delicate, with a ruby in the base. He was fascinated by it." Brian gestured for Mary to follow him. "Come on, there's something I want to show you."

He led her to a glass-fronted cabinet filled with sample products. Carefully, he pulled out a chalice and handed it to Mary.

"This is a replica of the one brought in for repair," Brian explained. "Your dad made a copy, said it wasn't anywhere near as delicate as the original. Couldn't match the clay, he said."

Mary turned the chalice over in her hands, marveling at its craftsmanship. "What happened to the original?"

Brian shrugged. "Your father said he'd try to find another pottery that might be able to repair it. Haven't seen or heard of it since."

A thought occurred to Mary. "Do we have any record of who brought it in?"

"We might," Brian nodded. "Let's check the old order books."

They made their way to the archives, pulling out dusty ledgers. After some searching, Brian's finger landed on an entry. "Here it is. It belonged to a Mr. G Benn. That's the man who brought it for repair."

Mary's breath caught. "G Benn? As in Gordon Benn?"

Brian looked at her, puzzled. "Could be. Why? Does that mean something to you?"

Mary's mind was racing. Could this be the chalice Ms. Rodriguez had mentioned in her drunken confession? And how was Gordon Benn, the murdered handyman from Wilton Manor, connected to all this?

She made her way back to her office, the weight of this new information heavy on her mind. The formal offer from Cerámica Innovadora still lay on her desk, its figures taunting her with the promise of financial security. But now, the decision to sell seemed even more complicated.

As she sat down, Mary couldn't shake the feeling that she was on the verge of uncovering something much bigger than a simple business deal. The mystery surrounding the pottery had just deepened, and she realized that the Spanish company's offer was likely just the beginning of a much larger and more dangerous game.

Whatever connection existed between the Dolfin chalice, Gordon Benn, and the Egremont estate, Mary was determined to uncover it – no matter the cost.

A knock at the door startled her from her thoughts. It was her Uncle Brian, his face creased with concern.

"Have you made a decision yet, love?" he asked gently.

Mary sighed. "I don't know, Uncle Brian. This offer... it's more than generous. It could secure all our futures."

Brian nodded, taking a seat across from her. "But?"

"But this place is more than just a business," Mary said, her voice catching. "It's our heritage, our family's legacy. And now, with what Ms. Rodriguez said about the chalice..."

Brian leaned forward, his interest piqued.

Mary recounted Ms. Rodriguez's drunken confession about the fine china chalice, allegedly stolen from monks by Vikings and hidden in the old monastery.

Brian's eyes widened. "Good Lord," he whispered. "You don't think..."

"That it might actually exist? That it might be here somewhere?" Mary finished for him. "I don't know. But it would explain the Spanish company's interest, wouldn't it?"

Just then, Mary's phone rang. It was Doreen Thornton.

"Mary, we've found something," Doreen said without preamble. "Hetherington uncovered financial transactions linking the Wyndham estate to the Spanish company. We think the Earl might be behind this offer."

Mary felt her heart racing. "But why? Because of the chalice?"

"Possibly," Doreen replied. "But there might be more to it. The chalice, if it exists, could be just the tip of the iceberg. We think there might be other artifacts, maybe even documents, hidden at the pottery site. Documents that could expose secrets the Earl desperately wants to keep buried."

As Mary hung up, she turned to her uncle, her mind whirling. "Uncle Brian, I think we're in the middle of something much bigger than we realized."

Brian nodded slowly. "So what do we do?"

Mary stood up, a new resolve settling over her. "We can't sell. Not now. There are too many unanswered questions, too much at stake."

"But the business, Mary," Brian protested weakly. "We're barely staying afloat as it is."

"I know," Mary said, her voice firm. "But we'll find a way. We always have."

She picked up the phone again, this time dialling the number for Cerámica Innovadora. "Ms. Rodriguez? This is Mary Postlethwaite. I'm calling about your offer..."

As Mary politely but firmly declined the Spanish company's bid, she couldn't shake the feeling that this decision would have far-reaching consequences. The pottery, it seemed, was not just her family's legacy, but potentially the key to unravelling the mysteries surrounding the Wyndham family and the dark secrets of Egremont's past.

Later that evening, as Mary locked up the pottery, she noticed a car parked across the street, its occupant watching the building intently. A chill ran down her spine as she realized that her decision had likely set in motion events that she couldn't begin to predict.

Whatever secrets lay hidden within the walls of the old pottery, she was now committed to uncovering them, no matter the cost.

As she walked home through the darkening streets of Egremont, Mary's mind raced with possibilities. The chalice, the documents, the Wyndham family secrets – how were they all connected? And more importantly, how far would the Earl go to keep those secrets buried?

Mary realized that her decision to keep the pottery wasn't just about preserving her family's legacy anymore. It was about uncovering the truth, no matter how dangerous that truth might be.

Chapter 41

The halls of Wilton Manor buzzed with tension as Detective Inspector Williamson and Sergeant Thompson methodically worked their way through the staff, collecting statements, DNA samples, and fingerprints. The murder of Gordon Benn, the estate's handyman, had cast a pall over the grand house, and secrets long buried were threatening to surface.

In a small anteroom, Williamson sat across from Agnes, the head housekeeper, her wrinkled hands fidgeting in her lap.

"And when was the last time you saw Mr. Benn?" Williamson asked, his pen poised over his notepad.

Agnes furrowed her brow. "It must have been the evening before... before it happened. He was arguing with someone in the garden. I couldn't hear what was said, but he seemed very agitated."

"Did you see who he was arguing with?"

Agnes hesitated, then shook her head. "It was too dark, sir. But..." she leaned in, lowering her voice, "there have been rumors, you see. About Mr. Benn knowing things he shouldn't."

Meanwhile, in a secluded corner of the estate grounds, Nigel Wyndham paced nervously, waiting for Paul Brankenwall to arrive. When Paul finally appeared, Nigel's relief was palpable.

"Paul, thank God you're here," Nigel said, his voice low and urgent. "Things are getting out of hand. The police are everywhere, questioning everyone."

Paul nodded grimly. "I know. It's about Gordon Benn, isn't it? What do you know, Nigel?"

Nigel ran a hand through his hair, his face etched with worry. "I've been doing some digging, like we discussed. There's something you need to see."

He led Paul to a hidden entrance near the old wing of the manor. As they descended a narrow staircase, the musty smell of age and decay grew stronger.

"What is this place?" Paul asked, his voice echoing in the darkness.

"An old cellar," Nigel replied, his flashlight beam dancing across damp stone walls. "It used to be... well, a dungeon, if you can believe it. My father never let anyone come down here. Said it was too dangerous, structurally unsound. But I think that was just an excuse."

As they reached the bottom, Nigel's light fell on something that made Paul's blood run cold. Partially buried in the earthen floor were unmistakable human remains.

"Jesus Christ," Paul whispered. "Are those..."

Nigel nodded grimly. "Bones. Human bones. And I'd bet my life they're connected to those rituals at Matty Benn's Bridge that Gordon was always muttering about."

Paul turned to Nigel, his face pale in the dim light. "Nigel, why are you showing me this? Why are you helping me?"

Nigel's expression hardened. "Because I'm sick of it, Paul. The secrets, the lies, the whole bloody legacy. When I found out you were the rightful heir... I was relieved. This family needs a clean slate, and you're it."

Back in the manor, the investigation continued. Thomas Carter, the farmer who had found Angela Benn's body on Cold Fell, sat across from Williamson in the kitchen, his weathered hands clasped tightly on the table.

"Mr. Carter," Williamson began, "I understand you're well acquainted with the Wyndham family."

Carter nodded, his eyes darting nervously around the room. "Known them for years. Good people, the Wyndhams."

"And the Countess? I hear you're particularly close to her."

Carter's face flushed. "I... I don't know what you mean."

Williamson leaned forward. "Mr. Carter, we know about your relationship with the Countess. We also know about your connection to Nigel Wyndham. What we don't know is how this all ties in with Gordon Benn's murder."

The Colour drained from Carter's face. "It's not what you think," he stammered. "The Earl... he knows. About me and the Countess. He doesn't mind, what with him being ill and all."

"Go on," Williamson prompted.

Carter took a deep breath. "A few days before it happened, the Earl called me to his study. Said Gordon was becoming a problem. Talking too much about family business, about the rituals at Matty Benn's Bridge. He asked me to... to take care of it."

"To murder Gordon Benn?" Williamson asked, his voice hard.

Carter's eyes widened. "No! Not murder. Just to scare him, to shut him up. But when I went to confront him..." He trailed off, his hands shaking.

"What happened, Mr. Carter?"

"He was already dead," Carter whispered. "Someone had got to him first. I panicked. I... I moved the body, tried to make it look like an accident. I thought I was protecting the family, but..."

As night fell, Paul and Nigel met again, this time in the garden where Agnes had last seen Gordon Benn.

"Who do you think did it, Nigel?" Paul asked, his voice barely above a whisper. "Who killed Gordon?"

Nigel shook his head, his face grim. "I don't know for certain, but I have my suspicions. Gordon knew too much, and in this family, knowledge is dangerous."

Paul nodded slowly. "We need to be careful. If they killed Gordon..."

"They won't hesitate to come after us," Nigel finished. "But we can't stop now, Paul. We're close to exposing everything. The rituals, the murders, all of it. We owe it to those girls in the cellar, to Gordon, to everyone who's suffered because of this family's secrets."

As they stood there in the gathering darkness, both men felt the weight of the task ahead. The truth was within their grasp, but the path to it was fraught with danger.

"Whatever happens," Paul said, placing a hand on Nigel's shoulder, "we're in this together."

Nigel nodded, a grim smile on his face. "Together. It's time the Wyndham legacy meant something good for a change."

As they parted ways, Paul cast a final glance at Wilton Manor. For a moment, he thought he saw a flicker of movement in one of the upstairs windows - a shadow shifting behind the glass. He blinked, and the window was still, leaving him to wonder if he had simply imagined it.

Shaking off the uneasy feeling, Paul reminded himself that the manor was supposed to be empty. Still, he couldn't quite dismiss the sensation of being watched. As he turned to leave, he was acutely aware that their investigation into Gordon Benn's murder had set in motion events that would shake the very foundations of Egremont. No one – not Paul, not Nigel, not even the Earl himself – could predict where it would all end.

Chapter 42

The Carlisle Crown Court buzzed with tension as spectators, journalists, and legal teams filed into the imposing Victorian building. Today marked the beginning of what many were already calling the trial of the century: The Crown vs. The Right Honourable William Angus Charles Wyndham,, 6th Earl of Egremont.

Doreen Thornton stood on the courthouse steps, her face a mask of determined calm as she addressed the scrum of reporters.

"We are confident that justice will be served," she stated firmly. "The evidence we will present will show beyond any doubt the extent of Lord Egremont's crimes."

Inside, Paul Brankenwall sat beside Hetherington, his lawyer, in the gallery. His eyes were fixed on the dock where his father – the man he had only recently discovered was his father – would soon stand accused of heinous crimes.

"You alright?" Hetherington murmured.

Paul nodded tightly. "Let's just get this over with."

The murmur of the courtroom fell to a hush as the clerk called out, "All rise for the Honorable Justice Ellington."

As the distinguished judge took his seat, the door to the dock opened, and Lord Egremont was led in. Once an imposing figure, the Earl now looked frail and diminished in his wheelchair. Yet his eyes, scanning the courtroom, still held a glint of defiance.

THE CLERK READ OUT the charges: "William Angus Charles Wyndham, 6th Earl of Egremont, you stand accused of conspiracy to commit murder, accessory to murder, perverting the course of justice..."

As the litany of charges continued, Mary Postlethwaite, seated a few rows behind Paul, felt a chill run down her spine. The scope of the accusations was staggering.

The prosecution's opening statement, delivered by a steely-eyed QC named Victoria Holbrook, painted a damning picture.

"My Lord, members of the jury," Holbrook began, her voice ringing clear in the hushed courtroom. "Over the course of this trial, we will present evidence of a decades-long conspiracy of silence, intimidation, and murder. We will show how the defendant, Lord Egremont, used his position and influence to conceal unspeakable crimes."

As Holbrook continued, outlining the case against the Earl, Paul felt a hand on his shoulder. He turned to see Nigel Wyndham, slipping into the seat beside him.

"Didn't think you'd come," Paul whispered.

Nigel's face was grim. " He may be a monster, but I still considered him to be my father.... until you came on the scene. And besides," he added, his voice hardening, "I want to see justice done as much as anyone."

The defense, led by a renowned barrister named Jonathan Fitch, seemed subdued in comparison. "My Lord, members of the jury," Fitch began, "we ask that you keep an open mind. The prosecution's case is built on circumstantial evidence and the testimony of unreliable witnesses. We will show that Lord Egremont is the victim of a vindictive campaign to destroy his reputation and seize control of his estate."

As the first day of the trial progressed, with preliminary motions and procedural matters being addressed, the tension in the courtroom grew. Everyone knew that the real drama would unfold in the days to come, as witnesses were called and evidence presented.

During a recess, Doreen conferred with Hetherington in a quiet corner of the courthouse.

"We need to be prepared," she murmured. "Fitch is going to try to discredit our key witnesses. Mary, Thomas Carter, even Paul..."

Hetherington nodded. "We've prepared them as best we can. But you're right, it's going to get ugly."

As they spoke, neither noticed the Earl's eyes following them from across the room, a calculating look on his aged face.

Back in the courtroom, as the judge adjourned proceedings for the day, Paul found himself staring at the back of his father's head. The Earl, as if sensing his gaze, turned slightly. For a brief moment, their eyes met, and Paul felt a jolt of... something. Recognition? Regret? Challenge? He couldn't be sure.

As the courtroom emptied, Mary approached Paul and Nigel. "Well," she said, her voice shaky, "that's day one done."

Nigel nodded grimly. "And tomorrow the real battle begins."

Paul looked between them, then back at the dock where his father had sat. "Whatever happens," he said softly, "the truth will come out. It has to."

As they left the courthouse, stepping into the fading light of the evening, all three felt the weight of what was to come. The trial of the Earl of Egremont was more than just a legal proceeding – it was the culmination of decades of secrets, lies, and buried truths. And before it was over, none of their lives would ever be the same again.

Chapter 43

As the trial of William Angus Charles Wyndham, the sixth Earl of Egremont, entered its second week, the atmosphere in the Carlisle Crown Court grew increasingly tense. Today marked the beginning of witness testimonies, and the gallery was packed with spectators, journalists, and those whose lives had been irrevocably altered by the Earl's alleged crimes.

Paul Brankenwall sat rigid in his seat, Nigel beside him. The two men, bound by a complicated web of family ties and shared purpose, exchanged a grim look as the first witness was called.

"The Crown calls Sarah Jennings," announced Victoria Holbrook, the prosecuting QC.

A woman in her sixties, her gray hair pulled back in a severe bun, made her way to the witness stand. As she was sworn in, her eyes briefly flicked to the Earl, a mixture of fear and long-suppressed anger evident in her gaze.

"Mrs. Jennings," Holbrook began, "can you tell the court about your relationship with the defendant, Lord Egremont?"

Sarah's hands trembled slightly as she clasped them in her lap. "I... I worked at Wilton Manor in the 1960s. I was young, just eighteen when I started there as a maid."

"And did you have any interactions with Lord Egremont during this time?"

Sarah's voice grew stronger, fuelled by years of pent-up anguish. "Yes. He... he took an interest in me. At first, I was flattered. He was charming, powerful. But then..."

As Sarah recounted the abuse she had suffered at the hands of the Earl, including a pregnancy that had been forcibly terminated, a hushed horror fell over the courtroom. Paul felt his fists clench, his knuckles white with suppressed rage.

Nigel leaned in, whispering, "I had no idea. All these years, and I never knew."

Paul nodded tightly. "That's how he operated. Secrets and silence."

The defense barrister, Jonathan Fitch, tried to discredit Sarah's testimony during cross-examination, suggesting her memory might be faulty after so many years. But Sarah remained steadfast, her quiet dignity more damning than any shouted accusation could have been.

As Sarah stepped down, visibly shaken but relieved, the next witness was called.

"The Crown calls Thomas Carter," Holbrook announced.

The farmer's weathered face was ashen as he took the stand. His testimony about his relationship with the Countess, his connection to Nigel, and the Earl's request to "take care of" Gordon Benn painted a picture of a man who ruled his domain through fear and manipulation.

During a recess, Doreen conferred with Hetherington in a hushed corner.

"Carter's testimony is crucial," Doreen murmured. "It ties the Earl directly to Gordon's murder, even if he didn't carry it out himself."

Hetherington nodded. "Fitch will try to paint Carter as an unreliable witness, given his affair with the Countess. We need to be prepared."

As the trial resumed, the atmosphere grew even more charged. The next witness was Mary Postlethwaite.

Mary's voice was steady as she recounted her discoveries at the pottery, the Spanish company's suspicious offer, and her conversations with Gordon Benn before his death. Her testimony provided crucial links between the Earl's activities and the broader conspiracy of silence that had allowed his crimes to continue for so long.

During cross-examination, Fitch attempted to undermine Mary's credibility.

"Miss Postlethwaite, isn't it true that you have a personal stake in this case? That you've developed feelings for Mr. Brankenwall, the man claiming to be Lord Egremont's heir?"

Mary's chin lifted defiantly. "My personal feelings are irrelevant. I'm here to tell the truth about what I've witnessed and uncovered."

The courtroom fell silent as the next witness was called. "The Crown calls Margaret Wyndham, Countess of Egremont," announced the prosecutor.

A tall, elegant woman in her early fifties made her way to the witness stand. Despite her composure, there was a hint of nervousness in her eyes as she was sworn in.

"Lady Egremont," the prosecutor began, "when were you married to the Earl?"

"On January 25th, 1942," she replied, her voice clear but tinged with a subtle bitterness.

The prosecutor nodded. "And were you aware that the Earl had married another woman, Annie Brankenwall, just two months earlier on November 5th, 1941?"

A ripple of shock went through the courtroom. The Countess's eyes widened. "No," she said, her voice barely above a whisper. "No, I did not know that."

As the questioning continued, a picture emerged of a loveless marriage built on deceit. The Countess revealed that not only did she not love the Earl, but he openly despised her, often calling her cruel names like "ugly bitch."

"Your ladyship," the prosecutor continued, "can you tell us about your relationship with Thomas Carter?"

A soft smile touched the Countess's lips for the first time. "Tom was my only friend at the manor. He... he became more than a friend."

"Is it true that Thomas Carter is the biological father of your son, Nigel?"

"Yes," she replied, her voice steady despite the weight of the admission.

The courtroom buzzed with whispers. Paul glanced at Nigel, who sat rigid in his seat, his face a mask of conflicting emotions.

The questioning turned to Nigel's upbringing, revealing that while the Earl had provided a nanny and later a tutor, Thomas Carter had no involvement in raising his son.

"The tutor's name was Edward Blackwood, correct?" the prosecutor asked.

"Yes," the Countess confirmed. "I had little to do with him or the nanny, but I didn't like Blackwood. There was something... odd about him."

As the Countess's testimony continued, she painted a picture of life at Wilton Manor that was far from the idyllic aristocratic existence many had imagined. She spoke of isolation, of turning a blind eye to the Earl's frequent absences and strange behaviors, of the suffocating weight of secrets and lies.

When asked about the rituals and the missing girls, the Countess claimed ignorance, but her body language suggested a deep unease. "I heard rumors," she admitted finally. "But I never... I never wanted to believe they could be true."

As the Countess stepped down from the witness stand, her eyes met the Earl's for a brief moment. The look that passed between them was one of mutual loathing and shared guilt – two people bound by a loveless marriage and the weight of terrible secrets.

Mary, watching from her seat, felt a complex mix of emotions. Pity for the Countess, anger at the web of lies that had ensnared so many lives, and a renewed determination to see justice done.

As Mary's gaze shifted to Paul, their eyes met. A moment of unspoken understanding passed between them, a shared recognition of the toll this case was taking on all involved.

The day's testimonies concluded with a surprise witness: an elderly priest from France, Father Bétron, who had officiated the secret marriage between the Earl and Paul's mother.

As Father Bétron confirmed the validity of the marriage certificate and recounted the circumstances of the ceremony, Paul felt a strange mix of emotions. Validation of his claim as the Earl's legitimate heir warred with the horror of learning more about his father's crimes.

Nigel, sensing Paul's turmoil, placed a hand on his shoulder. "He may be a monster," Nigel said quietly, echoing his words from earlier, "but I still considered him to be my father until you came on the scene. Now... now I'm just glad the truth is finally coming out."

As Father Bétron concluded his testimony about the Earl's marriage to Annie Brankenwall, the prosecutor, Victoria Holbrook, approached the judge.

"Your Honor," she said, her voice clear and determined, "in light of this new evidence, the Crown would like to add the charge of bigamy to the list of offenses against the defendant, William Angus Charles Wyndham, the sixth Earl of Egremont."

A murmur of shock rippled through the courtroom. The judge, after a moment's consideration, nodded gravely. "The charge will be added. Counsel for the defence, do you wish to respond?"

Jonathan Fitch, the Earl's lawyer, stood quickly. "Your Honour, the defence requests time to consider this new charge and its implications for our case."

"Granted," the judge replied. "We'll recess for one hour. When we reconvene, I expect both sides to be prepared to address this new development."

As the courtroom emptied for the recess, Paul turned to Mary, his face a mix of shock and anger. "Bigamy," he said, shaking his head in disbelief. "As if murder and conspiracy weren't enough."

Mary squeezed his hand supportively. "It's another piece of the puzzle, Paul. Another example of how your father believed he was above the law."

Nearby, Nigel sat lost in thought, the revelation about his own parentage still fresh in his mind. The added charge of bigamy seemed to be the final nail in the coffin of the Egremont legacy he had once believed in.

When the court reconvened, Victoria Holbrook wasted no time in addressing the new charge.

"Your Honor, members of the jury," she began, "the charge of bigamy further illustrates the defendant's complete disregard for the law and for the lives of those around him. This wasn't a mere oversight or a youthful indiscretion. This was a calculated decision to marry two women, to live a double life, fully aware of the illegality and immorality of his actions."

She went on to explain how this charge tied into the broader pattern of deception and manipulation that had characterized the Earl's reign.

The defence, caught off guard by this new development, struggled to mount an effective counter-argument. Fitch attempted to downplay the significance of the bigamy charge in light of the more serious accusations, but it was clear that this additional evidence of the Earl's duplicity had struck a chord with the jury.

As the day's proceedings came to a close, the judge addressed the court once more. "In light of today's revelations, particularly the charge of bigamy, we will adjourn until tomorrow to allow both sides to fully prepare their cases. This court is in recess."

The revelations of the day had stripped away the last vestiges of the Earl's carefully constructed facade, leaving exposed the dark and twisted reality of the Egremont legacy. The addition of bigamy to his list of crimes served as a stark reminder that his transgressions extended beyond the occult rituals and murders, permeating every aspect of his life and relationships.

As Paul left the courtroom, he felt a strange mix of vindication and sorrow. The truth about his parents' marriage was finally coming to light, but with it came the painful realization of just how deeply his father's web of lies and deceit had extended.

As the judge adjourned proceedings for the day, the courtroom buzzed with shocked murmurs. The Earl, who had remained impassive throughout much of the testimony, now looked noticeably shaken. The revelations of the day had stripped away the last vestiges of his carefully constructed facade, leaving exposed the dark and twisted reality of the Egremont legacy.

Outside the courthouse, reporters clamoured for statements. Doreen, flanked by Paul and Nigel, addressed the press briefly.

"Today's testimonies have shed light on decades of abuse and manipulation," she stated firmly. "We are confident that as the trial progresses, the full extent of Lord Egremont's crimes will be revealed, and justice will be served."

As the crowd dispersed, Paul found himself staring at the imposing facade of the courthouse. The weight of the day's revelations, the pain in the witnesses' voices, the shocking truths about his father – it all pressed down on him.

"You okay?" Mary asked softly, appearing at his side.

Paul shook his head slightly. "I'm not sure I'll ever be okay again. But we have to see this through. For Sarah, for Gordon, for all the others who suffered in silence for so long."

As they walked away from the courthouse, the sun setting behind Carlisle's ancient buildings, Paul, Mary, and Nigel knew that while the day's testimonies had been grueling, they were only the beginning. The fight for justice was far from over, and the darkest secrets of Wilton Manor and the Egremont legacy were yet to be revealed.

As the trial entered its third week, the prosecution prepared to present what they believed would be the most damning evidence yet against William Angus Charles Wyndham, the sixth Earl of Egremont. The courtroom was thick with tension as Victoria Holbrook, the prosecuting QC, called her next witness.

"The Crown calls Detective Inspector Williamson," she announced.

Williamson took the stand, his face grim but determined. After he was sworn in, Holbrook began her questioning.

"Detective Inspector, can you tell the court about the evidence you uncovered regarding the Earl's involvement in the death of Gordon Benn?"

Williamson nodded. "During our investigation, we recovered a voice recording from Mr. Benn's residence. It appears to be a conversation between Mr. Benn and the defendant, Lord Egremont."

A murmur ran through the courtroom. The Earl, who had been stoic throughout much of the proceedings, visibly stiffened in his wheelchair.

Holbrook turned to the judge. "Your Honour, the prosecution would like to play this recording for the court."

As the judge granted permission, Paul felt his heart racing. Beside him, Nigel leaned forward, his face pale.

The scratchy audio filled the courtroom:

Earl's Voice: "Gordon, you've become a liability. Your loose talk about the rituals, about the girls... it ends now."

Gordon's Voice: "My Lord, I've been loyal for years. I would never-"

Earl's Voice: "Enough! I've instructed Carter to deal with you. If you value your life, you'll disappear. Am I understood?"

Gordon's Voice: "You can't do this! I'll go to the police, I'll-"

The recording cut off abruptly. A stunned silence fell over the courtroom.

Holbrook turned back to Williamson. "Detective Inspector, based on your investigation, what do you believe this recording represents?"

Williamson's voice was steady. "We believe this is clear evidence of the Earl ordering the death of Gordon Benn. It corroborates the testimony of Thomas Carter and provides a direct link between the defendant and Mr. Benn's murder."

The defence barrister, Jonathan Fitch, objected vigorously, questioning the authenticity of the recording, but the damage was done. The jury's faces showed a mix of shock and disgust.

As Williamson stepped down, Holbrook called her next witness: Nigel Wyndham.

Paul watched as Nigel made his way to the stand, their eyes meeting briefly. Nigel's face was a mask of determination.

After Nigel was sworn in, Holbrook began. "Mr. Wyndham, you recently made a discovery at Wilton Manor, is that correct?"

Nigel nodded. "Yes. In a hidden cellar, formerly used as a dungeon."

"Can you describe what you found?"

Nigel took a deep breath. "Human remains. Multiple sets of bones, partially buried in the earth floor of the cellar."

A gasp rippled through the courtroom. Mary, sitting behind Paul, covered her mouth in horror.

"And what did you do upon making this discovery?" Holbrook prompted.

"I immediately contacted the police," Nigel replied. "A forensic team was brought in. They've identified at least seven distinct sets of remains so far, all young women."

As Nigel continued to describe the grim discovery and the subsequent investigation, Paul couldn't help but look at the Earl. For the first time since the trial began, he saw genuine fear in his father's eyes.

During cross-examination, Fitch tried to distance the Earl from the remains. "Mr. Wyndham, isn't it true that this cellar had been sealed off for decades? How can you be certain of your father's involvement?"

Nigel's voice was steady. "The cellar may have been sealed, but not forgotten. I found financial records in my fa- in the Earl's study, detailing payments for 'cellar maintenance' as recently as five years ago."

As Nigel stepped down, he paused briefly next to Paul. "I'm sorry," he murmured. "I know how hard this must be for you."

Paul nodded, unable to speak. The weight of his father's crimes seemed to press down on him, making it hard to breathe.

The day's proceedings concluded with a statement from the forensic anthropologist who had examined the remains. Her clinical description of the victims - all young women, all showing signs of trauma before death - painted a horrifying picture of decades of abuse and murder.

As the court adjourned for the day, the mood was somber. Reporters clamoured outside, but for once, Doreen declined to make a statement. The evidence spoke for itself.

Later that evening, Paul, Mary, Nigel, and Doreen gathered in a quiet pub near the courthouse.

"What happens now?" Mary asked, her voice barely above a whisper.

Doreen sighed heavily. "The defense will present their case next week, but after today... I can't see how they can possibly justify or explain away what we've heard."

Paul stared into his untouched pint. "All those years, all those lives destroyed... and for what? Power? Control?"

Nigel shook his head. "I don't think we'll ever fully understand. But at least now, the truth is out. The victims will have justice."

As they sat in contemplative silence, each lost in their own thoughts, they knew that while the trial was far from over, a significant turning point had been reached. The legacy of the Earls of Egremont would forever be tarnished, but perhaps from the ashes of these revelations, something new and better could arise.

Paul looked around at the faces of his allies - Nigel, no longer a rival but a brother in all but blood; Mary, whose strength and determination had been crucial in uncovering the truth; Doreen, whose legal acumen had brought them to this point. He realized that whatever the outcome of the trial, whatever challenges lay ahead, he was no longer alone in facing the dark legacy of his newfound family.

Chapter 44

As the trial of the Earl of Egremont continued to shock the nation with its revelations, Mary Postlethwaite found herself caught between two worlds. While her testimony had been crucial in the courtroom, she knew there was still more to uncover.

Mary turned her attention to another pressing matter. Her uncle Brian was waiting for her in the pottery's small office, his face creased with worry.

"Mary, love," he began, "I know you're caught up in this trial business, but we need to talk about the future of the pottery. The Spanish company has reached out again."

Mary sighed, feeling the weight of her family's legacy pressing down on her. "What are they offering now?"

Brian slid a document across the desk. "They've increased their offer by 20%. And they're promising to keep on all current staff for at least five years."

Mary studied the figures, her mind racing. The offer was generous – more than generous. It could secure the financial future of her family and the pottery's employees. But something still felt off.

"Have we done any more digging into this company, Uncle Brian? Who's really behind it?"

Brian shook his head. "It's all very corporate, very above board on paper. But..." he hesitated.

"But what?" Mary prompted.

"I've been asking around. There are whispers that the company has ties to some old Spanish noble families. Families that might have connections to the Wyndhams going back centuries."

Mary felt a chill run down her spine. Could this all be connected to the mysterious chalice Ms. Rodriguez had mentioned? To the "Egremont Legacy" referenced in the diary?

"We need more time," she said finally. "Tell them we're considering their offer, but we need to conduct our own due diligence."

As Brian left to make the call, Mary's phone buzzed. It was a text from Paul: "Need to talk. Meet me at the usual place in 30 minutes."

Mary grabbed her coat, her mind whirling. As she locked up the pottery, she couldn't shake the feeling that she was standing at the centre of a web that stretched far beyond Cumbria, beyond England, perhaps even beyond this century.

She arrived at the small Crab Fair café where she and Paul often met to find him already there, his face grave.

"What is it?" she asked, sliding into the seat across from him.

Paul stood up and greeted her with a kiss on the cheek. "Yesterday Nigel handed over the Earl's diary to the police, according to Nigel it contains some very incriminating details."

"That was very brave of Nigel don't you think?

Paul nodded and leaned forward, his voice low. "The defence team is making moves. They're trying to paint you as an unreliable witness, claiming you have a personal stake in seeing my father convicted."

Mary felt a flare of anger. "Of course I have a stake in this. We all do. It's about justice, about the truth."

Paul nodded, reaching across the table to take her hand. "I know. But Mary, they're going to dig into everything – your family, the pottery, your past. Are you prepared for that?"

As Mary opened her mouth to respond, her phone buzzed again. It was Doreen.

"Mary," Doreen's voice was tense. "The Earl's diary's been authenticated. The prosecution wants to introduce it as evidence, but the defence is fighting it tooth and nail. They're calling for an emergency hearing tomorrow morning. You need to be there."

As she hung up, Mary met Paul's worried gaze. "It's all coming to a head," she said softly. "The trial, the pottery, the Spanish company... it's all connected somehow. I can feel it."

Paul squeezed her hand. "Whatever happens, we're in this together. All of us – you, me, Nigel, Doreen. We'll see this through to the end."

As they sat there, the weight of what was to come settling over them, Mary knew that the next few days would determine not just the outcome of the trial, but the future of Egremont, the pottery, and perhaps the uncovering of secrets buried for centuries.

Chapter 45

The final battle was about to begin, and Mary Postlethwaite found herself at its very centre. As she left the café, her mind reeling from the day's developments, she couldn't help but feel the weight of responsibility pressing down on her.

Meanwhile, in a quiet corner of the courthouse, Paul and Nigel sat together, their voices low and serious. The trial had brought them closer, forging a bond between them that neither had expected.

"How are you holding up?" Nigel asked, his eyes searching Paul's face.

Paul sighed, running a hand through his hair. "Honestly? I'm not sure. Every day brings new revelations, new horrors. It's hard to reconcile the man I'm seeing in that dock with the father I never knew."

Nigel nodded, understanding in his eyes. "I know what you mean. For years, I thought he was my father. Now..." he trailed off, shaking his head.

"Have you given any more thought to what we discussed?" Paul asked after a moment. "About Angela?"

Nigel's face softened. "Yes. I think arranging a funeral for her in Brittany, at the convent where she grew up, is the right thing to do. It's what she would have wanted, I think."

Paul nodded, a lump forming in his throat. "She deserves peace, after everything. And closure for those who knew her there."

As they sat in companionable silence, the courtroom doors burst open. Jonathan Fitch, the defense barrister, strode out, his face set in grim determination. He was followed by a team of medical professionals, their presence causing a stir among the waiting journalists.

"What's going on?" Paul murmured, standing to get a better view.

Doreen appeared at their side, her expression tense. "The defense is making a move," she said in a low voice. "They're claiming the Earl is too ill to stand trial."

As if on cue, Fitch approached the gathered press. "Ladies and gentlemen," he announced, his voice carrying across the hall, "in light of Lord Egremont's deteriorating health, we are petitioning the court to declare him unfit to stand trial. The stress of these proceedings is taking a severe toll on my client's already fragile condition."

A buzz of excited chatter erupted among the journalists. Paul felt his heart sink. "Can they do that?" he asked Doreen.

She nodded grimly. "They can try. It's not uncommon in cases involving elderly or infirm defendants. But given the severity of the charges and the evidence we've presented, I don't think it will be an easy argument to win."

As they watched, Mary hurried into the courthouse, her face flushed with exertion. She made her way to their group, her eyes wide. "I just heard," she said breathlessly. "What does this mean for the trial?"

Nigel's face was grim. "It means they're desperate. They know the evidence is stacking up against him, so they're trying to avoid a verdict altogether."

Paul nodded in agreement. "But we can't let that happen. Too many people have suffered, too many lives have been destroyed. We need to see this through to the end."

The corridor outside the courtroom buzzed with hushed conversations. Paul and Mary stood to one side, watching as their solicitor, conferred with her team. Suddenly, a young clerk hurried up to the group, a folded piece of paper in hand.

"Ms. Doreen," he said, slightly out of breath. "Urgent message from the judge's chambers."

Doreen excused herself and stepped away to read the note. When she returned, her face was set in determined lines. "The judge wants to see counsel in chambers immediately. Something about new evidence."

As Doreen hurried off, Paul turned to Mary, concern etched on his face. "What do you think that's about?"

Mary shook her head, her voice low. "I don't know, but I've got a feeling it might be related to what I found out last night."

As the group dispersed to prepare for the next day's battle, Paul caught Mary's arm. "Are you okay?" he asked softly. "I know this can't be easy for you, with everything going on with the pottery as well."

Mary gave him a wan smile. "I'm holding up. But Paul, there's something you should know. The Earls diary apparently refers to something called 'The Egremont Legacy.' I can't help but feel it's connected to everything - the trial, the Spanish company's interest in the pottery, maybe even Angela's death."

Paul's brow furrowed. "The Egremont Legacy? What could that mean?"

"I don't know," Mary admitted. "But I have a feeling we're on the verge of uncovering something big, something that goes beyond just your father's crimes."

As they parted ways, each lost in their own thoughts, the atmosphere in the courthouse was charged with anticipation. The next day would be crucial - not just for the outcome of the trial, but for uncovering the truth about the Wyndham family's dark past and the mysterious legacy that seemed to connect everything.

That night, as Paul lay awake in his hotel room, he found himself thinking about Angela - the half-sister he never knew, whose death had set this whole chain of events in motion. He made a silent promise to her, wherever she was, that he would see this through to the end. Justice would be served, not just for her, but for all the victims of the Earl's crimes.

And as the first light of dawn began to creep through his window, Paul steeled himself for the battle ahead. Whatever happened in that courtroom today, he knew that nothing would ever be the same again. The final chapter of the Egremont legacy was about to be written, and he was determined to make sure it ended with the truth finally coming to light.

The Carlisle Crown Court was packed to capacity as Judge Ellington took his seat. The air was thick with tension; everyone present knew that today's proceedings would be crucial in determining not just the fate of William Angus Charles Wyndham, the sixth Earl of Egremont, but also the future of all those caught in the web of his crimes.

Paul Brankenwall sat rigidly in his seat, flanked by Nigel and Mary. Doreen Thornton stood at the prosecution table, her face a mask of calm determination. Across the aisle, Jonathan Fitch and his team huddled around the Earl, who looked frailer than ever in his wheelchair.

"All rise," the clerk called out, and a hush fell over the courtroom.

Judge Ellington cleared his throat. "Before we proceed with the trial, we must address the defense's petition to declare Lord Egremont unfit to stand trial due to ill health. I have reviewed the medical reports submitted by both sides, and I am prepared to make my ruling."

Paul felt his heart racing. He glanced at Nigel, who gave him a reassuring nod.

"While it is clear that Lord Egremont's health has indeed deteriorated," the judge continued, "I do not find sufficient evidence to halt these proceedings. The gravity of the charges and the public interest in seeing justice served outweigh the concerns raised by the defense. The trial will continue."

A collective sigh of relief swept through the prosecution's side of the courtroom. Fitch's face tightened, but he quickly regained his composure.

As the trial resumed, the prosecution called their final witnesses. Among them was a surprise addition: an elderly woman named Eleanor Blackwood, who had worked as a maid at Wilton Manor in the 1950s.

Victoria Holbrook, the steely-eyed prosecuting QC, approached Eleanor with a gentle demeanor. "Mrs. Blackwood, can you tell the court about your experiences working at Wilton Manor?"

Eleanor's testimony was damning. She spoke of young women brought to the manor late at night, of muffled screams from the cellars, and of the Earl's increasingly erratic and violent behavior over the years.

"And did you ever report what you saw?" Victoria asked, her voice filled with empathy.

Eleanor's eyes filled with tears. "I was young and scared. The Earl... he threatened my family. Said he'd make sure we'd never work again if I breathed a word."

As Eleanor stepped down, her testimony hanging heavy in the air, the defense began their case.

Fitch tried to paint a picture of the Earl as a misunderstood man, a product of his time and

Fitch tried to paint a picture of the Earl as a misunderstood man, a product of his time and station. He called character witnesses who spoke of the Earl's philanthropy and contributions to the local community.

But the tide had turned. The evidence was too overwhelming, the testimonies too consistent and horrifying to be dismissed.

As the trial neared its conclusion, Paul found himself struggling with conflicting emotions. This man, this monster, was his father. The legacy he had inherited was one of pain and suffering.

During a recess, he stepped out into the courthouse garden for some air. He found Mary already there, staring pensively at a bed of wilting roses.

"How are you holding up?" she asked as he approached.

Paul shook his head. "I'm not sure. Part of me wants this all to be over, but another part... Mary, what do I do with this legacy? How do I make things right?"

Mary turned to face him, her eyes soft with understanding. "You start by doing exactly what you're doing now. Seeking the truth, fighting for justice. And then... then you build something new. Something good."

As they stood there, the weight of the future pressing down on them, Nigel joined them. "They're calling us back in," he said quietly. "It's time for closing arguments."

The three of them made their way back to the courtroom, a united front in the face of the storm that was about to break.

Victoria Holbrook rose for the prosecution's closing argument. Her voice, clear and powerful, filled the courtroom. She wove together the testimonies, the physical evidence, and the long history of the Earl's crimes into a tapestry of guilt that seemed impossible to deny.

"Ladies and gentlemen of the jury," Victoria concluded, her eyes sweeping across the courtroom, "the evidence before you paints a clear picture of decades of abuse, manipulation, and murder. William Angus Charles Wyndham, the sixth Earl of Egremont, has hidden behind his title and influence for far too long. Today, you have the power to ensure that justice is finally served. Not just for the victims we know of, but for all those whose voices were silenced over the years. I urge you to consider the overwhelming evidence and return a verdict of guilty on all counts."

THE DOLFIN CHALICE

Fitch, in his closing, attempted to sow seeds of doubt, to suggest that much of the evidence was circumstantial. But even he seemed to realize the futility of his efforts.

As the jury filed out to begin their deliberations, an unexpected commotion arose from the defense table. The Earl, his face ashen, was clutching his chest.

"My client needs medical attention immediately," Fitch called out.

As paramedics rushed in, the courtroom erupted into chaos. Paul watched, stunned, as his father was wheeled out on a stretcher.

Hours passed in tense waiting. Finally, word came: the Earl had suffered a major heart attack but was stable. The judge, after conferring with both legal teams, announced that the trial would proceed.

It took the jury less than a day to reach their verdict. As they filed back into the courtroom, Paul felt as though he could hardly breathe.

"On the charge of conspiracy to commit murder, how do you find the defendant?"

"Guilty."

"On the charge of Bigamy, how do you find the defendant?"

"Guilty."

"On the charge of accessory to murder?"

"Guilty."

The litany continued, a drumbeat of justice long delayed but finally served. When it was over, William Angus Charles Wyndham, sixth Earl of Egremont, had been found guilty on all counts.

As the courtroom erupted into a cacophony of reactions, Paul sat still, feeling oddly numb. It was over, but in many ways, he realized, it was just the beginning.

Later that evening, as Paul, Nigel, Mary, and Doreen gathered in a quiet pub to process the day's events, they knew that their work was far from over. There were still mysteries to unravel, wounds to heal, and a legacy to reckon with.

"To justice," Nigel said, raising his glass.

"To truth," added Mary.

"To new beginnings," Paul said softly.

As they clinked their glasses together, each of them knew that while one episode had closed, another was just beginning. The verdict had been reached, but the real decisions - about the future, about healing, about what to do with the weight of history - those lay ahead.

And as they sat there, bound together by the trials they had faced, they knew that whatever came next, they would face it together.

Chapter 46

The days following the verdict were a whirlwind of activity and emotion. As news of the Earl's conviction spread, the nation watched in shock and fascination as centuries of aristocratic privilege came crashing down.

A week after the jury's decision, Paul, Nigel, Mary, and Doreen found themselves once again in the Carlisle Crown Court. This time, however, they were joined by an austere figure in ceremonial robes - the Lord Chancellor of the United Kingdom.

As the court was called to order, a hush fell over the room. The Earl, still pale and weak from his heart attack, was wheeled in, flanked by guards. Paul felt a complex mix of emotions as he looked at the broken figure of his father.

The Lord Chancellor stepped forward, his voice resonating through the courtroom:

"William Angus Charles Wyndham, in light of your conviction for numerous grave offenses against the Crown and its subjects, I am here to carry out a solemn duty. By the power vested in me by Her Majesty the Queen, I hereby revoke your title as the Earl of Egremont, along with all rights, privileges, and honors associated with it."

A collective gasp went through the courtroom. Nigel reached out and squeezed Paul's shoulder, a gesture of support in this momentous yet difficult moment.

The Lord Chancellor continued, "This decision is not taken lightly, but the crimes you have committed are so heinous, so contrary to the responsibilities and trust placed in a peer of the realm, that this action is necessary and just."

As the former Earl slumped in his wheelchair, Judge Ellington prepared to deliver the sentence. The courtroom was thick with tension as he began to speak.

"William Angus Charles Wyndham, you have been found guilty of multiple counts of conspiracy to commit murder, accessory to murder, perverting the course of justice, and various other serious offenses. The extent and duration of your crimes are almost without precedent in modern times."

The judge paused, his gaze sweeping the courtroom before settling on the defendant.

"Taking into account the severity and multiplicity of your crimes, I hereby sentence you to life imprisonment, with a minimum term of 30 years before possibility of parole. Furthermore, you are ordered to pay substantial compensation to the families of your victims, the details of which will be determined in subsequent hearings."

As the sentence was pronounced, Paul felt a strange sense of emptiness. The man before him - no longer an Earl, now just a convicted criminal - had cast a long shadow over so many lives. And yet, in this moment of justice, Paul felt no joy, only a profound sadness for all that had been lost.

Mary, sensing Paul's turmoil, gently took his hand. "It's over," she whispered. "We can start to heal now."

As William Wyndham was led away, Nigel turned to Paul. "So, what happens now? With the title, I mean."

Paul shook his head slowly. "I... I don't know. I'm not sure I want it, to be honest. Not after everything that's happened."

Doreen, overhearing, leaned in. "You don't have to decide right away, Paul. There will be a formal process to determine the succession. You have time to consider what you want to do."

As they left the courthouse, a sea of reporters awaited them. Victoria Holbrook, the prosecuting QC, was giving a statement:

"Today, we have seen that no one, regardless of their title or station, is above the law. Justice has been served for the victims of William Wyndham's crimes. While we cannot undo the harm he has caused, we hope that today's proceedings bring some measure of closure to those who have suffered."

Later that evening, as Paul, Mary, Nigel, and Doreen gathered once again in their usual pub, the mood was subdued but hopeful.

"To the end of an era," Nigel said, raising his glass.

"And the beginning of a new one," Mary added, looking at Paul.

Paul nodded slowly. "Whatever comes next, we'll face it together. There's still so much to sort out - the estate, the pottery, this 'Egremont Legacy' we've barely scratched the surface of..."

Doreen smiled. "One step at a time, Paul. For now, let's just be grateful that justice has been served."

As they clinked their glasses together, Paul realized that while one chapter of the Egremont story had indeed closed, another was just beginning. The title might have been revoked, the former Earl sentenced, but the true legacy - one of truth, justice, and redemption - was yet to be written.

And as he looked around at the faces of those who had stood by him through this ordeal, Paul knew that whatever challenges lay ahead, he wouldn't face them alone. The future of Egremont, whatever shape it might take, would be built on a foundation of friendship, integrity, and the unwavering pursuit of truth.

As the dust began to settle following William Wyndham's sentencing, Paul found himself facing another, more personal battle. The very day after the former Earl's fate was decided, Paul received a call from his lawyer in France.

"I'm sorry, Paul," the lawyer's voice crackled over the line. "The French court has ruled in favour of the insurance company. They won't have to continue covering Yvette's medical expenses."

Paul felt as if the ground had dropped out from under him. He sank into a chair, his mind reeling. "What... what does this mean for Yvette?" he managed to ask, though he feared he already knew the answer.

The lawyer's voice was gentle but firm. "I'm afraid it means that her life support will be switched off. The hospital can't continue to provide care without payment, and after ten years..." He trailed off, leaving the grim reality unspoken.

As Paul hung up the phone, he felt a wave of grief wash over him. Yvette, his first love, had been in a coma for a decade, the victim of a drunk driver who had shattered their lives one fateful night just 3 miles from their home. And now, just as one chapter of tragedy in his life was closing, another seemed determined to reopen old wounds.

Mary found him like that, slumped in his chair, his face ashen. "Paul? What's happened?"

He looked up at her, his eyes filled with a pain that seemed to go beyond words. Slowly, haltingly, he explained the situation - about Yvette, about the accident, about his long legal battle with the insurance company to keep her on life support.

"Oh, Paul," Mary whispered, taking his hand. "I'm so sorry. I had no idea you were dealing with all of this on top of everything else."

Paul nodded, grateful for her presence. "The drunk driver who hit her, he's still in jail. Five more years before he's even eligible for parole. But Yvette... she's the one who's truly been serving a life sentence. And now..."

He couldn't finish the sentence, but he didn't need to. Mary understood.

Over the next few days, as news of the French court's decision spread among their small circle, Paul found himself surrounded by a network of support he never knew he had. Nigel, upon hearing the news, immediately offered to use his connections to find specialists who might be able to help. Doreen dove into the legal aspects, looking for any possible avenue of appeal.

Even Inspector Williamson, who had become something of an ally during the trial, reached out. "I know it's not much," he said gruffly, "but I've got a cousin who works for the French police. If there's anything we can do to help with arrangements or... well, anything, just let me know."

A week after the court's decision, Paul found himself on a plane to Paris, Mary by his side. As they flew over the Channel, Paul stared out the window, his mind a whirlwind of memories and regrets.

"I keep thinking," he said softly, "about all the time I've spent fighting - fighting for justice for Angela, fighting against my father's crimes, fighting for Yvette. And now, it feels like I'm going to Paris to surrender."

Mary squeezed his hand. "You're not surrendering, Paul. You're letting go. There's a difference."

Chapter 47

The sentencing of William Angus Charles Wyndham, the sixth Earl of Egremont, had sent shockwaves through British society. Judge Ellington's 30-year sentence for the crimes of murder, conspiracy, perversion of justice, and bigamy had stunned the nation. The once-proud Earl, now a frail shadow of his former self, had shown no emotion as he was led away.

But fate had other plans. Just weeks into his sentence, the Earl's health took a dramatic turn for the worse. Diagnosed with late-stage cancer, he was transferred to a secure hospital unit.

Paul received the news with a complex mix of emotions. "I don't know how to feel," he confessed to Mary as they sat in his London flat. "He's still my father, but after everything he's done..."

Mary squeezed his hand supportively. "It's okay to have conflicted feelings, Paul. It's human."

Three days later, the call came. The Earl of Egremont was dead.

In the aftermath of the Earl's passing, a legal quagmire emerged. Paul found himself at the centre of a debate that reached the highest levels of British peerage law.

"It's unprecedented," explained Doreen Thornton, the lawyer who had been advising Paul throughout the ordeal. "Your father's title was in the process of being revoked, but it hadn't been finalized before his death. Technically, you could have a claim to become the 7th Earl of Egremont."

Paul ran a hand through his hair, his expression troubled. "Do I even want it? After everything that's happened, everything that title represents..."

The question of Paul's potential inheritance sparked heated discussions in legal circles and among the British aristocracy. Some argued that the sins of the father shouldn't be visited upon the son, that Paul had a right to claim his inheritance. Others felt that the Egremont title was too tainted by scandal and should be allowed to die out.

For weeks, Paul grappled with the decision. He spent long hours walking the grounds of Wilton Manor, now a shell of its former grandeur, trying to reconcile his complex feelings about his heritage.

"What are you thinking?" Mary asked him one evening as they stood watching the sunset from the manor's terrace.

Paul was quiet for a moment before responding. "I'm thinking about legacy. About how one person's actions can echo through generations. If I take this title, am I perpetuating something that should end? Or am I taking on the responsibility to make it stand for something better?"

In the end, after much soul-searching and lengthy discussions with Mary, Nigel, and his legal advisors, Paul made his decision. He would not claim the title of Earl of Egremont.

"The Egremont legacy is one of pain and suffering," he announced in a press conference that attracted national attention. "I believe the best way to honor the victims and begin to make amends is to let that legacy end. I am, and will remain, Paul Brankenwall."

His decision was met with a mix of reactions. Some praised his integrity, while others criticized him for turning his back on tradition. But for Paul, it felt right. He would forge his own path, create his own legacy - one built on truth, justice, and compassion.

As he and Mary left the press conference, hand in hand, Paul felt a weight lift from his shoulders. The shadow of the Egremont title no longer loomed over him. He was free to be simply Paul Brankenwall, and to shape his future on his own terms.

"So, Mr. Brankenwall," Mary said with a smile, "what's next?"

Paul squeezed her hand, a glimmer of excitement in his eyes. "I'm not sure, Ms. Postlethwaite. But whatever it is, we'll face it together."

As they walked away from the cameras and into an uncertain but hopeful future, both Paul and Mary knew that while one chapter had closed, another was just beginning. The Egremont legacy had ended, but their own story was far from over.

Chapter 48

At the hospital in Paris, Paul was struck by how little had changed in the decade since he'd last been there. The same antiseptic smell, the same hushed voices, the same feeling of life suspended in a fragile balance.

Yvette lay as she had for ten years, still and pale, machines beeping softly around her. Paul sat by her bedside, holding her hand, remembering the vibrant, laughing girl she had been.

"I'm so sorry, Yvette," he whispered. "I tried. God knows, I tried."

As the doctors explained the procedure for removing life support, Paul felt as if he were moving through a fog. It was Mary who asked the practical questions, Mary who made sure all the paperwork was in order, Mary who stood as a pillar of strength when Paul felt he might crumble.

The next morning, as the first light of dawn broke over Paris, Yvette Beaumont took her last breath. Paul, holding her hand to the very end, felt a chapter of his life close with a finality that left him both heartbroken and, paradoxically, free.

As they left the hospital, Mary turned to Paul. "What do you want to do now?"

Paul took a deep breath, looking out over the city he had once loved, the city that had given him so much joy and so much pain. "I want to honor her," he said finally. "All of them - Yvette, Angela, all the victims of my father's crimes. I want to use whatever resources, whatever influence I have, to make sure nothing like this happens again."

Mary nodded, understanding in her eyes. "Then that's what we'll do. Together."

As they made their way back to their hotel, Paul realized that while he had indeed lost the case against the insurance company, he had gained something far more valuable - a sense of purpose, a direction for the future, and a partner to face that future with.

The Egremont legacy, he decided, would no longer be one of privilege and hidden crimes. Instead, it would be one of justice, compassion, and healing. It was time to return to England, to face whatever challenges awaited, and to begin the work of building something new from the ashes of the old.

As the taxi wound its way through the Paris streets, Paul felt a sense of resolve settling over him. The battles might not all be won, but the war for redemption - both personal and for the Egremont name - was far from over. And this time, he knew exactly what he was fighting for.

As Paul grappled with the emotional aftermath of Yvette's passing and his newfound sense of purpose, Mary found herself facing her own crossroads back in Cumbria. The future of Postlethwaite Pottery hung in the balance, with the Spanish company, Cerámica Innovadora, growing increasingly insistent on their offer.

Mary sat at the old oak table in the pottery's office, surrounded by her siblings – Steve, the pragmatist; Andrew, the creative force; and his daughter, young Emily, still learning the ropes of the family business. Howards widow Jenny and Uncle Brian hovered nearby, his face etched with concern.

"WE CAN'T KEEP PUTTING this off," Jenny said, her voice tinged with frustration. "The Spanish offer is more than generous, and we're barely keeping afloat as it is."

Andrew leaned back in his chair, clay-stained fingers drumming on the table. "But it's not just about the money, is it? This place, what we do here – it's part of who we are."

Mary nodded, feeling the weight of generations pressing down on her shoulders. "You're both right," she said softly. "We can't ignore the financial realities, but we also can't just throw away our heritage."

Emily, who had been quiet until now, spoke up. "What if we didn't have to choose? What if there was a way to get the financial support we need without giving up everything?"

All eyes turned to the youngest Postlethwaite. Mary felt a surge of pride – and hope. "Go on, Em. What are you thinking?"

As Emily outlined her idea, Mary felt a plan beginning to take shape. Over the next few days, she engaged in intense negotiations with Cerámica Innovadora, pushing for a compromise that would preserve the essence of Postlethwaite Pottery while securing its financial future.

Finally, after what felt like endless meetings and late-night phone calls, Mary called her family together once more.

"I think we've found a solution," she announced, unable to keep a note of excitement from her voice. "Cerámica Innovadora has agreed to buy a controlling interest – 60% – but we'll retain 40% ownership and, crucially, creative control over our product lines."

A buzz of conversation filled the room as her siblings and Uncle Brian absorbed the news.

"What does that mean for us, day-to-day?" Steve asked, a hint of wariness in his voice.

Mary smiled. "It means we'll have the capital we need to modernize our equipment and expand our reach. But it also means we'll continue to design and create the pieces that have made Postlethwaite Pottery special for generations."

Emily nodded slowly, a look of relief spreading across her face. "And our jobs? The staff?"

"All secure," Mary confirmed. "In fact, part of the agreement includes plans for gradual expansion. We'll be hiring, not laying off."

Uncle Brian, who had been listening intently, finally spoke. "Your parents would be proud, Mary. You've found a way to honour the past while securing the future. It's not an easy balance to strike."

Chapter 49

The Postlethwaite family sat around the old oak table in the pottery office, the air thick with cigarette smoke and the weight of their decision.

"So, we're agreed then?" Steve asked, looking around at his siblings. "We'll partner with Cerámica Innovadora, but maintain control of the design and quality?"

Mary nodded, a smile playing on her lips. "It's a good compromise. We keep our heritage, but we get the resources to modernize."

Andrew leaned back in his chair, exhaling a plume of smoke. "I still think we could've got more out of them, but... I suppose it's not a bad deal."

"It's more than just a deal," Mary said, her voice firm. "It's a chance to reshape our legacy, just like Paul's doing with the Egremont estate."

As the family continued to discuss the finer points, Mary felt a weight lifting from her shoulders. The pottery would survive, evolve even, without losing its soul.

Later that evening, as Mary locked up the pottery, she paused by the old kiln. Her hand brushed against the weathered bricks.

"Penny for your thoughts?"

Mary turned to see old Tom, the night watchman, approaching with his thermos.

"Just thinking about all the history here, Tom. The secrets these walls must hold."

Tom chuckled. "Aye, and not just the walls. Have you heard the latest gossip about that chalice they found up at the old monastery?"

Mary's eyes widened. "No, what about it?"

"Well," Tom leaned in conspiratorially, "word is, it might be connected to the Egremont family somehow. Strange markings on it, they say."

Mary's mind raced. Could this be another piece of the puzzle? "Thanks, Tom. I'll have to look into that."

As she walked home through the quiet streets of Egremont, Mary's thoughts whirled with possibilities. The compromise with Cerámica Innovadora, the mysteries surrounding the Egremont legacy, the chalice - it all seemed interconnected somehow.

Passing the Blue Bell pub, she heard a familiar voice call out.

"Mary! Wait up!"

She turned to see Paul jogging towards her, a broad smile on his face.

"Paul! I thought you were in London," Mary said, surprised but pleased.

"Just got back," he replied, slightly out of breath. "Couldn't wait to tell you - I've had some ideas about the estate. About how we can honour the past while building something new."

Mary laughed. "Funny you should say that. We've just finalized a deal that does something similar for the pottery."

Paul's eyes lit up. "Really? That's fantastic! Listen, why don't we grab a quick pint and compare notes? I have a feeling our two projects might have more in common than we thought."

As they turned towards the pub, Mary felt a surge of excitement. There was still so much to uncover, so many possibilities to explore. But whatever challenges lay ahead, whatever mysteries still lurked in the shadows of Cumbria's ancient stones, she knew she wouldn't face them alone.

"You know, Paul," she said as they reached the pub door, "I think we're at the beginning of something big here. Something that goes beyond just the pottery or the estate."

Paul nodded, his expression thoughtful. "I think you're right. And I can't wait to see where it leads us."

With a shared smile, they stepped into the warm glow of the pub, ready to plan their next move in unravelling the mysteries that had brought them together.

Chapter 50

The summer sun hung low in the sky, casting long shadows across the grounds of Wilton Manor. Paul Brankenwall and Mary Postlethwaite stood before the small estate cottage where, months ago, the body of Gordon Benn had been discovered. The scene was markedly different now – gone were the police vehicles, the crime scene tape, the bustle of forensic teams. But the air still felt heavy with the weight of unresolved questions.

"It's hard to believe it's been almost a year," Mary said softly, her eyes scanning the quiet cottage.

Paul nodded, his expression grim. "A year since Detective Inspector Williamson got that early morning call. Since Freda found her father..."

Their minds drifted back to the accounts they'd heard, the details that had come out during the trial. The image of Gordon Benn's body, crumpled on the floor in a pool of blood. The devastated figure of Freda Benn, wrapped in a blanket on the cottage steps, finally ready to share what she knew.

"You know," Paul mused, "something's always bothered me about this case. Even after the trial, after my father's conviction, it feels... unfinished."

Mary turned to him, curiosity piqued. "What do you mean?"

Paul ran a hand through his hair, frustration evident in his gesture. "Think about it. The official story is that my father ordered Gordon's death because he knew too much, was talking too freely. But why here? Why so... messy? It doesn't fit with his usual methods."

As Paul and Mary surveyed Gordon Benn's cottage, their eyes scanning for anything the police might have overlooked, Mary's gaze settled on the kitchen.

"Paul, look," she said, moving towards the fridge. "There's something odd about this calendar."

Paul joined her, his brow furrowed as he examined the Lake District scenes adorning the calendar. But it wasn't the picturesque views that caught their attention - it was the markings on specific dates.

"June 15th, 1974," Mary read aloud. "It's circled and marked 'solstice.'"

Paul nodded, his finger tracing over other marked dates. "And look, some have 'FM' written next to them. Full moon, maybe?"

They exchanged glances, the implications sinking in. "The solstice," Mary whispered. "The rituals at Matty Benn's Bridge. We knew Gordon was involved, but this... this is concrete evidence of him tracking the dates."

Paul's eyes narrowed as he spotted a small note scribbled in the margin of the June page. The handwriting was cramped but legible:

"Can't go The girl . Must end."

"This sounds like he was having doubts," Paul said slowly, his mind racing. "And if he was thinking of backing out, that would give my father – or someone else – motive to silence him."

Mary nodded, her investigative instincts kicking in. "We need to look into this further. There's more to Gordon Benn's murder than what came out in the trial. And I have a feeling it might be connected to those poor souls we found in the dungeon."

They stood in silence for a moment, the weight of this new discovery hanging between them. The case they thought was closed had just blown wide open.

"We should document this," Mary said, pulling out her phone to take photos of the calendar. "This could be crucial evidence."

As they carefully examined the rest of the calendar, noting down all the marked dates and cryptic notes, Paul couldn't shake the feeling that they had stumbled upon something significant. The meticulous tracking of solstices and full moons, combined with Gordon's apparent last-minute doubts, painted a disturbing picture of the events leading up to his murder.

"We need to cross-reference these dates," Paul said, his voice tight with tension. "See if they match up with any of the disappearances or... or the bodies we found."

Mary nodded grimly. "Agreed. And we need to figure out who this girl was that made Gordon have second thoughts. She might be the key to unraveling this whole mystery."

As they prepared to leave the cottage, both felt a mix of excitement and apprehension. They were on the verge of uncovering a truth that had remained hidden for far too long - a truth that some people might kill to keep secret.Paul met her gaze, seeing his own determination reflected in her eyes. "You're right. We owe it to Gordon, to Freda, to all the victims, to uncover the whole truth." He paused, a wry smile tugging at his lips. "I don't suppose you fancy playing detective again, Miss Postlethwaite?"

Mary's answering smile was both excited and grim. "I thought you'd never ask, Mr. Brankenwall. Where do we start?"

As they made their way back towards the manor, plans already forming, neither of them noticed the curtain twitching in one of the upper windows of the cottage. Someone else was very interested in their discovery, and the secrets surrounding Gordon Benn's murder were far from fully revealed.

The hunt for the truth – and all the dark secrets it might uncover – had begun anew.

As Paul and Mary made their way back towards Wilton Manor, the weight of their discovery hung heavy between them. The summer breeze carried the scent of roses from the nearby garden, a stark contrast to the dark thoughts occupying their minds.

Paul broke the silence first. "You know, throughout the trial, I kept waiting for everything to make sense. For all the pieces to fall into place."

Mary nodded, her brow furrowed in thought. "But they never quite did, did they?"

They paused by an old stone bench, overlooking the sprawling grounds of the estate. As they sat, Paul pulled out the locket they had found, turning it over in his hands.

"Take Gordon's murder," he continued. "The official story is that my father ordered his death because Gordon knew too much and was talking. But why then? Gordon had been involved in... in the rituals for years. Why suddenly become a threat?"

Mary leaned in, her voice low. "And the manner of his death. It was so... brutal. From what we learned during the trial, your father preferred more discreet methods. Poisoning, staged accidents. This felt different."

Paul nodded grimly. "Exactly. It's almost as if someone wanted it to look like my father's work. But who? And why?"

They sat in silence for a moment, the implications of their words sinking in. The case that had seemed so neatly wrapped up at the trial was unraveling before their eyes.

Mary's gaze drifted to the locket in Paul's hand. "And now this. A hidden message, doubts about the rituals. It paints a very different picture of Gordon than what we heard in court."

"He was portrayed as a willing accomplice," Paul mused. "But what if he was having second thoughts? What if he was planning to expose everything?"

Mary's eyes widened. "That would certainly give someone a motive for murder. But not necessarily your father. It could have been anyone involved in the rituals who feared exposure."

Paul ran a hand through his hair, frustration evident in his gesture. "And what about Freda? She came forward as the anonymous caller, provided crucial testimony. But did she tell us everything she knew?"

"It must have been traumatic for her," Mary said softly. "Finding her father like that. Perhaps there are things she couldn't bring herself to say at the time."

They fell silent again, each lost in their own thoughts. The sun was beginning to set, casting a golden glow over the manor grounds. It was beautiful, peaceful even, but they both knew that beneath the serene surface lay a web of dark secrets still waiting to be uncovered.

"We're opening a Pandora's box here, aren't we?" Paul said finally, his voice a mix of determination and apprehension.

Mary nodded, her expression serious. "We are. And we need to be prepared for what we might find. This goes beyond just your father, Paul. We could be uncovering a conspiracy that involves some of the most powerful people in the region."

Paul met her gaze, seeing his own resolve reflected in her eyes. "I know. But we can't turn back now. Too many lives have been destroyed, too many truths buried. We owe it to Gordon, to all the victims, to uncover the whole truth."

Mary reached out, placing her hand over his. "We're in this together, Paul. Whatever we uncover, whatever dangers we face, we'll face them as a team."

As they sat there, the weight of their decision settling over them, they knew that the path ahead would be fraught with challenges. They were about to challenge the official narrative, to dig into secrets that powerful people wanted to keep buried.

But they also knew that in doing so, they had a chance to bring true justice to those who had suffered, to honor the memories of the victims, and perhaps, to finally put the ghosts of Wilton Manor to rest.

With a shared nod of determination, they stood, ready to begin their investigation in earnest. The sun had almost set now, casting long shadows across the grounds. As they walked back towards the manor, neither of them noticed the figure watching from a distant copse of trees, a figure with a vested interest in keeping the past firmly buried.

The hunt for the truth about Gordon Benn's murder – and all the dark secrets it might uncover – was about to begin in earnest. And the consequences of their investigation would reach far beyond the borders of Wilton Manor.

Chapter 51

As Paul and Mary made their way back to Wilton Manor, the sensation of being watched prickled at the back of their necks. Paul glanced over his shoulder, his eyes scanning the tree line.

"Did you see that?" he murmured, nodding towards a copse of trees in the distance.

Mary followed his gaze, squinting in the fading light. "I'm not sure. What did you see?"

"I could have sworn I saw someone duck behind those trees," Paul said, his voice low. "It's probably nothing, but..."

"But given what we're investigating, we can't be too careful," Mary finished for him. "Do you think it could be the same person we glimpsed watching from the upstairs window that day?"

Paul nodded grimly. "It's possible. Whoever they are, they seem very interested in our activities."

With a shared look of concern, they quickened their pace towards the manor. As they approached, they noticed a figure waiting on the front steps. It was Freda Benn, Gordon's daughter, looking pale and agitated.

"Mr. Brankenwall, Ms. Postlethwaite," Freda called out, her voice shaky. "I... I need to talk to you. It's about me dad."

Paul and Mary exchanged glances before ushering Freda inside. In the study, Freda fumbled in her bag, pulling out a battered old school exercise book.

"Found this," she mumbled, pushing it towards them. "Under a loose board in dad's room. Didn't know about it before. Just found it last week when I was... you know, sorting his stuff."

THE DOLFIN CHALICE

Paul carefully opened the book, his eyes widening as he scanned the pages. "It's not exactly a diary," he said. "More like... notes. Gordon's notes."

Mary leaned in, her breath catching as she looked over Paul's shoulder. The pages were filled with untidy scrawls, brief and cryptic jottings, and crude sketches.

"Look at this," Paul said, pointing to a page. The note read: "AB nice.. cousin. cant do it." Below was a poorly drawn sketch labeled "Countess is a bitch."

"And here," Mary added, indicating another entry. "Dates... and initials. FM, S... Full moon and solstice maybe?"

They flipped through more pages, finding rough sketches of girls, some bordering on pornographic, along with cryptic references to "ritual stuff" and "potential girls."

Freda shifted uncomfortably. "I... I didn't say everything before. At the trial. I was scared, you know?"

Paul looked up. "What do you mean, Freda?"

"The night me dad died," she said, her voice barely above a whisper. "I heard him arguing with someone. Weren't the Earl's voice though. Sounded younger."

Paul and Mary exchanged shocked looks. This new information cast everything in a different light.

"Freda," Mary said gently, "any idea who your dad might've been arguing with?"

Freda shook her head, wiping her nose on her sleeve. "Dunno. But... there was something else weird. After I found him... you know. His Saint Christopher thingy was gone. He always wore it. Always. But it weren't on him, and I never found it in the house."

———◦———

PAUL'S BROW FURROWED. "The missing medallion... it wasn't mentioned in the trial."

"I was too... too messed up to think about it then," Freda admitted. "But now, with this book... I dunno. It all seems important somehow."

The room fell silent as Paul and Mary pored over Gordon Benn's notebook, its pages filled with crude sketches and cryptic notes. Freda sat across from them, her eyes darting nervously between the couple and the floor.

Suddenly, Freda's composure crumbled. With a heart-wrenching sob, she lunged forward, throwing her arms around Mary and burying her face in the older woman's shoulder. Startled, Mary instinctively wrapped her arms around the girl, gently stroking her back.

"Freda, love," Mary murmured, "what is it? Why are you so upset about your dad's death?"

Freda's body shook with sobs. When she finally spoke, her words came out in a broken stammer. "N-no... I... I h-hate him."

Paul and Mary exchanged a worried glance over Freda's head.

"Why, Freda?" Paul asked gently. "What did he do?"

Freda's grip on Mary tightened. "When... when I was th-thirteen," she managed, her voice barely above a whisper, "he... he came home drunk and... and... he r.raped... me" tears flooded down her face.

Mary's heart sank as she realized what Freda was trying to say. "Oh, Freda," she breathed, holding the girl closer.

"He... he'd come to my r-room," Freda continued, her words tumbling out now. "Break the d-door if I locked it. Said he'd... he'd hurt me if I didn't..."

Paul's face had gone pale. "Freda, I'm so sorry. Did you ever tell anyone?"

Freda shook her head violently. "C-couldn't. Too scared. But now... with this n-notebook..." She gestured weakly towards the desk.

"I think... I think they k-killed him. 'Cause he was gonna tell. Tell everything."

As they absorbed this new information, Mary's expression softened with concern. "Freda, if you don't mind me asking, how have you been coping? Where are you staying now?"

Freda's shoulders slumped as she pulled away slightly. "With... with my aunt. In the v-village. She's nice, but... it's hard. The c-cottage... too many memories. And... and no one will give me w-work now."

Paul leaned forward, his voice gentle but firm. "Freda, what your father did... it wasn't your fault. None of this is your fault. And we're going to help you, I promise."

Mary nodded in agreement. "You're safe now, Freda. We'll figure this out together."

As they continued to examine the notebook, Paul and Mary realized they were looking at evidence of a much darker, more twisted story than they had imagined. Gordon Benn's crude jottings and Freda's hesitant revelations were painting a disturbing picture of rituals, exploitation, and a conspiracy that ran deeper than they had ever suspected.

The room felt heavy with unspoken truths and the weight of decisions yet to be made. But as Paul and Mary exchanged a determined look over Freda's bowed head, one thing was clear: they were in this together, ready to face whatever dark secrets still lurked in the shadows of Egremont's past.

Paul leaned forward, his voice gentle. "We want you to know that you're not alone in this, Freda. If there's anything you need - support, assistance, anything at all - please don't hesitate to ask."

Freda managed a small, grateful smile. "Thank you. That means a lot. I just... I want to understand what really happened to my father. I want the truth to come out."

As they absorbed this new information, a chill settled over the room. The case they thought was solved had just become infinitely more complex. Who had really killed Gordon Benn? Who was the mysterious figure watching them? And how deep did this conspiracy really go?

Paul closed the notebook, his expression grim but determined. "Thank you for bringing this to us, Freda. We'll do everything we can to uncover the truth about what happened to your father. And please, keep in touch. Let us know if there's any way we can help you."

As Freda left, visibly relieved to have shared her burden but still clearly struggling with her situation, Paul and Mary looked at each other, the weight of this new evidence heavy between them.

"We need to re-examine everything," Mary said. "The trial transcripts, the forensic reports, everything."

Paul nodded, his mind already racing. "And we need to find out who that reporter was that Gordon planned to meet. They might have crucial information."

As they began to plan their next steps, neither of them noticed the shadow that briefly passed by the study window. The mysterious observer was still out there, watching, waiting. And as Paul and Mary delved deeper into the mystery of Gordon Benn's murder, they were unwittingly drawing closer to a truth more dangerous than they could have imagined.

As the door closed behind Freda, Paul and Mary sat in stunned silence, the weight of their new discoveries hanging heavy in the air. Gordon's notebook lay on the desk between them, a Pandora's box of secrets and unanswered questions.

After a long moment, Mary spoke, her voice low but determined. "We can't ignore this, Paul. There's clearly more to Gordon's death than what came out at the trial."

Paul nodded, his brow furrowed as he flipped through the notebook again. Suddenly, his hand paused on a page. "Mary, look at this," he said, his voice tight with excitement.

Mary leaned in, her eyes widening as she saw a crude sketch map. At the centre was a roughly drawn building labelled "Pottery - Ravenglass."

Beneath the sketch was a cryptic note in Gordon's messy scrawl:

"Earl's cup – cracked but Ruby still there. Old man curious. Said he'd try to fix. Told him nothing. Must get it back before HE notices."

"The Earl's cup?" Mary breathed. "This must be related to the Dolfin chalice?"

Paul's mind raced. "It must be. But why would Gordon be taking it to a pottery for repair? And who's 'HE'? My father?"

Mary's finger traced the sketch map. "This is definitely the Postlethwaite pottery. My family's business." She paused, a look of realization crossing her face. "Oh, Paul, with all this going on, I completely forgot to mention my findings about the chalice."

Paul looked at her, surprise evident in his expression. "What findings?"

Mary took a deep breath. "I met with a Professor Cowan who'd done research on the chalice as a student at Oxford. He told me about its history - how it was made by nuns in Ravenglass, stolen by Vikings, and eventually ended up in the hands of the Lowther family."

She quickly briefed Paul on the chalice's long and twisted history, from its creation in the 12th century to its rumoured destruction by the 6th Earl of Egremont.

"But here's the thing," Mary continued, her voice growing excited. "This confirms what Uncle Brian told me. He said that Gordon Benn had been to the pottery to have the chalice repaired. They even made a replica of it."

Paul's eyes widened. "So the chalice wasn't destroyed after all?"

Mary shook her head. "It doesn't seem so. And now, with Gordon's notes here, we have proof that he was involved with it somehow."

"This is huge, Mary," Paul said, his voice low with the weight of the revelation. "If the chalice still exists, and if it's connected to the rituals my father was involved in..."

"It could be the key to unravelling this whole mystery," Mary finished.

They sat in silence for a moment, the implications of this connection sinking in. The notebook had already revealed so much about the rituals, the exploitation, and the dark underbelly of Egremont society. But this confirmation of the chalice's existence and its direct link to Gordon Benn added a new dimension to the case.

"We need to be careful," Paul said finally. "If this chalice is as important as it seems, there might be people who don't want us digging into its history."

Mary's face set with determination. "I know. But we've come too far to back down now. Whatever this cup is, whatever it means to the rituals and to your father, we need to find out."

As they began to plan their next steps, both Paul and Mary felt a mix of excitement and apprehension. The mystery of Gordon Benn's death had just become even more complex, intertwining with ancient artefacts and family histories in ways they never could have imagined.

The hunt for the truth about the Earl's cup and its connection to the dark events in Egremont had taken on a new urgency, with the chalice potentially holding the key to unlocking the secrets that had plagued the town for generations. "Maybe it was kept quiet," Paul mused. "If it's as valuable and significant as we think, Gordon might have been trying to keep it under wraps."

Mary nodded slowly. "We need to look into this.. And if it's connected to the rituals and Gordon's death..."

"It could blow this whole case wide open," Paul finished.

They sat in silence for a moment, the implications of this new discovery sinking in. The notebook had already revealed so much about the rituals, the exploitation, and the dark underbelly of Egremont society. But this connection to the Dolfin chalice and the Postlethwaite pottery added a new dimension to the mystery.

"We need to be careful," Paul said finally. "If this chalice is as important as it seems, there might be people who don't want us digging into its history."

Mary's face set with determination. "I know. But we've come too far to back down now. Whatever this cup is, whatever it means to the rituals and to your father, we need to find out."

Paul nodded, running a hand through his hair. "I agree. But reopening this investigation... it's not going to be easy. Or safe."

"I know," Mary said, meeting his gaze steadily. "But think about Freda, about all the other victims and their families. Don't they deserve to know the whole truth?"

Paul stood, pacing the room as he thought aloud. "We'll need to be cautious. The official case is closed. My father's been convicted. If we start poking around, asking questions..."

"We'll ruffle some feathers," Mary finished for him. "Powerful people might not want these secrets coming to light."

Paul turned to her, his expression a mix of determination and concern. "Are you sure you want to do this, Mary? You've already been through so much because of my family's legacy."

Mary stood, moving to join him. "Paul, I'm in this with you. Whatever we uncover, whatever dangers we face, we'll face them together."

A small smile tugged at Paul's lips, gratitude and affection clear in his eyes. "Thank you," he said softly. Then, squaring his shoulders, he added, "Alright, if we're going to do this, we need a plan."

They moved to the large desk in the corner of the study, clearing a space to spread out their thoughts and ideas.

"First," Mary said, pulling out a notebook, "we need to list everything we know and everything we need to find out."

Paul nodded, leaning over the desk. "Right. We have Gordon's notebook, which suggests he was planning to expose the rituals. We need to identify that reporter he was going to meet."

"And we need to look into the argument Freda overheard," Mary added, scribbling notes. "Someone younger than the Earl, someone Gordon knew well..."

"We should also re-examine the physical evidence from the crime scene," Paul mused. "The missing Saint Christopher medallion could be significant."

As they brainstormed, the list grew longer: people to interview, records to check, locations to revisit. The scope of their unofficial investigation was daunting, but also exhilarating.

"We can't do this alone," Paul said finally, straightening up. "We need help, someone with investigative experience and access to resources we don't have."

Mary's eyes lit up. "What about Detective Inspector Williamson? He led the original investigation. Do you think he'd be willing to help us off the record?"

Paul considered this, nodding slowly. "It's worth a try. He always seemed... unsatisfied with how neatly everything wrapped up. And he's a good man. I think he'd want the truth to come out, even if it means admitting the original investigation missed things."

"We should approach him carefully, though," Mary cautioned. "If word gets out that we're reopening this case, even unofficially..."

"It could spook whoever's really behind all this," Paul finished. "You're right. We'll need to be discreet."

As the night deepened outside, Paul and Mary continued to plan, their determination growing with each passing hour. They were under no illusions about the challenges ahead – the dangers they might face, the powerful interests they could be crossing. But the need for truth, for justice, outweighed their fears.

"We should start with his notes, doodles and scribbles," Mary said, stifling a yawn as the first light of dawn began to creep through the windows. "Go through it meticulously; look for any names or details that might give us leads."

Paul nodded, his eyes tired but alert. "And I'll reach out to Harry Williamson, feel him out about helping us."

As they prepared to call it a night – or rather, a very long morning – Paul paused, turning to Mary with a serious expression.

"Mary, whatever happens, whatever we uncover... thank you. For believing in this, for believing in me."

Mary smiled, squeezing his hand. "Always, Paul. We're in this together."

The investigation into the true circumstances of Gordon Benn's murder – and all the dark secrets surrounding it – was officially reopened. And as Paul and Mary would soon discover, the path to truth was fraught with more dangers and revelations than they could have ever imagined.

Chapter 52

The Cumbrian rain fell in a steady drizzle as Paul and Mary made their way to the small café just outside Carlisle. They had chosen this location carefully – far enough from Egremont to avoid prying eyes, but close enough to be convenient for Detective Inspector Williamson.

As they settled into a corner booth, Paul's eyes scanned the room nervously. "Are you sure about this, Mary? If we're wrong about Williamson..."

Mary reached across the table, squeezing his hand reassuringly. "We have to trust someone, Paul. And from everything we know about Williamson, he's a good man. He wants justice as much as we do."

The bell above the door chimed, and Detective Inspector Williamson entered, shaking raindrops from his coat. His sharp eyes found them immediately, and he made his way over, his face an unreadable mask.

"Mr. Brankenwall, Miss Postlethwaite," he greeted them, sliding into the booth. "I must admit, I was intrigued by your call. What's this all about?"

Paul and Mary exchanged a glance before Paul leaned in, his voice low. "It's about Gordon Benn's murder, Inspector. We've... we've come across some new information."

Williamson's eyebrows rose slightly, but he remained silent, waiting for them to continue.

Mary produced a manila envelope, sliding it across the table. "This contains copies of some pages from Gordon Benn's personal notebook. It was recently discovered by his daughter, Freda."

As Williamson leafed through the documents, his expression grew increasingly grave. When he looked up, his eyes were sharp with interest. "This suggests a very different scenario than what we presented at trial."

Paul nodded. "We believe there's more to Gordon's murder than what came out in court. We... we want to reopen the investigation. Unofficially."

A heavy silence fell over the table. Williamson's gaze moved between Paul and Mary, assessing them. Finally, he spoke, his voice low and measured.

"Do you two understand what you're getting into? This isn't a game. If what this book suggests is true, you could be stirring up something very dangerous."

Mary leaned forward, her voice earnest. "We know the risks, Inspector. But we also know that the truth needs to come out. For Gordon, for all the victims."

Harry Williamson sat back, his fingers drumming thoughtfully on the table. "I'd be lying if I said I was entirely satisfied with how the original investigation concluded. There were... loose ends. Things that didn't quite add up."

He paused, conflict clear in his eyes. "But to reopen this case, even unofficially... it could jeopardize my career. Hell, it could jeopardize all of us."

Paul met Williamson's gaze steadily. "We understand that, Inspector. We wouldn't have come to you if we didn't think it was absolutely necessary. But we need your help. Your expertise, your access to information. We can't do this alone."

Another long moment of silence stretched between them. Then, with a heavy sigh, Williamson nodded. "Alright. I'm in. But we do this my way. Carefully, methodically. And everything stays off the record. If anyone asks, I'm consulting on a cold case from another district. Understood?"

Paul and Mary nodded, relief and gratitude evident on their faces.

"Thank you, Inspector," Mary said softly. "We know what we're asking of you."

Williamson's expression softened slightly. "I became a detective to find the truth, to serve justice. If we've got it wrong... if the real killer is still out there... well, then we have a duty to make it right."

He gathered up the documents, tucking them securely into his coat. "I'll go through these thoroughly. We'll meet again in a few days to plan our next steps. In the meantime, be careful. Both of you. We don't know who might be watching."

As Williamson stood to leave, he paused, looking back at them with a mix of concern and determination. "We're stepping into murky waters here. But if there's truth to be found, we'll find it. Together."

With that, he was gone, leaving Paul and Mary to contemplate the enormity of what they had just set in motion. They had an ally now, a formidable one. But they also had a stark reminder of the dangers that lay ahead.

As they left the café, the rain had stopped, and a weak sun was breaking through the clouds. It felt, in that moment, like a good omen. The path ahead was uncertain, fraught with risk. But with Williamson on their side, they had taken a crucial step towards uncovering the truth about Gordon Benn's murder – and all the dark secrets that surrounded it.

The real investigation was about to begin.

The atmosphere in the makeshift forensic lab was tense. Paul, Mary, and Detective Inspector Williamson stood silently as Dr. Eleanor Sinclair, the forensic anthropologist, carefully examined the remains laid out on the sterile steel tables before them. The bodies from the Wilton Manor dungeon, long hidden and forgotten, were finally telling their stories.

"Most of the victims appear to be young women," Dr. Sinclair explained, her voice professional but tinged with sadness. "Ages ranging from approximately 16 to 25. Time of death varies, but the earliest remains could be up to 30 years old."

Paul felt a chill run down his spine. These crimes spanned decades, reaching back to before he was born. The weight of his family's dark legacy pressed down on him.

As Dr. Sinclair continued her explanation, the door opened and Nigel entered, his face pale and drawn. Paul moved to his side, concern etched on his features.

"Nigel, are you sure you want to be here for this?" Paul asked quietly.

Nigel nodded, his jaw set. "I need to know, Paul. If there's any chance... I need to be here."

Dr. Sinclair approached one of the tables, gesturing for them to come closer. "This victim has a unique identifying feature," she said, pointing to the skull. "There's a gap where the right front incisor should be. It appears the tooth was lost ante-mortem and replaced with a false tooth, which hasn't survived."

Nigel's sharp intake of breath was audible in the quiet room. His hands gripped the edge of the table, knuckles white.

"Nanny Alice," he whispered, his voice cracking. "She... she had a false front tooth. She used to play-fight with me, pretending to be a pirate with it when I was little."

The room fell silent as the implications of Nigel's words sank in. Mary moved closer, placing a comforting hand on his shoulder.

"Nigel," Williamson said gently, "can you tell us more about Nanny Alice? When did you last see her?"

Nigel closed his eyes, visibly struggling to maintain composure. "I was about six when she left. I remember being so upset... they told me she'd found another job, that she'd moved away. I never... I never questioned it."

Paul's mind raced. "That would have been around 1950, right? It fits with the timeline Dr. Sinclair mentioned."

Dr. Sinclair nodded, her expression grave. "The state of decomposition and the surrounding soil conditions are consistent with that timeframe. We'll need to run more tests to be certain, but..."

"But it's likely her," Nigel finished, his voice barely above a whisper. "All these years, I thought... God, I can't believe this."

As Nigel struggled with this shocking revelation, Paul found himself grappling with a horrifying realization. If Nanny Alice had been one of the earliest victims, that meant his father – the Earl – had been involved in these crimes from the very beginning of his reign.

"We'll need to get a DNA sample from you, Mr. Wyndham," Dr. Sinclair said softly. "To confirm the identification. And if you have any photos of Nanny Alice, they could help with facial reconstruction."

Nigel nodded numbly. "Of course. I'll... I'll look for photos when I get home."

As Dr. Sinclair moved away to prepare the DNA kit, Paul turned to Nigel. "I'm so sorry," he said, the words feeling woefully inadequate.

Nigel met his gaze, grief and anger warring in his eyes. "It's not your fault, Paul. But we need to find out who did this. All of it. No matter where the truth leads."

Williamson, who had been quietly observing, stepped forward. "Mr. Wyndham, when you feel up to it, I'd like to talk to you more about Nanny Alice. Any details you can remember might help us understand what happened."

As they continued to discuss the grim findings, Mary's attention was drawn to one of the other tables. "Dr. Sinclair," she called, "this victim... is that a Saint Christopher medallion?"

The anthropologist moved to examine the remains Mary was pointing to. "Good eye, Ms. Postlethwaite. Yes, it appears to be. It was found with the remains, likely worn by the victim at time of death."

Paul and Williamson exchanged meaningful glances. Could this be Gordon Benn's missing medallion? And if so, what did it mean that it was found with one of the dungeon victims?

As they left the lab later that day, each lost in their own thoughts, the magnitude of what they were uncovering weighed heavily upon them. The dungeon bodies were more than just evidence – they were people, with lives and stories of their own. Nanny Alice was no longer just a fond memory from Nigel's childhood, but a victim of unspeakable crimes.

The investigation had taken a deeply personal turn, and with it, the stakes had risen even higher. As they parted ways, each heading off to follow up on their respective tasks, one thing was clear: they were no longer just seeking justice for Gordon Benn. They were fighting for all the victims, giving voices to those who had been silenced for far too long.

And somewhere in the shadows, watching and waiting, was the person responsible for it all – a killer who had managed to hide their tracks for decades, but whose time was finally running out.

Chapter 53

Dr. Sinclair entered, her face grave as she carried a thick folder of reports. "Thank you all for coming," she began, spreading out several documents on the table. "I have completed a thorough analysis of the remains. What I've found is... well, it's disturbing, to say the least."

She pointed to a chart showing a timeline. "We have identified seven distinct victims. The earliest death dates back to approximately 1940, coinciding with when William Wyndham became Earl. The most recent appears to be from around 1973."

Nigel, now about 30 years old, visibly flinched at the implications, while Paul, approximately 33, felt a chill run down his spine. 1973 - that was just a year before Gordon Benn's murder.

Dr. Sinclair continued, "The victims range in age from 16 to 24 years old. All female. Cause of death varies, but..." she paused, taking a deep breath, "there's evidence of significant trauma in all cases. Some show signs of strangulation, others blunt force trauma to the head."

[...]

Nigel, who had been silent until now, spoke up. "What about... what about Nanny Alice? Was she...?"

Dr. Sinclair's expression softened as she turned to Nigel. "The remains we believe to be Alice date back to around 1951. She would have been one of the earlier victims. Her death appears to have been... quicker than some of the others. I'm so sorry, Mr. Wyndham."

A heavy silence fell over the room as they all absorbed this information. Paul's mind was whirling. The timeline suggested that these crimes had spanned his father's entire reign as Earl, starting from when he first took the title in 1940. How had no one noticed? How had it gone on for so long?

Williamson cleared his throat. "Dr. Sinclair, you mentioned a Saint Christopher medallion found with one of the victims. Were you able to date that particular set of remains?"

Dr. Sinclair nodded, rifling through her papers. "Yes, that victim dates to 1974. Given the state of decomposition and soil analysis, I'd estimate the time of death to be June or July of that year."

Paul and Mary exchanged meaningful glances. That timeframe aligned perfectly with Gordon Benn's murder.

"There's one more thing," Dr. Sinclair added, pulling out a small evidence bag. Inside was a tarnished locket. "This was found with the most recent victim. We managed to get it open."

She carefully extracted a small, faded photograph from the locket. It showed a young woman, smiling brightly at the camera.

Nigel leaned in, his eyes widening in recognition. "I know her," he said softly. "That's Jenny. Jenny Cartwright. She used to work in the village shop. I remember the Countess mentioning she'd moved away suddenly."

Williamson's expression sharpened. "Mr. Wyndham, do you remember when this was?"

Nigel thought for a moment. "It would have been... summer of '73, I think. Yes, because I had just returned from university."

The detective made a note, his face grim. "That fits with Dr. Sinclair's estimate for the most recent victim. We'll need to look into missing persons reports from that time, see if we can match any other names to our victims."

As they continued to discuss the findings, Paul found himself overwhelmed by the scope of the crimes. These weren't just bodies in a dungeon anymore. They were Jenny Cartwright, who worked at the village shop. They were Nanny Alice, who played pirate games with a young Nigel. They were daughters, sisters, friends - all cruelly taken, their stories silenced for decades.

"We need to identify all of them," Paul said suddenly, his voice firm with resolve. "Not just for the investigation, but for them. They deserve to have their names known, their families informed. They deserve to be remembered."

Mary nodded, her eyes shining with unshed tears. "Paul's right. These women were more than victims. They had lives, dreams. We owe it to them to uncover the whole truth."

As they left the lab that day, each carrying the weight of what they'd learned, their determination had only grown stronger. The forensic analysis had provided them with crucial information, timelines, and potential leads. But more than that, it had renewed their commitment to seeking justice.

For Gordon Benn, for Nanny Alice, for Jenny Cartwright, and for all the others whose names they had yet to discover - they would unravel this dark mystery, no matter where it led them. The truth, hidden for so long in the shadows of Wilton Manor, was finally coming to light. And with each revelation, they drew closer to uncovering the identity of a killer who had evaded justice for far too long.

The Egremont Public Library was quiet as Paul, Mary, and Nigel pored over old newspapers, yearbooks, and local records. They had been at it for hours, cross-referencing the information from Dr. Sinclair's report with local history.

"I think I've found something," Mary said suddenly, her voice hushed. She pointed to an article in a yellowed newspaper from 1958. "Look at this. 'Local girl, Emily Fawcett, 17, reported missing. Daughter of prominent businessman Henry Fawcett.'"

Paul leaned in, his brow furrowed. "The age and date match one of our victims. And Fawcett... isn't that the family that owns half the shops in town?"

Nigel nodded grimly. "Yes, and they've always been close to the Wyndhams. I remember countless dinners with the Fawcetts at the manor."

As they continued their research, a disturbing pattern began to emerge. Many of the victims had connections to influential families in the area. There was Lucy Hartley, whose father had been the local magistrate. Sarah Tindall, niece of the former Chief Constable. Each discovery sent a chill through the group, the implications becoming increasingly clear.

"It's not just that these girls were local," Paul said, his voice tight with anger. "It's that they were specifically chosen. Daughters of people with power, influence."

Mary's face was pale as she added another name to their growing list. "But why? Was it about control? Blackmail?"

Nigel ran a hand through his hair, looking shaken. "Or maybe it was about who wouldn't ask too many questions. Who could be... persuaded to accept a story about their daughter running away or having an accident."

The weight of this realization hung heavy in the air. It wasn't just about individual crimes anymore; it was about a systemic abuse of power that had corrupted the very fabric of their community.

As they were about to call it a day, Paul stumbled upon something that made his blood run cold. In a school yearbook from 1965, he found a photo of a smiling young girl named Catherine Benn.

"Mary, Nigel, look at this," he said, his voice barely above a whisper. "Catherine Benn. Any relation to Gordon, do you think?"

Mary's eyes widened as she looked at the photo. "The age fits one of our unidentified victims. And look at the resemblance to Freda."

Nigel quickly flipped through their notes. "Catherine Benn isn't listed among Gordon's known family members. But if she was a victim..."

"It could explain why Gordon was involved with the Earl's activities," Paul finished. "Blackmail, or maybe a misguided attempt to find out what happened to her."

The implications were staggering. If Catherine was indeed related to Gordon and one of the dungeon victims, it added a whole new dimension to Gordon's murder and his involvement with the Earl.

As they left the library, each lost in their own thoughts, they nearly collided with an elderly woman at the entrance. Paul recognized her as Mrs. Pemberton, widow of the former bank manager.

"Oh, I'm so sorry, Mrs. Pemberton," Paul apologized.

The old woman squinted at him, a flicker of recognition passing over her face. "My goodness," she said, her voice quavering slightly. "You look just like... are you related to Annie Brankenwall, by any chance?"

Paul's eyebrows shot up in surprise. "Yes, she was my mother. Did you know her?"

"Oh, yes," the woman nodded, a sad smile playing on her lips. "Annie and I were friends, long ago. I'm Mrs. Pemberton." Her gaze shifted to Nigel, and a shadow seemed to pass over her face. "And Nigel Wyndham. I... I haven't seen you in years."

There was something in her tone, a mixture of sadness and... was it fear? That caught their attention.

"Mrs. Pemberton," Mary said gently, "we're actually doing some research into local history. Would you mind if we asked you a few questions?"

The old woman hesitated, her eyes darting between them. "I... I suppose. What sort of questions?"

Paul took a deep breath, intrigued by this unexpected connection to his mother. "We're looking into some... events that happened over the years. Particularly involving young women who may have gone missing."

Mrs. Pemberton's face went pale. "Oh. Oh, I see." She was silent for a long moment, then spoke in a voice barely above a whisper. "You know, I had a sister once. Younger than me. Beautiful girl. She... she went to work at Wilton Manor in 1943. We never saw her again."

The three exchanged shocked glances. Another victim, another connection they hadn't known about.

"Mrs. Pemberton," Nigel said softly, "would you be willing to tell us more? It could be very important."

The old woman looked at him, tears in her eyes. "After all these years... yes. Yes, I think it's time someone knew the truth."

As they led Mrs. Pemberton to a nearby café, Paul, Mary, and Nigel knew they had stumbled upon a vital piece of the puzzle. The connection to local families ran deeper than they had imagined, and with each new revelation, the scope of the conspiracy grew.

THEY WERE NO LONGER just investigating a series of murders. They were unraveling a web of secrets, lies, and complicity that had ensnared their entire community for decades. And somewhere at the centre of it all was the truth about Gordon Benn's murder – a truth that now seemed more complex and far-reaching than they had ever imagined.

The Crab Fair café was quiet as Paul, Mary, and Nigel sat with Mrs. Pemberton, absorbing the shocking details of her story. Her sister, Elizabeth, had vanished without a trace after going to work at Wilton Manor in 1943. The official story was that she had run off with a soldier, but Mrs. Pemberton had never believed it.

"We were told not to make a fuss," Mrs. Pemberton said, her voice trembling. "The Chief Constable himself came to our house.

Said it would be better for everyone if we just... accepted things as they were."

Paul exchanged a troubled glance with Mary. "Mrs. Pemberton, were there others who had similar experiences? Other families who lost someone?"

The old woman nodded slowly. "There were whispers, you understand. Nothing openly said, but... yes. Over the years, there were others. Young women who disappeared, families who suddenly stopped asking questions."

As they left the café, the weight of this new information hung heavy between them. They walked in silence for a while, each lost in their own thoughts.

"It's not just about the Earl," Mary said finally, her voice low. "It's not even just about the people directly involved in the crimes. It's... it's the whole town."

Nigel nodded grimly. "A conspiracy of silence. People who knew, or suspected, but chose to look the other way. Officials who covered things up. It goes deeper than we ever imagined."

They made their way to the local pub, the Three Tuns, needing a quiet place to process what they'd learned. As they settled into a corner booth, Paul noticed the photos on the wall – a timeline of local history, faces of prominent citizens beaming out from faded black and white images.

"Look at this," he said, pointing to a photo from the 1950s. "There's the Chief Constable Mrs. Pemberton mentioned, standing right next to my father at some town event. And there," he indicated another photo, "that's Henry Fawcett – Emily's father – receiving an award from the Mayor."

Mary's eyes widened as she scanned the photos. "They're all connected. The police, the local government, the business leaders. It's like a web, with Wilton Manor at the centre."

As they continued to study the photos, piecing together connections, they overheard a conversation from a nearby table. Two elderly men were reminiscing.

"Have you heard if they've got the fella that battered old Gordon Benn to death?" one asked

. "No, Terrible business, that."

"Remember when Tom's daughter went missing?" the other one said

The other nodded sagely. "Aye, but what could be done? You didn't cross the Wyndhams in those days. Still don't, if you know what's good for you."

Paul, Mary, and Nigel exchanged shocked glances. Even now, decades later, the culture of silence persisted.

"We need to be careful," Nigel said in a low voice. "If this conspiracy runs as deep as we think, there could be people in power even now who have a vested interest in keeping the past buried."

Mary nodded, her expression determined. "But we can't let that stop us. We owe it to the victims, to their families, to uncover the truth."

Paul ran a hand through his hair, frustration evident in his gesture. "The question is, how do we break through this wall of silence? How do we get people to talk after all these years?"

As they debated their next steps, a young woman approached their table. She looked nervous, glancing around as if to ensure no one was watching.

"Excuse me," she said quietly. "I couldn't help overhearing... are you really looking into the old disappearances?"

They nodded cautiously, and the woman took a deep breath. "My grandmother... she worked as a maid at Wilton Manor in the 60s. Before she died, she told me things. Terrible things. I always thought she was confused, that it couldn't be true. But now..."

As the young woman, Kate, began to share her grandmother's story, Paul, Mary, and Nigel realized they had stumbled upon another thread in the complex tapestry of Egremont's dark history.

The conspiracy of silence had held for decades, maintained by a combination of fear, complicity, and a desire to preserve the town's reputation. But now, with each new revelation, that silence was beginning to crack.

They knew their investigation was not just about solving Gordon Benn's murder anymore. It was about unravelling a web of deceit that had ensnared an entire community for generations. And as they delved deeper, they were acutely aware that they were not just uncovering old secrets – they were challenging the very foundations of power and influence in Egremont.

The path ahead was fraught with danger. Those who had maintained the silence for so long would not give up their secrets easily. But as they listened to Kate's story, Paul, Mary, and Nigel knew they had to press on. For the victims, for their families, and for the soul of Egremont itself, the truth had to come out.

Chapter 54

Paul, Mary, and Nigel sat in the dimly lit study of Wilton Manor, surrounded by stacks of documents, old photographs, and newspaper clippings. They had spent days piecing together Gordon Benn's life, trying to understand the man whose murder had set this whole investigation in motion.

"Here's something interesting," Mary said, holding up a document from 1940. "It's a record of Gordon Benn's exemption from military service. Granted by... the Earl of Egremont."

Paul leaned in, his brow furrowed. "So their connection goes back that far. The Earl was already exerting his influence to keep Gordon close."

Nigel nodded, his expression thoughtful. "It makes you wonder what hold he had over Gordon even then. Or what services Gordon was providing that made him so valuable."

As they continued their research, a picture began to emerge of a man whose life had been intertwined with the Wyndham family for decades. They discovered records of Gordon's marriage in 1950 to a woman named Margaret, and the birth of their daughter, Freda, a year later.

"Look at this," Paul said, pointing to a death certificate. "Margaret Benn, died 1953. Cause of death... complications during childbirth."

Mary's brow furrowed. "That must have been devastating for Gordon. Left alone with a toddler and a newborn."

Nigel was leafing through employment records. "It seems that's when he started working full-time at Wilton Manor. The Earl must have offered him the job... perhaps as a way to help him cope with his loss, or to tighten his control."

They found a photograph of Gordon from the mid-1950s, standing proudly in front of Wilton Manor. Around his neck, clearly visible, was the Saint Christopher medallion that had become such a crucial piece of evidence.

"He never took it off, according to Freda," Mary mused. "I wonder if it was a gift from someone. His wife, maybe?"

As they delved further into Gordon's history, they uncovered a pattern of financial troubles in the years following his wife's death. Unpaid debts, a mortgage in arrears, and then suddenly, in 1955, everything seemed to stabilize.

"This is odd," Mary mused, comparing documents. "His salary at Wilton Manor doesn't account for this sudden financial turnaround. Where did the money come from?"

Paul's expression darkened. "Maybe that's when the Earl started involving him in... other activities. Using his financial troubles to manipulate him."

They spent hours poring over every detail they could find about Gordon's life. His involvement with the local church, his reputation as a skilled handyman, the way he doted on his daughter. But always, there were shadows, hints of a darker side that didn't quite fit with the public image.

As night fell, Nigel made a startling discovery. "I think I've found something about Catherine," he said, his voice tight. "A birth certificate from 1949. Mother's name is listed as Alice Benn."

"Gordon's sister?" Mary asked, leaning in to see.

Nigel nodded. "Must be. And look at this - there's a note in Gordon's notebook from 1965. 'Sixteen years since we lost little Cathy. The pain never goes away.'"

The implications hung heavy in the air. If Catherine was indeed one of the dungeon victims, it added a whole new layer to Gordon's involvement with the Earl's crimes.

"He must have known," Paul said softly. "Or at least suspected. Maybe that's why he stayed involved for so long. Trying to find out what happened to her."

As they continued to piece together Gordon's life, a complex picture emerged of a man trapped between loyalty, fear, and a desperate search for truth. They found evidence of his growing unease in the years leading up to his death - cryptic entries, attempts to reach out to old friends, even a half-written letter to a newspaper editor that was never sent.

"Look at this," Mary said, holding up his worn notebook. "It's some kind of code. Dates, initials, locations. This must be how he kept track of... of the victims."

Paul studied the notebook, his face grim. "This could be the key to unravelling everything. No wonder someone wanted him silenced."

As dawn broke, casting long shadows across the study, they sat back, exhausted but filled with a grim determination. Gordon Benn's life had been a tapestry of tragedy, manipulation, and ultimately, a desperate attempt at redemption.

"We need to talk to Freda again," Nigel said. "There might be more she can tell us now that we know all this."

Paul nodded, his mind racing. "And we need to look into this Alice Benn. If she was Gordon's sister and Catherine's mother, she might be the link we've been missing."

Mary stood, stretching tired muscles. "Whatever happens, we're closer to the truth now. Gordon Benn wasn't just a victim or a perpetrator. He was a man caught in something much bigger than himself, trying to find a way out."

As they prepared to continue their investigation, each of them felt the weight of Gordon's tragic life. They were no longer just solving a murder; they were unravelling a complex web of secrets, lies, and long-buried truths that stretched back decades.

The mystery of Gordon Benn's past had opened up new avenues of investigation, but it had also raised new questions. Who else had been manipulated by the Earl? How many other families had been torn apart by the dark secrets of Wilton Manor?

As they left the study, Paul paused at the door, looking back at the scattered evidence of Gordon's life. "We'll find the truth," he said softly. "For the perverted Gordon Benn, for Catherine, for all of them. No matter where it leads us."

Chapter 55

As the investigation into Gordon Benn's past deepened, Paul, Mary, and Nigel found themselves venturing into increasingly disturbing territory. Their search led them to Matty Benn's Bridge, a seemingly innocuous structure on the outskirts of Egremont that had featured prominently in Gordon's coded notebook.

Standing on the weathered stones of the bridge, Paul felt a chill that had nothing to do with the cool breeze. "So this is where it happened," he murmured, his voice tight. "The rituals, the... sacrifices."

Mary nodded grimly, consulting the notebook. "According to Gordon's notes, they gathered here on specific dates. Solstices, equinoxes, and... other dates that seem to have some significance we haven't figured out yet."

Nigel, who had been examining the structure of the bridge, called out suddenly. "Over here! There's something carved into the stone."

They hurried over, and in the fading light, they could make out a series of symbols etched into the underside of the bridge's arch. The markings were weathered, but still discernible - a crescent moon, a five-pointed star, and what appeared to be a stylized tree.

"These symbols," Mary said, her voice hushed, "they match some of the drawings in Gordon's notebook. He must have been documenting the rituals, maybe even... participating in them."

Back at Wilton Manor, they pored over the notebook, cross-referencing Gordon's cryptic entries with local records and the information they had gathered about the missing women.

"Look at this entry," Paul said, pointing to a page dated June 21, 1965. "It says 'M.B.B. - Full moon. E.W. leads. G.B. assists.' The initials..."

"Earl Wyndham and Gordon Benn," Nigel finished, his face pale. "And M.B.B. must be Matty Benn's Bridge."

As they delved deeper, a horrifying picture began to emerge. Gordon's role had evolved over the years, from reluctant participant to key facilitator. His handyman skills had been put to sinister use, preparing the ritual site and, more disturbingly, disposing of evidence.

They found references to a hidden chamber beneath the bridge, accessible only during certain water levels. Mary's research into local folklore revealed old tales of the bridge being a site of pagan worship long before the current structure was built.

"It's like they co-opted these ancient traditions," Mary said, her voice shaking slightly. "Twisted them into something... monstrous."

One particularly chilling entry caught their attention. Dated 1970, it read: "Cannot continue. The guilt... but E.W. threatens F. Must protect her "

"F must be Freda," Paul said softly. "The Earl was using her as leverage to keep Gordon in line."

Nigel nodded, his expression grim. "It explains why he stayed involved for so long, even as his doubts grew. He was trying to protect his daughter."

As night fell, they made a shocking discovery hidden in the back of the notebook. A list of names, dates, and locations - a record of the victims. Among them, they found confirmation of their earlier suspicions about Catherine Benn.

"July 15, 1965 - C.B. (A's daughter). Failed to protect. Never forgive."

The weight of this revelation hung heavy in the air. Gordon's involvement in his own niece's death seemed to have been a breaking point, the moment his reluctant participation turned into a desperate search for redemption.

"We need to go back to the bridge," Mary said suddenly. "Maybe being there will help us make sense of Gordon's notes."

Under the cover of darkness, they returned to Matty Benn's Bridge. The night was unusually still, the silence broken only by the occasional bleat of sheep in the nearby fields. As they approached, the old stone structure loomed before them, its arch a dark mouth against the starry sky.

Paul switched on his flashlight, the beam cutting through the mist that had begun to gather around the bridge. "It's eerier than I remember," he muttered.

Mary nodded, suppressing a shiver. "Look at the sheep," she whispered, pointing to a group of the animals huddled unusually close to the bridge. Their eyes reflected the flashlight beam, creating an unsettling, almost watchful presence.

As they walked onto the bridge, the sound of their footsteps echoed hollowly. Paul pulled out Gordon's notebook, flipping through the pages. "According to this, the rituals usually took place on the downstream side," he said, moving towards the spot.

Mary followed, her flashlight beam dancing across the weathered stones. "Look here," she said, indicating some faint markings on the bridge's base. "These symbols... they match some of the sketches in Gordon's book."

They spent the next hour examining the bridge, comparing what they found to Gordon's crude notes and drawings. The more they discovered, the more disturbing the picture became. Traces of candle wax in crevices, strange markings carved into hidden spots, even what looked like old bloodstains in one secluded corner.

"God," Paul breathed, his voice tight. "It really happened here. All of it."

A sudden gust of wind made them both jump, and the sheep in the field let out a chorus of alarmed bleats. For a moment, the mist seemed to take on shapes in the moonlight - dancing figures, reaching hands.

Mary grabbed Paul's arm. "Did you see that?" she whispered.

Paul nodded, his face pale. "It's just the mist," he said, but his voice lacked conviction.

As they continued their examination, the weight of Gordon's involvement became increasingly clear. His notebook, filled with dates, crude drawings, and cryptic notes, painted a picture of a man trapped in a world of dark rituals and terrible secrets.

"He was in deep," Mary said softly, looking through the notebook again. "But these later entries... it seems like he wanted out."

Paul nodded grimly. "And it got him killed. We need to take this to Williamson. With the notebook and what we've seen here, we can finally bring the truth to light."

As they prepared to leave, a sheep suddenly darted past them, startling them both. For a split second, Paul thought he saw a figure standing in the shadows beyond the bridge - but when he looked again, there was nothing there.

"Let's go," he said, unable to shake the feeling of being watched. "We've seen enough."

As they hurried back to their car, the mist swirling around their feet, both Paul and Mary knew that their visit to Matty Benn's Bridge had changed everything. The secrets of this place, long buried in shadow and silence, were finally coming to light - and the consequences would shake Egremont to its core.

The investigation into Gordon Benn's murder had led them to uncover a web of ritual killings, ancient practices twisted for evil purposes, and a conspiracy that reached the highest levels of local society. But as they were about to discover, exposing the truth would come at a price they might not be prepared to pay.

Chapter 56

Following their discovery of Gordon's notebook and the revelations about the rituals, Paul, Mary, and Nigel decided to bring Detective Inspector Williamson to Matty Benn's Bridge for a more thorough investigation. They arrived at the site early one misty morning, the bridge looming ominously before them.

Williamson surveyed the area with a practiced eye. "So this is where it all happened," he muttered, his face grim. "Hard to believe something so ordinary could hide such dark secrets."

As they began their search, guided by the information from Gordon's notebook, Mary noticed something odd near the base of the bridge. "Look here," she called out, crouching down. "These markings... they look fresh."

The others gathered around. In the soft earth, partially hidden by overgrown grass, were strange symbols carved into the ground. They matched some of the drawings in Gordon's notebook, but the soil disruption looked recent.

Williamson frowned, examining the markings closely. "This can't be more than a few days old," he said, his voice tight with concern.

Paul felt a chill run down his spine. "But that's impossible. The Earl has been in custody for months and now he's dead. These rituals should have stopped."

"Unless someone else is continuing them," Nigel said quietly, voicing the fear they all shared.

They spread out, searching the area more intensely. Near the water's edge, partially hidden by reeds, Mary found something that made her blood run cold.

"Over here!" she called, her voice shaking slightly.

The others rushed over. There, half-submerged in the shallow water, was a small, ornate dagger. Its blade was dark with what looked horribly like dried blood.

Williamson carefully retrieved the dagger, placing it in an evidence bag. "We'll have this analysed immediately," he said, his professional demeanour barely masking his shock.

As they continued their search, more signs of recent activity emerged. Candle wax drippings in the crevices of the stones. A scrap of fabric caught on a bramble, the material modern and brightly coloured. And most disturbingly, a small pile of bones hidden in a hollow beneath the bridge – animal bones, but arranged in a pattern that matched one of the diagrams in Gordon's notebook.

Williamson, surveying the area, suddenly turned to Mary. "Ah yes, this is where we found your bike, Mary. It's at the station. I'd forgotten all about it... remind me to send it round to you."

Mary blinked in surprise, momentarily distracted from the grim discoveries. "My bike? I'd almost forgotten about that myself, given everything that's happened."

Paul's brow furrowed. "Your bike being here... it connects you directly to this place, Mary. We need to be careful. Whoever is continuing these rituals might see you as a threat."

"This is madness," Nigel said, running a hand through his hair in frustration. "Who could be continuing these rituals? And why?"

Mary's face was pale as she flipped through Gordon's notebook. "According to this, the next significant date for a ritual would be... the summer solstice. That's less than a week away."

The implication hung heavy in the air. Someone was not only continuing the rituals but potentially planning another one in the very near future.

Williamson's jaw was set as he surveyed the evidence they had gathered. "We need to set up surveillance here," he said firmly. "Catch whoever is doing this in the act."

As they prepared to leave, each lost in their own thoughts about the disturbing discoveries they had made, the urgency of their investigation had taken on a new dimension. It was no longer just about uncovering past crimes and solving Gordon Benn's murder. Now, they were in a race against time to prevent another tragedy.

The rituals that they thought had ended with the Earl's arrest were clearly on-going. Someone – or perhaps a group of people – was carrying on his dark legacy. And with the summer solstice approaching, the clock was ticking.

Paul, Mary, Nigel, and Williamson knew that their next steps would be crucial. They needed to identify who was behind these continued rituals, protect potential victims, and put an end to this cycle of violence once and for all. But as they drove back to town, they couldn't shake the feeling that they were being watched, that somewhere in the shadows, the true mastermind behind these horrors was always one step ahead.

The mystery of Matty Benn's Bridge had deepened, and the danger was more present than ever. The final confrontation was approaching, and the stakes couldn't be higher.

Chapter 57

The small café on the outskirts of Carlisle was nearly empty when Paul, Mary, and Williamson arrived. They had chosen this location for its privacy, away from prying eyes in Egremont. In a corner booth, a woman sat alone, her hands wrapped tightly around a mug of tea.

Sarah Collins was in her early fifties, but the lines on her face spoke of hardships beyond her years. As they approached, her eyes darted nervously between them, settling finally on Williamson's reassuring presence.

"Mrs. Collins," Williamson said gently, "thank you for agreeing to meet with us. I know this isn't easy for you."

Sarah nodded tightly. "When you contacted me, I... I almost didn't come. I've spent years trying to forget."

As they settled into the booth, Mary leaned forward, her voice soft. "We understand how difficult this must be, Mrs. Collins. But your experience could be crucial in stopping these crimes from happening again."

Sarah's hands trembled slightly as she took a sip of tea. "I was seventeen when it happened," she began, her voice barely above a whisper. "Summer of 1960. I was working as a maid at Wilton Manor, saving money for college."

Paul and Mary exchanged glances. The timeline fit with what they had uncovered about the Earl's activities.

"There was a party at the manor," Sarah continued. "Grand affair, lots of important people. I was helping in the kitchens when one of the other staff – I think his name was Gordon – told me the Earl wanted to see me."

THE DOLFIN CHALICE

At the mention of Gordon's name, Williamson leaned in. "Gordon Benn?"

Sarah nodded. "Yes, that sounds right. He seemed... uncomfortable. Like he didn't want to be doing it. But I didn't think much of it at the time."

As Sarah recounted her story, a horrifying picture emerged. She had been drugged, taken to Matty Benn's Bridge in the dead of night. There were others there – men in robes, chanting in a language she didn't understand.

"I remember the Earl," she said, her voice shaking. "He was leading it all. There was a knife, an altar of some kind. I thought... I thought I was going to die."

Mary reached out, gently placing her hand over Sarah's. "But you escaped. How?"

A flicker of something – pride, perhaps, or defiance – flashed in Sarah's eyes. "They underestimated how strong the drugs were. When they untied me for the... the ritual, I managed to break free. I ran into the woods. I don't know how long I ran, but eventually I made it to the road. A truck driver found me, took me to the hospital."

"Did you report it to the police?" Williamson asked, though he suspected he knew the answer.

Sarah laughed bitterly. "I tried. But who was going to believe a maid's word against the Earl of Egremont? The police chief himself told me it would be better if I just forgot about it. Said it must have been a nightmare brought on by too much drink at the party."

As they continued to talk, Sarah provided details that corroborated much of what they had already uncovered – the layout of the ritual site, the symbols used, even descriptions of some of the participants. But it was when they showed her photographs of known victims that the most chilling revelation came.

"This one," Sarah said, pointing to a photo of a young woman. "I remember her. She was there that night, helping with the ritual. But she looked... scared. Like she was being forced to participate."

Paul studied the photo. "That's Jenny Cartwright. We found evidence that she was one of the victims a few years later."

Sarah nodded sadly. "I always wondered what happened to her. She helped me, you know. When I was running away. She distracted the others, gave me a chance to escape."

As their conversation wound down, Sarah turned to them, her eyes filled with a mix of fear and determination. "You really think these rituals are still happening? After all this time?"

Williamson nodded gravely. "We have evidence of recent activity at the bridge. Mrs. Collins, would you be willing to make an official statement? Your testimony could be crucial in bringing those responsible to justice."

Sarah was quiet for a long moment, her internal struggle visible on her face. Finally, she straightened her shoulders. "Yes. Yes, I'll do it. For Jenny, for all the others who didn't escape. It's time the truth came out."

As they left the café, each lost in thought about Sarah's harrowing story, Paul turned to Mary and Williamson. "We need to look into the other staff from that time. If Jenny was coerced into participating before becoming a victim herself, there might be others."

Mary nodded, her face grim. "And we need to identify the other participants Sarah mentioned. Some of them might still be involved in the current rituals."

Williamson's expression was one of grim determination. "We're getting close. With Sarah's testimony and the evidence from the bridge, we might finally have enough to bring this whole dark chapter to a close."

But as they drove back to Egremont, none of them could shake the feeling that they were racing against time. The summer solstice was approaching, and somewhere out there, the ones continuing the Earl's legacy were preparing for another ritual. The question now was: could they stop it in time?

Following their meeting with Sarah Collins, Paul, Mary, and Williamson gathered in the detective's office to analyse the new information. The weight of Sarah's testimony hung heavy in the air as they began to piece together its implications.

"Sarah's account gives us a clearer picture of the Earl's direct involvement," Williamson said, pinning a timeline to his cork board. "We now have eyewitness testimony placing him at the centre of these rituals as far back as 1960."

Mary nodded, flipping through her notes. "And it's not just his presence. Sarah described him as the leader, the one directing the entire ceremony. This wasn't just him turning a blind eye to others' actions – he was the driving force behind it all."

Paul leaned back in his chair, his face grim. "What strikes me is the scale of it. Sarah mentioned other participants, people in robes. This wasn't just the Earl and a few close associates. It was an organized group."

"A cult, essentially," Williamson added. "With the Earl at its head."

They turned their attention to Gordon Benn's role. Mary referred back to her notes. "Sarah's description of Gordon is interesting. She said he seemed uncomfortable, like he didn't want to be involved."

Paul nodded. "It fits with what we've pieced together about him. A reluctant participant, at least initially. But Sarah's testimony puts him there in 1960 – that's earlier than we thought his involvement began."

"It makes you wonder," Williamson mused, "how long had the Earl been grooming him? How did he go from that reluctant participant to the man we know was deeply involved in later years?"

They discussed the possibility that Gordon's initial involvement might have been under duress, perhaps blackmail or threats to his family. This added a new layer of complexity to their understanding of his character and motivations.

Mary brought up another crucial point from Sarah's testimony. "The mention of Jenny Cartwright is significant. We knew she was a victim, but now we know she was coerced into participating before becoming a victim herself."

"It suggests a pattern," Paul said, his voice tight with anger. "The Earl and his associates might have been grooming young women, forcing them to participate in smaller roles before... before making them the centrepiece of the ritual."

This realization led them to revisit the list of known victims, looking for others who might fit this pattern. It also raised questions about other staff members at Wilton Manor who might have been involved or victimized.

Williamson added another note to his board. "We need to look into the truck driver who found Sarah. If we can track him down, his testimony could corroborate her story and potentially provide additional details."

As they continued to analyze Sarah's testimony, they found themselves with a clearer but more disturbing picture of the Earl's crimes. The rituals were more organized, more deeply rooted in the community, and had been going on for longer than they had initially believed.

"There's one more thing," Mary said, her voice hesitant. "Sarah mentioned symbols, chants in a language she didn't understand. It suggests these rituals have a specific origin or tradition. We might need to consult an expert in occult practices to fully understand what we're dealing with."

Paul nodded, though the idea clearly made him uncomfortable. "Agreed. The more we understand about the nature of these rituals, the better chance we have of predicting their next move and stopping them."

As their meeting concluded, each of them felt the weight of what they had learned. The Earl's crimes were more extensive, more organized, and reached further back in time than they had imagined. Gordon Benn's involvement was longer-standing but also more complex, raising new questions about his journey from reluctant participant to key player.

They had gained valuable insights, but with each new piece of information, the case seemed to grow more complex. As they prepared to pursue these new leads, they knew they were racing against time. The summer solstice was approaching, and somewhere out there, the Earl's legacy continued.

The truth was coming to light, but the darkness they were uncovering was deeper and more terrifying than any of them had imagined.

Chapter 58

The study at Wilton Manor had become a makeshift investigation headquarters. Papers, photographs, and timelines covered every available surface. Paul, Mary, and Williamson had been working tirelessly, piecing together the complex puzzle of Gordon Benn's murder and its connection to the broader conspiracy.

"Something's not adding up," Mary said, frowning as she compared two documents. "Look at this. The Earl was supposedly in London on the day Gordon was murdered, attending a hospital appointment. We have multiple witnesses confirming his presence there."

Paul leaned over to examine the evidence. "But that doesn't necessarily mean he didn't order the hit. He could have arranged it from a distance."

Williamson shook his head, a thoughtful expression on his face. "True, but remember what we learned from Sarah's testimony. The Earl was always present for the rituals. He led them personally. It doesn't fit his pattern to delegate something this important."

As they continued to review the evidence, more inconsistencies began to emerge. The brutality of Gordon's murder stood out as particularly odd.

"The Earl's previous victims were all killed as part of the rituals," Paul mused. "Clean, almost ceremonial. But Gordon's death was messy, violent. It doesn't fit the Earl's usual method."

Mary nodded, her brow furrowed in concentration. "And then there's the timing. Gordon was killed just days before he planned to go to the authorities. How did the Earl know that if he was in London?"

A heavy silence fell over the room as the implications of their observations sank in. It was Williamson who finally voiced what they were all thinking.

"What if we've been looking at this all wrong?" he said slowly. "What if the Earl didn't order Gordon's murder at all?"

The idea was shocking, challenging everything they had believed about the case. But as they began to re-examine the evidence with this new perspective, a different picture started to emerge.

They revisited Gordon's diary entries from the weeks leading up to his death. There were cryptic references to disagreements, tensions within the group involved in the rituals.

"Look at this entry," Paul said, pointing to a passage. "'T.C. becoming unstable. Worried about what he might do if pushed too far.' T.C... could that be Thomas Carter?"

Mary's eyes widened. "Thomas Carter, the farmer who found Angela Benn's body? We know he was involved with the Countess, but could he have been part of the rituals too?"

As they dug deeper, they uncovered more evidence suggesting that there had been a power struggle within the group. Gordon's growing desire to confess and expose the truth had created factions. Some, like the Earl, wanted to silence him quietly. Others, it seemed, had more violent intentions.

"What if," Williamson posited, "Gordon's murder wasn't sanctioned by the Earl at all? What if it was a rogue action by someone who feared exposure more immediately?"

The pieces began to fall into place. The brutality of the murder suggested a crime of passion rather than a calculated hit. The timing aligned with Gordon's plans to go to the authorities, information that someone closer to him might have discovered.

"We need to look into Thomas Carter more closely," Paul said, his voice tight with the tension of their discovery. "And anyone else who was closely involved with Gordon in those final weeks."

As they worked to realign their investigation with this new theory, the complexity of the case became even more apparent. The Earl was still at the centre of the broader conspiracy, but Gordon's murder now appeared to be a separate, though related, crime.

MARY SAT BACK, RUNNING a hand through her hair. "If we're right about this, it means the killer might still be out there. Someone who was part of the Earl's inner circle but acted on their own."

Williamson nodded grimly. "And someone who might be continuing the rituals even with the Earl in custody. This could be the key to understanding the recent activity at Matty Benn's Bridge."

The realization added a new urgency to their investigation. Not only were they trying to uncover past crimes, but they were also potentially dealing with an active threat. Someone who had killed once to keep the secrets of the rituals and might be willing to do so again.

Chapter 59

As the investigation into Gordon Benn's murder and the cult's activities intensified, Paul found himself drawn back to the beginning of their journey. He remembered Mary's account of her bike ride, her rest at the ancient stone circle on Cold Fell - the Druid's Circle.

"Mary," he said suddenly, interrupting a strategy meeting with Williamson, "what if Matty Benn's Bridge isn't the only ritual site?"

Mary's eyes widened with realization. "The Druid's Circle on Cold Fell," she breathed. "Of course. How could we have overlooked it?"

Williamson leaned forward, intrigued. "What are you two talking about?"

As they explained about the ancient stone circle, a new picture began to emerge. They quickly organized an expedition to the site, bringing along Dr. Eleanor Sinclair, the forensic anthropologist who had examined the dungeon victims.

Upon reaching the Druid's Circle, they were struck by the eerie atmosphere. The ancient stones loomed against the skyline, their weathered surfaces holding centuries of secrets.

Dr. Sinclair moved methodically around the site, her trained eye picking up details the others might have missed. "Look here," she called, pointing to a barely visible marking on one of the stones. "This symbol... it matches one we found in the dungeon at Wilton Manor."

As they continued their examination, more connections emerged. Traces of wax, similar to what they'd found at Matty Benn's Bridge. Disturbed earth that, upon closer inspection, yielded bone fragments.

"These aren't ancient," Dr. Sinclair confirmed grimly. "They're recent. Within the last few decades, I'd say."

The implications were staggering. Not only had the cult been active at multiple sites, but they had been tying their rituals to ancient practices, perhaps seeking to tap into old power.

As they delved deeper into this new angle, more disturbing connections came to light. Historical records revealed that the land containing the Druid's Circle had changed hands multiple times over the centuries, always passing between a select group of families.

"Look at these names," Mary said, poring over old land deeds. "Wyndham, of course. But also Jenkins, Blackwood, and... Alderson."

Paul's head snapped up. "Alderson? As in Mayor Alderson, The guy who has run Egremont council for years?"

Williamson's face was grim. "This conspiracy goes deeper than we imagined. It's not just about the Earl or even this current generation. This has been going on for centuries."

As they continued to unravel the threads of this wider conspiracy, more powerful figures came into focus. The current Lord Mayor of Carlisle was descended from one of the families linked to the land. A prominent Member of Parliament had attended Oxford with Edward Blackwood.

"It's like a shadow government," Mary said, her voice hushed. "These families, these individuals... they've been wielding power from the darkness for generations."

The resolution of Gordon Benn's murder - now clearly tied to his threat to expose not just the Earl, but this entire centuries-old conspiracy - had led them to uncover something far more vast and terrifying than they had initially imagined.

Paul ran a hand through his hair, his mind reeling. "How do we even begin to tackle something like this? These people... they have connections everywhere."

Williamson's jaw was set with determination. "We do it piece by piece. We've already exposed some of them. We keep pulling at the threads until the whole tapestry unravels."

As they gathered their evidence and prepared to take their findings to higher authorities, they knew they were stepping into dangerous territory. The conspiracy they were unraveling had tentacles reaching into every aspect of power in the region, perhaps even beyond.

Mary voiced what they were all thinking: "We're not just solving a murder anymore. We're not even just exposing a cult. We're challenging a power structure that's been in place for centuries."

Paul nodded, his expression a mix of determination and apprehension. "And they're not going to give up that power without a fight."

As night fell over Cold Fell, the ancient stones of the Druid's Circle standing silent witness, the team knew they were on the precipice of something monumental. The final confrontation wouldn't just be with Edward Blackwood or the immediate cult members. They were challenging an entire hidden system of power and corruption.

The murder of Gordon Benn had been just the tip of the iceberg. As they prepared to dive deeper into this vast conspiracy, they knew the dangers ahead were greater than anything they had faced before. But the truth - and justice for countless victims over the centuries - drove them forward.

Chapter 60

As night fell over Wilton Manor, the team knew they had reached a turning point in their investigation. The true killer of Gordon Benn was still at large, and the web of conspiracy surrounding the Earl's crimes was even more tangled than they had imagined.

Paul looked at the others, his expression a mix of determination and concern. "We need to move carefully from here. Whoever killed Gordon might realize we're getting close to the truth. We could be putting ourselves in danger."

Mary nodded, her face set with resolve. "We've come too far to back down now. For Gordon, for all the victims, we need to see this through."

Williamson began pinning new notes to their investigation board, rearranging the connections between suspects and events. "First thing tomorrow, we start digging into Thomas Carter and anyone else who was close to Gordon in those final weeks. The killer made a mistake somewhere, and we're going to find it."

As they prepared to delve deeper into this new line of inquiry, each of them felt the weight of their discovery. The case had taken an unexpected turn, but with it came the hope of finally uncovering the full truth behind Gordon Benn's murder and the dark legacy of the Earl's rituals.

The hunt for the true killer had begun, and the stakes had never been higher.

As Paul, Mary, and Williamson continued to re-examine the evidence surrounding Gordon Benn's murder, they found themselves questioning everything they thought they knew about the case.

"We know Thomas Carter reported finding Angela's body," Williamson mused, "and he was forthcoming about his involvement with the Countess. It seems unlikely he'd kill Gordon and not report it, given his past behaviour."

Mary nodded, flipping through her notes. "You're right. We need to look at this from a different angle. Who else was close to the Earl, someone who might have had the motive and opportunity to kill Gordon?"

Paul's eyes widened as a thought struck him. "What about Nigel Wyndham's former tutor? Remember, Nigel mentioned him a few times - Edward Blackwood. He was a constant presence at Wilton Manor for years."

Williamson quickly pulled out the file on Blackwood. "Edward Blackwood, hired by the Earl in 1960 to tutor young Nigel. He lived on the estate until 1975... the year Gordon was killed."

As they delved deeper into Blackwood's background, a disturbing picture began to emerge. Born in 1930 in London, Blackwood had shown early promise as a scholar, specializing in ancient languages and folklore. His academic career, however, had been derailed by his growing obsession with the occult.

"Look at this," Mary said, pointing to an entry in Gordon's notebook. "'E.B. becoming more erratic. Talks of taking the rituals further. Must speak with the Earl about controlling him.'"

Paul leaned in, his brow furrowed. "E.B. - Edward Blackwood. It fits."

They began to piece together a new theory. Blackwood, brought into the Earl's inner circle through his position as Nigel's tutor, had become deeply involved in the rituals. But unlike the Earl, who seemed to view them as a means to an end, Blackwood had become fanatical.

"What if," Williamson posited, "Blackwood saw Gordon's plan to confess as a betrayal of the rituals themselves, not just a threat to the Earl?"

Mary nodded slowly. "It would explain the brutality of the murder. Not a calculated hit, but a crime of passion, a ritualistic killing in itself."

As they dug further, they discovered that Blackwood hadn't disappeared as they initially thought. He had been living quietly in Egremont all along, in a terraced house on East Road.

"He's been right under our noses this whole time," Paul said, disbelief evident in his voice.

Williamson's jaw set with determination. "We need to move on this. Now."

Within hours, a team was assembled. As dawn broke over Egremont, police vehicles converged on East Road. The quiet terraced house, unremarkable among its neighbours, suddenly became the centre of intense activity.

The raid was swift and decisive. Blackwood, now in his mid-60s, offered no resistance as officers burst through his door. But it was what they found inside that sent shockwaves through the investigation team.

The house was a treasure trove of incriminating evidence. Ancient texts on occult practices lined the shelves. Ritual objects, some stained with what looked horribly like dried blood, were carefully arranged on altars. And in a locked study, they found detailed records of the rituals performed over decades, including the names of participants.

As Williamson and his team pored over the evidence, a chilling realization dawned. The list of cult members included names of prominent local officials - the police chief, several town councillors, even a judge.

"This goes deeper than we ever imagined," Williamson said, his face grim.

Under questioning, Blackwood finally broke. He admitted to killing Gordon Benn, describing in chilling detail how he had turned the murder into a ritual sacrifice.

"Gordon was a weak pervert," Blackwood spat, his eyes wild. "He would have destroyed everything we had worked for. I did what had to be done to protect the sacred rites."

As Blackwood was led away in handcuffs, Paul, Mary, and Williamson gathered to assess the situation.

"We've got Blackwood," Williamson said, "but this is far from over. The cult's tentacles reach into every level of local government. Rooting them all out is going to be a massive undertaking."

Paul nodded, his expression determined. "Whatever it takes. We've come too far to back down now."

Mary squeezed his hand supportively. "We're in this together. All of us."

As they left Blackwood's house, now swarming with forensic teams, they knew that while they had solved the mystery of Gordon Benn's murder, they had uncovered an even larger conspiracy. The dark legacy of Egremont ran deeper than they had ever imagined, and bringing it fully to light would be the challenge of a lifetime.

But with Blackwood's arrest and the evidence seized from his home, they had taken a crucial first step. The truth was finally coming to light, and with it, the hope of justice for Benn and all the other victims of the cult's dark rituals.

Chapter 61

The small conference room at the Egremont police station had been transformed into a makeshift command centre. Walls were covered with photos, timelines, and family trees. In the centre of it all stood Paul, Mary, and Detective Inspector Williamson, surrounded by a team of forensic experts and social workers.

"We're ready to start notifying families," Williamson said, his voice solemn. "Thanks to the information from Gordon's notebook and the records we uncovered, we've been able to identify most of the victims from the dungeon."

Mary nodded, her face pale but determined. "How many?"

"Fifteen," Williamson replied. "Fifteen lives, fifteen families who've been waiting for answers for years."

The weight of this number hung heavy in the air. These weren't just bodies in a dungeon anymore; they were daughters, sisters, friends - each with a name and a story.

Paul picked up a file. "Catherine Benn," he said softly. "Gordon's niece. We should start with Freda. She deserves to know what happened to her cousin."

The next few days were a blur of emotional meetings and heart-wrenching revelations. Each notification was different, but all were marked by a mix of grief, relief, and often, a quiet anger at the years of not knowing.

Freda Benn sat stoically as they explained about Catherine, her hands clenched tightly in her lap. "I always hoped..." she said, her voice barely above a whisper. "Even after all these years, I hoped she'd just run away. That she was living a happy life somewhere."

Mary reached out, gently covering Freda's hand with her own. "She never forgot you," she said softly. "We found notes in Gordon's book. He wrote about how much Catherine loved you, how she always talked about her little cousin Freda."

Tears spilled down Freda's cheeks as years of uncertainty finally gave way to grief - and a measure of peace.

Not all notifications went as smoothly. The parents of Emily Fawcett, one of the earliest victims, reacted with disbelief and anger.

"You're lying," Mr. Fawcett shouted, his face red with fury. "Our Emily wouldn't have got mixed up in anything like that. The Earl was a family friend!"

It took time and patience to help them understand, to show them the evidence that proved their daughter had been a victim, not a willing participant.

One of the most poignant moments came when they identified Jenny Cartwright, the young woman who had helped Sarah Collins escape. Her elderly mother wept as they told her of Jenny's final act of bravery.

"That's my Jenny," she said through her tears. "Always thinking of others, even at the end."

As the identifications continued, the impact on the community became palpable. Families who had lived with whispers and sideways glances for years now stood tall, their loved ones' names cleared of any implied wrongdoing.

The process took an emotional toll on the investigators as well. Mary found herself staying late one night, staring at the wall of photos.

"It's overwhelming, isn't it?" Paul's voice came from behind her. "Thinking about all the lives affected, all the years of pain."

Mary nodded, wiping away a tear. "But at least now they know. At least now they can properly mourn."

As the final identifications were made, a memorial service was planned. The whole town seemed to turn out, standing in solidarity with the families of the victims. Where once there had been secrets and shame, now there was a community united in grief and a determination to heal.

During the service, Paul stood to address the gathering. "These women were more than victims," he said, his voice carrying across the hushed crowd. "They were daughters, sisters, friends. They had dreams, hopes, lives that were cut tragically short. By remembering them, by speaking their names, we ensure that they are not defined by how they died, but by how they lived."

As he read out the names of the victims, a bell tolled for each one. Catherine Benn. Emily Fawcett. Jenny Cartwright. Fifteen names, fifteen lives, finally honored and remembered.

The identification of the victims marked a turning point in the investigation. It brought a measure of closure to long-suffering families and helped to heal old wounds in the community. But it also steeled the resolve of Paul, Mary, and Williamson to see the case through to the end, to ensure that justice was served not just for Gordon Benn, but for all the victims of this decades-long conspiracy.

As they left the memorial service, they knew that their work was far from over. The wider conspiracy still loomed, powerful figures were still to be brought to account. But they had given names to the nameless, voices to the silenced. And in doing so, they had taken the first crucial steps towards true justice and healing for Egremont.

Chapter 62

The arrest and confession of Edward Blackwood had sent shockwaves through Egremont. In a surprising turn of events, Blackwood had stepped forward, admitting to the murder of Gordon Benn. His motive, he claimed, was to protect the ancient cult to which they both belonged. Benn, it seemed, had been on the verge of exposing their activities, a betrayal Blackwood couldn't allow.

The subsequent trial was brief but intense. Blackwood, his face a mask of grim determination, had pleaded guilty to the murder. Despite pressure from the prosecution and his own defense team, he steadfastly refused to implicate any other members of the cult. His loyalty, even in the face of a life sentence, was unwavering. The judge, noting the severity of the crime and Blackwood's lack of remorse, handed down the maximum sentence: life imprisonment.

As Blackwood was led away from the courtroom, many questions remained unanswered. Who were the other members of this mysterious cult? What activities had Benn threatened to expose? And what secrets did Blackwood still hold, even as he faced a lifetime behind bars?

It was these lingering questions that led Paul and Mary to request a meeting with Blackwood in prison. Despite initial reluctance from both Blackwood and the prison authorities, they had finally secured an interview. As they sat across from the man who had confessed to murdering Gordon Benn, they hoped to unravel the mysteries that still surrounded the case.

The stark fluorescent lights of the prison visiting room cast harsh shadows across Edward Blackwood's gaunt face. Paul and Mary sat across from him, the metal table between them cold and unyielding.

The stark fluorescent lights of the prison visiting room cast harsh shadows across Edward Blackwood's gaunt face. Paul and Mary sat across from him, the metal table between them cold and unyielding.

"I don't know why I agreed to this," Blackwood muttered, his eyes darting between them.

Paul leaned forward. "Because deep down, you want to talk. You want someone to understand."

Blackwood snorted. "Understand? You couldn't possibly-"

"Try us," Mary interjected softly. "We know about the rituals, Mr. Blackwood. We know about the Dolfin chalice."

At the mention of the chalice, Blackwood's demeanor changed. His eyes flashed with a mixture of anger and reverence. "The chalice," he hissed. "Its loss was... catastrophic. A piece of history, nearly ten centuries old, gone."

"What made it so special?" Mary pressed, her voice gentle but probing.

Blackwood's lips curled into a bitter smile. "Special? In the right hands, in the right situation, it had... power. Power you couldn't begin to comprehend."

Paul exchanged a glance with Mary before asking, "Is it true the Earl smashed it during an argument with the Countess?"

"Lies!" Blackwood spat. "It had a small chip, nothing more. We tried to have it repaired."

"At the pottery in Ravenglass," Mary said, her heart racing. "Where it was originally crafted by nuns."

Blackwood's eyes narrowed. "How do you-"

"We've done our research," Paul interrupted. "But what we don't understand is why you didn't retrieve it."

Blackwood leaned back, a sardonic chuckle escaping his lips. "Bureaucracy. It was registered to Gordon Benn. They wouldn't release it to me."

"But you have plans to get it back," Mary stated, watching Blackwood's reaction carefully.

A slow, unsettling smile spread across Blackwood's face. "Oh yes. We're buying the pottery."

"We?" Paul questioned.

"The Dolfins," Blackwood replied, his voice taking on a reverent tone. "Our high priest... he communes with the gods. Finding the money was trivial for him."

As Blackwood began to describe the structure of the cult - the Elders, Warriors, Initiates, and the "chosen" virgins - Mary felt a chill run down her spine. The details of the rituals, from the chanting in Old Norse to the herbal mixtures and symbolic sacrifices, painted a picture both fascinating and horrifying.

"And the chalice?" Mary asked, her voice barely above a whisper. "What role did it play?"

Blackwood's eyes took on a faraway look. "When the high priest poured the liquid into the chalice... magic happened. Steam and smoke would rise, and from it... the spirits of our Viking ancestors emerged."

Paul and Mary exchanged sceptical glances, but Blackwood seemed lost in the memory.

"Sometimes, on the bridge, old Matty herself would appear, blessing the virgins in the water."

As they left the prison, Mary turned to Paul, her face pale. "We can't let them get the pottery. If they think the replica is the real chalice..."

Paul nodded grimly. "We need to find the real one. Your father was the last to know its whereabouts. There must be some clue."

Chapter 63

The late afternoon sun cast long shadows across the living room as Mary sat with her mother, both nursing cups of tea that had long since gone cold. The weight of recent events hung heavy in the air.

"Mum," Mary began hesitantly, "I need to ask you about Dad... about the chalice."

Her mother's hands tightened around her mug. "I wondered when we'd have this conversation," she said softly. "Your father... he was so secretive about it towards the end."

As her mother spoke of her father's growing obsession with the chalice, his late nights in the study, and his cryptic comments about 'protecting history,' Mary felt a mix of emotions wash over her - curiosity, sadness, and a tinge of frustration at the secrets kept even from family.

"You know," her mother said, a wistful smile playing on her lips, "we haven't touched his study since... since he passed. Maybe it's time we did."

Together, they climbed the stairs to the small room that had been her father's sanctuary. Mary hesitated at the door, her hand on the knob. With a deep breath, she pushed it open.

The smell hit her first - old books, leather, and the faint scent of her father's pipe tobacco. It was like stepping into a time capsule. Dust motes danced in the sunbeam streaming through the window, settling on piles of papers, books, and curios that cluttered every surface.

"Oh, John," her mother whispered, running a hand along the back of her father's chair. "Always the collector."

As they began to sift through the papers on the desk, memories flooded back. Mary found a dried flower pressed between the pages of a book - a souvenir from a family picnic years ago. Her mother discovered a drawer full of birthday cards they'd given him, each one carefully preserved.

"He kept everything," Mary marveled, her throat tight with emotion.

It was as they were examining the old rolltop desk that Mary noticed something odd. "Mum, look at this," she said, pointing to a slight disColouration in the wood grain of one panel. "It doesn't match the rest."

Together, they pressed and prodded until, with a soft click, a hidden compartment sprang open. Inside, nestled in velvet, lay an object wrapped in soft cloth.

With trembling hands, Mary lifted it out and slowly unwrapped it. As the last fold fell away, the chalice gleamed in the fading sunlight, its surface catching the light and throwing it back in dazzling patterns.

"It's beautiful," her mother breathed.

Beneath where the chalice had lain were several unfinished letters. Mary read them aloud, her voice shaking slightly. They were addressed to various Staffordshire potteries, inquiring about restoration services for a "delicate and historically significant artifact."

"He was trying to restore it," Mary realized. "But why didn't he finish? Why hide it away?"

Her mother shook her head, tears glistening in her eyes. "Your father always said that sometimes, keeping something safe was more important than making it perfect. I never understood what he meant until now."

As they sat there, the chalice between them, surrounded by the remnants of her father's life, Mary felt a profound sense of connection - to her father, to her family's history, and to the weighty responsibility that now fell to her.

"What do we do now?" she asked softly.

Her mother reached out, squeezing her hand. "We do what your father would have wanted. We protect it, and we find the truth."

As the sun dipped below the horizon, casting the study into shadow, Mary knew that this discovery was just the beginning. The real challenge lay ahead - unravelling the mysteries of the chalice, the cult, and the legacy her father had left behind.

As Mary and her mother made their discovery in the study, Paul was deep in conversation with his lawyer, Hetherington. The news Hetherington shared left Paul stunned.

"You're saying the money behind Cerámica Innovadora... it's from the Wyndham estate?" Paul asked, his voice barely above a whisper.

Hetherington nodded gravely. "It appears your father, or someone with access to the estate's finances, set up a complex series of shell companies. The trail leads back to Wilton Manor."

Paul sank into a chair, his mind reeling. "So if the sale of the pottery goes through..."

"You'd essentially be buying it from yourself," Hetherington finished. "As the likely inheritor of the Wyndham estate, you'd be on both sides of the transaction."

Mary picked up the receiver and dialed Paul's number, her heart racing. After a few rings, his voice came through the line.

"Hello?"

"Paul, it's Mary," she said, trying to keep her voice steady. "We've found it. The real chalice. It was in Dad's study all along."

There was a moment of stunned silence before Paul responded. "Are you certain? Mary, this is... this is incredible. I'll come right over."

"Yes, please do," Mary replied. "And Paul... be careful. We don't know what this means yet."

As she hung up the phone, Mary turned back to her mother, who was still examining the chalice.

"What do you think Dad knew about this?" she asked softly.

Margaret shook her head, a mix of emotions playing across her face. "I'm not sure, love. Your father kept many things close to his chest. But I have a feeling we're about to uncover some long-buried family secrets."

Mary nodded, her mind racing with possibilities. The chalice, sitting innocuously on her father's desk, seemed to pulse with the weight of history and hidden truths.

The sound of a car pulling up outside broke the moment. Paul had arrived, and with him, the promise of answers – and likely more questions. As Mary moved to let him in, she cast one last glance at the chalice. Whatever secrets it held, they were about to be revealed, for better or worse.

When he arrived at Mary's house, she pulled him aside before showing him the chalice. "Paul, there's something you need to know," she began, her eyes searching his face. "We found letters... my father was trying to get the chalice restored. He was writing to potteries in Staffordshire."

Paul took a deep breath. "Mary, I've just learned something too. The Spanish company, the one trying to buy your family's pottery? The money... it's coming from the Wyndham estate."

Mary's eyes widened in shock. "But that means..."

"If the sale goes through, and if I inherit as we expect, the pottery would end up belonging to me," Paul finished.

They stood in silence for a moment, the weight of this revelation hanging between them.

"We need to tell my family," Mary said finally. "This changes everything."

As they gathered Mary's mother and siblings to share both the discovery of the chalice and the news about the Wyndham estate's involvement, the complexity of their situation became clear.

"So what do we do?" Mary's brother Steve asked, looking between Paul and Mary. "Do we still sell? Do we keep the real chalice secret?"

"And what about the cult?" Mary's mother added, her voice tinged with worry. "If they find out we have the real chalice..."

Paul and Mary exchanged a look, both realizing that their next steps would have far-reaching consequences. The chalice, glinting innocently on the table before them, seemed to hold not just centuries of history, but the key to their future.

"Whatever we decide," Paul said slowly, "we need to be careful. This isn't just about the pottery or the chalice anymore. It's about unraveling the last of Egremont's secrets, and maybe... maybe finally putting an end to the cult's influence."

Chapter 64

The late afternoon sun cast long shadows across the manicured lawn of Wilton Manor. Mary and Paul sat on a weathered stone bench, the chalice nestled between them in a velvet-lined box. Its jewels caught the fading light, throwing prisms across their faces.

Paul ran a hand through his hair, his brow furrowed. "It's ironic, isn't it? Something so beautiful, yet it's caused so much pain."

Mary nodded, her fingers tracing the chalice's delicate engravings. "I keep thinking about all those girls, the rituals. How many lives have been ruined because of this thing?"

"And now it's our responsibility," Paul sighed. "What do we do with it?"

Mary bit her lip, considering. "I almost wish we could destroy it, you know? Just end its legacy once and for all."

Paul shook his head. "I understand the feeling, but... it's a piece of history. Destroying it won't undo what's been done."

"No, you're right," Mary agreed. "But keeping it feels wrong too. Like we're just waiting for history to repeat itself."

They sat in silence for a moment, the weight of their decision hanging heavy in the air.

"What about Dr. Harrison?" Paul suggested suddenly. "The coroner. He's dealt with evidence from the case. Maybe he'd have some insight."

Mary's eyes lit up. "That's not a bad idea. He'd understand the importance of preserving evidence, but also the need to keep it safe."

The next day, they found themselves in Dr. Harrison's cluttered office. The coroner listened intently as they explained the situation, his weathered face thoughtful.

"It's quite a conundrum you've got there," he mused, leaning back in his creaky chair. "You're right to be cautious. Objects with this kind of history... they tend to attract the wrong sort of attention."

"What would you suggest?" Mary asked.

Dr. Harrison stroked his beard. "Have you considered the British Museum? They have the facilities to study it safely, and the security to keep it out of the wrong hands."

Paul and Mary exchanged glances. "That... actually makes a lot of sense," Paul said slowly.

"It would be preserved, studied," Mary added. "But out of reach of anyone who might misuse it."

Dr. Harrison nodded. "Exactly. And it would be a way to honor the victims, don't you think? Bringing the truth to light, but in a controlled, respectful manner."

As they left the coroner's office, Mary felt a weight lift from her shoulders. "It feels right," she said. "Like we're finally breaking the cycle."

Paul squeezed her hand. "I'll make some calls to the British Museum. Let's end this chapter of Egremont's history the right way."

The next morning found Paul in Hetherington's office, surrounded by stacks of legal documents. Sunlight streamed through the windows, illuminating motes of dust dancing in the air.

Hetherington peered at Paul over his reading glasses. "You're sure about this, Paul? Withdrawing the investment is no small matter."

Paul nodded, his jaw set. "I'm sure. I can't be part of buying Mary's family business, especially not with money from my father's estate. It's... it's not right."

Hetherington leaned back in his chair, studying Paul. "You understand the implications, I assume? This could significantly affect your inheritance. The estate's finances are... complex."

"I understand," Paul said firmly. "But some things are more important than money. I need to do this, for Mary, for her family... and for myself."

A small smile tugged at Hetherington's lips. "Your father would never have made this decision, you know. You're a better man than he was, Paul."

Paul blinked, taken aback by the unexpected compliment. "I... thank you. I'm just trying to do what's right."

Hetherington nodded, reaching for a thick folder. "Well then, let's get to work. We'll need to untangle this investment carefully. It won't be easy, but we'll make it happen."

As he turned back to the financial labyrinth before him, he felt a sense of peace. Whatever challenges lay ahead, he knew he was on the right path.

THE FAMILIAR SCENT of clay and glaze filled the air as Mary gathered her family in the pottery's main workshop. Afternoon light streamed through the high windows, illuminating the dust motes swirling above the wheels and kilns. Uncle Brian, Steve, and Andrew sat on stools, their expressions a mix of curiosity and concern.

Mary took a deep breath, steeling herself. "Right, so as you all know, the deal with the Spanish company has fallen through."

"Bloody hell," Steve muttered, running a hand through his hair. "So we're back to square one, are we?"

Uncle Brian leaned forward, his weathered hands clasped. "Not necessarily, lad. Mary's been working on alternatives, haven't you, love?"

Mary nodded, a small smile playing on her lips. "That's right. Remember Plan B we discussed a few weeks back? I think it's time we revisited that."

Andrew's eyes lit up. "You mean opening up to the public? The whole tourism angle?"

"Exactly," Mary said, her enthusiasm growing. "Look, we all agreed that selling wasn't ideal. This pottery, it's more than just a business. It's our heritage, our family's legacy. So why not share that with others?"

She moved to the large whiteboard on the wall, quickly sketching out a rough plan. "We partner with the Ravenglass and Eskdale Railway. They're always looking for new attractions to bring in tourists. We offer tours, workshops, demonstrations. Really show people the art and craft of what we do."

Steve looked skeptical. "And you think people will be interested in watching us make pots?"

Mary grinned. "Not just watching. Doing. Imagine pottery classes where people can make their own pieces. We've got the space, the equipment. And think about it - every tourist who makes something here is taking home a piece of Postlethwaite Pottery. It's marketing and production rolled into one."

Uncle Brian nodded slowly, a smile creeping across his face. "You know, your father always talked about doing something like this. Said the pottery had stories to tell."

"Exactly," Mary said softly. "And now we can tell those stories. Not just about our family, but about the whole history of pottery in this region. The chalice, the connection to the abbey - it's all part of a rich tapestry we can share."

Andrew, who had been quiet, suddenly spoke up. "What about seasonal events? Christmas markets, summer festivals. We could really make this place come alive year-round."

Mary beamed at him. "That's brilliant, Andrew. We could collaborate with other local artisans too. Make it a real celebration of Cumbrian craftsmanship."

Steve, still looking unsure, sighed. "It sounds great in theory, but what about the practical side? We'd need to renovate, hire more staff. That all costs money we don't have."

Mary nodded, acknowledging his concern. "You're right, it will take investment. But think about it - we're not just selling individual pieces anymore. We're selling an experience. And with the tourism board behind us, I really think we can make this work."

She looked around at her family, her voice softening. "I know it's a risk. But isn't it a risk worth taking? To keep this place, this legacy, alive and thriving?"

There was a moment of silence as everyone considered her words. Then Uncle Brian stood up, placing a hand on Mary's shoulder. "Your father would be proud, love. I say we go for it."

Andrew nodded enthusiastically. "I'm in. This could be exactly what we need to breathe new life into the place."

All eyes turned to Steve. He looked around at the workshop, taking in the wheels, the kilns, the shelves of finished pieces. Finally, he cracked a smile. "Alright, alright. Let's give it a shot. But I'm not dressing up as a Victorian potter or anything, just so we're clear."

Laughter filled the workshop as the tension broke. Mary felt a wave of relief and excitement wash over her. "Right then," she said, grinning. "Let's get to work. We've got a pottery to reinvent."

As they began to discuss the details, throwing ideas back and forth, Mary couldn't help but feel a sense of rightness. This was how it should be - the family coming together, honouring their past while looking to the future. Whatever challenges lay ahead, they would face them together, just as the Postlethwaites always had.

Chapter 65

The evaluation room at the British Museum was bathed in stark, white light, designed to reveal every minute detail of the artifacts examined within. Mary and Paul stood to one side, watching with a mixture of anticipation and trepidation as Dr. Eleanor Fairfax, the Sotheby's expert, carefully lifted the chalice from its protective case.

Dr. Fairfax's eyes widened almost imperceptibly as she turned the chalice in her gloved hands. "Extraordinary," she murmured, almost to herself. "The workmanship is simply exquisite."

She looked up at Mary and Paul, her professional demeanor barely concealing her excitement. "This piece is truly remarkable. The age alone would make it valuable, but the quality of the craftsmanship and the gemstones... well, it's quite exceptional."

Paul leaned forward slightly. "Can you tell us more about the stones?"

Dr. Fairfax nodded, holding the chalice under a magnifying glass. "The centrepiece is what we call a 'moonlight ruby' - a rare, almost translucent variety. This one is approximately 15 carats, and in this condition... I'd estimate its value alone at around £12 million."

Mary gasped softly, her hand finding Paul's arm. Dr. Fairfax continued, her voice taking on a tone of reverence.

"Then we have these diamonds - six of them, each about 3 carats, of exceptional clarity. And these smaller emeralds... the way they're set is unlike anything I've seen from this period. It's as if the artisan was centuries ahead of their time."

She carefully set the chalice down, removing her gloves. "Taking into account the gemstones, the craftsmanship, the historical significance, and its provenance... at auction, we'd be looking at a value between £30 to £40 million. Possibly more, given its unique nature."

Paul let out a low whistle. "That's... that's incredible."

Dr. Fairfax smiled. "It truly is a national treasure. You've done a great service by bringing it to light."

Later that afternoon, Mary and Paul found themselves in the office of Dr. Jonathan Blackwood, the British Museum's curator of medieval artifacts. The chalice sat on his desk, seeming to glow in the warm lamplight.

Dr. Blackwood leaned back in his chair, his eyes twinkling with excitement. "I cannot express how grateful we are to you both, and to the Postlethwaite family. This chalice... it's going to revolutionize our understanding of medieval craftsmanship and religious artifacts."

Mary smiled, though there was a hint of sadness in her eyes. "We're just glad it's somewhere it can be properly studied and protected."

Dr. Blackwood nodded understanding. "Indeed. And we intend to honor your family's role in preserving this piece of history." He leaned forward, his tone becoming more formal. "On behalf of the British Museum, we'd like to offer a finder's fee of £6 million to Postlethwaite Pottery."

Paul's eyebrows shot up. "That's... extremely generous."

"It's well deserved," Dr. Blackwood insisted. "This isn't just about the monetary value of the chalice. Your actions have preserved a priceless piece of our shared cultural heritage. That's something we take very seriously here."

Mary's mind was racing. "That kind of money... it could secure the pottery's future. Fund all our plans for renovation and expansion."

Dr. Blackwood smiled warmly. "I'm glad to hear it. We'd very much like to maintain a relationship with Postlethwaite Pottery.

Perhaps we could discuss future collaborations? Educational programs, special exhibitions..."

As they left the museum, stepping out into the busy London street, Mary and Paul were quiet, still processing the enormity of what had just transpired.

"It doesn't seem real, does it?" Mary said finally. "All that value, tied up in one small object."

Paul nodded, his expression thoughtful. "And yet, the real value isn't in the gold or the jewels. It's in the history, the stories... and in finally bringing the truth to light."

Mary squeezed his hand. "We did the right thing, didn't we? Bringing it here?"

"We did," Paul affirmed. "It's safe now. No more dark rituals, no more secrets. Just... history, as it should be."

As they hailed a taxi to take them back to their hotel, both felt a sense of closure. The chalice, with all its beauty and darkness, was now where it belonged. And they were free to write the next chapter of their own story.

Chapter 66

The sun was setting over Egremont, casting long shadows across the grounds of Wilton Manor. Paul and Mary sat on a stone bench in the garden, the weight of their discoveries heavy on their shoulders. The past few weeks had been a whirlwind of revelations, each more shocking than the last.

Paul broke the silence first. "I keep thinking about my father," he said softly. "When my mother told me about their secret marraige in France, I had this image of him as this distant, almost mythical figure. The Earl of Egremont. And now..."

Mary reached out, gently squeezing his hand. "Now you know the truth. It's a lot to process."

Paul nodded, his eyes distant. "The Egremont legacy. It's always been a part of me, even when I didn't fully understand it. But now I see it for what it really was - a mask for unspeakable crimes, a centuries-old conspiracy."

"But that's not all it has to be," Mary said, her voice firm. "You have the power to reshape that legacy, Paul. To turn it into something positive."

They sat in thoughtful silence for a moment, considering the enormity of that task.

"I've been thinking about the victims," Mary continued. "About how we can honor them, bring some kind of closure to their families."

Paul turned to her, curiosity in his eyes. "What did you have in mind?"

"A memorial," Mary said, her eyes lighting up with purpose. "Not just a statue or a plaque, but something living. A garden, perhaps, here on the grounds of Wilton Manor. A place where families can come to remember their loved ones, where the community can heal."

Paul nodded slowly, the idea taking shape in his mind. "And a foundation," he added. "We could use the Egremont resources to set up a foundation in their names. To help other families of missing persons, to fund research into solving cold cases."

As they continued to discuss their ideas, the weight of their discoveries began to feel less like a burden and more like a responsibility - a chance to make amends for the sins of the past.

"You know," Paul said, a hint of wonder in his voice, "when I first came here, I was so focused on uncovering the truth about my father, about Gordon Benn's murder. I never imagined it would lead to all this."

Mary smiled softly. "Life has a way of taking us on unexpected journeys. But I think we're exactly where we need to be."

Their conversation turned to the future, to the challenges that still lay ahead. The wider conspiracy was still to be fully unravelled, powerful figures brought to justice.

"It won't be easy," Paul mused. "These people, this network - they've had centuries to embed themselves in every level of society."

Mary's face set with determination. "No, it won't be easy. But it's necessary. For the victims, for their families, for the whole community. We've started something here, Paul. We can't stop now."

As they walked back towards the manor, both felt a sense of purpose that went beyond solving a mystery or uncovering a conspiracy. They were part of something larger now, a movement to right long-standing wrongs and bring light to dark places.

Chapter 67

At the centre of the garden stood a simple stone monument, engraved with the names of the dungeon victims. Surrounding it, flowers of every Colour bloomed - a vibrant testament to the lives that had been lost and the hope that now grew in their memory.

Paul's hand rested on the cool stone, his fingers tracing the names etched there. "It's hard to believe how much has changed in such a short time," he said softly.

Mary nodded, her eyes taking in the peaceful scene. "From uncovering your father's crimes to saying goodbye to Yvette... it's been quite a journey."

They walked slowly through the garden, the gravel path crunching softly beneath their feet. The air was filled with the gentle sound of a nearby fountain - a sound of life and renewal.

"I've been thinking about what you said," Paul began, "about using the Egremont title to make real changes. I think... I think that's what I need to do. Not just for the victims and their families, but for the whole community."

Mary smiled, a mix of pride and affection in her eyes. "I think that's a wonderful decision, Paul. The title of Earl of Egremont has been associated with darkness for too long. It's time to bring it into the light."

They paused by a bench overlooking the garden. In the distance, they could see the pottery, its chimneys standing tall against the sky.

"And what about you, Mary?" Paul asked. "How are things progressing with the pottery, it must help knowing you have so much financial backing?"

"It's been challenging," Mary admitted, "but also exciting. We're finding ways to blend tradition with innovation, just as you're doing here at Wilton Manor."

Paul chuckled, shaking his head. "Always another challenge to solve, isn't there?"

"Speaking of which," Mary said, her tone growing serious, "Williamson called this morning. They've made some progress on tracing the wider conspiracy. It seems the rabbit hole goes deeper than we thought."

Chapter 68

The Parisian summer sun cast long shadows across the cemetery as Paul Brankenwall stood before a freshly covered grave. The headstone, simple yet elegant, read "Yvette Beaumont Brankenwall, 1944-1975 Beloved and Never Forgotten."

Mary Postlethwaite stood a respectful distance away, her presence a silent pillar of support. As the last of the mourners dispersed, Paul turned to her, his eyes red-rimmed but clear.

"It's strange," he said softly. "For ten years, I've been fighting to keep her alive. Now that she's gone, I feel... I don't know. Sad, of course, but also..."

"Free?" Mary offered gently.

Paul nodded, a look of guilt flashing across his face. "Is that terrible of me?"

Mary shook her head, taking his hand. "No, Paul. It's human. You've been carrying this weight for so long. It's okay to let it go."

As they walked through the quiet paths of the cemetery, Paul found himself talking about Yvette – not the comatose woman he'd visited in the hospital for a decade, but the vibrant, laughing girl he'd fallen in love with in his youth.

"She loved life so much," he said, a faint smile playing on his lips. "She would have hated being trapped in that hospital bed. I think... I think maybe it's better this way. She's free now too."

They made their way to a small café near the Seine, the same one where Paul and Yvette had shared their first date all those years ago. As they sat down, Paul looked out over the river, his expression thoughtful.

"What now?" Mary asked, sensing the shift in his mood.

Paul turned back to her, a new resolve in his eyes. "Now we go home. There's work to be done."

The flight back to England was a quiet one, both Paul and Mary lost in their own thoughts. As the plane descended towards Carlisle Lake district airport, Paul broke the silence.

"I've been thinking about the Egremont estate," he said. "About what to do with it all."

Mary nodded encouragingly. "And?"

"I want to turn it into something good," Paul said, his voice growing stronger with each word. "A foundation, maybe. Something to help victims of abuse, to fund research into coma patients. To make amends, in some small way, for all the harm my father caused."

Mary squeezed his hand. "That sounds wonderful, Paul. And the title? Have you decided what you'll do about that?"

Paul shook his head. "I'm still not sure. Part of me wants to refuse it entirely, but another part thinks... maybe I could use it. Use the influence it brings to make real changes."

As they drove from the airport towards Egremont, a comfortable silence settled between Paul and Mary, both lost in thought about recent events. Finally, Paul broke the quiet.

"So, how are things progressing with the pottery?" he asked, glancing at Mary. "I've been wondering how it all worked out after I withdrew support from the Spanish company."

Mary's face lit up with a mix of excitement and relief. "Paul, I can't thank you enough for that. At first, I was worried, but it turned out to be the best thing that could have happened."

Paul raised an eyebrow, intrigued. "Oh? How so?"

"Well," Mary began, her voice animated, "when the Spanish deal fell through, we had to fall back on Plan B – you know, opening up to the public, working with the railway, all that. And then, with the British Museum's finder's fee... it's like all the pieces just fell into place."

Paul nodded, a smile spreading across his face. "That's fantastic, Mary. How's the family taking it?"

Mary chuckled. "Oh, you should have seen it. Steve and Andrew were skeptical at first, kept going on about how we'd be 'selling out' our heritage. But once I showed them the numbers and laid out the full plan, they came around pretty quickly."

"And the rest of the family?"

"Jenny – Howard's widow – she's been our biggest cheerleader," Mary said, her voice softening. "I think she sees it as a way to honor Howard's memory while securing the pottery's future. And Uncle Brian... well, he's just thrilled to see the place buzzing with activity again."

Paul reached over and squeezed Mary's hand. "You've done an amazing job, Mary. Balancing tradition with progress, just like we talked about. And to think, if the Spanish deal had gone through..."

Mary nodded, her expression turning serious for a moment. "We might have lost everything that makes the pottery special. Your decision, Paul... it gave us the push we needed to forge our own path."

"Team effort," Paul said with a grin. "We make a pretty good pair, don't we?"

As they drove on, the familiar landscape of Egremont coming into view, both felt a sense of accomplishment and anticipation. The pottery's future was secure, but more than that, it was evolving in a way that honored its past while embracing new possibilities.

"You know," Mary said thoughtfully, "I think this is just the beginning. With the museum connection and all the new ideas we're implementing... who knows where we'll be in a few years?"

Paul nodded, his eyes on the road ahead. "Wherever it is, I'm glad I'll be there to see it. Partner," he added with a wink.

Mary laughed, the sound full of joy and promise. As they approached the town, both felt ready for whatever new adventures – and challenges – lay ahead.

As they crested the hill overlooking Egremont, the ancient town spread out before them, Paul felt a surge of emotion. This place, with all its history and secrets, was his heritage. But it was also his responsibility.

"There's still so much we don't know," he mused. "The Egremont Legacy, the mysterious chalice, the connection between our families..."

Mary smiled. "Sounds like we've got our work cut out for us."

The next few weeks were a whirlwind of activity. Paul met with lawyers to discuss the establishment of the Egremont Foundation. Mary dove into the modernization plans for the pottery, working closely with her syblings ensuring that the Postlethwaite traditions were maintained.

One evening, as they sat in the garden of Wilton Manor – soon to be the headquarters of the new foundation – Nigel joined them, a bottle of wine in hand.

"To new beginnings," he said, pouring three glasses.

As they clinked glasses, Paul felt a sense of peace settling over him. Yvette was at rest, his father was facing justice, and he had found a way to move forward that honored the past while working towards a better future.

"You know," Nigel said thoughtfully, "there's still the matter of Angela's funeral in Brittany. We should start making arrangements."

Paul nodded. "Yes, it's time. She deserves to be laid to rest properly, back where she began."

Mary leaned forward, her eyes sparkling with an idea. "What if we combined the trip to Brittany with some research? The convent where Angela grew up might have records that could shed light on some of our unanswered questions."

Paul and Nigel exchanged excited glances. "The Egremont Legacy," Paul murmured.

"The chalice," Nigel added.

"The truth," Mary concluded.

As the sun set over Egremont, casting the ancient town in a golden glow, the three friends raised their glasses once more.

"To the future," Paul said.

"To the past," Nigel added.

"To the journey," Mary finished.

And as they sat there, bound by friendship, shared experiences, and the promise of mysteries yet to be unraveled, they knew that while one chapter had closed, another – equally thrilling and full of possibility – was just beginning.

"You know," Paul said, breaking the comfortable silence, "with everything that's happened, I've been thinking a lot about the vineyard in St. Giles."

Mary nodded, remembering. "The one you told me about when we first met on Cold Fell? With your French number plates, I should have guessed you had deeper connections to France."

Paul smiled, a mix of fondness and sadness in his eyes. "Yes, that's the one. My mother and I moved there from Brittany when I was young. It wasn't until later that I discovered the Earl – my father – had bought it for us."

"He must have felt guilty," Mary mused, "about abandoning his rightful heir."

Paul nodded, his expression thoughtful. "I think so. It's strange to think about now, knowing everything we do. The vineyard has always been a symbol of... well, of complicated things. My mother's love, my father's absence, and now..."

"And now?" Mary prompted gently.

"Now, I'm not sure," Paul admitted. "It's been a part of my life for so long, through everything with Yvette, and even during these past months of upheaval. Jean-Pierre, my manager there, he's been keeping things running smoothly. I've neglected it terribly, but somehow, it's still there, waiting."

They paused by an old oak tree, its gnarled branches stretching out over a small pond. Mary turned to face Paul, her expression serious.

"How are you really doing, Paul? With everything – Yvette, your father, the trial, all of it?"

Paul was quiet for a moment, his gaze distant. "It's... complicated," he said finally. "There's a part of me that feels relieved, I suppose. Relieved that Yvette is at peace, that my father can no longer hurt anyone. But there's also this overwhelming sense of... I don't know, responsibility? Like I've inherited not just a title and an estate, but a duty to make things right."

Mary nodded, understanding. "And the vineyard? Where does that fit into all of this now?"

Paul's eyes lit up slightly. "You know, I'm not sure yet. But thinking about it now, I wonder if it might be a place to... reconnect with my past while also looking to the future. To honor my mother's memory and perhaps... perhaps even find a way to reconcile the complicated legacy my father left behind."

"That sounds like a powerful idea, Paul," Mary said, squeezing his hand encouragingly.

As they continued their walk, Paul asked, "And you, Mary? How are you coping with everything?"

Mary took a deep breath, considering her words carefully. "It's been a whirlwind, that's for sure. There are moments when I feel completely overwhelmed, like I'm in over my head. But then I think about my family – Steve, Andrew, Jenny – how we've all come together through this. And I think about the pottery, all the generations of Postlethwaites who've poured their lives into it. It gives me strength, you know?"

Paul nodded, understanding all too well the power of legacy – both its burdens and its gifts.

"And then there's us," Mary continued, her voice softening. "Everything we've been through together, everything we've uncovered. It's terrifying and exhilarating all at once."

They found themselves at the edge of the property, looking out over the Cumbrian landscape. The first stars were beginning to appear in the darkening sky.

"You know," Paul said thoughtfully, "perhaps we should plan a trip to the vineyard. After Angela's funeral in Brittany and our research at the convent. It could be a chance to... I don't know, come full circle in a way. To revisit the place where my journey really began."

Mary's eyes lit up. "That sounds perfect. And who knows? Maybe the vineyard holds some clues of its own. About the Egremont Legacy or any of the other mysteries we've yet to solve."

Paul chuckled, shaking his head in amusement. "Always the investigator, aren't you?"

"Look who's talking," Mary retorted with a grin.

As they made their way back to the manor, a comfortable silence fell between them. Both were lost in thoughts of the future – of foundations to be built, mysteries to be solved, and new chapters to be written.

"You know," Paul said as they reached the main house, "for the first time in a very long time, I'm actually looking forward to what comes next. Despite everything – or maybe because of it – I feel... hopeful."

Mary smiled, linking her arm through his. "Me too, Paul. Whatever comes next, we'll face it together."

As they entered the warm glow of Wilton Manor, now a symbol not of dark secrets but of new beginnings, both Paul and Mary felt a sense of peace settling over them. The past few months had been a crucible, testing them in ways they never could have imagined. But they had emerged stronger, wiser, and more united than ever.

The future, with all its unknowns and possibilities, awaited them. And for the first time in a long while, they were ready to embrace it with open arms.

Chapter 69

In the weeks following the, Postlethwaite Pottery buzzed with a new energy. The influx of capital had brought with it both excitement and apprehension, as the family business entered a new era.

Mary stood in the newly renovated design studio, watching as her brother Steve worked a new line of vases. The sight of cutting-edge technology alongside traditional pottery wheels was still jarring, but Mary was beginning to see the potential in this blend of old and new.

"What do you think?" Steve asked, holding up a delicate, intricately patterned vase fresh from the kiln.

Mary examined it closely, running her fingers over the fine details. "It's beautiful," she admitted. "But can we replicate this level of intricacy with traditional methods?"

Steve grinned. "That's the beauty of it. We use computorised prototyping, then our skilled artisans recreate it by hand. We're marrying technology with craftsmanship."

As if on cue, Andrew walked in, his hands clay-stained from working on the wheel. He eyed the vase with a mix of skepticism and curiosity.

"I have to admit," he said grudgingly, "it does open up some interesting possibilities."

Later that afternoon, Mary met with Jenny, Howard's widow, in the pottery's small café. The space had been renovated as part of the modernization efforts, now serving as a showcase for Postlethwaite pieces and a gathering place for staff and visitors alike.

"How are you finding the changes?" Mary asked, stirring her tea.

Jenny looked around, a soft smile on her face. "It's different, certainly. But I think Howard would have approved. He always said the pottery needed to evolve to survive."

Mary nodded, feeling a pang at the mention of her late brother. "I just hope we're doing right by his memory, by the family legacy."

"Oh, Mary," Jenny reached out, squeezing her hand. "You've done wonderfully. Look around – the pottery is thriving. We're reaching new markets, creating new designs, all while maintaining the quality and craftsmanship that's always been our hallmark."

As the day wound down, Mary took a walk through the pottery, observing the seamless blend of traditional and modern that now defined the space. In the main workshop, long time employees worked alongside new hires, sharing knowledge and techniques. The gift shop, once a small afterthought, had been expanded and modernized, showcasing both classic Postlethwaite designs and the new, innovative pieces born from the Museums financing.

Outside, construction had begun on a new visitor centre, which would include a museum detailing the history of Postlethwaite Pottery and its connection to the region. Mary paused by the construction site, remembering her conversations with Paul about honouring the past while embracing the future.

As she stood there, lost in thought, she felt a presence beside her. It was Uncle Brian, his weathered face creased in a smile.

"Quite a change, isn't it?" he said, nodding towards the construction.

Mary nodded. "Sometimes I wonder what Great-Great-Grandfather Postlethwaite would think of all this."

Uncle Brian chuckled. "I reckon he'd be right proud. He was an innovator in his day, you know. Always looking for ways to improve, to push the boundaries of what was possible with clay and glaze."

Later that evening, as Mary locked up the office, she paused to look at the old family photograph on the wall – generations of

Postlethwaites standing proudly in front of the pottery. She thought about the mysterious chalice, the connection to the old monastery, the secrets still waiting to be uncovered.

With a smile, she realized that the pottery's tale, like her own, was far from over. There were still pages to be filled in their story, mysteries to be solved. And with the support of her family and her evolving relationship with Paul, she felt ready to face whatever challenges and adventures lay ahead.

As she walked home, Mary's mind was already racing with ideas for the future – new designs to explore, markets to enter, and perhaps, just perhaps, a few more family secrets to uncover along the way.

The pottery, like the Postlethwaite family itself, was adapting, evolving, and thriving. And Mary couldn't wait to see what the next chapter would bring.

Chapter 70

Epilogue: New Beginnings ....The gentle lapping of waves against the hull of the small yacht was a soothing counterpoint to the warm Mediterranean breeze. Paul Brankenwall stood at the helm, his eyes scanning the horizon as he guided the vessel along the coast of southern France. Behind him, Mary Postlethwaite emerged from the cabin, two glasses of wine in hand.

"I still can't believe you talked me into this," Mary said, a smile playing on her lips as she handed Paul a glass.

Paul grinned, accepting the wine. "A working holiday, remember? We're supposed to be tracking down leads on that Spanish connection."

"Is that what we're calling it?" Mary teased, settling beside him.

As the sun began to set, painting the sky in brilliant hues of orange and pink, they reflected on the whirlwind of the past year. The resolution of the Egremont case, the establishment of the victim's memorial, the ongoing work with the foundation - and through it all, the slowly evolving nature of their relationship.

"You know," Mary said softly, "there were times I thought this would never happen. Us, here, like this."

Paul's expression softened as he gazed at her. "I know. For so long, I couldn't let myself even consider the possibility. But now..."

He didn't need to finish the sentence. They both knew how much had changed since Yvette's passing. The night they had finally come together, weeks after the funeral, had been a culmination of years of unspoken feelings and growing trust.

"Do you ever wonder," Paul mused, "what might have happened if we hadn't met that day on Cold Fell? If you hadn't been so persistent in uncovering the truth?"

Mary chuckled. "Knowing me, I'd probably still be trying to solve the mystery of the missing bike. And you'd be..."

"Lost," Paul finished simply. "I'd be lost."

As the last rays of sunlight disappeared below the horizon, Paul set the autopilot and turned to face Mary fully. "I never properly thanked you, you know. For believing in me, for standing by me through everything. Even when I couldn't offer you anything more than friendship."

Mary reached up, cupping his cheek gently. "You offered me the truth, Paul. And in the end, that was worth waiting for."

Their kiss was soft, unhurried, filled with the promise of a future neither had dared hope for not so long ago.

As they broke apart, Paul took a deep breath, his hand reaching into his pocket. "Mary, there's something I've been wanting to ask you."

Mary's eyes widened as Paul dropped to one knee, producing a small velvet box. Inside nestled a ring, its design reminiscent of the intricate patterns they'd seen on the Dolfin chalice.

"Mary Postlethwaite," Paul began, his voice full of emotion, "you've been my partner in solving mysteries, in facing the darkest parts of my family's legacy, and in building a new future. Will you be my partner in life? Will you marry me?"

Tears welled in Mary's eyes as she nodded, barely able to speak. "Yes," she whispered. "Yes, of course I will."

As Paul slipped the ring onto her finger, they both marveled at how far they'd come. From that chance meeting on Cold Fell to this moment, their lives had been transformed in ways they never could have imagined.

The stars were beginning to appear, twinkling against the darkening sky. In the distance, the lights of a coastal town beckoned - another stop on their journey, another lead to follow.

"So," Mary said finally, a hint of mischief in her voice as she admired her ring, "what's our next mystery to solve? Hidden treasures? Ancient conspiracies? Or are we just going to enjoy being together for a while?"

Paul laughed, pulling her close. "Why can't we do both? After all, we've got pretty good at balancing the extraordinary with the everyday."

As the yacht sailed on through the night, Paul and Mary stood together at the helm, ready to face whatever adventures lay ahead. The ghosts of Egremont still lingered, and there were undoubtedly more secrets to uncover. But for now, they had each other, and the open sea before them - a new beginning, full of possibility.

Back in Egremont, the newly renovated Postlethwaite Pottery Visitor Centre was thriving. Tourists from the Ravenglass and Eskdale Railway filled the workshops, eager to try their hand at the potter's wheel. In a glass case near the entrance, a replica of the Dolfin chalice gleamed, a testament to the rich history they now shared openly with the world.

At Wilton Manor, the Egremont Foundation was making strides in supporting victims of abuse and funding research into historical crimes. The victim's memorial garden bloomed with new life, a place of reflection and hope.

The yacht cut through the inky waters, leaving a trail of phosphorescent foam in its wake. Paul and Mary stood at the helm, their figures silhouetted against the gradually lightening sky. The first tentative rays of sunlight began to paint the horizon, turning the clouds into a canvas of pink and gold.

Mary leaned into Paul, her voice barely above a whisper. "It feels like we're sailing right off the edge of the world, doesn't it?"

Paul nodded, his arm tightening around her waist. "Into uncharted territory. Rather fitting, I'd say."

As the coastline of Egremont faded into the distance, the weight of the past seemed to lift from their shoulders. The grand old house, with its centuries of secrets and sorrows, was now just a speck on the horizon - significant, but no longer looming over them.

"Do you think we'll ever truly understand it all?" Mary mused, her eyes fixed on the point where sea met sky. "The legacy, the chalice, the connections between our families?"

Paul was quiet for a moment, considering. "I'm not sure we're meant to understand it all," he said finally. "But I think we've done what matters most - we've brought the truth to light, and we've chosen to move forward rather than being trapped by the past."

As if in agreement, a pod of dolphins suddenly appeared alongside the yacht, their sleek bodies arcing gracefully through the waves. Mary laughed in delight, the sound carried away by the sea breeze.

"Look at them, Paul! It's like they're showing us the way."

Paul smiled, drinking in the joy on Mary's face. "To new adventures, my love. And new mysteries to solve."

The sun climbed higher, its warmth chasing away the last vestiges of night. In the distance, a flock of seabirds took flight, their cries echoing across the water. It was a new day, full of promise and possibility.

As Paul and Mary sailed on, the legacy of Egremont Dawn's First Light

The yacht cut through the inky waters, leaving a trail of phosphorescent foam in its wake. Paul and Mary stood at the helm, their figures silhouetted against the gradually lightening sky. The first tentative rays of sunlight began to paint the horizon, turning the clouds into a canvas of pink and gold.

Mary leaned into Paul, her voice barely above a whisper. "It feels like we're sailing right off the edge of the world, doesn't it?"

Paul nodded, his arm tightening around her waist. "Into uncharted territory. Rather fitting, I'd say."

As the coastline faded into the distance, the weight of the past seemed to lift from their shoulders. The grand old house, with its centuries of secrets and sorrows, was now far from the horizon - no longer looming over them.

"Do you think we'll ever truly understand it all?" Mary mused, her eyes fixed on the point where sea met sky. "The legacy, the chalice, the connections between our families?"

Paul was quiet for a moment, considering. "I'm not sure we're meant to understand it all," he said finally. "But I think we've done what matters most - we've brought the truth to light, and we've chosen to move forward rather than being trapped by the past."

The sun climbed higher, its warmth chasing away the last vestiges of night. In the distance, a flock of seabirds took flight, their cries echoing across the water. It was a new day, full of promise and possibility.

As Paul and Mary sailed on, the legacy of Egremont travelled with them - not as a burden, but as a tale of redemption, of darkness transformed into light. The ghosts of the past might still whisper on the wind, but their power had been broken. What lay ahead was a future of their own making, a story yet to be written.

The yacht pressed on, a tiny speck of hope and love on the vast expanse of the ocean. And as the new day bloomed around them, Paul and Mary stood ready to face whatever lay beyond the horizon - together. with them - not as a burden, but as a tale of redemption, of darkness transformed into light. The ghosts of the past might still whisper on the wind, but their power had been broken. What lay ahead was a future of their own making, a story yet to be written.

The Egremont legacy, once a source of darkness and pain, had led them here - to truth, to justice, and finally, to love. Whatever challenges the future held, they would face them together, two investigators bound by a shared quest for truth and a deep, hard-won affection for each other.

As the coastal town grew closer, Mary squeezed Paul's hand. "Ready for our next episode?"

Paul smiled, his eyes shining with affection and anticipation. "With you? Always."

And so, under a canopy of stars, their journey continued - a story of mystery, redemption, and love, still unfolding with each passing day.

Author's Note

"The Egremont Legacy" is a work of fiction set in the rich and atmospheric landscape of West Cumbria. While the author has drawn inspiration from the region's history, legends, and geography, the characters, incidents, and dialogues are products of the author's imagination and are not to be construed as real.

Any resemblance to actual persons, living or dead, events, or locales is entirely coincidental. The historical events, local customs, and place names have been used fictitiously and do not intend to represent or depict any actual historical figures or current inhabitants of the region.

This novel is a celebration of West Cumbria's mystique and beauty, woven into a tapestry of mystery and imagination. The author hopes it will inspire readers to explore the real wonders of this remarkable area while enjoying the fictional narrative presented within these pages.

About the Author

From UK Roots to Spanish Shores

I'm originally from the UK, where I spent my formative years and received my education. Life then took me on an exciting adventure to sunny Spain, where I now happily reside.

Beyond enjoying the Spanish climate and culture, I'm an avid bridge player. The strategic thinking and social aspects of the game keep me mentally sharp and provide opportunities to connect with like-minded individuals.

However, my true passion lies in the digital realm. I've had the pleasure of creating and launching several websites, immersing myself in the world of web development. But my greatest satisfaction comes from successfully developing online businesses that generate income. It's a constant learning process, but the thrill of building something from scratch and seeing it flourish is incredibly rewarding.

When I'm not glued to the screen, you might find me out on the water as a keen yachtsman. There's something truly invigorating about sailing, the feeling of freedom, and the challenge of harnessing the power of the wind.

Whether it's bridge games, building online ventures, or navigating the open seas, I'm always up for a challenge and enjoy the journey of continuous learning. Feel free to browse my work or connect with me if you share similar interests!

www.ingramcontent.com/pod-product-compliance
Ingram Content Group UK Ltd.
Pitfield, Milton Keynes, MK11 3LW, UK
UKHW010645280525
6111UKWH00012B/151